Fiona McIntosh was born and raised in Sussex in the UK, but spent her early childhood commuting with her family between England and Ghana in West Africa where her father worked. She left a PR career in London to travel and found herself in Australia where she fell in love with the country, its people and one person in particular. She has since roamed the world working for her own travel publishing company, which she runs with her husband. Fiona lives with her young family in South Australia.

Read about Fiona or chat to her on the bulletin board via her website www.fionamcintosh.com

Find out more about Fiona McIntosh and other Orbit authors by registering for the free monthly newsletter at www.orbitbooks.net

D0267342

By Fiona McIntosh

The Quickening Trilogy
Myrren's Gift
Blood and Memory
Bridge of Souls

The Trinity Trilogy
Betrayal
Revenge
Destiny

Percheron
Odalisque
Emissary
Goddess

BLOOD AND MEMORY

THE QUICKENING BOOK TWO

FIONA McINTOSH

www.orbitbooks.net

ORBIT

First published in Great Britain in 2005 by Orbit
Reprinted 2006 (twice), 2007, 2008, 2009, 2010

Copyright © Fiona McIntosh 2004

The moral right of the author has been asserted.

A CIP catalogue record for this book
is available from the British Library.

ISBN 978-1-84149-374-9

Typeset in Garamond 3 by Palimpsest Book Production Limited,
Polmont, Stirlingshire
Printed in the UK by CPI Mackays, Chatham ME5 8TD

Papers used by Orbit are natural, renewable and
recyclable products sourced from well-managed forests and certified
in accordance with the rules of the Forest Stewardship Council.

Mixed Sources
Product group from well-managed
forests and other controlled sources
www.fsc.org Cert no. SGS-COC-004081
© 1996 Forest Stewardship Council

FSC

Orbit
An imprint of
Little, Brown Book Group
100 Victoria Embankment
London EC4Y 0DY

An Hachette UK Company
www.hachette.co.uk

www.orbitbooks.net

In blood and in memory of my own . . .
for William Richards

ACKNOWLEDGEMENTS

It would be easy to write a simple but huge Thank You at the front of this book and hope that everyone connected with it knows how grateful I am for their support. There are always those, however, whose contribution makes such a diffeence that they deserve individual recognition. That list includes:

Gary Havelberg and Sonya Caddy – draft readers I've now come to rely on for guidance. Then there's Robin Hobb, my long-distance friend and mentor, whose own work continues to inspire and drive me harder as does the work of Guy Gavriel Kay – they both make me appreciate what a long journey is still ahead for me! My parents, Fred and Monica Richards, for looking after our children while I roam the world for my work and for freeing me up to write without guilt. Pip Klimentou, who ensures with her daily morning call that I don't sleep in after late nights of writing. No thanks are complete without a mention for my agent, Chris Lotts, who gave me the fab Orbit team and the opportunity to work with terrific editor, Darren Nash.

Finally, love and endless thanks to the three patient men in my life – Will and Jack and their father, Ian.

Fx

PROLOGUE

WYL SLID OFF THE saddle on to unsteady feet. Too flustered to tether the horse, he trusted it to remain where he left it as he stumbled deeper into the copse and retched. The sickening need to be rid of the curse, to rip the sorcery free from its sinister grip, seemed to last an eternity. At the rim of his tortured mind Wyl acknowledged that this cold moonlit night was too beautiful for death . . . once again.

He believed he could taste the taint of the magic which had claimed his body hours earlier. Wyl did not want to remember it, but it was so fresh, so horrific in his mind, that he could not expel it. Commander Liryk of Briavel had smiled when the man called Romen Koreldy, newly banished from the realm, had suggested the Forbidden Fruit for their overnight stay before leaving for whichever border he chose. Liryk had understood that the mercenary wanted to drown his sorrows in the soft and welcoming embrace of a whore in the region's well-known brothel. And he had smiled even wider when Romen had accepted the offer of the woman Hildyth. The commander had enjoyed her on a previous occasion and knew there would be no better place for his grieving companion to lose himself for a few hours.

Wyl Thirsk, trapped in Koreldy's body, had felt the same . . . until the whore buried a stiletto deep in his heart, in an attempt to take his life. Except she did not. Romen's body released its trapped guest so it could travel into the assassin's and claim her life instead.

It was not a new experience for Wyl. He had felt that same wrenching sense of despair once before, and even now could hardly believe it had happened again. He was dry-retching now; knew he must force himself to stop. He looked at his hands – his smooth woman's hands – gripping the tree he leaned against and angrily rubbed them on the rough bark to force himself to accept that he was living, not dreaming this nightmare.

Don't think about who you've become. Remember who you are, he reminded himself. *Remember who you are!*

'I am Wyl Thirsk, son of Fergys Thirsk of Argorn,' he croaked with his new and strange voice. He hated its feminine pitch. 'I am Wyl Thirsk, General of the Morgravian Legion.

'I am alive,' he said, his voice becoming stronger and steadier, his mind accepting, his spirit resolute.

He repeated his mantra until the nausea finally subsided and his cramping muscles stopped answering the call to expel the enchantment. It was not possible anyway, he knew. Myrren's gift was his to keep, unless he could find a way to stop it.

Wyl Thirsk raised his head to the starry skies and screamed his despair. It was a cry without hope. He knew all too well that no shaking of fists nor howling to the heavens could bring to an end the dark enchantment which doomed him to cheat death. Whoever might try to take his life, the curse that was Myrren's gift would ensure that he claimed their life instead. Wyl did not know if it would ever end, only that he could not rest until he had found the key to unlock the mystery.

A wave of sadness crashed over him as he remembered Romen Koreldy, his first victim. Now Romen's body was dead too. Wyl felt gutted to have lost the comfort of that vessel which had welcomed him, sheathed him, given him succour and life. At first so strange, it had become familiar – Romen's essence had lived on with Wyl whilst Wyl's true body was mortifying in a tomb. The two of them had become one . . . and now perhaps they must consider themselves three with this woman who embodied them. She was their shield; they were her secret.

Wyl limped to the narrow brook nearby. The water glinted in the silvery light and he threw himself down at its edge and cleansed his mouth of the taint. Lying there, he succumbed to tears; deep heartfelt sobs that shuddered through his new, womanly body. But the grief belonged only to Wyl Thirsk.

I live, he told himself again, fumbling in his pockets for the piece of linen that held the key to his life for the time being. Wrapped within it lay the bloodied ring finger of Romen Koreldy of Grenadyn, noble, mercenary and the lover of Queen Valentyna of Briavel. Wyl had retrieved it from the chamber at the Forbidden Fruit . . . and now he would use it. Wyl calmed his thoughts, drawing on his skills as a strategist to think through what he must do. He would send Koreldy's finger to Celimus, the treacherous King of Morgravia, to convince him that Romen

Koreldy was dead and confirm that the mysterious assassin had succeeded where others had failed. And in doing so, he would allow Morgravia's sovereign, the betrayer, to live within a false cocoon of safety.

Wyl knew that the neighbouring realm of Briavel was Celimus's main concern now, and his plans to wed its Queen, Valentyna, would be occupying his time. In his disguise as Romen, Wyl had aided Valentyna to hinder those marriage plans through diplomatic strategy, but Wyl knew she could not do so with ease again. He understood all too well what a tightrope of politics she was treading. Her own nobles and counsellors were pressing for the marriage and the peace and prosperity it would bring to Briavel. In fact, both realms were clamouring for a royal wedding, captivated by the romantic notion that the joining of their sovereigns would create harmony, and possibly an heir who would once and for all unite the realms.

It made perfect political and strategic sense. When Celimus had first broached the subject with him, Wyl could hardly believe the far-sighted plan this young king had devised to force the two warring realms to set aside their history of hate once and for all. He had even agreed to help shape such a union, until his inner sense warned him that Celimus's intentions were not as straightforward as they at first seemed. His decision not to support the King's wishes led to the slaughter of his best friend, Alyd Donal, and the imprisonment and degradation of his own sister, Ylena. It was with the knowledge that Ylena's life lay in his hands that Wyl had agreed to travel into Briavel, escorted by a band of mercenaries, to win its princess for the King of Morgravia.

How could he have guessed that even deeper treachery

lay behind Celimus's plotting? Not only had the King planned to win Valentyna's hand in marriage by using the Thirsk name to gain an audience with King Valor, but he had ordered the deaths of Wyl and Valor by an assassin once the betrothal agreement had been made. More twisted yet was the dark mind of Celimus, who had contrived that the blame for King Valor's death should fall on Wyl himself, relying on the skill of the assassin, Romen Koreldy, to kill Wyl and also on the sheer weight of numbers of the other treacherous mercenaries to then murder Koreldy. The Grenadyne knew too much; his life could not be spared.

Celimus, however, had not reckoned on the integrity of the assassin, Koreldy. A blood pact made between Wyl Thirsk and Koreldy ensured that whichever of them survived a duel to the death would expose the King's treachery. But little did any of them know an even darker menace lurked mysteriously within Wyl Thirsk himself; brutal and without loyalty to anything but itself. It was a gift from the Witch Myrren to Wyl for his kindness during her trial torture and it had waited patiently to wreak its havoc. When it had finally struck it was savage and shocking, forcing Wyl's spirit out of his dying body, mortally wounded by Koreldy's sword blow, and into Koreldy's body instead, thereby claiming the mercenary's life. And now Myrren's gift had struck again and Wyl had lost Koreldy's form and was forced to inhabit the body of the whore, Hildyth.

Wyl surfaced from his troubled thoughts, realising that his mind was rambling over old ground. He could not change what had gone; he could only move forward now and work to protect his sister — the last of the Thirsks —

and somehow thwart Celimus's intention to control Briavel through marriage to Valentyna. But before he could do either, he had to find a means of bringing to an end this foul curse.

The seer who had first identified the magic in Wyl had told him to seek answers from the manwitch, Myrren's true father. And that was where Wyl had to turn his attention now – he must track down the manwitch and find the answer to the enchantment.

In making the decision to let go of the past Wyl's intense regret was knowing that Valentyna, whom he had loved from the moment she had first breezed in to his life when he was General Wyl Thirsk of the Morgravian Legion, had fallen in love with him as Romen Koreldy. His own feelings for her had only intensified during his time as Romen and he could never forgive himself for risking that love and allowing her to think that he had betrayed her when she had so relied on him.

A headache was gathering. He must find out more about who he had now become before his pain and grief over his love for the Queen claimed him completely. Valentyna could never love him now, and his punishment was to love her from afar in this strange and female body. Wyl could not bring himself to look at his new body just yet, nor touch it. But he held no such reticence regarding the woman's memories. What remained belonged to Wyl now. They were his to remember and use.

He leaned back against a tree, exhausted, and delved. Wyl learned that he was not Hildyth the whore – that was simply a guise. He was Faryl of Coombe, a brilliant assassin, born in the midlands and familiar with places far away from Morgravia or Briavel . . . and riddled with secrets.

I

THE QUEEN HAD SUFFERED a sleepless night, churning over her decision to banish Romen Koreldy. Valentyna had measured the dark hours by listening to the muted noises of the guard changing before stillness claimed the night again . . . until the next time. The only other distraction was the distant howl of a dog — or was it a wolf? She wondered if it was caught in one of the traps laid by poachers; or, more whimsically, she decided it had lost its mate and was venting its despair. She understood such things, for the sorrowful cry served as an echo of her own loneliness.

Valentyna asked herself the question yet again. Could she have kept the man she loved and still appeased an angry king? A king, she might add, with more than enough fighting power to overwhelm Briavel. The answer, whichever way she approached the problem, was no.

'Damn duty!' she murmured into her coverlets. She punched the feather pillow which brought no comfort this night.

To add to her misery, a vision of Fynch haunted her.

She would never forget the way he had looked at her. He too had grown to love Romen, despite his initial misgivings about the man. In that she and her young friend were alike, and they had shared so much in the short time they had known one another. But that closeness was shattered now. Fynch was avoiding her because she had deliberately distanced herself from Romen and ordered him to be expelled from Briavel. She had cast aside the man she loved over Celimus — a man they all hated. Even a child could see that her actions made no sense. And Fynch was no ordinary child; his serious, deep-thinking manner made him special. She did not want to lose his companionship but it seemed that the day just gone had dawned solely to bring loss to her life.

King Celimus, she realised, kicking off her blankets with irritation, would probably be close to the border by now, possibly even crossing into Morgravia. Nevertheless she had no doubt his spies would keep him updated on events in Briavel and Koreldy's banishment would feature prominently in their missives. It suddenly occurred to her that the King, on hearing this news, might have Romen tracked down. Surely Romen would be cautious? He had been warned not to set foot into Morgravia at risk of certain execution. Failing Romen's good sense, she trusted that her own Commander Liryk would counsel him. Hopefully they had ridden through the night and would be headed north, back from where he had come. 'Where Cailech, King of the Mountains, awaits him,' she whispered sorrowfully.

The last time Valentyna had wept passionately was on the death of her father; the time before that was a decade ago when she had fallen from a horse. She considered herself resilient but heavy tears finally overtook her as she realised the enormity of her command. Romen had nowhere to go. Briavel alone represented safety. Beyond its borders to the north and west, people wanted to kill him. The south offered the ocean and to the east lay only fear in the little-known Wild. Fynch knew it too. She had seen the accusation in that final chilling glance he had given her. It spoke of betrayed friendships.

And he was right. What *was* Romen thinking during that sword fight! It was clear he had meant to kill Celimus, and where would that have left Briavel but in intense danger?

He knew how precarious her position was. *What had been his intention?* She had not had a chance to consider it, in truth. She had not had the luxury of thinking it through but had been forced to react swiftly in the only way possible for a monarch in her situation. She knew her decision was political but this reassurance was cold comfort.

Her heart ached. She loved Romen and she had sent him away. Briavel no longer recognised him as friend. Romen Koreldy would not be permitted to set so much as a toe inside its borders again. If recognised, he would be captured and imprisoned. Her actions had trapped him as surely as that wolf she had heard howling in the distance. Whichever way he turned, whichever borders he finally crossed, he was as doomed as their new and fragile love.

Valentyna twisted beneath her remaining sheet, trying to escape thoughts of his touch which brought a new kind of ache to her body. She would have given herself gladly to him that night before the tourney, but his had been the voice of calm amongst the waves of passion. It was

Romen who had pulled back, Romen who had made her
understand the reason for holding onto the most precious
commodity for a new Queen. Virginity was wealth, he
had counselled. More importantly, it was power. A virgin
Queen was an irresistible magnet for appropriate suitors.
Except she wanted no husband . . . unless it was Koreldy.

She rubbed her tired but stubborn eyes and sat up.
This would not do. Pulling on a soft robe against the
chill, Valentyna moved to the window and looked out
towards the dark woodland she loved so much.

'It might work,' she murmured, as an idea gathered
resonance in her thoughts. She could meet him somewhere outside of Briavel's borders, somewhere safe where
they could rendezvous in secret. If only she could feel his
kiss just once more it would be enough, she reasoned,
hardly believing it herself. She would take Fynch too.
Between them they would mend friendships, renew loyal-
ties, rekindle the flame which had burned brightly
between them all. She could apologise for making the
hardest of decisions, and she knew Romen already understood – his eyes had told her so when they regarded her
so gently despite her harsh words. She could ask him
why he had risked so much. They could set things
straight between them. Perhaps she could even find a
way around the expulsion order, when time had passed
and life was less precarious. Perhaps there was a chance
for them one day.

'Where are you now, Romen?' the Queen of Briavel
whispered towards the trees, longing to see her lover one
last time, not knowing that at this very moment he was
just a few miles from entering her own castle's walls.

Far sooner than she could have imagined, Valentyna

would cast her eyes upon Koreldy once more; kiss him again as she had so desired.

Liryk's expression was grim; beneath it anger seethed. This should not have happened. The Queen had deliberately granted Koreldy the chance to make a new life elsewhere when she could so easily have commanded death. There was friendship between the two, possibly more if his intuition served him well. He could not blame her. Who could help but fall under Koreldy's spell?

The Briavellian Guard emerged from the cover of the woodland that surrounded the northern border of the palace grounds. Commander Liryk glanced to his left, where the corpse of the man he hardly knew but had comfortably called friend lay in a cart, wrapped in sacking. Combined sorrow and guilt threatened Liryk's stern demeanour, forcing him to look back towards the castle.

They had arrived at the famous Bridge of Werryl where past sovereigns, remembered faithfully in marble, stood proudly either side to guide visitors into the palace. He raised his hand towards the ramparts where he knew his guards had seen their fellow soldiers approaching through the light mist of dawn. The gate was up, he noticed. He grimaced; he would have to take a hard look at security again and ensure the castle remained closed to all visitors until permission was formally granted. After Valor's sudden death everyone had been extra careful but recently he had noticed a general slackening of vigilance. With an assassin on the loose who knew what could happen. Their Queen must be better protected.

In the courtyard he handed his horse's reins to the stableboy and gave orders for Koreldy's body to be taken to the chapel and laid out. Like his men, Liryk was tired. They had ridden through the night, determined to bring the body back as quickly as possible to ensure that gossip disappeared with the evidence. With no body, no sign that an assassination had occurred, the story would rage for a day and then hopefully be forgotten. The Forbidden Fruit's women would be entertaining in that same chamber this very night, all sign of the recent bloodshed washed away. His mouth twisted at the thought. Poor Koreldy. He deserved better.

Tired or not, the next hour would be the most difficult. Liryk suspected that no matter how he counselled her, their headstrong Queen would want to see this corpse for herself. He shook his head, resigned. Valentyna was an early riser. Best to see her immediately and get the ugly business done with.

Liryk made his presence known to Krell, the Queen's Chancellor and former servant to King Valor. He was a calm and solid force amongst Valentyna's advisers and Liryk liked the man. He wondered if Krell ever slept, for the Chancellor always seemed to be available.

'May I ask if it is urgent, Commander Liryk?' Krell said, shifting papers around on his desk. 'This is an irregular hour to be requesting an audience.'

The soldier nodded. 'Something unexpected. She must be told.'

'Bad news?' the Chancellor enquired. Liryk's expression was enough to foreshadow this would not be a happy meeting.

'It is, I'm afraid. Koreldy is dead.'

The Queen's servant looked up sharply from the orderly piles of paperwork which he dealt with daily for his monarch, sorting tasks into priorities and keeping Valentyna's mind firmly on her duties. He understood that the woman needed space to still enjoy her youth and had single-handedly eased Valentyna into her challenging role as sovereign, allaying her fears, guiding her with informed skill, instinctively knowing what her father would have expected. In terms of administering the realm, he was a blessing to them all, a man who could rarely be ruffled. However, the expression on his normally well-guarded face was all shock at this moment. Liryk was convinced that Krell wanted to ask if he was quite sure but had checked himself.

Liryk confirmed it anyway. 'I've had him laid out in the chapel. I imagine the Queen will want to view the body.'

'Indeed. She will not be persuaded otherwise,' Krell replied. He walked around from behind his desk. 'This is dark news, Commander. I'm sorry to hear it. In spite of the reason for his expulsion, Koreldy was a good man for Briavel and . . .'

Liryk guessed that the Chancellor wanted to add that Koreldy was a good man for Valentyna as well; instead the Chancellor held his tongue and asked the Commander to wait while he sought an appointment with her majesty immediately. He left Liryk alone with his bleak thoughts and fatigue.

When Liryk was shown into her study, he could see Valentyna had not slept well. Her eyes lacked their usual sparkle and dark smudges beneath made them appear hollow in the much too pale face. He wished once again he could escape this task and hoped Krell had forewarned her of the tidings.

She was wearing a satin robe and had obviously come in a hurry straight from her chambers, not caring about her state of dress, but then Valentyna had never been one for vanity. He had known this fine young woman since she was newborn and she had always treated him as a kindly uncle — she still did, in fact. He noticed she managed to muster a smile for him, rising above the concerns that had troubled her slumber.

'I am glad to have you back, Commander Liryk,' she said formally. She crossed the room and took both his hands in her own, falling into her usual, less regal manner. 'Now, ease my worry,' she said. 'Tell me it all went smoothly.'

Liryk glanced towards Krell who was passing behind her majesty with some papers. The Chancellor shook his head slightly and Liryk felt the weight of his task settle like a stone in his throat. Krell was following protocol — he had left the bad news entirely for Liryk to deliver.

Valentyna was searching his face, a confused smile on her lips now. 'What is it? Krell tells me you have news which cannot wait. I presume you wish to report that Romen Koreldy was seen safely to a border. But which border? I must know,' she said, her words coming out in a rush.

Liryk's eyes came back to rest sadly upon her own. 'May we sit, your highness?'

'Oh, of course, how remiss of me. You've obviously been riding through the night to be back here so fast.' She gestured towards one of the comfy armchairs. 'Please.'

'Thank you.' He sat slowly, taking every last moment he could before he had to share his tidings with this lovely young Queen. So much grief around her. He wished Krell had remained in the room, but knew the man had done the right thing once again and given them privacy.

Valentyna sat in the chair opposite.

'You look very pale, your highness.' He blurted his thoughts aloud.

She nodded. 'You know me too well. I did sleep badly. I've anguished over yesterday's decision, Liryk. It was the appropriate action to take for Morgravia's King and the dutiful thing for Briavel. But oh, it was a poor decision for me personally. I miss Koreldy more than most would realise.'

Liryk was shocked. He sensed the friendship had run deep but had no idea it had progressed so far and so quickly. He leaned back in his chair and closed his eyes, risking her further confusion whilst he gathered up his anguished thoughts.

'My apologies, sir. I should not burden you with affairs of my heart,' Valentyna said to fill the awkward pause, sorry that she had spoken as she had.

She noticed the sad expression on Liryk's face when he opened his eyes and sat forward again. He even took her hand, held it gently but firmly in his large, gnarled soldier's hands. He sighed heavily and when he said, 'Your majesty,' as though his shoulders carried the very weight of the realm, her intuition told her she did not want to hear whatever it was he had to report. She had to bite her lip to prevent herself from begging him to say no more.

He began to speak, his tone measured, his words carefully chosen. Valentyna looked at Liryk's hands covering hers, trying to shut out the voice, concentrating on the gingery hair there which made her think of Wyl Thirsk of all people. Poor lovely Wyl Thirsk with his thatch of orange hair and freckles. She recalled the way he had blushed whenever her eyes glanced towards his, and that his smile, so hard to win, was bright and joyful when it came. He should never have died. He had fought courageously for a realm which was not even his own, in order to save the life of his enemy. She had liked him the instant they met; had felt a connection to him somehow, which was hard to shake. The young man entered her mind at the oddest of times to this day and there were moments – not that she would admit openly to it – when Fynch's suggestion that Wyl Thirsk was still amongst them rang true with her.

It was an odd situation. Normally she did not take to people so readily; she was wary of folk by nature and downright suspicious of strangers from Morgravia. But Wyl was not what she had expected. He was forthright and humble. Just a little in awe of her father, which she had appreciated because it showed respect – even between enemies. And her father had liked him and, more importantly, had trusted him. That much was obvious. She recalled how Romen had told her that Wyl had fallen desperately in love with her on that first meeting. How shocked she had been and, strange though it sounded, how flattered. There had been something special about Wyl Thirsk. Despite his lack of stature, about which she had gently poked fun at him, he had a strong presence . . . and there had been a chemistry of sorts between them. Valentyna recalled how he had not felt ashamed to weep in front of her and her father, or accept her comfort for the loss of his friend and fear for his sister. She had loved that about him.

Liryk's voice spoke on. As though from a distance, she

heard him talking about a place called the Forbidden Fruit. It sounded like no establishment she would ever visit and yet she would like to. She wished she could see such things, understand them better. Apparently Romen had gone with a woman there. She knew what this meant but she tried to ignore it. She wanted to believe that the bathing and smoothing had been an innocent activity to ease the tension of that strange and joyless day. But it was more than that – she could read as much in the way Liryk told of it.

She heard the name Hildyth. A hateful name. She despised the woman, a stranger she had never met nor ever would. A whore. *Romen's whore.*

She imagined the stranger laughing with him, unselfconscious at being naked with this handsome man. The whore would feel his fingers on her body, his tongue, his lips . . . Valentyna tried to convince herself, as these visions raged, that Romen had used the whore because he could not have his true love, his Queen. His Queen had banished him, had marked him as no friend of hers, or of Briavel's. He had to bury his grief somewhere and he had chosen to do so at the Forbidden Fruit, sheathing himself within a woman called Hildyth. Was this what Liryk was so hesitant to tell her – that Romen had spent the night with a paid woman, she thought bitterly.

It seemed not. There was more to this tale. As he continued, her throat caught . . . and then began to close as though it meant to stop her breathing. Liryk was speaking of a knife, of a fingerless hand.

She looked up suddenly, as though the picture he was describing had only now become clear. The Commander stopped speaking, disturbed by the change in her manner.

'I . . . Liryk . . . I don't understand.' There was a tremor in her voice and she hated it. Hated it almost as much as she hated Hildyth for taking pleasure in Romen's body when he was meant for a Queen.

It broke every protocol but Liryk did not care – the Queen of Briavel, loved by all since a little girl, needed comfort. He moved to sit beside her and put his arm around his young sovereign, pulled her to his broad chest as a dear uncle might. She allowed him to because she was scared. She had heard the words but did not believe them. She would need him to say them again.

He spoke in a near whisper this time, his lips close to her hair which smelled of fresh lavender. 'Your highness,' he said gently, 'Romen Koreldy was murdered last night. We have nothing more than the whore's description of a man she saw running down the hall. Understandably she was distraught, so the details are somewhat vague . . .' He stopped, not sure of what else to say.

As he pulled away the Queen's gaze was locked on his face but her expression suggested her mind was far away. 'Dead?' she said, as though testing the word on her tongue. He nodded.

Valentyna moved fast, leaping to her feet, grabbing her Commander's shirt in her fists. 'Romen's dead?'

'Yes, my Queen. He was murdered,' Liryk answered as gently as he could.

He was relieved when the door clicked softly open and Krell entered, carrying a mug of steaming liquid. Liryk caught a waft of dramona. It was a wise choice. The medicine was strong and would help with the shock.

Valentyna became aware of Krell and his presence helped her to compose herself. She released her grip on

Liryk and felt for the chair behind her to sit down again. She realised she was wringing her hands and clasped them firmly together until she had regained control of them. The Queen took a long, deep breath. She remained silent for a moment or two longer and then lifted her chin, fixing with a steady dark blue gaze the man whose news had just stuck a blade into her heart. There was some pleasing symmetry to that notion, she thought bitterly, for if her ears had heard correctly, a blade in the heart was the manner in which Romen had died.

'Commander Liryk, you will tell me everything once again so I understand thoroughly the events which unfolded last night.' The Queen's words fell like ice crystals now. They matched the wintry expression which had frozen her lovely face. She was not to be argued with.

And so for the third time that morning Liryk told his sad tale, this time sparing her no detail. He delivered his report in the detached military manner he knew best, devoid of emotion and embellishment.

'It was only later that we discovered his ring finger had been removed,' he concluded.

'Why?'

'A trophy perhaps, although I do believe, your highness, that this was an assassination. People who kill for money must provide proof of the death before they are paid in full. It is my belief that Koreldy was murdered by someone's order.'

'Whose order?'

One name hung silently between them. Neither dared speak it. If they did it would become truth, and the repercussions should they act upon that truth were too daunting to contemplate.

Instead Liryk chose a safer path. 'We have no firm evidence as to who perpetrated this.'

'Other than the blade,' she replied.

'Yes, highness. Other than the weapon.'

Krell took this moment to offer the Queen the mug of medicine. 'Drink it all, your majesty,' he whispered before taking his leave.

Valentyna smelled the dramona, knew its intention and put it aside. They would not sedate her. 'Did Koreldy say anything to you before he died?'

The Commander nodded. 'He told me that he did not kill your father. He wished you had given him a sign that you knew him to be innocent of all accusations levelled at him.'

Valentyna's newly calmed expression faltered at the words. She knew Liryk had not meant to drive a further wedge of pain into her. She expected him to be truthful, after all. What she did not suspect was that his honesty carried only to a certain point. Liryk had told Koreldy that he would not do anything to dissuade the Queen from marriage with Celimus, even though Koreldy had begged him to. He held his tongue now. For Briavel's sake, the marriage should go ahead.

Valentyna drew on every ounce of her courage to remain composed and not crumple. That would come later. Right now she had to learn everything she could about why Romen had died.

'The whore . . .'

'Hildyth?'

'Yes,' she said, irritated to hear the name again. 'Where is she now?'

'She asked if she could leave after she had told us

everything she could. She was very upset, as you can imagine.'

'Did it not occur to you, Commander, that the whore might have been involved? She could have allowed the killer entry? Could even have killed Koreldy herself?'

'Yes, your majesty.'

'And?'

She watched the colour rise in her chief of security. 'She could not have killed Koreldy because he would have been too strong for her. You know what an artful fighter he was. As for her being involved – yes, it had occurred to me, but I decided she was innocent.'

'Why?'

There it was again – the hesitancy, a flush of red at the neck. 'I have met her before, highness. She did not strike me either as violent or anything more than a young woman trying to make the best of her situation.'

'I see,' said Valentyna, understanding perfectly. Romen Koreldy was not the first of her acquaintances to lie with this woman. Clearly Liryk had intimate knowledge of Whore Hildyth. 'I want soldiers sent immediately to bring this woman to the castle for questioning. Can I leave that with you?'

Liryk nodded, embarrassed. 'Of course.'

'Where is Romen now?' she asked, just managing to keep her voice steady as she said his name.

'In the chapel, your highness.'

'Thank you, Commander Liryk. I know you must be extremely tired. Please take your rest. We shall speak again when you are refreshed. I apologise for having kept you so long . . .' and then her voice softened '. . . and for losing myself there for a few moments. It was a shock.'

She watched Liryk's relief at her words. Perhaps her cool detachment had unsettled him, although was this not the very quality a Queen must exhibit? She could not be prey to shrieking hysterics but must control her own emotions and deal calmly with any situation.

'I understand fully, your majesty. In truth, I don't believe I have come to terms with it myself yet.'

'He died as a result of a blade through the heart, that's right, isn't it?'

He nodded. 'Driven into his chest with expert precision. The killer knew what he was doing.'

'So it would have been quick?'

'Dead before Koreldy even realised he'd been struck,' he assured her, although not quite believing it himself.

She nodded that he may depart and he stood and bowed gladly, flooded with relief that his ugly task was done.

2

KNAVE KNEW. THE DOG had woken him in the night with a howl so sorrowful it hurt Fynch to hear it. They had been sleeping rough in the woods because Fynch could not bear to be in the castle after all that happened. Most of all, he could not face the Queen. She had done something so unexpected that he had been unable to disguise his feelings over her actions – not that he had any right to disapprove of someone so above him in status. They were friends, though. Friends did not cast each other aside. She needed Romen – why could she not see that?

It was true that he too had been wary of Romen originally; how could he not be? It was Fynch who had overheard King Celimus plotting with Koreldy to assassinate Wyl Thirsk. But it was also Fynch who had noticed the curious attachment Wyl's dog, Knave, had shown for Koreldy when they had tracked him back to Pearlis. Fynch had been shocked to see the mercenary with Ylena and to hear that he had brought Wyl's corpse back to Stoneheart for the formal burial it was due. It was he alone who had worked out that something very strange had occurred, something magical.

Fynch believed in magic and so did not suffer from the same wariness of it as most Morgravians, or dismiss it like the Briavellians. His suspicion that Wyl Thirsk was somehow still amongst them had been gradually confirmed: firstly by Knave's affection for a stranger, and secondly by Koreldy's uncharacteristic actions regarding Ylena and his desire to clear the Thirsk family name. Fynch's intuition was rewarded when Koreldy had admitted to being Wyl Thirsk, and told him of the Quickening, the frightening phenomenon that had given him life and taken that of the real Romen Koreldy.

But Wyl had forbidden Fynch from sharing this knowledge with Valentyna, which was why the Queen's decision to banish Koreldy had been so painful for the boy. He loved Valentyna and wished he could tell her the truth outright, but he knew it would be in vain. How could anyone, especially one who could not conceive of sorcery, believe such a tale?

He had hoped to see Romen before the guards escorted him from Werryl – that way he could have heard Wyl's plans, however thin they may be. But it had not been permitted. Knave had wanted to follow Wyl's trace, but Fynch had exerted his own authority for once and told his companion they should wait. They needed to plan their next move. The boy sensed that the dog would always find its master, and they could catch up with Wyl later. Now he needed time to 'tidy his mind', as he liked to think of it, to consider all options. So the woods had become their hiding place.

Fynch had expected to spend a few days there, but outside events began to have their own crushing impact.

No amount of shooshing or cajoling had quieted Knave's howling during the night. It was a strange sound, filled with despair. The dog was closed to him, so he could not work out what was troubling him, and neither did Knave want to be touched or spoken to. So Fynch had tossed and turned all night, trying to shut out the terrible keening. He had finally fallen asleep, only to be roused again by the dog at first light. The boy sleepily obeyed the beast's wish to be followed. Clearly Knave had an objective.

They slipped into the castle grounds, waving to the guards and getting a familiar raised hand back. Knave was making for the main courtyard. The reason why became all too clear with the arrival of Commander Liryk and the Guard.

The boy and the dog had watched the soldiers enter the bailey. Liryk looked grave and weary. They saw him hand the reins to the stableboy and heard him give an order to his men, although Fynch had not been able to make out the words.

As Liryk left the courtyard and entered the castle, Fynch noticed that Knave was no longer at his side. Instead the dog was moaning by the cart which had rolled in after Liryk. He watched as the men struggled to lift something out of the cart, and felt a claw around his throat, squeezing tight and hard. Instinctively he knew they were carrying the corpse of Romen Koreldy. His heart felt as though it had cracked in two.

Distraught, he followed the soldiers into the cool chapel with its exquisite carved whitestone and simple yet sophisticated structure whereby six slim, smooth pillars somehow held up the entire building. The ceiling was frescoed with mythic scenes depicting the glory of Briavel. But none of its beauty impacted on the silent handful who entered its glorious space this morning.

Fynch felt relieved to be granted permission to be present. He stood, rigid with despair, next to the body, disturbed by its pallor. Romen had been browned from the sun; he should not be this ghostly. A guard, sensitive to the friendship which had existed between the dead man and this child, gently explained that a great deal of blood had drained from the body at the time of death which would account for its pale appearance. Fynch was not so sure he had needed to hear the reasoning, but he whispered his thanks all the same and was glad when the man stepped away.

The soldiers, all known to him, murmured their sympathies. One even apologised for not keeping Romen safe. Fynch wanted to cry out that Koreldy could take care of himself, but he had obviously been duped then murdered. Instead he accepted their commiserations silently and, relieved, watched them gradually depart.

He and Knave were alone at last with their friend and he felt it would be all right now if he cried. He reached out and smoothed back a few stray hairs from Romen's face. Wyl had adopted Koreldy's fastidiousness and would not like his hair to look so scruffy. Those who had dealt with the body in Crowyll had done their best, mercifully wiping away most traces of blood and putting him in a fresh shirt. Still, he was hardly tidy and he would hate to be seen so dishevelled. Fynch kissed his friend's forehead before laying his own head on Romen's cool chest and allowing his sorrow to echo through the chapel.

The dog sniffed the body long and carefully. Presumably satisfied that his master no longer breathed, he lay at Fynch's feet. Knave was patient. It was as though he understood that it was Fynch's turn now to grieve.

Valentyna felt her composure slip as she stepped quietly into the chapel, flanked by Krell and Liryk who had insisted on accompanying her. On seeing the child draped over the corpse, she felt the sickening lurch of a cry rushing into her throat. It was real; death was here. Krell's guiding hand – a gentle, well-timed touch steering her down the short aisle – rescued her. She fought the grief back and was able once again to view the poignant scene before her.

Fynch looked so small, so vulnerable. She desperately wanted to hold him in her arms, to cling to the living. Instead, as she silently drew up beside him, she risked taking his hand. She knew she chanced a rebuke, for who could blame a youngster for not keeping his emotions in check? She was relieved when he did not pull away from her touch but straightened and stepped back from the corpse to stand next to her. Valentyna looked down into the tear-stained face and was rewarded by a watery smile. It was enough.

'We lost him,' he whispered, his voice leaden with sorrow.

'Yes,' she replied, now finally finding the courage to look fully upon the body of the man she had loved.

Neither Krell nor Liryk stirred, and Fynch and Knave too stood like statues, whilst Valentyna stared at Romen, seeing nothing for the moment other than how handsome he was in such stillness.

'May I?' she asked, pointing tentatively towards his shirt.

Liryk's sad eyes blinked. He nodded gently, knowing what she wished to see.

'He's so pale,' she whispered.

'There was a lot of blood lost,' Fynch replied, his voice coming as though from far away.

She felt herself lurch inwardly again as a picture of Romen's body spewing forth its lifeblood swam into her mind. Undoing the shirt buttons she revealed his chest, no longer warm and filled with love for her. Valentyna needed to see the ugly wound where the blade had been expertly driven into his flesh to puncture his heart, all of its love draining out on to the floor of a brothel while a whore called Hildyth shrieked as she watched him die. *Or had she killed him?* The nagging thought would not leave her.

Knowing looks passed between the two men as the Queen lingered over the corpse. 'Your highness,' Krell uttered, after clearing his throat lightly. 'Do not torture yourself any further.'

'But I must. I sent this man to his death.'

'No, your highness!' Liryk spoke up. 'You gave him his life . . . and a chance to make a new one. King Celimus would surely have had him killed.'

'Perhaps he did,' Fynch muttered to himself, but they all heard it.

Valentyna tore her gaze from Romen and turned to Fynch. 'Tell us what you think.'

She and Liryk held their breath. If even the youngster was thinking it, then surely their unspoken yet shared conclusion could not be far off the mark.

'Celimus wanted Romen dead. Now he is,' Fynch said tonelessly.

'We cannot prove such a thing, lad,' Liryk replied, his voice gruff with rebuke.

'No. That's the point though,' Fynch said, staring at the corpse. As he spoke he suddenly sounded a lot older. 'You need not be a physician to see that this was an expertly achieved death. Celimus could not be seen to have bloody hands.'

All three Briavellians noted his casual use of the Morgravian monarch's name. 'You sound familiar with the King, boy,' Liryk said.

'I know him. Certainly enough about him to accept that Romen's death could easily be by his design. We already know that Celimus thinks nothing of hiring mercenaries to kill a sovereign.' There was a sharp intake of breath from both men, although Valentyna seemed not to react. Fynch continued as though they were discussing the weather. 'What makes you think he would not order the death of a troublesome noble? Someone who knows too much about the comings and goings of Morgravia?' He stopped suddenly, his look defying them to contradict him.

'He's powerful, son, and more than capable of such commands,' Liryk said, impressed with Fynch's grasp of the situation. 'I just can't prove the King of Morgravia is behind Koreldy's death.'

'No, and that's why we must be very careful about what we say aloud,' Valentyna warned. 'Please, all of you – what has been aired here must remain between the five of us.'

Fynch found an inward smile. It amused him that the Queen counted Knave amongst them. He too believed the dog heard and understood everything. Knave sidled up towards him again and he laid his hand on the large head, glad of the comfort.

Without warning, a familiar dizzy sensation claimed him. Valentyna spoke again but her words sounded distant. 'Krell, I know this is unusual, but you and I will wash Koreldy's body.'

'My Queen! I cannot permit—'

'No, you cannot permit me anything,' she said kindly. 'This is my order, although I prefer it be a request of you.'

The old man nodded, an unhappy expression on his face.

'I am doing this so we may keep knowledge of Romen's death between as few people as possible.'

He is not dead! Wyl lives! A voice spoke inside Fynch's head, which began to throb. He saw only swirling grey mist before him but he heard the words clearly. Then the mist cleared and he saw a small town fringed by fields of hops. He had no idea of its significance.

Find him. He walks in another body now, the voice urged.

The swirling sensation dissipated as fast as it had arrived and the voices of the people in the chapel no longer sounded as if spoken from the bottom of a well. Intense pain and shock reverberated through his body as he tried to think about what had happened. He knew now that the voice had come to him through Knave; he just did not know why.

Fynch felt distracted and nauseated. His mind was in turmoil. If Knave's information was correct, then they were needlessly grieving over a man who was not dead. *He walks in another body now.* Had it truly happened again? Had Wyl Thirsk become the person who had killed Romen Koreldy?

Valentyna deserved to know, but what could he say to her? She would not even hear him out. She was liberal in most ways, and he would describe her as tolerant – she certainly had been of his views on magic – but she was not a believer. The Queen would probably banish him as well if he started talking about transference into another body. No. This he would have to keep to himself for the time being.

The Queen was still speaking to her Commander and Fynch struggled to bring his attention back to the people around him. 'Liryk, I want that Hildyth creature at the palace by sunset tomorrow. Bring her before me alone. Did many other people at this place know of the murder?'

Liryk was grateful for the Queen's tact. 'Several, your highness. But none of them would know Koreldy. He was a stranger there. It was not crowded either, so those whose ears have already heard probably do not know his name – simply that a man was killed.'

'Good. Your men will spread the rumour that this man was Briavel's prisoner but that we had granted him a new life outside our borders. So far this is true. The seed you will plant, however, is that we suspect a Briavellian loyalist took offence at Koreldy's actions at the tourney and took it upon himself to rid our realm of a troublemaker. Make sure everyone understands how keen Briavel is to pursue the betrothal. No official word, mind,' she cautioned. 'Tell the story into a few inns where loose mouths lurk. I will provide coin. Fret not that the story may become warped as it is retold; as long as people believe it was purely an internal problem.'

'Why?' Krell asked, unable to follow his Queen's rapid line of thought.

Liryk could not help a grim smile of appreciation. He bowed: 'Inspired, your highness.' He turned to his companion. 'Because, Chancellor Krell, as it's supposedly our own work the rumours will die quickly. There is less intrigue, you see, around the death of a prisoner rather than the assassination of a noble, particularly one we supported. More importantly, in designing this plan, our Queen has deflected any potential damage to Briavel. Whether or not the person we suspect is behind this, he can only be privately grateful to her majesty for being so without guile and accepting blame in Briavel's name.'

'I see,' the Chancellor replied, impressed. 'Your majesty has inherited her father's quick mind for strategy.'

Valentyna gave a brief, harsh laugh. 'Oh, I do hope so. We are entering challenging waters, gentlemen, and we shall need all our wits to navigate the safest channel.'

Both men nodded their agreement.

'What of the body, your highness?' Krell asked gently.

The Queen sighed, inwardly proud that she had so far held on to her grief in front of these men. They were obeying her now as they would have her father. She had truly become their sovereign.

'Liryk, to anyone nosing around, you can say the prisoner's body was buried quickly in an unmarked grave. Make out you left it for others to do, and so it passes down the chain of command until no one really knows who took responsibility. Give the impression that neither do we care.'

'Yes, your highness.'

'Krell, you and I will prepare the body. Whom can we trust to bury him?'

'Father Paryn is a good man, my Queen. He will help us to send off Koreldy with some dignity.'

'Dignity, yes,' she said, seeing once again her version

of Hildyth enjoying her evening's work with Romen. 'He will be buried at a private ceremony. No one is to speak of it with anyone other than Father Paryn. Krell, please make arrangements for a site near my father.'

'In the royal crypt, your majesty?' His tone carried sufficient surprise that she knew he was not happy with such an arrangement.

'Yes,' she said firmly. 'He deserves as much. He fought to save my father's life; he certainly saved mine. He was also . . .' She paused, forcing herself to hold back the words she longed to speak. It would serve no purpose for these men to know her true feelings for Koreldy. She took a breath. 'This is what I want.'

'As you wish,' Krell said, bowing.

'Liryk, what of the men who accompanied you?'

'All reliable, your highness. If you will excuse me, I shall round them up now and make our orders clear.'

'Each to be paid double salary for this moon cycle. They are to understand that their silence is appreciated at the highest level.'

He nodded and bowed before taking his leave.

'Clothes,' Krell muttered. 'I should organise some fresh garments for him.'

Valentyna looked again at her beloved Romen in his dusty travelling clothes.

'He looks best in dark grey,' she said. 'It sets off his eyes.' The sorrow in her voice was thick.

Krell looked sharply at his sovereign and then away. The expression of pain on her face at that moment was too raw. He knew she needed privacy.

'At once, your highness. I shall go find Father Paryn now,' he murmured.

Valentyna heard the door of the chapel close quietly. 'Lock it, Fynch,' she begged, 'I need some time.' And she broke down, her soft cries heartbreaking as she bowed helplessly over the cold corpse. No longer a Queen having to follow protocol or keep her emotions in check, but a young woman grieving over the death of the man she loved.

'His killer took his bracelet as well,' she said through her tears. She felt no shame at showing her sorrow with Fynch.

'Yes, highness, I noticed it was missing. But it was worth nothing. He told me his sister had plaited it for him, the beads were hers from childhood.'

'A trinket, yes, but worth everything to Romen, I imagine, and perhaps more to his killer.'

'How so, my Queen?'

She shrugged. 'I suppose further proof that he is dead. Anyone who knew Romen would have noticed he habitually wore that tiny bracelet.'

Fynch nodded, remaining silent.

'He looks so peaceful,' she admitted, her eyes drawn to the damaged hand where a finger had been carelessly hacked off.

Fynch saw she had refastened the shirt buttons to hide the brutal wound.

'Asleep even,' he ventured.

'Yes. Except Romen was never still, was he? He had a special energy. We shall never hear his laugh again, or that way he mocked everyone with gentle affection.'

Fynch took a chance. 'If I suggested this was simply a dead body and not really the Romen Koreldy you loved, what would you say?'

Valentyna looked at him, disturbed, wiping away the helpless tears. 'I would call you cruel. Why should you suggest such a thing when you know how I feel . . . felt about Romen?'

It was pointless pursuing this conversation but he tried anyway. At least later he could reassure himself he had made the attempt. He swallowed. 'Although Romen's corpse lies here before us, I don't believe that the man you knew – the man you loved, your highness – is dead.'

She looked at him aghast. 'Fynch, whatever are you talking about? Stop now. This is hurtful.'

He sighed, dropped his head. 'My apologies, your highness.'

She wanted to retain his friendship so much and yet here she was pushing him farther from herself. Valentyna moved swiftly to be beside him and then crouched so she could look directly into his large, serious eyes. 'No, I am sorry. He is dead because I banished him. This is my cross to bear – not yours. You would never have done this to a friend, but oh, my dear Fynch, I am bound by duties and royal protocol.'

'I understand. Really. I think I've got it straight in my mind why you did what you did.'

'It's your forgiveness I seek. I don't want to lose you, Fynch. You and even your strange dog there are my closest friends in the world.'

Her words touched him. 'Then you must trust me.'

'I do.'

'And understand what I must do.'

She noted the grave tone. 'What must you do?' she asked, frowning now.

'I am leaving, your highness.'

The shock of his words stopped her tears. 'No! Why?'

'There is something I must pursue.'

'Fynch, speak plainly. Tell me,' she commanded, searching his guileless face for clues.

'You cannot understand.'

'Make me.'

He smiled. It was shy and rare, full of kindness. 'I cannot, your highness. I have tried before.'

She took a deep breath, then laid her hands lightly on his shoulders. 'Is this about Wyl Thirsk . . . and – what was it? Romen taking on his duties . . . his desires? You said you felt his presence.'

Fynch nodded. His expression was sombre. 'More than that, but I cannot explain yet.'

'Magic.' She spoke the word as if it was poison in her mouth.

'Just trust me,' Fynch repeated.

'But where will you go?' There was a plaintiveness in her voice.

'To track down Romen Koreldy's murderer.'

The Queen rubbed a hand over her face. He could not tell whether she felt frustration, anger, despair or a combination of all.

'You are a child,' she said, hating to state the obvious and working hard at keeping her voice level.

'All the more reason I shall go unnoticed, your highness. Who would bother with a child?'

'And your purpose?' she blurted, irritation spilling over, sarcasm evident in her tone.

If Fynch noticed he did not react. He spoke evenly. 'I mean to see his killer with my own eyes.' He kept as close

to the truth as possible for lies did not come naturally to
him.

'And?'

Fynch was silent. She waited, knowing he was considering how best to answer her. He was always very careful
in how he spoke.

'I will decide then,' he answered.

The cryptic reply annoyed her further. She stood and
turned away, her voice hard. 'It is your decision and you
will be missed. Will you remain for the burial?'

'There's no point,' he said quietly. 'I prefer to leave
immediately, unless you wish it differently.'

'I do. We must honour him.'

'But it is not him any more, your highness.'

'Stop it, I beg you!' she beseeched, the pain of his words
cutting through her.

Fynch's gaze was unblinking and honest. 'Once again
I ask for your faith. I will not let you down. Neither will
he,' he said, nodding towards the corpse.

Valentyna wanted to scream at him, shake his bony
shoulders and force some sense into his head. She did
neither. 'I shall spend some time with him alone now. I
insist on your presence at the burial.'

Fynch bowed but she had already turned away from
him.

The burial was swift. The body was surrounded by small
candles which would be permitted to burn out. A few spoken
words, a quick prayer, and then Father Paryn was asking
them to lay their gifts next to the body. Koreldy's spirit
would move beyond, whilst his body remained surrounded
by possessions from those who had cared for him.

Liryk laid down a blade. He now dearly wished he had given Koreldy one — perhaps he might have saved himself if he had. Krell laid down a quill, the symbol of his duties for Briavel. It was all he could think of to leave with a man he had not known well but had respected. Fynch cut off a twist of his own hair and some from Knave. He laid it on Koreldy's chest. It was the most personal item which would travel with Romen into the next life.

Finally, Valentyna placed her offering of a small wreath of mint, basil and lavender she had bound with one of her own ribbons intertwined with a thong Romen had used for his hair — beneath his crossed hands. That the wreath was heart-shaped was missed by no one. *May it remind you of where love's tentative touch first embraced us*, she cast silently, hoping his spirit might hear.

Two soldiers, trustworthy men who had accompanied Liryk and Koreldy on their fateful trip into Crowyll, slid the heavy stone slab across the tomb in which Romen had been laid. It was unmarked.

Valentyna lifted her head. 'No one is ever to speak of this.' She eyed each of the men who stood with her. 'Or I shall have his tongue cut out. This is a secret which Briavel shall hold.'

They nodded as one.

'Thank you, gentlemen,' she said, relieved she could trust them, even without the threat.

Fynch was the last person to leave the crypt. As he stepped out into the brightness of day he was momentarily blinded, but as his eyes adjusted he noticed a soldier making fast passage towards the chapel.

'What news?' Liryk asked, all formalities dispensed with. It was one of his most trusted men.

'Your majesty,' the man said breathlessly, going down on one knee. 'Sir,' he added, addressing his Commander, 'may I speak freely?'

'You may. Please report.'

'The woman is no longer at Crowyll. She left her lodgings during the night of the attack or possibly the next day. None of the people who live nearby remember seeing her that morning.'

Liryk's brow twitched in annoyance. 'You checked her place of employment?'

The man was sucking in air; he had obviously ridden at speed. 'Yes, sir. Everywhere else that we have been told she frequented. There is no trace of her.'

'The plot thickens, Liryk,' Valentyna said as she strode away. She was convinced now that the whore had been in on the deed. 'Fynch, a word.'

Fynch hurried behind her until they had reached the quiet herb garden.

'And so you leave me now?'

'Yes, your majesty. I must.'

'Then I shall miss you until I see you again.'

'Likewise, your highness.'

The Queen pulled a pouch from one of her pockets. 'I don't understand this journey of yours, Fynch, but I see I have no choice but to let you go.'

He shook his head sadly, unsure of what to say.

'I know,' she said more quietly. 'I must trust you.'

When he looked up she was making an effort to smile. He knew it did not come easily to her after what they had just done. No doubt she was in great personal pain and his leaving only magnified her loneliness. He hastened to offer some reassurance. 'As soon as I have found out what I need to know, I shall return, your majesty.'

'I wish I understood what it is you need to know.'

Sensibly he remained silent.

'Here, Fynch. Please take this,' she said, holding out the pouch. He took it and it rested heavily in his hand, suggesting gold and silver within. He hesitated and looked at the Queen, who immediately said: 'No, don't fight me on this. You will have need of it. This is a dangerous person you go headlong to meet. I wish I could stop you.' She forced herself to pull her hand away, although every instinct told her to grab him and hold him, to stop him leaving as everyone she had ever loved had left her.

'You cannot. But you must be strong, my Queen,' Fynch replied. 'Koreldy would expect it of you.'

She gave him a sad smile. 'Everyone expects it of me, my friend. Shar speed you safely, Fynch.'

Valentyna allowed him to kiss her hand, then walked away, too fearful to hug him farewell. He recalled how she had turned from Romen in the same manner. Now they had both hurt her. He left quietly to find Liryk, Knave padding silently behind.

Fynch refused the offer of a horse but pressed a surprised Liryk to tell him all he knew.

Liryk, surprised at the boy's queries, gave him all the information he had on the assassination, even down to an accurate description of the woman.

'Where do you go, son?' he asked, his curiosity piqued by the boy's questions and distant manner.

'To find Hildyth,' Fynch replied.

3

CELIMUS MUNCHED ON AN almond cake baked fresh that
morning. It mattered not to him that his pastry cook
would have had to leave his bed many hours prior to dawn
to craft this specialty. It not only meant a great deal of
tedious preparation in skinning and crushing the nuts,
the dough also required proving prior to its energetic
kneading and shaping into the complex designs. The
fiddly cakes were normally reserved for celebrations, but
Celimus had a particular liking for them and, on a whim
just before midnight, had ordered some to be served with
his breakfast. No one dared put forward an objection.
Celimus was King. Whatever he wanted he would have.

Celimus glanced at the second cake he held, relishing
the anticipation of its chewy texture and delicate flavour,
before looking back at the strange gift which had arrived
this morning by courier. The King picked it up again
from the linen it had been wrapped in; he had not been
able to take his eyes from it since its arrival. He twirled
it between his fingers – it gave him immense satisfaction
to hold it at last. He wished he could preserve it somehow

and thus retain the grim pleasure of glancing at it from time to time, knowing that once again he had triumphed.

He considered Koreldy. He had rather liked the mercenary's sardonic manner and had appreciated his carrying out of Wyl's murder, but Koreldy's execution had become necessary after Celimus realised he could not rely on the man's loyalty.

His strange behaviour in the cathedral during Thirsk's funeral was odd to say the least, and once Koreldy had fled Stoneheart with Thirsk's sister, Celimus understood he could not trust this man to keep their dark secret. There was too much at stake – not just the annexing of Briavel to Morgravia but his own crown. If the Legion ever suspected that he had anything to do with Thirsk's death then his sovereignty would be vulnerable in the extreme. The Legion was too powerful; even without Thirsk at its head it could take over the realm.

No, he thought, flicking crumbs absently from his chin, ridding himself of Koreldy was regrettable but wise, especially as the man hailed from Grenadyn. Who knew what links he might have with the Mountain King. Risking the passage of Morgravian secrets into the hands of Cailech would be tempting fate indeed.

'Best without him,' he murmured, replacing Koreldy's severed ring finger into the box it had arrived in.

Celimus was looking forward to showing his new prize to Jessom, his Chancellor. It was unusual to have circumvented the man's thorough inspection of all deliveries into the palace, and had occurred purely by chance. He had been talking with his personal horse handler when the messenger had arrived, entering the main bailey at full gallop.

'Find out what's so urgent,' the King had ordered at a passing page, interrupting the intense discussion with the horse handler about a new stallion shortly due to arrive in the royal stable.

The startled boy, unused to contact with the King, had looked terrified, unsure whether to bow or run the errand immediately. He had attempted both, clumsily. When he returned, he stammered that it was a package . . . a delivery for his majesty.

Celimus had strolled towards his guards. 'You have a delivery for me?'

'Yes, your highness,' the most senior of the men had replied, nodding his head repeatedly to show the required subservience demanded by his King.

'Well, give it to me. I can't stand around here all day.'

'Er, sire . . . Chancellor Jessom has ordered that all—'

Celimus's anger had always been swift to rise, and he was bored – a deadly combination. Impatient for his new horse and impatient with the tedious days of routine which had followed his return from Briavel, his ire had sparked. The package was a small diversion but a diversion nonetheless.

'I don't give a flying fig what the Chancellor has ordered. Give it to me now or, Shar help me, you'll be cleaning the latrines for the rest of your career . . . after I've had your feet cut off!'

The man visibly swallowed, unprepared for such an assault. He would be in serious trouble with Jessom but that paled in comparison to his King's wrath. He motioned to the gatekeeper to pass over the parcel, then bowed low and handed it to Celimus, face burning from the embarrassment of being shamed in front of the other soldiers.

He had tried to salvage some small pride. 'Apologies, my King. I am following orders.'

'Indeed,' Celimus had replied drily, his anger quietened. 'It looks like something of no matter anyway. I've been expecting some new jesses for my hawk. It's most likely those,' he had lied, wondering if the contents could possibly be what he dreamed of holding in his hands.

'Yes, sire,' the man had said. He had bowed once again for good measure, and sighed with relief as he watched the King stride away to pick up the conversation with his horse handler as though no interruption had occurred.

Celimus smiled now to himself as he chewed another mouthful of his favourite cake. There was no warmth in the expression though, only malice. 'Farewell, Koreldy,' he whispered, wondering whether the finger had been cut off before his enemy died. He certainly hoped so. Romen would have known it to be an assassination – and on whose orders.

There was a knock at his chamber door. It would be Jessom. He covered Romen's finger with the linen and closed the lid of the box. 'Come,' he called.

Jessom entered, his hands full of parchments. 'Good morning, sire. I need you to sign some papers, if you please.'

He noticed the King was suppressing some mirth. He had already heard about the parcel's delivery, but had not yet connected the two.

'I'm rid of him, Jessom.'

'Rid of whom, sire?' the man asked absently, setting down the papers and shuffling them into a neat pile before the King.

'Koreldy, of course. Care to take a look?' Celimus pushed the small box towards him.

Jessom felt a thrill of elation. She had done it! He forced his expression to remain unchanged, however, except for a contrived confusion passing across it for the King's benefit.

'Whatever is this, my King?' he said, staring at but not yet picking up the proffered parcel.

'Open it.'

He did as asked, lifting back the linen and pausing theatrically, knowing the delay would drive Celimus to distraction.

'Well?' the King said irritably. 'Your man triumphed.'

Jessom carefully shut the lid on the bloodied finger. 'As I see.'

'Do you not share my glee?' Celimus was indignant now.

'Of course, your highness. I am delighted we achieved your desire. It is always my aim to please you, sire.'

Celimus ignored the maddening obsequiousness. 'And your man?'

'Hmmm?' Jessom deliberately busied himself with the papers. He did not want to answer any questions about the woman he knew as Leyen, and she would certainly not appreciate him divulging any information about her. 'These are quite urgent, my lord.'

Celimus pushed them away. Some fluttered to the floor. 'Jessom, you appear rather vague about this person.'

'Do I, sire? It is not my intent.'

'Then tell me his name.'

'My King, we have discussed this previously. I do not wish to involve you in any matters which may incriminate you. By knowing the name of the killer, you become part of the intrigue.'

'But *I am* the intrigue, Jessom.' The olive-green gaze narrowed.

Jessom knew he must never play Celimus for a fool. The King was pretentious, often petulant, and had many qualities which a less perceptive person might consider rendered him a dolt. They would be mistaken. Jessom knew that Celimus possessed the sharpest of minds, the cruellest of tongues, and felt absolutely no remorse for any suffering. The King missed very little. He would have to tread carefully now.

'Bring him here to Stoneheart,' Celimus demanded, reaching for his third cake.

Jessom's throat constricted. This was everything he did not want. 'I am not sure I can do that, sire.'

'Why not?' Celimus casually brushed cake crumbs from his shirt. He slumped further in his chair, lifting one leg to rest on a nearby stool. 'Tell me why this is impossible.'

Jessom knew not to trust the relaxed stance. 'This assassin is not easily contacted, I must admit.'

'Then find him. I wish to meet with him.'

'May I ask why, my King?'

'Because, Jessom, someone who has done my bidding where others have failed rises in my esteem. This man is useful to me. I wish to speak with him, perhaps even discuss further . . . tasks.' He chose his words with care. 'Have you paid in full?'

'The last instalment is due on proof of death, sire,' Jessom answered unhappily.

'And now you have it. Your man will have to collect that payment and, when he does, you will bring him before me. Do you understand?'

'I shall try, sire.'

'No, Jessom. You will not try. You will do.' The voice was no longer casual. There was clear menace in those softly spoken final three words.

The Chancellor nodded. Keen to change the subject he said lightly, 'So you are free of the Thirsk influence, my King. This must make you happy.'

'Not yet free.'

'Oh?' Jessom bent to pick up the spilled papers.

'There is still the matter of the sister. Once she is dealt with, I shall have rid myself entirely of all connections to the Thirsk family. So this is what I propose: I want you to find out everything you can about the disappearance of the lovely Ylena. Where did Koreldy take her? He pulled the wool over my eyes on that occasion. I really believed he was going to use her and cast her aside. It suited my needs, I suppose, and I allowed myself to be duped. I shall find her though.'

Jessom was not surprised at how quickly the King's temper changed. Suddenly he was charged with energy, all previous threats pushed aside. He fought the temptation to shake his head at the unpredictable nature of the monarch. It made him a very dangerous individual. 'How much do we know of Koreldy's movements?' Jessom said.

'Nothing, in truth. He and Ylena slipped out of Stoneheart on the evening of Thirsk's funeral feast. No one saw them leave, although I'm told one of my guards spoke to Koreldy earlier in the day in a little-used court-yard.'

'It had a gate, I presume?'

The King nodded. 'The same gate where, apparently, Thirsk's dog caused a commotion that night.'

'Ah, that was the diversion then, not that I understand

how one gets a dog to co-operate,' the Chancellor said, picking up the King's line of thought. He was pleased to see Celimus nod. 'Where does the closest road lead, your highness?'

The sovereign frowned. 'That would be towards Farnswyth, I suppose.'

'It's a start. I shall make enquiries. By the way, did you make provision for any staff for Koreldy during his brief stay?'

'A page, I think. I know not which one. Why?'

'Thank you, sire. You never know what a servant might overhear. I will look into it.'

'Good. Now about my lost taxes and revenue – any progress?'

'I have men infiltrating the entire Legion, sire.'

'You remain convinced it is someone from within our own ranks?'

'Yes, sire.'

Celimus became quiet for a few moments. Jessom knew something bad was coming. Tax collectors from all over the realm were being ambushed far too regularly for it to be random bandit raids. It had to be someone from the inside leaking information.

'In that case,' the King said finally, 'from today and for every day that we fail to identify the culprit, two men from the Legion will be impaled. Take strong, healthy men – I don't care how they are selected. Fear will spread like plague. They'll yield the perpetrator very quickly.' He took another cake.

His servant bowed and moved towards the door. The King stopped him. 'And Jessom . . .'

'Sire?'

'When you find Ylena Thirsk . . .'

'Yes, your majesty.'

'. . . I want her killed.'

'Consider it done, my lord.'

Jessom left the King's chambers troubled. He had not successfully deflected Celimus from his desire to meet the assassin, Leyen. It was going to be hard work to persuade her to come to Stoneheart, but he had no choice now but to try. She had to be tracked down. As for Thirsk's sister, that edict did not rattle him nearly as much.

He despised killing just for the sake of it and he was concerned that Celimus often demanded death on a whim. The whole Rittylworth escapade was a disaster for the realm and the amount of damage it could do if the truth came out would be catastrophic for Celimus's reign. Sadly, Jessom thought, the King could not seem to grow beyond his own sense of omnipotence when subtlety was so urgently required. However, with regard to Ylena Thirsk Jessom could appreciate the necessity of her death. She was a dangerous person on the loose, for her name alone commanded such respect across the realm and particularly with the Legion. It was not a task he relished certainly but Jessom believed her death was critical to the continuing power of Celimus.

'I'm coming for you, Ylena,' he muttered as he stalked through the corridors of Stoneheart towards his own rooms.

4

CAILECH, THE MOUNTAIN KING, stood over the prone figure slumped on filthy straw in the cell that saw neither day or night. Buried deep in the mountain out of which the fortress had been hewn, it might as well have been a tomb. Gueryn, the prisoner, hoped it would be.

'Is he dying?' the King asked, his jaw working to temper the anger he felt. Cailech rarely wasted words and the man he spoke to knew to offer the same courtesy. The gaoler nodded. 'Willing himself to death, my lord. He hasn't taken food in a long time.'

'Water?'

The man shook his head. 'Doesn't talk; doesn't move much either.'

'I should have been told,' Cailech said, disgusted. 'Summon Rashlyn immediately.'

The gaoler disappeared, well aware that he had not pleased his King. He called for a runner and a message was sent to the strange, dark man who was barshi to the sovereign.

Inside the cell, Cailech paced as he thought. He had

no idea who this man was, other than a soldier of the
famous Morgravian Legion. Initially his delight in
capturing him came purely from the opportunity to make
an example of the Morgravian through torture and humiliation, to salvage some revenge for those of his people
slaughtered by the cruel King from the south. The senseless killing of innocent youngsters, not even warriors, had
offended Cailech deep into his soul. He would make the
brash new King pay. But then Romen Koreldy had
returned to the Razors, despite a warning from his
previous visit that he risked death by doing so. Koreldy
– whom Cailech could not help but like and, to some
degree, admire – had spun a web of excuses, none of which
resonated as truth to the Mountain King, but he could
not prove otherwise. Even more strangely, Koreldy had
seemed to recognise the Morgravian prisoner, even though
the soldier claimed no knowledge of Koreldy. Why then
had Koreldy argued to save the prisoner's life? And why,
in turn, had this man gladly given up his own chance at
escape, bravely attempting to lead the Mountain warriors
away from the trail of his fellow escapees, Koreldy and
the woman, Elspyth of Yentro?

And so King Cailech, who could tease at a secret as a
dog gnawed at a bone, did not kill this Morgravian soldier
as his heart wanted to. Instead, driven by an instinct he
was still unsure about, he had incarcerated him. Had even
had the man's near fatal wounds healed, in order that he
might live and prove useful in luring Koreldy back to the
Razors and to death.

Cailech had not taken the escape of his prisoners with
any grace. If not for the recapture of Gueryn le Gant he
would have had his own men executed for allowing the

three Morgravians to slip past their guard. They had had
help of course, from Cailech's own second-in-command.
Lothryn's deceit was a matter which continued to make
the King's gut twist, for they had been the closest of
comrades. As brothers, no less. It seemed unthinkable that
Lothryn had chosen betrayal, and Cailech was uncertain
yet of his reasons. Whether it was out of affection for the
female Morgravian, or out of grief for the loss of his wife,
who had died in birthing the King's son. Or, more likely,
a result of their argument about the near cannibalism of
le Gant and the other prisoners. Whatever it was, it
mattered little now. Loyalty had been asked, Lothryn had
refused to give it and now he was paying the price.

Returning his mind to the prisoner in the cell, the
King felt sure that Koreldy was not finished with this
one yet. He would come back to rescue him and then
Cailech would deal with them both. He smiled humourlessly at the thought.

His musings were disturbed by movement from le
Gant. A flicker of the prisoner's eyelids told him that the
starving man was aware of the King's presence. The candle
which the gaoler had lit threw a warmer pallor over the
Morgravian than he possessed. The chill of the cell was
biting and the constant drip of water in one corner was
enough to send most mad. It had created a mossy slime
down one rough wall but the earthy smell did little to
mask the stink from le Gant, who had long ago given up
caring for himself or his health. In fact, he had deliberately laid in his own dirt, hoping that infection would
find his old arrow wound – a gift from Cailech – and kill
him. He was clearly determined to die.

All of this enraged the King but he held onto his

famous temper as he spoke to his prisoner. 'Understand, le Gant, that I will keep you alive. I must, for you will bring Koreldy back. Not only will I have his secret, but I will take his life. I know you hear me, soldier.'

The man moved then, enough to let Cailech know that he was paying attention.

'Why the silence, Morgravian? I would have thought you would welcome some company.'

'Not yours,' the voice croaked, weak but still tinged with anger.

Cailech nodded, pleased with the recognition. At least the prisoner had not lost his wits.

'We will make you well, le Gant. And then you will return here.'

'And I will repeat the process,' Gueryn said defiantly, still not opening his eyes.

'As will I. You might crave death, soldier, but I will not grant it. Get used to the idea and make it better for yourself. Choose to live. Who knows, you might even see Koreldy again before you both die at the time and in the manner of my choosing.'

'You are so naive, Cailech,' Gueryn chided, weak as he felt. 'No wonder Celimus isn't worried about a threat from the north,' he lied. 'He knows you can be provoked into thoughtless rage and your kingdom dismantled at the time of his choosing and manner.'

Gueryn knew the echo of his words would enrage the man who stood above him, and he waited for the kick or punch that would surely come. Instead he heard a choking sound as the King of the Mountains swallowed his anger.

'Don't be so sure, soldier. Your King is the ruin of Morgravia and I shall be its ultimate destroyer.'

Gueryn had no time to respond. He heard footsteps and knew this would be the healer arriving, the strange man who had brought him back from the brink of death once before.

'Sire,' said the new voice.

'I want him made well again – no matter what it takes,' the King growled.

Rashlyn nodded. 'I shall see to it.'

'And this time he's to be force-fed and watered daily.'

'It will be done, my lord.'

Gueryn was moved from the dungeon to a room he recalled from his nightmares. It was here he had watched Cailech execute the kind, brave woman called Elspyth. She was a Morgravian, captured with Koreldy. How he had cheered inwardly when she had stood up to the King. It was she who had patiently cut away the stitches that bound his eyelids together so that he might look upon his rescuers. The one he had thought was Wyl, had heard speak in a strange voice yet with such a striking similarity to Wyl's manner, turned out to be a handsome mercenary from Grenadyn. The man had certainly known Wyl but the disappointment had cut through Gueryn as keenly as a blade.

Elspyth was every bit the feisty woman he had guessed she would be and pretty too, whilst his previous torturer, Lothryn, had turned friend. Gueryn could not imagine what fate had befallen the Mountain man who had betrayed his King. He had been Cailech's second-in-command and so the defection would have been a damaging blow to the King. Gueryn was glad. He wished he could deal some damaging blows of his own, but he was pathetically weak, his only way of fighting back being to try and kill himself. That had been a fight in vain. The cruel healer was preparing to bring Gueryn back to full strength so they could continue laughing in his face.

At this moment Gueryn had never felt closer to tears. He was not a man given to emotional outbursts; trained by the stoic Fergys Thirsk, he kept his thoughts and emotions in check. He had had many reasons to weep in his life. Since adulthood he had given into none of them, but he had never felt more like doing so than now. He felt useless – a senior soldier of the Morgravian Legion and personal attendant to the Thirsk family, and unable to offer any resistance to the enemy.

He spat on the ground in disgust.

'Save that,' Rashlyn called over his shoulder. 'No use in wasting precious liquid, or I'll do just as my King asks and subject you to the added humiliation of having men hold you down and force food and water into your throat.'

Gueryn sighed. He remembered Elspyth's sad end and how her blood had gushed from the savage cut made by Cailech. It had congealed around Gueryn's boots, marking him as her killer because he would not relent and tell them what they wanted to hear. Blackmail was only one of Cailech's weapons. Gueryn remembered how Rashlyn had smiled as Elspyth died, his eyes sparkling with pleasure. He would not hesitate to hurt Gueryn, if given authority. But for now his job was to heal and Gueryn came to the painful realisation that the King of the Mountains was right. It was pointless fighting it, for they would continue the cycle and keep him alive – if not fit – until he was of no further use. But perhaps if he regained his health he could be of some use and strike some of those damaging blows. He could not think clearly enough yet, for his mind was dulled by starvation and thirst, but he promised himself to plan ways to hurt Cailech.

'There's no need to force me,' he murmured, his voice cracking from lack of use.

'Oh?' Rashlyn said, turning now.

'I'll eat and drink.'

'Good, the other method is rather messy.' The wild-looking man cackled horribly.

'I make a demand, though, for this co-operation.'

'You are in no position to make demands,' Rashlyn replied softly.

'Your mad King wants me well and healthy. I will make this easy for you, for all of us, if he'll allow me time outside to breathe fresh air and to work my muscles. If he won't permit this then I will fight you, and I will promise you that I will find a way to die and anger him. Remember whose head will be on the chopping block then, Rashlyn,' Gueryn warned.

There was silence whilst the man he spoke to digested the import of his words.

'I shall speak to the King. But now you eat,' he said. He clapped his hands to summon a bearer with food.

'You will remain here until I release you. Consider yourself lucky, Morgravian. You have a window to look out of and a comfortable pallet to sleep on.'

'I want to be allowed outside for periods and for that I'll exchange your comforts for the dungeon.'

Rashlyn acted as though Gueryn had said nothing. 'You will remain chained for the entire time you are in my care. Have no delusions, soldier. There is no escape, not even if you breathe the air of outside.'

'I did it once before,' Gueryn said, more out of defiance than any real threat.

'With help. It will never be offered again.'

'Where is Lothryn?' he asked and hated the sound of the other man's cruel laughter.

'Nowhere you can help him,' Rashlyn answered, delighted that he could hurt with words.

'Is he alive?'

'Hardly,' came the cold reply. 'Although it was a lot of fun dealing with him.'

Despite his lack of strength, Gueryn threw himself at the small dark man, his body toppling towards the King's barshi out of pure will rather than an ability to move freely.

But Rashlyn held his hand up the moment he heard Gueryn move and for the first time in his life Gueryn felt real terror, spine-tingling fright that made the hairs on his arms and at the back of his neck stand on end. For at Rashlyn's gesture the soldier found himself pinned in mid-air. The thought flitted through his mind that this must look comical but then his wits were flooded by the realisation that something awesome and terrible had just occurred. Rashlyn was a sorcerer and had wielded magic upon him.

'I will make it hurt next time,' the barshi said softly. 'Never try that again, Morgravian. If you have never believed it before, then believe it now that magic exists. You and the rather strange position you hang in are testimony to that. Remember how it feels, le Gant, for I can immobilise you like this for eternity if I so choose.'

Rashlyn removed the spell and Gueryn crashed painfully to the ground. He groaned in agony and gut-wrenching despair as he grasped the full terror of what he was up against.

5

FYNCH SAT AT THE back entrance to the Forbidden Fruit. Knave had followed his friend's suggestion to remain hidden for the time being but he had good vision from his quiet spot and could see the boy kicking at a stone, biding his time until someone arrived who might speak to him.

Several women had already hurried past and in through the dark doorway, but they had not struck Fynch as being the friendly target he was looking for. He trusted his instincts, knew the right person would come along. It had been a couple of hours now. Winter was mild this year but still cool enough to chill his thinly covered bones. He must have looked cold, sitting on the fence stump, when the young woman arrived. She seemed in no rush and he could not see if her full-length cloak covered a revealing gown. With no firm knowledge of how a brothel actually operated his mind bothered at such minor detail.

'You'll catch your death out here,' she said, eyeing him around her hood.

He recognised the Briavel accent. So she was a local. 'Yes, it's right cold today,' he replied in a strong northern dialect he had picked up from listening to some of the other lads, sent by their families to work at the kitchens of Stoneheart. He pitched it perfectly, masking his own less distinctive southern accent.

'You're far from home, boy. Morgravia?'

Bullseye, he thought. 'That I am, madam. How sharp you are.'

She smiled. 'Are you waiting for someone?'

Fynch nodded. 'My sister.'

'Oh? And who might that be?'

'Her name is Hildyth. I've travelled many days to see her. Our mam's dead. I was sent to find her.'

Her expression melted as he had anticipated it would. 'You poor mite – she's not here, love. Come on inside. Let's warm you up a bit.'

Fynch followed, and as they walked past some of the other women, he heard them use her name.

'Thank you, Rene,' he said as she pulled up a chair by a stove and sat him down.

'There, that should warm those thin bones of yours. Now, how about something to eat? You must be hungry – boys are always hungry.'

He was not; hunger rarely entered Fynch's mindset. 'I'm starving,' he said, forcing a grin, not enjoying beguiling this kind soul.

'I knew it. I've got a couple of young nephews and their bellies are always grinding.' She ruffled his hair and set about gathering some items to tempt him.

A few women moved into and about the parlour, but they ignored Fynch and he them. He stared into the flames of the stove, ensuring he looked cold, scared even, and not open to conversation with others. As he became lost in his thoughts, he realised he had already begun thinking about Romen's murderer as being Wyl. He wondered whose shoes Wyl walked in now. Fynch had no doubt the whore was involved, even though Liryk had looked shocked at the Queen's insinuation. He intended that she would lead him to Wyl.

'There you are, sweetie,' Rene said, arriving at his side and dragging his thoughts back to the warm kitchen. 'Cheese and home-made chutney is the best I can do. And here's a knuckle of bread. I've put a glass of milk behind you on the table. What's your name by the way?'

Fynch hated milk. 'I'm Fynch. Rene, you're very kind.'

'I just feel badly you've come so far for nothing,' she said, her expression soft. 'My little brother died some years past. He would have been ten summers now, a few years older than you.'

Inwardly he sighed. He was ten summers but knew he looked younger. 'You must miss him,' he said, forcing himself to munch on the food.

'So much. He was a lovely lad. Shouldn't have drowned. It was an accident but still . . .'

He had opened an old wound. 'I'm sorry, Rene.'

She forced herself to brighten. 'I know. You remind me of him a little with your light colouring. Somehow I don't think he would have trekked so many miles to find me though. You must love your sister very much to have come so far.'

'I had to. We need Hildyth. Father is sick too and there are five wee ones, all younger than me.' He laid the accent on thickly, suggesting he was becoming upset. He was, in truth, for lying was not Fynch's style.

'Oh, now, now. Come on. Hildyth is no longer working

here – in fact, I know she's left Crowyll. Let me see if I can find out any more for you.'

He nodded, pushing more bread into his mouth so he would not have to lie any further to such a decent person.

She disappeared for a few minutes and returned whispering with someone. Another woman, slightly older, regarded him. 'You're Hildyth's brother?'

He nodded, not allowing himself to fib any more. Her eyes were narrowed. 'She never said anything about a brother.'

'Hush,' Rene said. 'His mother's just died. There's several children. Be gentle.'

The other woman shook her head. 'Hildyth's gone. She left on the night of that fellow's death, the one who got stabbed.'

Fynch wrinkled his brow in confusion. Rene rolled her eyes at her companion's heavy tongue. 'We had a mishap here not so long ago. A noble. We don't know anything about him, but obviously someone wanted him dead. Hildyth was . . . well, she was with him – or I should say looking after him at the time. I took her home.'

The other woman bent down. 'Do you know what your sister does for a living, boy?'

Again he nodded. 'She makes men happy,' he said seriously and saw Rene's face soften once again with affection.

'That's right, love, she does that,' Rene said. 'Go on, tell him.' She grimaced at the woman beside her.

This time her friend sighed. 'She came back much later that night, must have been in the early hours of the morning, when all the fuss had died down. Everyone was asleep or gone back to their homes. I just happened to be still around and I saw her.'

'What did she say?' Fynch asked, listening intently now.

'Nothing, really. I mean, she looked terrified and who wouldn't be with what she'd just been through. I asked her what had happened.' The woman shrugged. 'She told me briefly about the man's death, said she was leaving.'

'Why did she come back, I wonder?' Rene queried.

'She said she'd left something behind in the room, but she didn't want to see all those soldiers again so she'd waited until the place was quiet.'

'What was it?' Fynch hoped for a clue.

Irritatingly the woman shrugged again. 'How would I know? She just stepped inside one of the chambers and was out again almost straightaway.'

'Did she tell you where she was going?' Fynch held his breath.

'I didn't know she was going anywhere to even ask. She was acting strangely, I recall – I mean, apart from being scared there was something else. It was as though she was drunk, but I smelt no liquor on her.'

'What do you mean?' Rene asked. Fynch was glad she did.

'Well, I can't really say. You know, staggering a little, unsure of her words, couldn't hold my gaze. I just figured she was upset, but she seemed really uncomfortable around me which would explain why she left me so suddenly.'

Fynch tried to phrase his question differently. 'Did Hildyth say anything that might help me find her?' His accent slipped in his determination to learn as much as he could but neither of the women seemed to notice.

'No. Perhaps she decided to go home, not that I know where that is. She said a name . . . a girl's name. I didn't catch it. Miriam or something. I don't know anything else.'

'Does that help you, Fynch?' Rene asked, her face filled with hope.

He hated doing it but he shook his head, adopting a glum expression. 'No, but I'll just keep looking,' he said. Inside, his heart lurched at the mention of Myrren, which was surely the name Hildyth had spoken. 'Thanks rightly for the cheese and bread,' he said to Rene. 'And to you, miss.' He nodded at the other woman.

She gave her habitual shrug and left, Fynch already forgotten.

'Can I pack you a little food?'

'No, Rene. I'll be fine.'

'Good luck, then.'

Fynch surprised himself by giving her a hug. After all his sadness it was uplifting to have such a positive lead. 'I'll come back and see you some day.'

She smiled, knowing he would do no such thing.

He left to find Knave and they quickly moved away from the Forbidden Fruit. Fynch's mind was racing. 'I'll explain everything in a moment,' he said to the dog. 'Let's just get away towards the woodland.'

Drinking water from the same stream that Wyl had in his new body, Fynch gathered his thoughts. He found it helpful to speak them aloud to his silent friend, arrange them neatly before storing them tidily away.

'Wyl is alive – I'm convinced of it. The vision told me so. I have to believe it's happened again and that he now walks as his executioner. If I'm right, then it was Hildyth who killed Wyl, and then Wyl had to lie about the man breaking in and stabbing Romen.' Fynch adjusted his position to lean against the big dog. Knave licked him. 'I suppose he discovered himself as this woman and disappeared from the scene as fast as he could.' The boy shook his head, imagining how distressed Wyl must have been. 'The woman at the brothel remembers Hildyth muttering a name. She said Miriam but I think she means Myrren. Only a handful of people know about Myrren – none of them in Briavel save our Queen and us. I'm certain he's become Hildyth. We have to find her.'

Knave wandered away. Fynch assumed the dog was hungry and would probably hunt down a careless rabbit. He settled back against a tree and closed his eyes to ponder. When he needed to think things through he had taught himself to let go. To stop teasing at one strand of thought and let his mind roam amongst all its wealth of gathered information. Invariably he found that clues began to show themselves as threads intertwined. Where would Wyl go, he wondered. The memory of his recent vision slipped into his mind. He went back over what had been said and the image of the town and the fields of hops. Why had that picture been given to him? Where had Myrren come from?

Fynch sifted through his recollections of overheard conversations between excited city folk during the witch trial. He relaxed, turning his face up to the watery sunlight that filtered through the canopy of leaves. It came to him moments later. *Baelup!* Could that be where Wyl was heading? Baelup was where the realm's best ale was made – he knew this from listening to the soldiers reminiscing about trips to the tiny town. Hops were used in ale-making. It was a clue. Perhaps Wyl was trying to track down Myrren's family.

The dog returned. It carried something in its mouth

but it was no creature. Knave dropped it into Fynch's lap. It looked like a ragged thong until Fynch realised it was the bracelet Romen used to wear.

'It's a sign, Knave! He must have hidden here on the night he became Hildyth. Wyl left this deliberately, I'm sure. Perhaps he hoped you would find it, you clever dog.'

He scratched Knave's ears and hugged the animal close. 'We're going to Baelup,' Fynch whispered to his friend. 'I shall need a horse. Valentyna's purse will be put to good use.'

Wyl had collected a tiny stash of coins from a hiding spot in Crowyll, the whereabouts of which Faryl's memory had released. She had similar hides located across both realms, he realised, so she could access money relatively swiftly. This was very little here – he would need more, much more. He took the time to write down the locations, in case Faryl's essence and memories faded. He learned that her mind was tidy and her ways thorough. He was impressed.

If you must be a woman, then be glad it's this one, he reminded himself constantly.

Faryl was not just good at her chosen work, he discovered, she was the very best. Her kills shocked him. Highly placed and influential people from so many different cities, and even realms across the ocean, had drawn their last breath as a result of her actions. She felt nothing for her victims; Faryl was cold. More than that . . . she was bitter. *Why?* This he could not tease out from where it was buried deep. It was connected with her family, he sensed, but no more would come through. Wyl left it. It might surface, as so many vague recollections of Romen's had.

Wyl was riding towards Morgravia, destination Baelup.

It was a start. He knew that Myrren's mother had left that town almost immediately after her family's traumatic deaths. Lymbert had reluctantly given him details of where they had found Myrren, and Wyl had travelled to Baelup to collect the dog, Knave, as he had promised the girl. He had met the mother only briefly – they had not even swapped names. He had tried to explain that he was from Pearlis, a member of the Legion, but she had hardly paid him any attention. She was almost out of her wits, packing her belongings frantically.

He had told her that he had promised Myrren he would pick up her pup, which the mother had been glad to hand over without further questions. Where she had gone after that he could not guess, but it was the only lead he had.

Drawing on Faryl's good sense he had donned a disguise. It definitely felt more comfortable to be travelling as a man and helped somewhat to ease the despair of the last couple of evenings. Until this moment, it was all he could ask of himself not to grab his blade and open his wrists.

That bleak thought had been well and truly scrutinised the night before. He had come close, too. It had seemed the only answer when every demon came to haunt him as he slept rough beneath a hidden moon. He hated being a woman, despised the very sight of the body that had not so long ago stirred him to thoughts of lust when it belonged to Hildyth. The thought of being trapped in that body forever convinced him there was no point trying to live on.

Somehow he had talked himself through the urge to draw blood and allow it to leak away quickly and strongly. Thoughts of Valentyna swirled in his mind and he could not do it. Valentyna, Ylena, Fynch, even Elspyth – they all needed him to stay alive.

Remembering Elspyth inevitably led him to think on Lothryn. Wyl had given Elspyth a promise, one he knew he could not break, that he would go back to find out Lothryn's fate. At the back of his mind too was the thought that he must recover Gueryn's body and bring it home to Argorn.

Argorn! His eyes watered as he remembered his father. No, he could not kill himself. The Thirsks were a proud line and he was its last son, even if the world no longer recognised him as such. He must fight on and expose the root of all this evil: Celimus.

And so Wyl now found himself on a lonely, dusty road, a man in a woman's body, dressed plainly as a man and carrying weapons. No one who glimpsed those would mistake him for a vulnerable lone traveller. He displayed them deliberately in order that any thief who may consider tackling him would think twice at the sight of the sword. His blades were once again close to his chest, lying uncomfortably against the breasts he had bound tightly to flatten. He had not been tempted to look at himself in the mirror amongst Faryl's belongings. It was too much for his mind to bear right now. He preferred the discomfort of the bindings to the disarming weight and swell of his breasts when they moved freely.

He *had* been tempted to hack off her hair, but had resisted, reasoning that he may well be grateful for the female disguise Faryl offered. Instead he pushed it under a wig – made by a master craftsman, he could tell – and pulled a cap down over it. He also wore a false beard, again of such quality that he knew the pieces had been purchased at high cost from craftsmen who asked no questions and accepted only gold. The beard was his greatest comfort, together with the artful hair glued to the back of his hands. In this guise, he could convince himself he was a man again.

Wyl estimated he was now a day from the Morgravian border and a couple of days' ride then to Baelup. The trail he was hoping to pick up was almost a decade cold and, although he had no choice but to try, he doubted he would find the scent of Myrren's mother. The thought reminded him of Knave. He hoped the dog had sensed his death; it seemed to know when he was in trouble. If so, then perhaps Knave had already led Fynch to Crowyll and tracked down the bracelet. It would resonate in Fynch's sharp brain and set the lad thinking. Wyl felt confident his young friend would work it out and then come looking for him. He would like both of them close by when and if he finally found the manwitch.

He refused to allow himself to think on Valentyna beyond wondering whether she would know by now. Of course she would. Would she be grieving? He hoped so, but then again perhaps she would see it as a fitting end to a flawed relationship. He could not forget the grief in her eyes, well-masked but evident to him. The accusation of treachery was clear in that pained glance. Her public accusation of his treachery was almost more than he could bear, but borne it he had, for he loved her more than he had ever loved anyone or any thing, including himself. He would gladly die for her. Wished that he could do so now – leave this wretched existence and save her the agony of Celimus. But he could not be sure of saving himself or Valentyna. All he could do was grit his teeth and go on, holding onto hope.

Wyl spurred his horse into a gallop. There was no time to waste in sorrowful musings.

6

ENTERING GRIMBLE TOWN WYL knew he could not stand the tight bindings around his chest for much longer. The temptation to spend the night at one of the two inns got the better of him. He quickly found stabling for his horse. The stablemaster hardly looked twice at him as he promised sweet water and fresh hay for the mare. Wyl reminded himself to stop being quite so self-conscious.

'Which inn do you recommend, Master Paul?' Wyl asked, adding some extra coin to the amount required. It was an old habit, one Gueryn had drummed into him from an early age. *Pay well for whoever looks after your horse. His care might save your life one day*, his mentor used to say.

Wyl extended the creed to all areas of his life. A few extra coins, especially silver, in someone's palm often made that person unwittingly his through the subtle bond of generosity. Thinking of Gueryn brought a wave of sadness which he blinked back fiercely.

The stablemaster replied, 'Well, the Four Feathers be as good an inn as you'll find in these parts. The ale is watered only lightly and Kidger's wife does an honest stew.'

'Thank you,' Wyl said. 'I'll see you on the morrow.'

'That you will, sir,' Master Paul said, already bending towards the buckets of water to wash the horse. Wyl smiled. Gueryn had been right. His horse would be fresh for tomorrow's long ride having been rubbed down properly and well fed.

He strolled into the town proper as late afternoon settled upon it with the stillness that often comes as the sun lowers. At this time of year, once the sun had dipped low in the sky the temperature plummeted and the evenings became crisp. Wyl could feel it chilling as he cast a glance about Grimble Town's main square. It was a neat, sleepy place, known mostly for its orchards which yielded Morgravia's tastiest almonds and prized cherries. Come early summer the town swelled as transient workers flooded in to help with the harvest. It was also handily positioned not far from one of the main routes into Pearlis so it enjoyed valuable seasonal trade from merchants.

Right now it was quiet, which suited Wyl. He made his way towards the Four Feathers and was relieved when Kidger paid no special notice to the bearded stranger asking for a room. Faryl had a skill in pitching her voice low enough to be acceptably manly, so it drew no attention. He understood from her memory this had taken years of practice and silently thanked her for her diligence.

Wyl paid in advance for a night's lodging and meals. Hearty smells wafted through from the kitchen and he suddenly realised how hungry he was. 'That smells good. What's on tonight?' he asked.

'The missus has got some lamb stew simmering or there's chickens on the spit.'

Both sounded delicious. 'I'll have stew.'

'Thank you, sir,' Kidger replied. 'The girls will be serving from dusk.'

Wyl nodded and gratefully made his way to his room. He sank on to the bed with such pleasure it might have been down-filled and covered with fine linen rather than worn sheets over a horsehair mattress. Nevertheless the bed and the room were clean and a pleasant draught of air came from the open window. He had meant to undress straightaway. Instead he dozed off, the bindings forgotten as sleep claimed him. A loud clatter of pans beneath his window woke him abruptly less than an hour later and the pain across his chest reminded him the bindings were still in place. He ordered a bath to be brought up and filled.

'The bathhouse in town is very reasonable, sir,' said the somewhat sullen girl who took his request.

Wyl realised she did not fancy hauling up a tub or the water. He grinned through the beard, hoping it looked friendly. 'I know, but I don't feel like leaving my room. Here.' He handed her two crowns, an exorbitant sum in her small world.

'Oh, sir! I . . .'

'Please. And bring my water quickly.'

She grinned, tucking the money beneath her blouse. 'At once, sir.'

Impressive, Wyl thought. If he ever allowed himself to be seen as Faryl, he must remember that trick.

True to the girl's word, hot water was soon steaming in the tub and she sent up soap as well as scented oil. He thanked the two lads who had dragged up the pails and the tub. Obviously the serving girl had coin enough now to pay for lackeys.

When the door closed and he was finally alone, Wyl stripped down. He struggled to untie the lengths of torn sheeting which held his breasts flat, and when they eventually loosened he sighed with relief at the wondrous sensation of being free again. He refused to look down at himself. Instead, he poured a few drops of the musky oil into the tub to soften the water, then, after checking the latch was firmly on the door once again, he climbed in, immersing his body as much as he could, averting his eyes from the smoothly muscled yet clearly feminine legs which bent at well-shaped knees.

Wyl had thought to have a flask of wine sent up as well and he sampled it now, glad he had paid that little bit extra to Kidger, for the first swallow told him it was of an acceptable quality. He closed his eyes, blanked his mind and focused on nothing but the soothing sensation of the water warming his tired, unfamiliar body. He soaked the beard and eyebrows then pulled them away from his face, the glue dissolving as Faryl's memory had told him it would. Wyl placed them on a nearby chair next to the wig; these were valuable possessions to him now.

Unpinning his hair he let it fall loose, marvelling at its heaviness as it dropped, its ends curling into the water. Wyl ran his hands through it to push it off his face. Gone was his own coarse red hair; gone was Romen's smoothly combed plait. Instead he boasted these lustrous locks of a curious darkly golden hue. He touched them, unable to resist, and was rewarded by the feel of their soft texture. He remembered the sensation of Faryl's hair against his body when she bent over him, seemingly to begin his smoothing; in reality, to end his life with the punching of the blade into his heart. Wyl shuddered from the memory of that powerful and shocking sensation, and then the equally terrifying tearing away from Romen's body as his spirit moved into his killer's flesh.

His eyes remained fixed on the wall opposite, where a small dresser stood. He knew that on the other side of the chamber was a table with a mirror, which he had ignored and intended to go on ignoring. He had no desire to see himself as a woman. Feeling his hair with wonder was as close as he wanted to get to knowing this strange new body.

Again he closed his eyes and his thoughts roamed to Myrren's mother and the knowledge that she had betrayed her husband. Had Myrren's father known he was raising another man's child? That question led him to consider Lothryn's sadness at giving up his newborn son to Cailech, even though the babe was not truly his but had been sired by the King. Cailech had reclaimed him now to nurture and raise as his heir. Wyl shook his head and worried again at how Cailech would have dealt with brave Lothryn. He knew the King of the Mountains was too vengeful to simply kill his once-loyal second, his best friend.

Lothryn's certain suffering prompted thoughts of Elspyth and his promise to her that he would return to the Razors to find the man she loved. He wondered where she was and how she would get on with Ylena, and his spirits plummeted further as he thought of these two women travelling alone – frightened, despairing at the loss of loved ones, their happy lives shattered because of him. He could not even protect them; instead he needed them to be courageous and fend for themselves until he could return to them. He sent a silent plea to Shar to watch over them.

The act of prayer put him in a sombre mood. He finished his soak swiftly, deliberately ignoring the chance to soap himself. He could not bring himself, just now, to touch the body he resided in. Wyl stood to reach the towel. The tub rocked on its uneven base and, in that moment of alarm that he may tip it all over, Wyl caught sight of his naked body in the mirror. The shock was complete.

He fought back the surge as his gorge rose and opened his eyes again. Reflected was the image of a striking woman. She was not exquisitely pretty like Ylena or classically beautiful as Valentyna; instead Faryl possessed something else which was hard to describe. It blossomed from confidence. He noticed the arrogant twitch of a smile on the neat, clearly defined lips. The eyes were feline and sensual in an oval face that was tanned lightly from the sun. Her hair, he mused, was probably her vanity. If not, she would have cut it short for it was an encumbrance to her trade. Digging into her rapidly fading essence he realised that Faryl needed her hair to feel feminine, to remind herself she was a woman, because she spent so much of her life posing as different men as well as following a brutal profession. The body itself was a marvel to his eyes. Curvy but strong. She ran to keep herself fit apparently, favouring hills for her exercise for they tested her stamina but also gave her cover. He nodded. She would make an excellent soldier of the Legion with her rigorous fitness routines and high level of fighting skills. She favoured the blade but was handy with a sword and skilled with a bow.

Feeling foolish he smiled at himself in the mirror, and was rewarded by a relaxing of Faryl's normally intense look into a softness he had not glimpsed previously. She rarely used this expression, he realised, just as Fynch rarely lost his sober look, but her neglect was for different reasons. Fynch was just a serious sort whereas Faryl, Wyl now knew, had little to smile about. He tried to find specific memories, but the source of her grim outlook on life was still hidden from him. He must be patient. It would yield itself eventually. He stared at the smile on the face looking back at him. It touched the feline eyes, sparking them into girlish michievousness. Despite hating Faryl for what she had done to him, Wyl wished he could have glimpsed that smile when she was alive. Any man could fall head over heels for it.

Many minutes had passed; he was almost dry in fact. Then, as he stood there feeling like a peeping Tom stealing a look at a naked woman, he uncovered the disturbing memories. Wyl flinched as buried hurts emerged from Faryl's youthful years. Her elder brothers — twins — had raped her regularly, as had her father. The younger boys — she had five brothers in all — knew of the rapes but were too scared of their burly elders to do anything about it, except, after the vile couplings were done, to help her to the brook nearby to wash herself clean. Her youngest brother, just ten, would cry as he dabbed at her bruises with witch-hazel spirit and she would weep at having to share this atrocity.

Wyl's heart lurched as he learned that Faryl's mother also knew of the rapes, but was helpless to prevent them so cowed and battered was she by her brutish husband. And so the abuses continued, until Faryl took her life into her own hands and killed her father. She stuck a blade into his stretched throat as he lay above her, taking his pleasure with his only daughter. She had relished his blood gushing over her; it was cathartic. Then she had pushed his corpse from between her legs and walked to the brook, as she had done on so many previous occasions. This time she was not weeping and she was not scared. Naked, she took her time bathing and cleaning herself.

Her twin brothers had come then, trembling in fury and fright. She had defiantly raised her catlike eyes to the handsome, perverted pair. 'Watch your backs, boys,' she had threatened. 'One day I'll be coming for you.'

Her calmness and the demonic look in her eyes had stilled their tongues and rattled their minds. Neither moved, too shocked by the sight of the bloodied corpse in the empty stable.

'I'm leaving now,' she had said, climbing out of the water and, not even bothering to dry herself, pulling on some clothes. 'You're evil, both of you. I hope Shar finds a way to take you soon.'

She spat on the ground between them, picked up her cleaned blade and, just fourteen, walked away from her life of despair, vowing never to desire a man. She had enjoyed the sensation of killing her father and, in her bitterness, looked forward to doing the same to other men. Her only regret was that her youngest brother might suffer for her bravery.

'If you lay a finger on Tye, I'll kill you both, and horribly,' she said as a final warning over her shoulder.

She had not needed to carry out her threat. It seemed Shar had heard her plea, and the brothers died in a freak accident when their horse was startled, overbalanced their cart and they plunged down a ravine to their death.

Wyl, eavesdropping on Faryl's memories, realised that

she had indeed looked after Tye, sending money home in secret for him. One day, a few years after she had escaped, she had met him covertly and taken him away. She had continued to send money to what remained of her family. Faryl had lost track of Tye, but no longer worried about him for her brother was now rich and enjoyed a new life as a merchant.

Wyl felt hollow as he returned his gaze to the mirror and Faryl's reflection. He felt pity, but understood that she had long ago rejected any such sentiment. She preferred to be utterly in control of her life and remained contemptuous of most men. Faryl's coldness would never have warmed. She was an assassin and enjoyed her work. He learned how killing Koreldy in the brothel was a thoroughly satisfying task until it ended so badly for her.

He shook himself clear of her memories and noticed with pleasure that she was a tall woman — he had got used to towering above people as Romen. Flat and trim though her belly was, it felt empty and interrupted him now with a loud grumble. He felt hungry enough to eat all the stew and a helping of the fowl. Towelling himself unnecessarily, he felt the sombre mood dissipate slightly and he was grateful, for it clouded his thinking. He was glad his curiosity had won through. Learning about Faryl's past had enabled him to turn the key on it. *He* was Faryl now. He had no choice but to use her body to all of its best advantages and not lose sight of his mission to find Myrren's true father and learn the secret of her gift. It was frustrating having to give over so much time and energy to chasing down strangers whilst Valentyna remained vulnerable to Celimus. But, as with Elspyth and Ylena, he was useless to the Queen of Briavel until he

solved this nightmarish curse. He had no intention of
being killed again; that said, he could hardly bear the
thought of remaining as Faryl for the rest of his living
days. The temptation to choose a victim himself flitted
through his mind, but the seer had told him that he could
not control this gift of Myrren's. He could not choose who
to become. It would be murder anyway, he reminded
himself. No, the answer to this curse remained with the
manwitch and finding him remained his priority. Wyl
prayed once again that Shar would protect the three
women he loved from the dark grasp of the man he hated.

Reluctantly he lifted the strips of linen which would
help him look like a man again. Wyl sighed, knowing it
was only for an hour or two, then wasted no further time
in binding his breasts flat and climbing into fresh clothes.
He swished his previous garments in the still warm bath
and rubbed at them with the soap, congratulating himself
as he realised this simple act brought all three of his
personalities together: Faryl's diligence, Romen's need to
be neat and tidy and Wyl's training to take advantage of
every opportunity. He squeezed the clothes out and hung
them wherever he could position them on a chair to enjoy
the draught.

Darkness had fallen. He should hurry down to eat.
Checking his room for any giveaway signs of Faryl, he
was convinced all had been well hidden. He re-glued the
beard to his face and donned the wig, pinning his hair
very carefully this time because he did not have the luxury
of the hat to hold things in place. He would need to be
vigilant tonight. Still, he was not planning to do anything
more than eat his meal quickly and return to his room.
Tidying away the glue, he satisfied himself in the mirror

that he was now Thom Bentwood again – his alias for this journey.

He headed downstairs into the common dining room, marvelling at how easily Faryl's body slipped into a masculine stride. His mind turned hungrily towards the lamb stew. He swept the chamber with a practised gaze without being obvious, taking in that the common room was busy with a group of men, some of them Legionnaires.

Wyl's heart skipped but he settled his nerves. None of these soldiers could possibly know him. He did recognise one; a man older than himself whom he had never had much time for when he had been General. Wyl remembered the fellow to be lazy, the sort who looked for short cuts and always on to some lurk or another. He was loud of personality, though, and tended to impress the younger soldiers with his wit and confidence.

Wyl took a swallow of ale, deliberately looking away and around the room as he tried to remember the fellow's name. It came to him. Always good with the ladies, he recalled, as he watched the man give one of the serving girls a brash smile. Wyl fiddled with his beard as he waited, trying not to think of his breasts which had sounded a fresh ache, threatening to ruin his appetite.

'Lamb stew, wasn't it, Master Bentwood?' a plump young girl asked, startling him as she set down a huge clay plate. He nodded distractedly and she smiled. 'I'll be right back with some bread. Can I bring you some more ale, sir?'

'Please,' he replied, relieved that his hunger had remained intact as he eyed the meat which had been simmered to render itself into a deliciously rich and sticky stew. Vegetables and some dumplings floated in the dark gravy.

'Perfect,' he said quietly and began eating. He became so focused on his pleasurable chewing that the large serve was gone very quickly. He realised he must have been extremely hungry to wolf it down so fast. He pushed his plate aside and hardly noticed when it was cleared away and the new ale deposited before him. He felt sated and peaceful at last. He leaned back against the wall, turning his body so he could surreptitiously watch the rest of the room whilst not really seeming to be staring at anything in particular from beneath his bushy eyebrows. His attention was drawn back to the soldiers. There were three of them and they sat amongst five civilians clearly known to them. These five looked dusty and road-weary. They were travellers. Wyl wondered at the easy connection between the two groups and their increasingly loud behaviour. He noticed it was not just ale flowing freely but wine also. Money was plentiful, he could tell. All had eaten here, and if the night wore on much longer he believed they may even be staying here. Legionnaires did not normally stay at Grimble Town, and if they did there would be a small company of them passing through, certainly more than this trio.

He puzzled at it but could come up with no answer, other than a vague suspicion that the soldiers were not meant to be here at all. There was no officer present which was further damning. Three foot soldiers in a tiny town? He let it go. Right now he was Thom Bentwood and he had a mission. Whatever these members of the Legion were up to, it was not his business any longer.

Wyl finished his ale. As he drained his mug he saw that one of the civilians was watching him. He was big, built like a bear. The man averted his eyes immediately, rejoining the merriment around the table, but he somehow did not seem to belong there. Not that it mattered to Wyl — it was time to go. He stood and felt light-headed momentarily. Too much ale on top of the wine earlier. He noticed that he had managed to down two jugs of the liquid.

I need some air, he told himself and, against his original plan, decided to step outside the inn for just a few minutes before retiring. He waved his thanks to the girls, left some coin at the table — which he knew would be pounced upon as soon as his back was turned — and made his way to the main door. He did not even glance towards the group that had previously held his interest.

Stepping outside, the freshness of the night hit him and he felt sober straightaway. He allowed himself the luxury of a short stroll up the street, with the plan to head back upstairs just as soon as his large meal had settled. On his return, he was barely fifty paces from the door of the Four Feathers when he noticed a figure leaning against the wall of the building next to the inn. It was one of the men from the group; he recognised the chap's hat. He wanted to believe the fellow was merely taking some fresh air too, but all his senses were on instant alert.

Wyl walked briskly towards the inn. He was not daunted by the presence of a single man, and farther down the street a few locals were going about their business — closing up for the night, walking home, perhaps even headed for the Four Feathers . . . although probably not, as the darkened shadows were moving with purpose but not towards him.

As Wyl drew close to the figure, confident now he would pass without incident, the man began to whistle

softly. It was too obvious. Wyl's body clenched in anticipation, and his fears were confirmed as several other
shadowy figures melted out of an alley. They manhandled
him into the unlit area and dragged him around the corner,
behind the sheds of the inn.

There would be no help here, so Wyl allowed his body
to go limp rather than fight. He counted five of them,
one of them the soldier he had recognised, Rostyr. He
obliged Wyl now with one of those fake smiles he hated
so much. 'What were you doing watching us?'

Someone held a candle close to Wyl's face. Wyl shook
his head, feigning confusion. 'I don't know what you mean.
Get these men off me,' he said, hoping he sounded like
an offended merchant.

'Oh yes you do, friend. You were far too interested in
us back in the inn.'

'Good fellow,' Wyl spluttered, realising he should have
allowed Faryl's instincts to rule rather than his own – she
would not have allowed herself to be noticed, 'my name
is Thom Bentwood, I am a merchant and I have never
seen you or your companions before this evening. You're
a soldier, anyway. What in Shar's name could I want with
you?'

'My question entirely,' Rostyr said with unnerving
calm. 'Perhaps we should help his memory along,' he
added. Wyl felt the first blow land and his breath
whooshed out of him, leaving him struggling to fill his
lungs. He coughed. The next blow, delivered with precision, doubled him over. The third brought him to his
knees.

'Pick him up,' Rostyr ordered.

Wyl was hauled back to his feet where he hung between

the two men who held him, sucking in air, his face battered, all of him hurting. He realised his beard had gone askew. So did his tormentor, who at first looked baffled then began to laugh.

'It's a lad,' he said. 'Let's hear you squeal the truth now, boy,' he added, gripping between Wyl's legs.

It would only be much later that Wyl would enjoy the memory of the shock on Rostyr's face. Expecting to squeeze the truth from the impostor, Rostyr found his large hand gripped nothing.

'What the . . .' He jumped back. 'Pull his breeches down!' he yelled.

'Are you mad?' someone asked, then laughed. 'Do it yourself!'

Rostyr, angry now as well as confused, did just that. 'Bring the candle here.'

Wyl closed his eyes. He had not thought he could hate Myrren any more for her gift, but right now he believed he was plumbing new depths. His trousers were torn down to reveal the truth of what he had become. 'It's a fucking woman,' a dismayed voice said.

Rostyr's expression coalesced into something new and horrible in the glow of the candlelight.

'Now this bitch will give us the truth all right. Hold her down.'

Wyl could not believe what was happening. He watched with horror as Rostyr, snarling menacingly, struggled to free himself from his clothes. Then some internal defence forced Wyl to close his eyes and not witness this. He felt the abomination of probing fingers, then something else pushing inside, and from deep within he began to scream. It was Faryl's true voice this time, primal and

angry. A filthy hand clamped itself over his mouth. He
tried to bite it and succeeded. Wyl filled Faryl's lungs to
scream again but someone hit him on the head and his
world filled with sparks of light before misting over.

When his vision cleared, he saw an altogether different
scene. Rostyr's body was arched, but not from the anticipated release, rather because a knife had just penetrated
his lung. He spasmed then coughed, spattering Wyl's face
with bright blood. His body was hauled up and flung
away like a rag doll.

Wyl looked around. Others were dead, one still dying.
The candle was extinguished so now only a huge shadow
loomed. Wyl thought he was almost certainly going to
be run through with the knife too. *It wouldn't be the first
time*, he thought wryly and wanted to laugh at his own
dark humour as he imagined becoming the man who
towered above.

The figure stepped over him and finished off the
groaning man. Wyl held his breath, or thought he did;
he could still hear someone breathing short and shallow
and realised it was in fact him.

A face appeared close to his own.

'Come,' the voice said and he was lifted as easily as if
he weighed nothing.

'Who are you?' Wyl slurred.

'Aremys.'

The dizzying mist returned and this time it enveloped
him entirely.

When he woke he was in a bed. He opened his eyes slowly.
A large man sat in a corner watching him. Wyl remembered now – it was the bear from the dining room. He

realised he was naked beneath the sheets. For some reason he found this deeply disturbing with the huge stranger nearby. He dimly recalled the man's name.

'Aremys?' he said, careful to use Faryl's real voice this time as it was obvious the man knew he was a woman.

'I'm here.'

'Why?'

'I don't like women being attacked.'

Wyl could not agree more. 'You were one of them, I thought. The bear.'

The man smirked at the title, as though it had been levelled at him often before. 'Not really one of them.'

Wyl remembered how the huge man had seemed distant from the others. He nodded, let it pass for now. 'All dead?'

'Yes.'

'The bodies?'

'Taken care of,' the bear reassured.

'Taken care of?' Wyl could not keep the incredulity from his voice. 'Five corpses!'

'Seven actually.'

Wyl took a sharp breath. The bear had been with seven other companions and he had killed them all.

'Why?'

'That seems to be a favourite question of yours,' Aremys replied, the suggestion of a smile behind his words.

'It's a good question under the circumstances!' Wyl countered, a suggestion of anger behind his words. He moved stiffly to sit up. 'May I have some water?'

The bear moved smoothly for a big man. He took his time, lighting a second lamp nearby before pouring a mug of water which Wyl gratefully swallowed in a single draught before falling back on the pillows. His body ached everywhere.

'Tell me what happened . . . please.'

Aremys gave a reluctant nod. 'It's a long story.'

'I'm not going anywhere.'

The man's mouth twitched as if to smile but it did not eventuate. He sighed instead. 'Let me pour myself a wine.'

'Where are we?' Wyl could see this was not his own chamber.

'My room. The other inn.'

'I see. Whose side are you on?' It was a loaded question.

'Yours, it seems.' He leaned over to pour himself a cup of the wine from a nearby carafe.

'Who undressed me?'

'I averted my eyes,' Aremys said and then a smile did ghost across his face.

Wyl could not remember a moment in his life when he had felt more embarrassed.

'*You* took my clothes off?' It came out in a girlish shriek, which he hated even more.

'You've got lovely tits,' Aremys added, fuelling Wyl's discomfort, making his cheeks burn.

The big man laughed. 'Couldn't help myself.'

It felt good to share a joke, despite the awkwardness. Wyl smiled. 'I'm glad you appreciate them.'

Their mood became serious again as Aremys attempted to apologise. 'I'm sorry I didn't arrive in time to stop them . . . well, you know . . .'

Wyl closed his eyes in distress at the memory of the violation and the deeper memory of Faryl's early life. 'I know,' he said, softly, wanting to put it behind him, but wondering if women who were attacked in this way ever could. Faryl had never succeeded. She had hated men ever since. 'Is that why you killed them?'

The man sipped from his cup then looked over its rim at Wyl. 'No, but your plight made it easier for me to do it.'

It fell into place. 'You're a mercenary?'

Aremys nodded. 'Is it that obvious?'

'Let's just say I've known a few.' There was a wryness which his companion heard but did not pursue. 'In whose service?' Wyl added.

'The realm's.'

'Celimus?' It came out choked.

'I suppose. His monkey, Jessom, hired me. I gather royal revenue has been going missing with alarming regularity. Jessom suspects it's someone from within the Legion.'

'Rostyr,' Wyl murmured. 'How fitting.'

Aremys shrugged. 'I don't care. I'm not Morgravian but anyone who can steal back taxes has my vote. Except your King has no sense of humour,' he said, drily. 'Jessom paid me a fortune to track down the culprits. It turned out to be three of them and I managed to infiltrate their group. It took me many weeks to find them and then the most of this winter to win their trust. Rostyr was the leader. Cluey fellow too. He used bandits to do the deed but he was the brains behind the jobs.'

'I see,' Wyl said, trying to straighten himself on his pillows again. 'A lot of money stolen?'

'Enough to fire a king's wrath.'

'Did they hurt anyone?'

'Yes, on a couple of occasions. It wasn't intentional but it happened.'

'Soldiers?'

'Yes. You seem very interested in them.'

'Can you blame me after being raped by them?' Wyl bristled. 'It hurts, Aremys. I'm not sure many men realise quite how much!'

'Apologies. That was blunt of me.'

Wyl accepted it graciously although the part of him that was Faryl was angry. 'And so why did you choose tonight to kill them?'

'They were planning something daring. It would mean more innocent deaths and someone of note also. I could not allow that to happen – it was the right time to deal with them as I was instructed.'

'Poison?' Faryl's senses told him this would be the best mode.

Aremys nodded. 'Good guess. That was my plan, until you decided to enter the dining room and ruin it. I had to use a messier method.'

'I'm sorry to have spoiled things. What have you done with the bodies?'

'Tomorrow they'll be carted back to Pearlis as proof. I've already sent a messenger to inform Jessom of my findings.'

'Not to mention requesting final payment.'

Wyl's barb had no effect on the man, who simply shrugged his burly shoulders.

'And so now it's your turn,' Aremys said, setting down his mug. 'I'm all ears.'

'For what?'

'To hear the intriguing tale of Thom Bentwood, a woman in disguise as a merchant passing through a town whose season for merchants is long over.'

Wyl mentally kicked himself. Faryl's instincts had niggled at him along these lines and he had ignored them. Aremys had him nailed good and proper.

He tried for the obvious. 'It's not easy being a woman travelling alone,' he replied. 'The disguise helps.'

'I accept that. But the point is, why do you travel alone?'

'Do I need a reason?'

Aremys fixed his dark gaze on the bruised woman before him. Secrets. That was all right; he had them too. 'No, I suppose not. But will you tell me anyway?'

That was unexpected. Wyl felt flustered.

Aremys could see this. 'Perhaps tomorrow. Right now I suspect sleep is what you need.' He sensed the woman's relief. 'Will you allow me to tend the injuries to your face?'

Wyl nodded. 'Are they bad?'

'I shan't be giving you a mirror tonight.'

'Oh, that alarming,' Wyl said, disappointment strong in his voice.

Aremys was rifling through an old leather sack. He pulled out a small flat glass box. 'It would be if I didn't have my miracle salve with me.'

He moved to the bed. 'I'll have a bathtub brought up tomorrow,' he said absently, digging a finger into the cloudy ointment. He daubed it on to Wyl's face, which soon began to tingle as the big man gently rubbed the salve into the injured spots. 'The bruises will surface and disappear quickly,' he assured his patient. 'Now rest.'

'Where are you going?'

'Not far. I'll be here on the floor beside you. I'll leave a fresh candle burning.'

Wyl was touched. He could more than take care of himself under normal circumstances but it felt rather comforting to have someone looking out for him. It reminded him of being a youngster again, with Gueryn making all his decisions for him. He missed being looked after. He missed Gueryn. On that sad thought he closed his eyes and turned on his side. Sleep would come fast tonight.

He listened to the sounds of Aremys trying to make himself comfortable on the hard floorboards. Wyl was grateful to him for not pursuing the story of Thom Bentwood further tonight.

'My name is Faryl,' Wyl said quietly into the darkness, surprising himself for giving the other man the truth . . . and for finally acknowledging it himself.

7

THE DAYS AT RITTYLWORTH passed slowly, following their own particular rhythm as the men of Shar kept to their routine of worship and work. For some, their duties were in the library, poring over texts and carefully scribing passages; others who were artistic spent hours patiently copying ancient illuminations. For many, their daily toil was in the vegetable gardens and orchards, or tending to the sheep and goats which kept them fed. Others looked after the few cows which sustained the gentle community with fresh milk for drinking, as well as producing the rich cream, butter and famed cheese of the region.

Rittylworth Bruise took its name from the dark wax the monastery's cheesemakers dipped their proud product into for maturing and preserving. The shiny violet rounds of hard cheese were stored in a special room beneath the chapel, which maintained a steady temperature through all seasons. But even this room was not as deep into the ground as the secret grotto – a place that few outside the monastic Order knew about.

It became Ylena's favourite place of all. Brother Jakub,

all too aware of their visitor's grief, had suggested within the first day of her arrival that she make it her own for a while. As much as Ylena enjoyed her sleeping room with its view over the orchards, it was to the grotto she escaped for solitude and it was there, alongside the gentle waters of the warm spring, that she had begun to slowly heal.

In the beginning, the healing process was purely physical: regaining an appetite, finding her voice again, the fading of bruises and swellings. Eventually, as her slim frame regained some of its strength and vitality, she found herself able to think of the horror she had experienced, and to begin to grieve.

In the dungeon at Stoneheart, forced to look upon her beloved husband's severed head, she had thought she would go out of her mind. Darkness had gripped her then, and she sank into its embrace willingly, finding strange comfort in that wilderness, for there was no pain there.

But at Rittylworth, surrounded by the monks' serenity and faith, Ylena felt a subtle change occur deep within. The storms of helpless sobbing grew less frequent and slowly she understood that she could not bring back her loved ones, no matter how hard she wept. And in accepting this, her feelings of weakness and the belief that she was incapable of living without those she loved began to dissipate.

It was not easy, and many times the grief threatened to carry her away again, but on those occasions Ylena would remind herself of her family name and the need to live up to it, to keep digging deeper towards the strength she knew she possessed.

Wyl had once spoken to her of how he had taught himself to accept the death of their mother and, more lately, their father. Ylena drew on that teaching now, directing the painful emotions inward and burying them in a safe dark place where they could no longer disable her.

Ylena would be the first to admit that she had led a pampered and spoiled life. But Thirsk blood ran in her veins and Wyl, Shar bless him, had never allowed her to forget that she came from the strongest of stock. And the knowledge gave her the resilience to fight the grief and despair and return to the light. She could think of Alyd and his execution now without being overwhelmed by the horror, and her shock at losing the only remaining member of her family, her dear, loving brother Wyl, had dulled to bitter acceptance. At times she still felt numb but she was learning to put that aside and 'walk out into the sun' as Brother Jakub so poetically put it.

It was Celimus of course who had contrived all of this death and suffering and on whose hateful name she should build her own hate. Killing Alyd was his petulant reaction to them denying him the right to Virgin's Blood during the tourney – how clever Wyl had been to suggest they marry within hours of learning Celimus's intention. And how sorrowful that she had lost both men who loved her so much. She had cried for the loss of Gueryn too, whom she presumed had been felled for similar jealous reasons. Celimus had systematically set about destroying the Thirsk family and its closest supporters.

And then there was Brother Jakub – calm and patient with searching eyes that seemed to see into the depths of her heart and the pain she had buried there. He had never asked directly about her dark experiences but it was obvious he knew what had happened and at whose behest. The old monk's patient care had contributed much to Ylena's recovery and she would be forever grateful to him.

And so, nourished by the calm of the secret grotto, Ylena had allowed the days to blend until her body and her mind returned themselves to her whole. Now, she sensed a resilience within she had never known before. Daunting though it was, she would do what was expected of her as a Thirsk — what her father would want; what Wyl would admire. Despite her fear, she would fight back. Somehow, as impossible as it seemed right now, she would make Celimus pay for his horrific deeds.

Crossing the main courtyard this bright morning, Ylena smiled at two brothers, who dipped their heads towards her but did not break the morning silence which was held until third bell – due any moment, she suspected. She wondered where Pil was. He was normally skipping around her by this time, making her laugh with his tall stories. The young novice monk took his role as her care-taker earnestly and she had to keep reminding him that she was not an invalid and preferred to do things for herself. He would smile shyly and apologise, then go right back to fussing around her. In truth, he was a large factor in her recovery. His almost childlike desire to make her smile and see her well again was infectious.

Pil was one of a big family who hailed from the north-west. His father was a fisherman, as were his brothers. His sisters and mother prepared and sold the catch. Everyone in their village was involved in the sea and its bounty but Pil was the only member of his family who felt no calling for it. In fact he would be the first to admit that he suffered the ocean sickness and hated anything to do with boats and fish. Saying such things was sacrilege in his village so he suffered in silence and did a terrible job of mending nets and helping wherever he could. His father finally gave up on him and on one particular evening of high frustration asked a travelling monk whether he would take his youngest, good-for-nothing son with him and teach him the ways of Shar. 'Perhaps he'll be some use to us then and can pray for our safety and prosperity,' Pil had haltingly repeated to Ylena one day. The monk had agreed and after travelling with the man for several months and discovering that he was not only interested to do Shar's work but that he was good at his letters, Pil began to feel a calling to become a monk himself. The kindly guardian had contacted his old friend Jakub at Rittylworth and by year's end, young Pil had found himself a new home and a new family who welcomed him with love and patience. He had fitted in easily and being the youngest had been spoiled with care and affection from the brothers. Ylena could see this and the love they had given him had manifested itself in Pil's ebullience at life and his desire to do his god's work with enthusiasm. She thanked her lucky stars that Pil had been so dreadful at fishing and had told him that not so long ago, enjoying watching him blush and stammer.

Truly, it felt as though she had lived here amongst the brothers for an age when in fact it was only weeks.

Despite the bright day, winter's last bite still nipped at the air, although the buds on the fruit trees suggested spring was not that far away. Ylena pulled her soft shawl more tightly around herself. She felt the cold and even the steaming bowl of cream oats sweetened with oozing honeycomb she had swallowed gratefully early that morning had not warmed her sufficiently. She shivered, relishing the thought of her daily soak in the soothing waters of the grotto, which was where she was headed now.

Her boots clicked on the flagstones of the great arched cloisters through which Ylena loved to walk. She turned her head, knowing Brother Tomas would be in the tiny courtyard to her left, lovingly tending his citrus trees. The peel of the akin fruit had healing properties, he had explained to her, and curiously it was at its most powerful in the morning. And so each day he checked the fruit at the same time, testing it for readiness. She waved and he nodded to her, holding up one of the bluish-green spheres and grinning. It was a good one obviously. Tomas had said that he was fortunate to coax one fruit per week from the trees when they were in season in early spring. They were one of nature's more stubborn follies and one needed extraordinary patience to tend and harvest them. It was easy to be patient at the monastery, Ylena thought, surrounded by its sleepy, tranquil atmosphere.

Skipping down some steps, she realised she felt the brightest she had in a long time. Happy was not quite the word she would choose, but she felt as though she was almost ready to consider a life beyond Rittylworth. Her first task would be to get herself to Alyd's people. After learning the fate of his son the powerful Duke of Felrawthy would surely help her in her quest to bring down Celimus – she was sure of it. Ylena was convinced the Legion would not take up arms against them when it learned of the truth behind its General's death and the execution of its popular Captain.

Third bell sounded and Ylena smiled: the silence for the day was over. It occurred to her that she had meant to call in on Brother Farley and get a gargle for the gritty throat she had developed during the night. Torn between longing to immerse herself in the warm waters of the spring, but not wanting to risk falling ill now that she felt so much better, Ylena hurriedly veered towards the old physic's rooms – and ran straight into Brother Jakub.

'Ah, my girl. You are a sight to gladden the heart of an old man.'

She hugged him. 'Good morning, Brother Jakub. Are you ailing?'

His face crinkled into his gentle smile. 'No, child. There are some sick children in the village and I want to speak with Brother Farley before he becomes too engrossed in his day's toil. I'd like him to look in on them this morning. And you?'

She touched her neck. 'Sore throat.'

'Well, my dear mother used to say that if you gad about with wet hair on cold days you're bound to catch a chill,' he said, wagging a finger in fair imitation of an old woman. She enjoyed his impression and he squeezed her hand, delighting in her joy. 'How good it is to hear you laugh.'

Ylena pulled a rueful face. 'Today, for the first time since I was married, I am pleased to be alive. I catch myself smiling and I feel almost guilty.'

'You mustn't,' Jakub counselled. 'This is the human spirit, child, restoring itself. It is how we heal; how we go on and deal with life which can be so ugly sometimes. Let your spirit soar when it is of a mind to. Trust it, for it means you have found hope again. Hope is a powerful weapon.'

She nodded, feeling tears welling at the goodness and generosity of this man. He sensed her emotion and, not wishing to upset her happy mood, changed the subject. 'Is Pil attending you well, Ylena?'

'Too well, Brother Jakub!' she replied, with mock despair.

'Ah, he's a good boy and takes his role of protector very seriously.'

'I know. He has been most kind . . . all of you have. But I must think soon of leaving.'

'Not too soon, I hope,' he said softly. 'Take your time. Be well.'

She took her chance. 'I shouldn't hold you up, Brother Jakub,' – he shook his head slightly to show it was of no consequence – 'but I wonder if I could ask you whether you have heard from Romen?'

'I've received no word,' he replied, guiding her into the warmth of the physic's chamber. Brother Farley was busy measuring out powders and breaking clumps of dried herbs into smaller pieces. He muttered to himself, hardly noticing them.

'Then may I impose on you further by asking whether he left something with you before he departed – something important for safekeeping?'

Jakub's expression grew grave and Ylena knew immediately that Romen had indeed left behind the sack containing the remains of her husband. She swallowed hard. 'It's all right. I can talk about it now. I'm much stronger.'

'I know you are, child. You are a marvel and it is not difficult to see that you come from strong stock.'

'Did you know my father?' she said, surprised.

'Of him, of course. I regret I never had the pleasure of meeting your fine father, or your brother, in person. They were good men as I hear it.'

'Thank you,' she whispered. 'So you do have it?'

He hugged her. 'It's safe. In the grotto.'

Ylena flinched at the realisation that she had been sharing her special place all this time with Alyd. 'Where?' she asked.

'There is a false back to the cupboard where we keep the candles. I hid it there. It has been preserved as Romen requested.'

'He did?' She had not counted on this and would kiss Romen right now if she could. It had been worrying her that Alyd's remains would have deteriorated beyond recognition and she would never be able to prove to his father how his son had died.

Ylena was about to speak again when the sounds of men yelling cut across the calm morning. Frowning, Brother Jakub told her to remain where she was and hurried outside to see what was happening. A few moments later he ran back in, face ashen.

He grabbed her hand. 'Ylena, hide behind this counter.'

'Whatever is going on?'

'Riders – king's men!' Pil burst into the room, a look of terror on his face. 'They're hurting the brothers.'

Ylena's eyes widened with disbelief and rising panic gripped at her throat, its soreness forgotten in an instant. 'What—'

'Do as I say,' Jakub ordered, his voice hard. 'Hide now, both of you, and as soon as you can, climb out of the window here and make for the grotto. You know what to do there, child,' he said sombrely to Ylena, then turned to Pil: 'Now is when you prove your worth, lad. Keep her safe. Get her away from here as soon as you can.'

'Jakub!' she began, her voice trembling with intense fear. 'It's me they've come for, isn't it?'

'But they'll never find you, my girl. Not as long as I draw breath.' He nodded at his colleague. 'Come, Farley, be brave now. We have nothing to share with these men.'

Jakub gave Ylena a searching look, kissed her briefly and whispered for her to be brave, then took the dismayed Brother Farley's hand and together the two old men walked out into the bright day.

Ylena was too stunned to move. Then she heard men's voices gruffly questioning her friends who had just left the room. 'Come on!' Pil hissed and dragged her around the counter.

They ducked behind Brother Farley's weighing bench and crawled underneath his shelves. Ylena held her breath as she heard boots clattering into the room. Pil put his finger to his lips, more out of a need to comfort himself she was sure, for his eyes were tightly shut.

She heard Jakub's voice. It was gentle, filled with the contrived confusion of an old man. 'There is no woman in our monastery, son,' he offered innocently, presumably to a soldier. 'But by all means you're welcome to search . . .' His voice trailed off as they left the chamber again. Mercifully the men were only carrying out an initial cursory search.

'They'll be back,' Pil whispered.

'I want to see what they're doing,' she mouthed.

He shook his head vehemently. 'I promised Jakub.'

Ylena knew he was right, just as she knew that these intruders had come for her. If they found her she might not live to enjoy her revenge. She was terrified but if they were to escape, they had to know what was happening. 'We can't risk running into greater danger, Pil,' she pleaded.

The young monk bowed his head, beaten. 'Perhaps we can see from the small tower,' he suggested.

The small tower used to be a special place of prayer for brothers who chose to live for a time in what was known simply as Solitary. Part of the floor had collapsed a few years back and Jakub had declared it too dangerous so the tower had been closed. Due to lack of requests from brothers looking to spend time in Solitary, its repair had still not been attempted.

'We can get there easily enough,' Pil added cautiously, 'and then we can access the grotto through the cheese pantry if we have to.'

He climbed out from under the counter and motioned that all was clear. They opened the small window and wriggled out – fortunately both were slight of frame. They tiptoed across the small clearing towards the tower, then heard voices.

'Quick! Someone's coming.'

The pair hurtled through the tower door with barely a moment to spare. Leaning back against the solid wood, they breathed hard and silently, listening to the sound of boots crunching on the small pebbles.

The boots stopped outside the door. 'Did you check in here?' a voice asked.

Ylena held her breath now, praying to Shar to keep them hidden.

'Yes. It's a ruin. No one there.'

'Right. Put a bar against the door so no one gets in . . . or out. Then all our boys will know this one's been checked.'

'At once, sir.'

The footsteps trailed off. Ylena looked towards the

pale-faced Pil and appreciated for the first time how very young he was. He could only be fifteen, she realised, and here he was risking his life for her. She would have to put her own fear aside and be strong now, just for him.

She took his hand and squeezed it. 'We'll find a way out, Pil. Trust me,' she said, surprised at the confident tone of her voice. She wondered where all this new courage was coming from, then remembered Jakub's words about the human spirit and hope being a powerful weapon. It's not really hope, she told herself; there was none, with Alyd and Wyl dead. Just the need to survive and see them avenged.

'Come on, lead the way,' she encouraged.

He gave a nervous smile and, holding on to her hand, began to ascend the narrow winding staircase. Slits in the wall let in air and Ylena felt a new fear claw at her heart.

'I smell smoke, Pil.'

He said nothing, just kept climbing. At the top he pointed out some rotten timbers. 'Be very careful,' he said softly.

'Are you all right?' she ventured.

'They were beating some of the brothers,' he said, his eyes bright with tears. 'I'm not sure I want to see any more.'

Ylena swallowed hard. How could she have been so insensitive? The men could not be Legionnaires, she decided. No Legionnaire would participate in something as heinous.

'Are you sure they are the King's men?'

'They carry his banner,' the young man said.

'Then Celimus must have amassed an army of paid mercenaries dressed as Legionnaires,' she mused. 'Wait here, I'll look.'

Pil did not argue. He pointed out where she must tread and she crossed the small area with ease. She reached the opening and gazed down on what was happening below.

At her first strangled sound, Pil slumped to the floor. He did not need to see it to know that the world he loved was being smashed to pieces. Ylena's throat closed in terror and her eyes confirmed what the wind blowing through the wall slits had told her. Fires had been lit. The monastery was burning.

Men she recognised lay in contorted positions in the gardens, their hoes and spades dropped beside them. They had been murdered where they were working – no warning, just a sword through the belly. Others, more bloodied, had tried to escape and been hacked to death. Some had arrows protruding from their backs.

She covered her mouth with her hands as she recognised the slumped figure of Brother Farley. He was still alive, barely, but one of his hands was missing and he was looking at the bleeding stump, bewildered. How will he measure out his powders now, she thought idiotically, knowing he would die from shock within minutes. Others still were being interrogated – in their midst was the tiny figure of Brother Jakub, rallying their spirits and trying to keep his human flock – what was left of it – from fighting back or giving offence. She could see him pleading with the strangers, begging for mercy for his men of Shar.

He was quickly singled out, beaten and nailed to a makeshift cross. Ylena knew in that moment that if she did nothing with her life but kill Celimus, she would have achieved something worthwhile. She choked back the scream that struggled to fly from her throat and watched the perpetrators throw liquid from a flask over Jakub's tortured body. A lit torch was flung towards the frail figure and he ignited. Now she did let out a heart-felt sob. 'Jakub,' she whispered.

Pil was crying, his hands covering his ears, but she knew that the anguish in her expression had told him all he needed to know. She did not need to see any more carnage to know that these men had not come to find her – they had come to kill her. They knew she was at Rittylworth and they were persecuting its community to discover where she was hiding.

They would not find her. The deaths of these kind, helpless men made it all the more necessary to escape and somehow expose Celimus's treachery.

She moved to where her young friend crouched against the wall. She pushed back her fear for his sake – he must not know how terrified she was or he would never have the courage to do what she needed of him now. She tried to keep her voice steady. 'Come, Pil. We must go.'

'Where to?' he sobbed.

'To the grotto first. There is something I must fetch, and we will be safe there to make our plans.'

'Is everyone dead?' he mumbled.

'I don't know.' It was a poor answer but it was truthful. She knew it would not help their cause if she told him all she had seen. 'We must hurry.'

'We can't get out,' he reminded her, trying to stop his tears.

'Yes, we can. We'll go out through this window behind you – they won't be able to see us.'

He looked at her as though she had lost her mind.

She stated the obvious. 'We can't stay here. They've

barred us in and they might come back and search through all of these places again.'

'It's too dangerous across the roof.'

'You know, Pil,' she said as gently as she could amidst her own swirling emotions and fears, 'you told me something important when I first came here and was too frightened to be left alone. You explained how Brother Jakub had taught you to fix your eye on the things that scare you and walk towards them — do you remember that?'

He nodded bleakly.

'Well, it was you who helped me to find myself again. You helped me to conquer my fear of what happened to me in Stoneheart.' She knew he had only scant information about those events, but the gravity of her words was enough to convey it had been a terrifying experience.

'I did?'

'Truly. And so now you have to take Jakub's advice again and stare this beast right back in its eyes and let it know you don't fear it. And I shall do the same.'

'How?'

'By running across the rooftop with me and helping me to get into the grotto so we can make our escape.'

His expression told her that he was now convinced she was mad.

'Trust me,' she begged.

'Where are we escaping to?' he asked, in some awe now of the courageous woman standing before him.

'We go to Felrawthy, to convince the duke to raise an army.'

8

AREMYS KEPT TO HIS WORD. In the morning a tub was brought up and filled with steaming water and some fragrant oils he had ordered. Once again Wyl was surprised by the thoughtfulness of this stranger.

Aremys turned at the door. 'I'll go out for a while. You take your time.'

'What have you told them about me?'

'Nothing. It's not their business. What they surmise is up to them,' he said and winked.

Aremys smiled at the look of dread that passed across the woman's face when she realised what he meant. He was glad to note her bruises had benefited from the salve; even with her injuries she was striking to look at.

'Lock the door behind me,' he suggested and left.

Wyl did, then for the second time in as many days slid with extraordinary relief into the comforting warmth of the tub. He gingerly touched the spots that hurt, avoiding them as best he could, scrubbed himself clean of the violators with the flannel and soap paste provided. It was the strangest of sensations — a woman's sex felt completely different from the other side, so to speak. He did not have the courage to explore further, and those parts felt raw anyway. Another time, he decided, embarrassed.

Wyl knew he could never feel the depth of despair a real woman might in a similar situation – he was still a man in his thoughts and emotions. Nevertheless he would never forget how physically vulnerable he had felt as Faryl against a group of lusty men without a skerrick of pity amongst them. He was glad Rostyr was dead. Justice had been done, thanks to Aremys – and indeed to Jessom. The threads that remained of Faryl certainly approved.

He wondered what penance had been meted out by Celimus before the tax thieves were discovered. Knowing the King as he did, he had no doubt that he would be seeking information on the thefts in far less subtle ways than his Chancellor.

He would not have to wait too long to learn the answer.

Wyl had taken care with his hair, brushing it until it shone before tying it back in Faryl's way as best he could. He was alarmed to see the extent of the bruises on his face – they would attract unwanted attention. On the positive side, however, although he pained in several places he knew his body was intact, with no bones broken.

Aremys returned to find Faryl much refreshed and wrapped in one of his huge shirts which she had dug into his saddlebags for. He swallowed at the sight of her. She really was an exciting-looking woman. He had never been one to fall for the breathily-spoken, pretty sort who looked as though they may break if squeezed in a hug. Nor did he find more obviously flirtatious women desirable – they were confident of their bodies and used their sexual attractiveness as a weapon. If he was honest, he had never truly fallen for anyone – unless he counted Elly from the farm next door when he was a young lad. But then Elly had been more tomboy than girl, which was probably why she still won through as his favourite. Elly could run faster, shoot arrows further and skin a rabbit quicker than he ever could. She had called him Bear too, and like Faryl wasn't conventionally pretty. She had a laugh, though, which could fill his heart and a wit that could cut anyone down to size.

Wyl felt instantly self-conscious at the way Aremys was staring. 'I thought I'd travel as myself today,' he said defensively.

The man nodded, approving, but remained just inside the doorway. He said nothing. An awkward silence stretched between them, neither knowing how best to handle the situation.

Wyl shrugged, touched a hand to a bruise on his face. 'You've been extremely kind to a stranger. I'm not sure how to say appropriate thanks, but consider it said and meant.'

Aremys found his voice. 'I've been back to the Four Feathers, picked up your things for you. I didn't think you'd care to go back just now.'

'Ah . . . I'm further in your debt then. Thank you.'

The mercenary took a step into the room and made a gesture to say it was no trouble. Struggling for something else to say as his mind raced to consider his next move, Wyl politely enquired as to whether there were any outstanding monies due at the inn he'd been staying at.

'No. You had prepaid everything. A woman after my own heart,' Aremys admitted. 'I always prepay . . . er, just in case I need to leave swiftly.'

It was Wyl's turn to nod. 'Well,' Wyl said, with an exaggerated brightness, 'time I left you to your own business. You've done more than enough for me.'

Aremys nodded. 'Where are you headed?'

Wyl cringed; they had moved to small talk. 'Oh, a little town a few days' ride from here.'

'Family?'

'Er . . . no, well . . . in a way. I'm trying to track down a friend's mother.' It was easier to stick close to the truth, Wyl decided. 'And you?' he added, hating how polite they both suddenly sounded.

'Nowhere really, now that I've finished my job for Jessom. I'm at a loose end you could say.' Aremys laced his large fingers together, undid them, put them behind his back, then hung them at his sides again. This happened in a blink but Wyl saw it all. It was time to go.

'I hope our paths cross again,' Wyl said, stepping forward to take the large hand in his. 'I'm grateful to you, Aremys,' he added, looking into the man's expressive eyes. 'Shar keep you safe.'

The dark eyes regarded him with what looked like sadness. 'I've fetched your horse as well.'

Wyl grinned briefly. 'Whatever made you do that?' he asked, bemused.

Aremys noted how the small smile made such a difference to Faryl's bearing. It touched her eyes and changed her serious, often sad visage into something light and lovely. He shook his head to suggest he was a little baffled himself. 'Well, I figured you may ride out as yourself and thus would not want to confront the stablemaster as Faryl demanding Thom Bentwood's horse.'

He decided to come clean. 'But . . . I also thought we

might leave together. There is only one road, and I'm guessing you're headed towards Pearlis rather than away from it – is that right?'

'Why, yes I am,' Wyl replied, taken aback at the suggestion and not able to think of a reason to contradict it.

'We could ride together for a while, then?'

It was time to be direct. 'Aremys, you don't need to worry about me. Contrary to how it seems, I can fend for myself.'

'I'm not worried about you. I can see from the tautness of your body and by the weapons you carry that you are not one to trifle with.'

'You went through my things?' Wyl's voice was suddenly harsh.

'I could hardly miss them, Faryl. I told you, I gathered up your stuff.'

'It seems there is nothing I can hide from you! What else did you look through?'

'I give you my word I wasn't prying.'

'You're a mercenary, Aremys. I'm not sure your word is worth much.'

Wyl could see he had struck hard. It was not necessary and surely undeserved. Why was he so touchy? This man had probably saved his life.

'I'm sorry. I'm edgy today, please forgive me. It's just the aftermath of what happened, I'm sure. I have a long ride ahead and should get going. I really do owe you thanks rather than criticism.'

'It's forgotten.'

Wanting to salvage something for Aremys's sake, Wyl capitulated. 'Look, I don't mind if we ride out together. I just want you to know that I'll be fine.'

Aremys nodded. 'Good,' was all he said.

It was not ideal, but it was only as far as the outskirts of Pearlis and then Wyl could branch off. 'Let me just climb into some clothes,' he said. 'I hope you didn't mind me throwing on one of your shirts?'

'Not at all. I don't mind you rifling through my stuff one bit,' Aremys replied, with just a hint of sarcasm.

Their departure from the inn was uneventful and Wyl had to admit he felt infinitely more comfortable physically – if not emotionally – travelling as Faryl, without the painful bindings and irritating hairy disguise. He was dressed simply in loose tan trousers, soft boots and a warm jacket over a shirt.

'You still look like a man,' Aremys said, but it was meant kindly. He watched Faryl climb on to her mare with practised ease. He could tell she was as comfortable in the saddle as she was drawing the weapon he had watched her strap on earlier. She had let him hold the knives – he had never seen such beautiful craftsmanship.

'Is your throw as exquisite as your blades?' he had asked facetiously back in the inn.

His answer had been a knife whooshing past his cheek, narrowly missing his ear and pinning some of his hair to a wooden beam. The speed and fluidity of her throw had left him stunned.

'Sorry . . . that was a bit theatrical of me,' Wyl admitted, stifling the grin of satisfaction that Romen's skill had stayed with him.

If Aremys had needed any further convincing that this woman could, for the most part, look after herself, that had done the trick.

As they rode through a particularly pretty patch of Morgravia's southern rural region Wyl felt himself relaxing for the first time in many days. They had been travelling in companionable silence for a long way now, which contributed to his peace.

Aremys finally broke it with a question. 'May I ask where you learned to throw a knife with such deadly accuracy?'

Wyl had expected the query far sooner, was ready for it. 'When you grow up with a host of brothers, you learn such skills.'

'I have six brothers. None of us learned how to throw a knife.'

'Six,' Wyl said, keen to direct the conversation elsewhere. 'I had only five. Where is your family home?'

'Minlyton is the village I was raised in.'

'Never heard of it,' Wyl admitted.

'I'm not surprised. It's on a small island off the far north coast.'

Wyl's every nerve sprang to high alert. 'Oh? Which one?' He hoped his voice sounded casual and that Aremys would not say the word he feared.

'Grenadyn.'

Wyl flinched, and because Aremys had turned his dark gaze towards him, attempted to cover it by flicking away a few strands of hair that had escaped their bindings.

'Do you know it?' Aremys enquired.

'Er . . . I've heard of it, of course.'

'But never been there?'

'No,' he said, grateful to answer truthfully. 'Why?' His tone was cautious.

'Oh, it's nothing. I just . . . well, there is someone from

Grenadyn who is as handy as you are with a knife. Actually, I understate his skill. He is a sensational wielder of the small blade and throws a knife with such deadly accuracy that, until I saw your talent, I had never thought to see anyone match it.'

Wyl's throat constricted. 'Oh yes? What's his name?'

'Romen Koreldy. A noble from a very wealthy family.'

This time Wyl could not hide his alarm. 'Did he know you?' The stupid question slipped out and Wyl, cringing, tried to correct it. 'I mean, do you see him?' His mind raced to dig amongst the little that was left of Romen to find information on this man.

'No, he was older than me. He used to lark around with my elder brothers but I was too young. I did see him once, showing off for the youngsters. I was about five. He was that good with a knife he could split a thread from twenty-five paces when he was little more than a youth.'

Something nagged at Wyl's attention but he ignored it. He was fascinated, for Romen's mind had not released any of this. No wonder his riding companion's name had meant nothing to him. 'And?'

Aremys shrugged. 'Nothing of note. Our family left Grenadyn not many years later and we came to the mainland. We didn't stay so long, a few years perhaps – we all missed home too much. In that time, Romen had left. There was some talk of a scandal amongst the Koreldys but I never found out what it was. I have not seen or heard of him since.'

It was time to move away from Koreldy. 'And you've never been back?' Wyl asked.

'To Minlyton?'

Wyl nodded.

'No, but now you mention it, once I collect my monies I may do just that.' Aremys straightened in the saddle, stretching. 'Time to break our fast, do you think?'

The mention of food ended that conversation and Wyl was relieved he had not been required to explain his skill with the knife any further. He had learned his lesson about not showing off. They shared the hearty meal they had asked the kitchen staff at the inn to pack, knowing it was an all-day ride to Pearlis. The servings of chicken, cheese, fruits and bread were generous, and afterwards both admitted they could easily lie back on the soft verge and take a nap. Instead they encouraged each other to saddle up again and continued their journey, falling back into easy silence for the next hour or so.

As they drew closer to Pearlis, Wyl's question was answered: Celimus had indeed been busy strong-arming the Legion for answers. 'Shar's wrath!' he exclaimed when they came across the first tortured soul.

The body had been well preserved by the cool weather and rotted slowly on the fearsome spike. The mouth was drawn back in agony, the limbs strangely twisted.

'This man died slowly,' Aremys commented. 'You can see they broke his bones first, and expertly done.'

'I've never seen such cruelty in Morgravia outside of its torture chamber,' Wyl murmured, shaking with anger. 'This is over the stolen taxes, isn't it?'

'I wouldn't know, Faryl. Come on, let's keep moving.'

They counted a further nine corpses, all soldiers, hanging from the poles on which they had been precisely impaled to cause maximum pain and ensure a slow death. Some had deteriorated more than others, suggesting

Celimus had set to with his vicious inquisition several days before the first victim they had seen.

'And these are only the bodies on this stretch of road. Shar knows how many more are rotting on the others that lead into Pearlis,' Aremys said.

The smell of putrid flesh threatened to spill their breakfast for them. Wyl was horrified that these men – his men – had been tortured like this over the likes of Rostyr. 'I hate him,' he whispered.

'Who?'

'The King,' he said, staring at the body contorted in its death spasm.

His companion was looking at him with a guarded expression. Wyl knew there was no point trying to take the words back. 'And if you repeat that to anyone, I won't miss with the knife next time.'

He sighed. 'I'm going now, Aremys. Here's where we part company. My road into the western counties is about four miles from here. Again, I thank you for your company.'

He almost made the farewell sign of the Legion, stopping himself just in time. Instead he reached over and clasped the man's shoulder. It was not a particularly feminine gesture but he had already decided that a woman who carried weapons was never going to be considered courtly.

'Faryl, please don't leave yet.'

'I must. It's time I was on my way.'

'What's so important?'

'Nothing. I just want to continue on my own now. I've seen enough to know I have no reason to travel through the city.'

'Sounds to me like you have something to hide from.'

Wyl bristled. *If only you knew*, he thought. 'Only my hate for this sort of thing,' he said, pleased to hear how calm his voice was. 'Just leave it, Aremys.'

'All right, I understand,' his friend said, then he grinned. 'Look, come with me as far as Smallhampton. It's just a few miles away and you can pick up a small track there to the western counties. It won't take you much out of your way.'

'Why?'

'I have a hide there. I want to pick up some money.'

'But you're going into Pearlis, surely, to be paid for your kill?'

'No. I've changed my mind – that money can be paid later. Since we began talking about Grenadyn I've decided to go home . . . see my family before I die or they do.'

Wyl was baffled. He swiped at yet more of the auburn hairs which had loosened on the ride and were flapping around his face. It was such an annoying sensation, and yet he recalled how attractive that same look had been on Valentyna. 'Well, that's good. But what has this to do with me?'

Aremys looked uncomfortable again. 'Nothing, in truth. I just want to continue riding with you a little longer. We can . . .' He stopped, embarrassed by his own awkwardness. 'I like you, Faryl. I just . . .' He struggled again. 'That is . . . I enjoy your company.'

Wyl did not know whether to feel flattered or cornered. It was true that going to Smallhampton would not take him much out of his way, and there would be a chance there for an ale and some food before heading out west, which would enable him to ride through the night. On the other hand, Aremys was sounding needy, which did not sit right with what Wyl knew of him so far. Aremys struck him as an independent type, used to a solitary existence. It just didn't add up. There was some secret here but as he tried to bring together those thoughts which had nagged at him earlier also, he noticed that Aremys would not meet his eyes. That, together with the slight flush to his cheeks, gave Wyl far more information than he wanted. *Shar save us!* he thought. *He's enamoured of me.*

'Please,' Aremys added softly, with perfect timing.

Knowing it was a bad idea, but flustered by the situation, Wyl conceded. 'All right. Smallhampton it is and then I'm going west . . . alone.'

Aremys loosed a broad smile, pleased with his win. 'We can share an ale at the inn there before you go.'

Wyl looked again at the putrefying body nearby. 'Let's just get away from here,' he said.

They moved off the road on to a small track and flanked some deserted fields before entering a copse.

'Know anything about hides?' Aremys asked.

'No,' Wyl replied, lying. Faryl had dozens all over various realms.

'Actually hired assassins tend to use them more than we mercenaries, but I like to be cautious. You should follow suit — it could save your life some time.'

'I don't live as dangerously as you. But yes, I may take that advice.'

There was an old disused hut on the edge of the copse. 'In there, is it?' Wyl asked.

'No. Too obvious. Any vagabond using it for shelter could discover my cache. I use the hut as a marker. Let me show you.'

He climbed down from his horse and pulled a small length of rope from his saddlebag.

Wyl got off his horse too. 'What's the rope for?'

'Wait and see.'

They approached the hut as far as its door, then Aremys turned his back to it. 'Now walk with me thirty strides.'

They did.

'And ten strides to our left.'

Wyl followed him to a hollow in an old tree but hung back as Aremys glanced into it.

'Bollocks!' Aremys exclaimed.

'Gone?' Wyl said, leaning over to look in too.

They were shoulder to shoulder now. Aremys turned and looked at the woman he liked very much – he had even allowed himself daydreams of bedding her. He was not an unattractive man, just large. Most women, once they got to know him, enjoyed him. He would have loved to have pleasured this woman. He hated doing this.

'I'm so sorry, Faryl,' he whispered into her hair. Then louder, 'Forgive me.'

'Forgive you? For what?'

In a blink Aremys had spun Wyl around and clamped his hands behind his back. He knocked his legs away so Wyl slammed to the ground, old wounds protesting angrily, new bruises flaring. Aremys used the rope to bind Faryl's hands. It would have been easier if he had been required to kill her, because she struggled furiously, nearly unbalancing him at one point. She was far stronger than he had anticipated. But he was bigger and he finally managed to sit on her legs and still her, which was fortunate because he was not sure he could have killed her for any amount of money.

'Aremys!' Wyl shrieked in the voice he despised. 'What are you doing?'

'Apologies, Leyen,' said a new voice, prompting Wyl to turn his head sharply towards the hut. 'I knew you wouldn't come to me on the strength of my bidding so I had to hire special help.'

'Jessom!' Wyl spat, remembering the Chancellor who had accompanied Celimus into Briavel.

Aremys lifted Faryl to her feet, moving to dust off her clothes. Wyl kicked at him, eyes burning with hatred towards his betrayer. 'Fuck you, Aremys!'

Jessom made a sound of disapproval. 'Dear me, Leyen. Language, language. So crude for a lady.'

Wyl stopped struggling and simply glared between the two men. There were soldiers too. No point in trying to run or even fight. He was trapped.

'What do you want?' he snarled.

'Well, my dear, you did such a good job on your last . . . er, task that you have impressed someone who wishes to meet with you.'

'I'm not interested,' Wyl said, every nerve on edge now. This was dangerous.

'I expected as much. You certainly are a private person. Is this a disguise you are wearing, bruises included?'

Wyl remained silent. Jessom looked towards Aremys.

'This is the real thing as far as I can tell,' the mercenary mumbled.

'Not that I'm complaining, for she is far more attractive than I have ever seen her. How can you be sure, though?' Jessom enquired, in no hurry.

'Does seeing her naked count?' Aremys growled, bristling now.

He did not care much for Jessom but the money was too good to ignore. The Chancellor had paid five times more than the price of a kill just for Aremys to track down and capture the woman. It all became too easy when she stumbled into his path and he was able to deal not only with the conspirators but with her as well. The disguises he discovered in her belongings and other give-away signs like how well she rode, her lean strong body, her private ways – they all added up to her being the woman Jessom searched for. But as soon as she threw the knife towards him, he no longer had any doubt this was his prey.

He hated himself for handing her over to Jessom. It was obvious Faryl had no desire to meet with the King. More secrets, he decided. *Take the money and leave. Don't get involved*, he told himself, not wanting to meet her gaze.

Jessom was laughing softly. 'Ah, that's very convincing. I'm glad you were able to enjoy a dalliance with this intriguing creature . . . and get paid for it. Surely you didn't give her the bruises as well? Tsk, tsk,' Jessom said.

Wyl wished he could reach his blades. There would be several dead men in the copse if he could. He said nothing, just levelled Aremys with the murderous stare he knew Faryl did so well.

Jessom became businesslike. 'I know her as Leyen. She is a master of disguise. Has she told you any different?'

Aremys considered. If Faryl's eyes were weapons he would be dead thrice over. She was a dangerous enemy to make, as she was surely going to be permitted to live. Perhaps the money was not worth it after all – he knew she would probably pursue him now, come hell or high water. And he had stupidly admitted where he came from.

Strange . . . he knew she had been honest with him up to a point, possibly shared things she would not with most, and that had made him truthful with her . . . up to a point. It was a mistake, though.

'Well?' Jessom prompted, irritated.

Aremys noted that Faryl's eyes were communicating something more than just the plain hate of earlier.

'Sorry, I was just thinking back over our conversations. No. I have known her only as Leyen,' he admitted. He saw relief flit across Faryl's face before she looked away.

'Good, then perhaps we have her real name now. Not that we can be absolutely sure, but it will do. Come, my dear, you are to be escorted back to Pearlis.'

'Why?' Wyl said.

'To meet with his royal highness King Celimus, whom you have impressed with your talents.'

9

ELSPYTH HAD STAYED TRUE to her promise to Wyl. Resisting the urge to head home after their farewell she had made her way slowly south, accepting rides with a family, a merchant convoy and a travelling band of musicians. All were very kind and would accept no money for their transport or hospitality. None were in a hurry and, in truth, neither was Elspyth, happy to meander at their pace, stopping off at towns to make their deliveries or perform. The musicians had helped her find her laughter again, even encouraging her to sing along with them around their nightly fire. They were taking a circuitous route towards Pearlis, hoping to earn good profits during the spring months and more than happy to have her in the group for part of their journey. She was surprised at how much she enjoyed her time with them, and quietly regretted their parting. The troupe gave her a fond farewell and the usual expressions of hope for meeting again.

Between all her new friends she had got as far as the outskirts of Rittylworth, about eleven days after her parting with Wyl. She was happy to walk the rest of the way, wondering how Wyl's sister would react to her and what she was going to say to the grieving young woman. Wyl had extracted a promise from her that would effectively see Elspyth telling lies from here on in to anyone who knew him. But she and Wyl – as Romen Koreldy – had been through too much together to forsake one another over a few lies. Furthermore, Wyl had given her his own oath and so she would keep true to him, anticipating reciprocal courtesy when the time came for him to return to the Razors.

Elspyth had no idea why Wyl needed to guard his identity so keenly. She did, however, understand part of his reluctance to share his tale, for people's suspicion of magic was deeply entrenched. This enchantment on Wyl was hardly a fairground trick; its enormity was too much for most to cope with. The fact that both she and Lothryn had accepted the sorcery was fortunate for Wyl, but they came from backgrounds that accepted the existence of magic in the world.

She remembered how Wyl had haltingly told them of the curse on his life – 'Myrren's gift' he had called it and laughed bitterly. As implausible as it had sounded, everything he had said corroborated that this magic had indeed been wielded on him. For Elspyth, it explained her aunt's strange reaction towards Wyl when he had visited the seer, and the curious comment she had made after the Pearlis tourney that, 'we haven't seen the last of that one yet'.

And Elspyth could see that Lothryn believed him too. She recalled how matter of fact the Mountain man had been, not at all perturbed by the suggestion of magic. She felt the same way. Another reason to love him. Her thoughts turned to how hard and quickly she had fallen for the big man who had wrenched her from her home and, against her will, taken her into the Razors, only to risk his life for her a few days later. It was seeing him weep for his dead wife while holding his newborn son in his arms that had caused her heart to fully melt for him, and no doubt he had felt similarly, for since that moment their relationship had changed. Suddenly there had been a burning connection between them, yet they had not so much as shared a kiss. How sad when she loved him as she did.

She remembered how he had turned to fight their pursuers on that lonely escarpment, begging her to run. And she had done so only because she had given her word to him that she would, and then Lothryn had pressed Wyl into running too. It hurt deeply to imagine what had befallen him after their escape. She had no doubt whatsoever that he would have been taken alive in order to stand before a wrathful Cailech and suffer whatever punishment was meted out. Would it have been death by some harrowing method which only the Mountain King could dream up?

Elspyth did not want to think about it. She wanted to believe that Lothryn lived, and distracted herself by turning her mind to Wyl. Trapped in Koreldy's body, he was trying to save the Queen of the realm which had killed his father and been his homeland's enemy for centuries, whilst sending Elspyth off to track down his grieving sister. What a tragic family, she thought, so much despair in their lives. But she had agreed to do this for him, and in exchange he had agreed to return to the Razors as soon as he could and find out what had happened to Lothryn.

She had put her trust in Wyl Thirsk. He was a good

man, and she would like to talk to him in happier times about what it feels like to become someone else. Wyl was lucky, she thought, that it was the darkly handsome Romen Koreldy's body he walked in. Imagine how it might have been if he had been killed by someone who was crippled or retarded, or someone of very lowly birth. Worse, she giggled to herself, a woman!

She found herself approaching the high ground from which she had learned she could look down into the valley and see the monastery with its village clustered nearby. Relief that she had made it this far coursed through her and she climbed the slope with a lighter heart than when she began.

Still smiling from the notion that Wyl could have become a woman instead of handsome Romen, she began to rehearse what he had instructed her to say to Brother Jakub. But as Elspyth crested the hill her smile died, taking with it her good mood.

The tiny enclave of Rittylworth was in ruins, parts of it still smoking from the fires. The monastery itself looked cold and silent. It was still whole, but even from this distance she could sense it was deserted. What had happened here?

She did not want to approach just yet, she needed time to gather her racing thoughts. She scrutinised the scene below, gathering as much information as she could. Noticing something odd in the far distance, she squinted then let out a sound of despair when she realised what it was. People . . . crucified. She could not tell whether they were corpses or still alive.

Elspyth did not pause for further thought but picked up her skirts and began to run.

As she drew closer, gasping for breath, her fears were confirmed. She could see that the village had been torched. It was desolate. There were no bodies, much to her relief, so she suspected the attack had occurred to teach the villagers some sort of lesson, perhaps as retribution for something. Presumably they had fled and would return to rebuild the village and their lives when they felt it was safe.

Panting now as breathing became easier, she discovered that the monks had not been so fortunate. The greater lesson had clearly been taught within the grounds of the monastery, where the smell of burned flesh was cloying. The light breeze carried the stench from the host of charred corpses suspended from a hastily erected series of crosses.

She had not realised she was weeping until a gust of wind blew the tears across her face. It was obvious that many of the monks had been set aflame and left to die in horrific pain wherever they writhed. She found herself stepping over the blackened remains of men . . . some boys too, and quickly averted her horrified gaze. It seemed that most had been working in the gardens or had gathered there when the raid began, for that was where the greatest number of bodies lay. Elspyth had no doubt there were more inside the monastery itself but she was not prepared to look within.

The horror of being nailed to a cross and then burned had been saved for selected monks – the most senior perhaps. She counted six. They all appeared dead although their bodies had not yet begun the process of decay. This made her skin prickle for it meant the attackers were not that long gone.

Needing to do something to combat her despair, but

unable to face going into the holy chapel of the monastery, she sank to her knees and began praying at the feet of one of the crucified. As she murmured her pleas to Shar, the body above her croaked something. Elspyth fell backwards with fright, looking up towards that tortured hairless head with the flesh hanging off it. She stood, petrified, yet craning as close to the man's moving lips as she could on tiptoe.

'Find Ylena,' he breathed. 'She lives. Pil took her.'

'Are you Brother Jakub?' she asked, frantic.

An almost imperceptible, clearly painful nod told her he was indeed Brother Jakub.

'Let me help you,' she cried, desperately looking around for a tool which might loosen the nails.

'Too late,' he croaked. She returned to look into his sightless eyes and charred flesh. 'Tell Romen . . .' he coughed, his breath rattling in his throat, 'that this was the work of the King.'

'Why would he do such a thing?' She could see his death looming.

'Thirsk . . . he . . .' was all the monk could get out before the last agonising breath wheezed out of his throat and he died.

Elspyth wept for his suffering and that of his brothers, all peaceful men of the cloth. She felt rage surfacing at this new King of Morgravia, understood now why Wyl's identity must be protected. She gently eased the lids down over the staring eyes of Brother Jakub. There was nothing more she could do here, other than bear witness to the atrocity. It would stay with her forever. She touched a shaky hand to the blackened cheek of the brave monk who had stayed alive long enough to give her the information she needed, then set off. She did not know where she was headed, only that she must find the young woman being hunted by a merciless king.

Elspyth trudged in something of a stupor for more than a day, only realising as she heard the haunting call of an owl that dusk was darkening to night. She was exhausted. Since leaving the smouldering village of Rittylworth she had met no travellers along the narrow roads through Morgravia's mid-north. Her mind too numb to think, she had put one foot in front of the other to gain as much distance between herself and death as she could. It had been many solitary hours.

She shivered now in the chill night air as darkness finally registered in her blurred thoughts. She burrowed into a small hollow beneath a bush for safety and collapsed there, not so much from fatigue as from the emotional trauma of the morning. She was convinced the smell of burned flesh still clung to her, and she could not forget the fire-torn voice of Brother Jakub courageously using his last breath of life to tell her what had happened. Elspyth wept quietly into the silence.

Inevitably, her despair led her to think on Lothryn again. Would she ever see him again? Deep down she believed that the man she loved still lived. Despite all her fears for him, something within begged her to believe that he was alive and so she must remain strong for him. And as firmly as she believed this, Elspyth instinctively trusted that Wyl Thirsk, now walking as Romen Koreldy, was the only person who might be able to restore Lothryn to her. Why this seemed so she could not say, except that her aunt had taught her to trust her instincts. Nothing

had been the same since that day in Pearlis when Wyl
Thirsk had entered the tent of her aunt, the Widow Ilyk,
and terrified her. *Her aunt*. Elspyth laughed bitterly. What
had become of her ageing relative? Was she dead? Injured?

She could so easily have returned home when she and
Wyl had parted company, but here she was, heading who
knew where after a woman she had never met.

Rittylworth had been torched because of the Thirsk
name. Holy men of peace, of love, had lost their lives
because of the Thirsk name. Even Lothryn had suffered
because of . . .

No, she must not follow that line of thought. She must
not blame the Thirsks or she would never survive this.

Elspyth sniffed. She dug in her cloak pocket and found
some nuts and dried fruit which her travelling friends had
provided. There was some hard biscuit too, but she decided
to keep that for the morning when hunger always seemed
at its sharpest. She chewed without interest in what she
ate, considering her path now. She must make some decisions – good ones, and quickly.

Brother Jakub said Ylena had escaped. The girl would
be on foot presumably, so not that far away from
Rittylworth herself. Elspyth wondered about this lad the
older man had mentioned, Pil. She presumed he was a
monk as well. Either way, Ylena would be confused, frightened, disoriented. The thought brought a sad smile to her
face. *Much like myself*, she admitted, realising that she was
also penniless, having used all her money to buy Wyl a
horse in Deakyn. They had assumed she would soon meet
up with Ylena and have access to funds again, but now
she had no coin nor means of getting any.

She shook her head clear of the doubts, swallowed the

last of the fruit and nuts and settled down to sleep. But her thoughts drifted back to her journey and where she must go. She could not know in which direction Ylena had fled, so she had to choose the path that best served her promise to Wyl. She had in her possession a letter for the Duke of Felrawthy from Wyl – that was where she should head next. But for now she was alone and defence-less, which meant she would need to find a new method of transport. Perhaps she could link up with another group of travellers heading east, find some temporary work to pay for food and lodging along the way?

Well, it was a plan. Something to wake up to the next morning. The owl hooted again, reminding Elspyth that her kind should be asleep whilst the creatures of the night went about their business. She wriggled into the least uncomfortable position she could find and cast her last conscious thought towards Lothryn, wherever he was.

Elspyth dreamed.

Lothryn was calling to her. Crying for her, in fact. He was in pain. Drowning in all-encompassing, mind-altering pain. It seemed to her that he could sense her presence as strongly as she sensed his. Why there was pain and who was inflicting it she could not tell. There was darkness. Anger too. She felt bitterness raging about Lothryn; it was not his own, but she could not see him or the person experiencing the emotion. Something else too . . . some-thing powerful. Magic . . . swirling around her . . . It knew she was there but it could not touch her.

Did she scream or was that Lothryn again?

Lothryn! she called into the pain.

His voice, barely audible, thick with agony. *Tell Wyl*

I will wait, he whispered. *I am no longer as he would expect*.

Elspyth did scream now, shrieking Lothryn's name into the darkness and its foul magic again and again, but her lover was gone. Their bond was viciously snapped, as if the power-wielder cut through the point where their minds had touched.

She awoke, still crying out, as dawn crept through a heavy mist that had settled about her during the night. Initially Elspyth panicked in the blindness, waving her arms and fighting the foggy swirls, but as her vision cleared slightly she was reassured of where she was, and her aloneness. Shallow breaths came rapidly; she needed to slow them. Painfully she stood from her uncomfortable hollow and sucked in deep gasps of air, filling her lungs and expelling it as slowly as she dared.

Tears streamed down her face as a new fear of what had become of Lothryn gripped her. Was he talking to her from the dead? Had he spoken at all or had she just experienced a nightmare of sorts? She forced herself to be practical even though she felt more fatigued now than before her distressing sleep. She wiped her eyes, relieved herself, then sat down to slowly consume the hard biscuit and think on what had happened. She was not hungry but the process of chewing and swallowing would help ease her alarm, she hoped, and so she forced herself to eat. Lothryn had made them eat when they were fleeing for their lives in the Razors. None of them had felt hungry, yet he had insisted and he had been right. She took the same advice now and nourished herself.

Elspyth had never felt more alone in her lonely life than at this moment. Lothryn's words, real or imagined,

were all she had to cling to now. She must succeed in her
task if Wyl Thirsk was to keep his promise.

She stood, brushed away the crumbs and patted at her
unruly hair. She knew she looked a fright but no longer
cared. Lothryn was suffering. He had spoken from life not
death – she knew it and trusted her weak sensitivity to
magic, even though she could not wield it herself. Magic
was strong in her maternal line but not strong in her.
Somehow it had avoided her with its riches, but she knew
enough to understand that Lothryn had truly reached her.
The means he had employed were irrelevant. She had heard
his voice: he needed help.

Setting her jaw in a way her aunt would recognise as
the stubborn manner of her forebears, Elspyth began to
walk, heading east towards Felrawthy.

IO

WHILE ELSPYTH WAS RUNNING down a lonely hill towards desolation, Fynch was entering the town of Baelup. He had made speedy progress from Crowyll out of Briavel and into Morgravia courtesy of a man in a hurry to make a delivery to Pearlis. Fynch had done him a good turn and the man had offered the boy a lift to his destination.

It was Knave who had done the good deed, in fact, frightening off a couple of thieves who were nosing about the man's cart whilst it was briefly unattended. Fynch had noticed their interest and, realising their actions were furtive, had sent Knave in. When the huge dog sounded his ferocious bark the men scurried away, understandably terrified.

The scene had brought to Fynch's face one of his rare smiles. As he was patting Knave in congratulation for his performance, the owner of the cart had returned. He too looked anxiously at the dog. Fynch explained what had occurred and the man's face lit up.

'Travel with me,' he had said. 'I'll pay you.'

Fynch was taken aback. 'Why?'

'This is the second time this has happened. Two months ago I lost half my goods to thieves. I suspect it is not the last time either, and it's more than my life is worth not to get this delivery to Lady Bench of Pearlis.'

'And how can I possibly help you?' Fynch asked, amused, thinking of how slight he was. Then it dawned on him. 'Oh, I see. My dog.'

'Precisely,' the man said. 'You do have control of it, don't you?' he added, nervously.

'Only when he wants me to. But fret not, he will not attack you.'

'Thanks be to Shar,' the man replied with relief. 'Is it a deal?'

'I need to get to Baelup.'

'Perfect. I can take you there as soon as I've made my delivery,' the man had said. 'Please . . . I have food for the journey and my intention is to drive the horses hard to Grimble Town, changing them there. We shall be in Baelup sooner than you can pick your nose. What do you say?'

Fynch liked the man and his amusing manner. He knew Hildyth's trail was cooling with each day he spent on foot and he could make up valuable time if he took the man's offer. 'All right.'

They had experienced no further robbery attempts and it had turned out that the man, Master Rilk, was a tailor, one of the best in Briavel, although modesty prevented him from claiming that he was in fact the most popular of all tailors with the nobles. Word had spread and now various Morgravian dignitaries were securing his services. Lady Bench was the most notable to date, and she had paid him a veritable fortune to tailor her daughter's latest dancing gown. She had insisted, however, that Master

Rilk personally deliver the gown just in case it required last-minute adjustments.

Rilk made pleasant, intelligent company for Fynch, and he in turn thoroughly enjoyed the serious lad, who was knowledgeable in the ways of the Morgravian court and seemed to know many of its nobles. Fynch had gladly passed on their names and dress tendencies, his attention to detail impressing the tailor. Master Rilk had plans to expand his business dealings in the Morgravian capital so this inside information was a blessing.

They had parted company at Baelup as friends, with a promise to meet again some time. Fynch had refused payment. He had been fed and watered well, as had Knave, at Rilk's expense, plus they had travelled swiftly and safely to their destination.

After they had waved goodbye, Knave made himself scarce and Fynch walked into the main square, wondering where to begin. Several hours later, having passed himself off as a distant member of the family bringing news of his own mother's passing, he had established that Myrren's mother, Emil, had left Baelup soon after learning of her daughter's ugly death. With her husband dead and her daughter burned as a witch, people had sympathised with her fears for her own life.

The blacksmith was the most helpful. He seemed to have known the family well, but claimed to have no idea where she had fled to.

'I can't offer much more help. I know a young fellow came here to see her the day after Myrren's death. He was with a tall chap, but I don't think the older one went in with him to see Emil.'

'Was the youngster's name Thirsk?' Fynch asked.

'I don't know, lad. I just saw him arrive and leave with the pup. I gather Myrren had asked him to take her dog. He was there barely minutes.'

'Can you remember anything about him?'

'Red hair. Does that help?'

Fynch grinned. 'It does. He was probably accompanied by a man called Gueryn. How did you come to meet them?'

'My missus and I were helping Emil pack her things, as I recall,' the man said, scratching his head. 'She was in a tearing hurry to leave. And once she had news of Myrren's end, she could only think of fleeing the house, the town, everything she knew. Shame. It was the second time in her life she'd done that. Myrren had funny eyes, you see, and those Witch Stalkers were after her. Poor mite – she deserved better. She was a lovely girl and a good daughter. The old man just dropped dead in front of the Stalkers. His heart gave out; he had feared such a thing for so many years.'

'Yes, I see,' Fynch said. 'And then what happened?'

'Well, after the bad news from Pearlis, Emil was only too happy to hand the pup over to this red-headed chappie, for she had no idea what to do with it anyway. Apparently the lad had shown Myrren some kindness at the time of her torture and she had wanted to give him a gift in return.'

If only you knew, Fynch thought.

'And then Emil left,' the man concluded. 'She never said anything more about the dog or its new owner. We didn't hear her conversation with him either, although I tell you it was only moments long. Emil could hardly string two sensible words together at the time.'

Fynch nodded in sympathy. 'She gave no mention of where she might have been headed?'

The man pulled a face. 'Wait now . . . I do recall her saying something about a sister. Where was it?'

'Please, it's important.'

'Er . . . let me think now. It was mid north. Perhaps Rothwell?'

'Where's that?'

'About three days from here. Tiny village. But I can't be sure now, lad. Truly, I can't remember what she said.'

There was little choice. Fynch decided to head north to Rothwell, just in case it brought him closer to Myrren's mother – or, more likely, Wyl – and so he filled up on a sweet pastry at Baelup's bakery and a mug of apple juice before he set off. He was sipping at the refreshing liquid, thinking that he must purchase some dry food, when it happened.

Onlookers watched in dismay as the small lad's mug crashed to the floor moments before he did, his body instantly limp amongst the spilled juice. Seconds later a huge black dog entered the shop, terrifying all with its fierce growl. The beast positioned itself above the boy, guarding him.

Then it waited, its head cocked as though listening . . .

Fynch could hear the familiar voice. It was not unkind but it was insistent. *Look at me, boy.*

Fynch turned his head. He saw himself prone on the floor of the baker's shop, apple juice around him and people fussing nearby. To all intents and purposes he was dead. Above him stood Knave, still as a statue, fearsome.

Am I dead? It was his voice – somehow he could talk with his mind.

No, came the reply. *Use your power, child. Send yourself to me.*

Fynch obeyed, finding that he was able to lock on to the voice and reel in its echoes of sound as though pulling on a rope. He willed himself along the connection, feeling insubstantial yet very much alive and aware.

Moments later he saw a figure facing him through a fine mist. Fynch reached out to touch it, but it was as unreal as he was in this place. But as the face smiled, its warmth reached through the mist to touch him.

Fynch surmised that the man seemed oddly short, but could not make out his age, or any features other than a suggestion of dark hair.

Who are you? Fynch asked.

A friend. There was caution in the voice.

What are you?

Wyl Thirsk knows me as the manwitch.

Myrren's father?

The man nodded.

Are you Knave as well?

There was the brief smile again, as though congratulating the boy. *In a way*, he spoke softly. *But he is real enough.*

What do you want with me?

Your help, Fynch.

How?

The manwitch, Elysius, shook his head. *Not now. Too dangerous like this. Come to me. Follow the dog. Trust him.*

But . . .

Go now. Send yourself back to your body. Forget Emil. We will talk soon.

Fynch did as he was told and woke to see the people

from the baker's shop crowded around him. Knave had disappeared. He came to his wits as if from a dream.

'What happened, lad?' someone asked.

'I'm sorry,' he said. 'I haven't eaten in days.'

He heard them muttering about how tiny and skinny he was. He was used to this. Hands lifted him from the floor; others pushed food into his lap as they sat him down. People talked to him, talked over him, and worried about whether that ferocious dog might reappear.

'No,' Fynch murmured, 'he won't.' He knew Knave would be waiting for him now, ready to lead him to wherever it was he had to go.

There was no longer any need to search out Myrren's mother. He was travelling to Elysius, where he hoped he would be reunited with Wyl – or whoever his friend might be by the time he reached the manwitch.

11

IT FELT STRANGE, AND dangerous, to be entering Stoneheart again. The last time he had ridden through its magnificent gates he had been Romen, bringing back the body of Wyl Thirsk to clear his name as well as rescue his sister. He thought of Ylena now, hoping she was safe with Elspyth.

Aremys's horse drew up alongside. 'I hope it was worth it,' Wyl said bitterly. 'Enjoy your money quickly, Aremys, because I shall hunt you down and kill you.'

'I regret it,' Aremys admitted.

'Too late,' Wyl replied. 'You can't begin to imagine what you've done.'

'I—'

But Wyl did not wait to hear what the mercenary had to say. He clicked his horse on and entered the bailey alongside Jessom.

'Be easy, Leyen,' the Chancellor said. 'The King does not want you dead. Believe me, I had no choice but to bring you in.'

'What does he want?'

The Chancellor grimaced. 'You achieved for him something important, something no one else could.'

'Payment is thanks enough for me,' Wyl snarled, handing his reins to the boys who had run towards the group.

'Not for him, apparently,' Jessom said, climbing down from his horse. 'Oh, and by the way, he thinks you're a man.'

Jessom had requested that Aremys join him and Leyen at the audience with the King. It was clear Aremys felt uncomfortable at the summons but he simply nodded. They followed Jessom to the orangery, an area the King had claimed as his own, including the chambers surrounding it.

It was another stab to Wyl's heart that this part of Stoneheart, designed specifically for Ylena by her guardian, King Magnus, was now enjoyed by Celimus. Wyl held his breath as the delicate fragrance of orange drifted towards them, bringing with it a flood of memories of happier times spent here with Alyd and Ylena.

'Let us hope the King is in good spirits today,' Jessom murmured as they stepped down into the sheltered courtyard, ringed by citrus trees laden with ripening fruit, that Wyl knew so well.

'My liege,' Jessom said, bowing low.

The King was staring out across the balustrades to the panoramic beauty of the meadows beyond. Wyl's whole body tensed with hatred as Celimus turned towards them. He wished he had a knife. One swift throw and the cruel man before him would be taking his last gasp. Being hanged, drawn and quartered would be worth the pleasure of seeing Celimus dead.

Wyl bowed low, hiding the look on Faryl's face from the man he so deeply hated.

'Ah, Jessom. Welcome to you and your guests.'

The smooth resonant voice was so reminiscent of old King Magnus, yet it made Wyl's flesh crawl.

Celimus stepped forward, tall and graceful. He flicked an appreciative glance towards the woman but his attention was securely on Aremys. He reached out his hand for Aremys to bend over and touch to his lips, which the mercenary dutifully did.

'You must be the man I have been looking forward to meeting. I wanted to thank you in person for your services. I trust we have rewarded you well?'

Aremys looked into the olive eyes of the handsome King he had heard so much about yet until now had never seen. Confusion passed across his face. 'My King, I . . . yes, the reward is ample.' He looked towards Jessom.

'Your highness,' Jessom said softly, 'this man is Aremys Farrow of Grenadyn. He has rid us of the Legionnaires responsible for stealing the royal monies.'

Celimus looked sharply at Jessom. 'Forgive me, Chancellor, I was under the distinct impression that you were bringing before me the person who relieved me of a certain mercenary who threatened the Crown.' The King's voice was suddenly icy. He did not appreciate being embarrassed.

The Chancellor moved smoothly on. 'I have, your majesty. May I introduce Leyen.'

The olive gaze slid from Aremys to look into the face Wyl hid behind. He held that familiar gaze steadily, despite the sensation that he was being slithered over by a deadly snake. Celimus said nothing for a moment; the small silence was sizzling with intensity.

'A woman?' he finally said.

Wyl bowed once again; he could hardly curtsy wearing these clothes. He was not so sure whether he would know how – perhaps Faryl might. These fragments flitted through his mind as the full weight of the monarch's scrutiny rested upon him. *Close enough to kill with a single stab*, Wyl thought, hoping his face remained as expressionless as he was trying to make it.

'I am without words,' Celimus admitted. 'Once again you surprise me, Jessom.'

'Your highness, I am your servant in all things,' Jessom oozed.

Then came what Wyl had been dreading. He blinked as he saw the hand of the King rise. He could not, would not kiss that hand. He would sooner die than swear allegiance to this King. Wyl bent over and reached for the hand, then exploded into a coughing fit. Celimus snatched back his hand and glared towards Jessom, who appeared equally alarmed.

It was Aremys who rescued Wyl. 'Your highness, forgive us. We have been riding hard for a couple of days without adequate food or water,' he lied. 'Leyen suffered a vicious attack at the hands of those same men whose corpses I sent you, your majesty. That is how we came to meet. She is in need of rest and attention.'

It was a long speech for Aremys. Perhaps a bit too long to be convincing, Wyl thought. Despite his misgivings about the man he was grateful for his intervention at this moment.

'I see,' Celimus said, not really seeing at all as Wyl

continued to struggle with his contrived cough. 'I have noted the injuries to your face, Leyen, and we will provide the attention you require. Jessom, see to it.'

The Chancellor bobbed his head in agreement.

The King continued, his irritation evident. 'Let us meet later then, when both of you have had sufficient time to recuperate.'

'Thank you, your highness,' Jessom said, embarrassed.

'Have them join me for a private supper tonight. I have things I wish to speak of to these people.' He spoke to Jessom as though neither Aremys or Wyl were there. Grateful to be ignored they bowed and followed the Chancellor out of the courtyard.

'Not an auspicious beginning,' Jessom spat as they moved out of earshot.

'My apologies,' Wyl lied. 'I really don't feel well.'

'Be brighter by tonight, Leyen,' Jessom warned. 'It will not go well with you if you displease the King a second time. He is unpredictable,' he added, in case neither of them were taking his advice seriously enough. 'Now follow me.'

Aremys was housed away from Wyl, in a separate wing close to the Legion's quarters. That suited Wyl; he had no desire for any further dealings with the man, beyond those which were absolutely necessary, such as the evening repast with the King. His own accommodations were sparse but comfortable. To his good fortune, he saw the page, Jorn, racing by, a worried look on his face. Wyl hailed him.

'Yes, madam,' Jorn enquired, clearly in a hurry but just as keen not to offend one of the King's guests.

Wyl wished he could tell this lad the truth. 'What is your name?'

'Jorn, madam. How may I serve you?'

'You seem to be a little rushed just now.'

'I am happy to help in any way I can,' the lad replied. He had grown up quickly at Stoneheart, it seemed, for the sparkle in his eye and his eager manner had gone, replaced by polite language, a cautious approach and a demeanour that suggested anything but happiness.

'Well, I was going to ask your advice, but may I request that you come by later when you are not quite so harried?'

Jorn looked surprised. 'Have you no lady assigned to assist you?'

'It seems not, but then I require such advice as only a young man such as yourself can provide.'

Now Jorn looked worried. 'In that case, madam, I shall return as soon as my immediate duties to his highness are complete.'

'You work for the King?'

'I am one of his personal messengers.'

'Thank you, Jorn. I look forward to seeing you when you can spare a minute.'

The lad bowed and hurried away. Wyl returned to his room to ponder this information. Jorn had personal access to the King's dealings; he may prove himself the ally the youngster had so badly wanted to be when Wyl, as Romen, was fleeing Stoneheart with Ylena. What to tell him, though? It needed further thought. For now his immediate problem was what to wear for dinner tonight – every woman's dilemma. Wyl scowled, hating that he should be concerned with such things.

He had nothing appropriate, obviously. He would have

to speak with Jessom. In the meantime a bath was very necessary and he made his way, grimacing, to the women's bathing pavilion.

Wyl had no idea what to do when he arrived there. He was entering a mysterious world which had never been even remotely available to him previously. To begin with, the atmosphere was hushed and tranquil in the special gardens that housed the pavilion. Outside the men's building it was normally raucous with young men jostling and jockeying with each other. Here the women entered and exited sedately, in quiet conversation with one another. They seemed to move in pairs, he noted, whereas the men tended to wander in as a boisterous herd. As General, he and his officers had a special area they could retire to for more peaceful bathing. Nonetheless, they tended to form what was essentially a smaller gang of the soldiers and were just as noisy and energetic. He hoped that Faryl's femininity would help guide him through this ordeal as she had surely visited bathhouses in the past, although there was no advice surfacing at present. Whilst he was thinking about all of this he had not realised that he was lurking at the entrance of the pavilion.

'Are you all right?' a voice asked.

It was a middle-aged woman, one he recognised.

'Er . . . this is my first time at Stoneheart. I'm a little daunted. It's very beautiful.'

And it was. The pavilion was delicate in design and decorated with beautiful glasswork of brilliant colours.

'Don't be, my dear,' the woman said. 'Come with me. I'll show you the ropes.' She linked her arm in Wyl's. 'What's your name?'

'Leyen.'

'Pretty. Not from Pearlis or around here then obviously?'

'No.' Wyl's mind raced. He had not thought about what background to give. He wanted no link to Faryl whatsoever. 'Er, I'm from a small village to the mid-north.'

'Oh yes? Which one?' She was not going to be put off easily he realised.

'Rittylworth.' It was the first name that came into his head.

'Shar's mercy. That poor place,' the woman said, her voice suddenly grave.

'Pardon?'

But his companion was distracted by a group of women hailing her. They sound like a gaggle of geese, Wyl thought, amazed by the laughter and sudden bursts of separate conversations that ensued.

'I won't desert you,' his new friend said, looking back and winking. 'Take a towel and a robe. We undress over there,' she added. 'I'll be with you in a moment.'

There was nothing for it; he had to follow her instructions or risk curiosity. Everyone seemed to be moving in the same direction. He chose an elegantly shuttered cubicle for modesty but most of the women just stripped off in the communal area. It was terrifying. Wyl felt way out of his depth now. He was going to have to walk naked to the baths.

He looked down at his full breasts and felt the familiar urge to gag at the sight. But it was the fear of discovery that troubled him most. He took several long, shuddering breaths. *You're Leyen*, he berated himself. *No one bar Aremys knows any different, and he knows nothing other than a name. They see only a woman's body. Now—*

'Leyen?' It was his friend knocking. 'Are you in there?'

He closed his eyes. 'Yes, I'm just coming,' he said as lightly as he could and reached for courage. He opened the door and stepped out, his gaze on the floor.

'My, but you're a modest one,' she said and chortled softly. 'Oh, my dear, with a body like yours you have nothing to fear here – other than all-consuming jealousy. I don't believe there is a flatter belly nor tauter thighs amongst us. Now come, let me show you around.'

'I don't know your name, I'm sorry,' Wyl lied, still not risking a glance towards the naked woman who walked beside him arm in arm, her doughy flesh touching his own.

'Oh, how remiss of me,' she chuckled. 'I am Lady Bench. But, please, as we have now strolled naked together, you must call me Helyn.' She smiled warmly and Wyl blushed.

'Thank you, Helyn,' he said, knowing he must do his best to start acting like a woman and less like an impostor.

He looked up at last and was rewarded with a sight any other man would give a limb for: fifty or sixty naked women, bathing, luxuriating, talking, some taking a smooth, others just being oiled. The atmosphere was serene yet playful – he wondered how they achieved that. His companion answered his thoughts.

'Welcome to the ladies pavilion, Leyen,' Helyn said. 'All we do is gossip,' she added. 'We're all talking about each other, of course . . . but carefully.' She winked again. Her mood was infectious and Wyl liked her.

The bath was hotter than he had expected as he stepped into the gently bubbling water. He could see a magnificent mosaic on the floor, similar in design to what he recalled from the men's pavilion. This building was more palatial though, with more glass, more light, paler marble, artworks adorning the walls, and smoothing tables made comfortable with cushions. Everything just a little more luxurious, a little softer, than the men enjoyed.

The chatter here was subdued – probably because of its needing to be kept 'just between us' he thought, and grinned to himself. *So this is what Ylena used to get up to.*

'Ah, you must share the joke. Nothing is private here, Leyen,' Helyn admonished in gentle fun. 'Follow me – over here is my favourite spot,' she said. The noblewoman gestured for Wyl to join her on a special seat built into the wall which allowed them to comfortably submerge themselves in the water's warmth whilst still being in a position to talk with ease. Steam was rising off the surface of the water. Wyl commented on it for conversation as they settled themselves, and to keep his eyes occupied rather than lecherous as they seemed determined to be.

'They keep the temperature of the water warmer in the ladies' pavilion than in the men's, I'm told. Apparently we women prefer it that way, to steam our skin and keep our complexions healthy.' She levelled an enquiring gaze upon Wyl. 'So, Leyen, who are you?'

'A guest,' Wyl replied. 'I am handling some correspondence for the King between realms.' The lie came quickly.

'No messenger I know of is accommodated as a guest of Celimus,' Helyn probed.

'No messenger you know of is a special courier to Briavel,' Wyl said evenly, wondering at the audacity of his own invention. He could thank Romen for that.

'Indeed,' she said, eyebrows raised, curiosity piqued. 'Briavel? This can only be about the marriage.'

'Press me no further, Lady Helyn. I am sworn to secrecy,' he added theatrically but hoping she might take the hint.

His words achieved the opposite, fuelling her need to discover more. This time her eyes narrowed. 'You don't look like a simple courier.'

'I am not and never will be simple, madam,' Wyl replied and laughed coquettishly, drawing on the mannerism Faryl had used to such effect at the Forbidden Fruit.

'I'll get to the bottom of you yet, Leyen of Rittylworth,' Helyn said, enjoying the intrigue.

'Which reminds me, Lady Helyn, what did you mean earlier when you spoke of my home village?'

She looked at him sideways, sober now. 'Have you family there still?'

'No,' he said carefully.

'You are fortunate then, and little wonder you have not heard that the place was torched.'

Wyl felt his chest constrict. 'Torched,' he repeated in a small voice, the sight of naked women suddenly forgotten. 'By whom?'

'They say bandits, but I have never heard of bandits who could be bothered torching a village. Ransacking it maybe, but they would not waste the time damaging it. To what end? You burn a village to teach its inhabitants a lesson, in my opinion.'

An attendant squatted by them with a tray of multi-coloured layers. Wyl looked confused.

'Oh dear, child, wherever have you been hiding your-self? These are soap leaves, my girl. Take a few. Each is scented differently.'

'Thank you,' Wyl said, feeling like a dullard. In the

men's pavilion they used soap paste, nothing so dainty as these leaves. In truth, part of his confusion came from shock at the news.

'I know only the dusty road, Lady Helyn, and am used to washing myself in a tin tub dragged up the inn's stairs. Forgive me my ignorance. But tell me, what of the monastery at Rittylworth?'

Lady Helyn sighed as she began soaping herself. Wyl looked away, embarrassed, locking instead on to the sight of an attractive pair of breasts on the other side of the pool.

'Well, that was the worst part of it, Leyen – and why any fool would know this was not the work of bandits. The monks were killed and not mercifully either. Everyone in the monastery was murdered.'

Wyl must have paled because his new friend reached out to steady him. 'I am so sorry to give you this news. You must have known many there.'

'Yes . . . yes, I did. You say everyone was murdered?'

'Mmm, it's true. My husband deals with many merchants. One who passes through Rittylworth regularly said he had recognised the body of the senior monk, Brother Jakub. He had been nailed to a cross and burned. Any visitors at the monastery were killed too . . . dreadful business.'

Lady Bench continued talking but Wyl had stopped listening. The horror was too much for him to bear. Ylena, dead? Her lovely face swam before him but he could not make it smile no matter how hard he tried. His memory of her now was sombre – her laughter had gone from the moment she had witnessed her husband's death and been committed to sorrow. Perhaps she had welcomed death, he wondered. His entire family was dead now then, including himself in a way.

He agreed with Lady Bench — the killers were no bandits. Only a sadist would do such a thing. A sadist with power. Celimus — who else? But how could the King possibly have known where Romen had taken Ylena? He had covered their tracks too well. Wyl's whole being fought back the urge to make his way to the King's rooms immediately and, come what may, kill him.

Then another horrific thought came. Had Elspyth perished too?

'When did this occur?' he demanded.

'Pardon me?' Lady Bench said, turning back towards Wyl from engaging someone passing by in a polite salutation. 'Oh . . . I would guess at about three days ago.' She waded off with her friend, throwing a wink back to Wyl as though she had latched on to some juicy gossip. 'Won't be long,' she mouthed.

Wyl was relieved she had given him a few moments alone. His mind felt dazed.

If she had travelled quickly, Wyl calculated, then Elspyth would have certainly been at Rittylworth when the attackers came, and there was no hope for either of them. He could only pray to Shar that she had reached Ylena before the massacre and got her away to safety. And then, irrationally, he hoped that Elspyth had ignored his needs, had broken her promise and gone directly to her home. But he knew she would not have done that. Elspyth was steadfast and true; she would have kept her oath to him and walked straight into danger. He had failed both the women he had sworn to protect.

Lady Bench floated back. 'My dear, you look very pale.'

'I'm sorry. The news of Rittylworth has upset me.'

'And I feel badly that I was the messenger of these painful tidings. Come, wash yourself and then you are to return home with me.'

Wyl wanted to be alone with his sorrowful thoughts, but he also did not want to be within Stoneheart.

'It is spitting distance from the palace,' she urged. 'We will share a light meal and you can spend some quiet time in my gardens. It will be better for you than here. I shall leave you in peace if you wish – you can even stay the night.'

'I am having supper with the King tonight,' Wyl said distractedly.

'Shar save us, girl! You *are* important.'

'Not really,' he said, wondering why he had blurted out that information. 'I have nothing to wear.'

'Well, I have plenty!' Helyn said, suddenly galvanised. 'I shall hear no argument. You are coming with me.'

Without further discussion Wyl found himself dried, dressed and in Lady Helyn's carriage bound for her home. She was alone right now – her husband away and her only daughter staying with friends – so she was glad of the company.

Wyl had to admit it was good for him to be diverted in this way. His inclination was to jump on a horse and ride for Rittylworth, but his soldier's mind told him there was little he could do. Whatever had happened would not change because of his arrival; the carnage would not become any less tragic. Besides, he had begun to convince himself that Elspyth had got to the monastery in time and that both women were together and on the run to Felrawthy. Jakub would not have allowed any harm to come to Ylena.

At the first hint of trouble he would have hidden her in the secret grotto and hopefully got her to safety.

Lady Bench was right. Wyl did feel better for the solitude, and she was as good as her word and left him alone for a while. Her home was a splendid sandstone affair, its design and furnishings testament to her wealth and excellent taste. The gardens were no less magnificent and Wyl was pleased to spend some time wandering their scented paths, thinking over his current situation and how he might make the best of it. Wyl was not completely taken in by the attention he was receiving from Lady Helyn. He knew she was a pivotal and indeed powerful member of the nobility, and she had sensed the chance to be privy to the secret dealings of the King. She herself had mentioned to Wyl how Pearlis thrived on gossip and hearsay, and she was no different to other women — a bored, wealthy woman was always going to be fascinated by intrigue. Wyl appreciated, however, that Lady Bench was intelligent as well as wise, for she knew when not to push for the information she so desperately craved. When she finally joined him, they talked about every subject under the sun, bar the King's marriage.

They sat sipping mint tea next to a pond filled with fat flame-coloured fish that occasionally broke through the water's surface decoration of delicate water lilies. Nearby, an aviary of chittering canaries was a mass of colour and movement. The garden was a sun trap and they were warm out there, with the help of some soft rugs, which Wyl did not need but politely accepted. 'Now, Leyen,' Lady Bench said, 'we must find you an appropriate gown and cloak for your rendezvous with the King this evening.'

'Lady Helyn, I hope you won't take it as rude when I say we are not necessarily of a size. I am taller for a start,' Wyl said, feeling clumsy. Despite his best efforts he believed he gave offence. No woman alive liked to hear that another was taller, slimmer, prettier . . . no matter how old they were.

'And infinitely trimmer too,' she said, laughing. She placed her glass on the small table beside her. 'I was thinking of something from my daughter's wardrobe. Shar knows, I lavish enough of my husband's fortune on that girl's back. She won't even notice them missing, my dear. Only the other day I took delivery from Amos Rilk, Master Tailor of Briavel, of my daughter's first formal ballgown – worth a small fortune in gold.'

'You use a tailor from Briavel?'

'None finer. They say he dresses the Queen.'

'Then he is privileged indeed,' Wyl replied, wishing he could dress Briavel's Queen in Master Rilk's place. He stifled a sad smile at the thought that he would actually prefer to undress her.

'Have you met her majesty?' Helyn enquired innocently.

'Yes.'

'And?'

'She is very . . .' He wanted to say easy to love, wonderful to kiss, but he did not '. . . statuesque. Rilk would surely be in raptures hanging his fabrics from her shoulders.'

'Hmm, I hear she is an extraordinary beauty.'

'She is. But Valentyna,' he saw Helyn's eyes widen in surprise at his casual use of the monarch's name '. . . er, I mean, the Queen, is not a vain woman from what I can gather. In truth, I have seen her more comfortable in riding breeches than a gown, with her hair falling down around her face rather than exquisitely braided.'

'You have mingled with her at formal occasions then . . . as well as less formal ones?'

'A couple.'

'As her guest, no doubt,' Helyn said, unable to hide the irony in her voice.

'Lady Helyn, forgive me. I have mentioned that much of my work between the monarchs is covert. I am not permitted to discuss it.'

'I understand. My apologies. I don't mean to pry but, as you can tell, we Morgravians are all very excited about this marriage.'

'Are you?'

'Of course! Aren't you? We all want peace. Valentyna will bring it by marrying Celimus. Perhaps she may also temper his wayward pursuits. And if you ever repeat that, Leyen, I shall publicly denounce you!'

Wyl laughed in spite of his churning emotions, and made the gesture of locking his lips with a key.

'I've been away on other business so must catch up on the latest news. How far have the plans for the wedding ceremony progressed?'

'I believe it will happen soon,' Helyn replied. 'Certainly the nobility is pressing through its own channels for a wedding by spring's end.'

'Spring's end,' Wyl murmured. Only weeks in which to save Valentyna.

'So tonight, no doubt, you will receive another message from Celimus for his beautiful Valentyna?'

'No doubt.' Wyl grimaced.

'He is very clever to use a woman for this role. Who would ever suspect? Now, let us choose something from my daughter's wardrobe to put him in a good mood.'

This was the last thing Wyl felt like doing. His mind was fraying just thinking about Rittylworth, but Faryl's essence kept him strong.

Lady Bench led Wyl to a dressing chamber, chatting along the way about the type of woman Celimus usually favoured. Wyl allowed her to ramble.

'I think olive green is your colour, my dear, with that lovely hair. Which reminds me, have they given you a maid?'

Wyl shook his head.

'Right, I'll send over one of my girls, with some flowers to dress your hair. Fresh gardenias from my glasshouse. I hope you don't find their perfume overwhelming?'

'No. But your generosity is, Lady Helyn.'

'Don't mention it. I want to cheer you after your news, and who knows, I may be responsible for helping you into the King's bed if we make you look as gorgeous as it's obvious you can be.'

She winked at her friend as a co-conspirator, then immediately apologised, alarmed by the look of horror on Leyen's face. 'Oh, my dear, just a little joke from a silly woman with nothing else to occupy her mind.'

12

WYL LOOKED AT HIMSELF in the mirror after Lady Helyn's
maid had departed. He hardly recognised this person as
the Faryl he had known since he had taken over her
grooming. Before him stood a tall, striking woman. Her
polished hair was swept up into an intricate design behind
her head and interwoven with tiny delicate gardenias. He
would require no perfume tonight as the fragrant flowers
more than compensated.

Helyn had decided against the olive green in the end
and chosen a soft cream gown. It was simplicity itself,
draping elegantly from his broad square shoulders, soft-
ening the long muscular arms. The maid had carefully
smoothed and creamed his lightly browned skin until it
too shone and then, to Wyl's fascination, she had dusted
it softly with a gold powder. The effect was to make his
skin shimmer as he moved – it was a stunning addition
for any woman looking to impress a man. For Wyl it was
a wondrous insight into the female arts of allurement.

Helyn had also sent one of her own items of jewellery:
a small ruby now hung at his throat like a drop of blood.

No other adornment was required after a dab of soft kohl at his eyes to deepen their dark intensity and a smudge of tawny colour on his lips. Wyl despised the taste and the gluey texture, but he knew Leyen looked superb and dared not wipe his mouth clean. The maid had trimmed and buffed his nails until they too shone mirror-like. He was complete.

As he stared at his reflection Wyl hoped that the King would not take an unprofessional liking to what he saw. He was relying on his own knowledge that Celimus had always tended towards flaxen-haired beauties whose fairness made his own swarthiness all the more dramatic. Wyl also knew that the King preferred weaker women, ones he could dominate, which was why he must allow Faryl's strong personality to shine. Such preferences made Valentyna a poor choice for Celimus – she neither suited his taste for golden-haired women nor did her feisty, regal style lend itself to his domineering manner.

Wyl realised, though, that it was not Valentyna whom Celimus loved but the riches she brought and the peace their union would achieve. The whole region would grow wealthier still, and Celimus's heir would rule over two great realms. Wyl grimaced at the thought of Celimus siring an heir upon Valentyna. Then it occurred to him that perhaps the King's ambitious eyes looked even further afield. With peace achieved in the southern realms, the new power could deal with the people of the Razors and their upstart Mountain King.

Spring's end. The thought nagged repeatedly.

There was a soft knock at the door, which turned out to be Jorn.

'Too late,' Wyl said, 'I've already chosen. Do you approve?' he added.

'My lady,' Jorn said, blushing, 'what could there be to disapprove of?'

'Well spoken, Jorn. Come in. You've been busy, I gather?'

'Yes, my lady,' he replied, stepping carefully into the chamber and leaving the door ajar.

'Close it, would you,' Wyl said.

The lad did so, clearly uncomfortable.

'Jorn, let me put your mind at rest. We have a mutual acquaintance.' This won the lad's attention. 'I am a friend of Romen Koreldy.'

The young man's eyes lit up. Wyl was pleased Romen had made a good impression.

'I am honoured, then, to know you. He is someone I admire.'

Guilt raged through Wyl. The truth would not work here, however. 'Tell me, how are you getting on?'

'Did he ask you to enquire after me?' Jorn said, his eagerness heartbreaking.

'Yes, in a way.'

'And the Lady Ylena? Tell me she is well, Madam Leyen.'

'In truth I have not seen Ylena in a long time. I—'

Jorn cut across his words. 'Because I have worried myself sick over the recent news that Rittylworth has been ransacked, knowing she had gone there.'

Wyl felt a twist in the pit of his stomach as the missing piece of the jigsaw slotted into place. It was Jorn who had told them; innocent, eager Jorn who had unwittingly led Celimus to Ylena like a cat to cream. He felt sick at the thought of kind and wise Brother Jakub, the young lad Pil, all those monks murdered so cruelly in the pursuit of the Thirsk line. A vision of Ylena lying broken and dead hit his thoughts like a clap of thunder. *No, she is alive*, he told himself.

He took a steadying breath, working hard not to betray his fear. He could not blame the boy. 'Jorn, did you know specifically where Koreldy was headed when he left Stoneheart?'

'Not really, madam. He mentioned something about the northwest and possibly Rittylworth, but he wasn't sure at that time as I recall.'

Wyl remembered wanting to bite out his own tongue when that slip had occurred. It was a pity the lad had such a good memory. 'And did you mention this to anyone?' he asked casually, busying himself fussing with his hair so as not to arouse suspicion in Jorn.

'I . . . um . . . I might have, yes. I think Chancellor Jessom was making some enquiries.'

'Ah, yes, I know Jessom,' Wyl said in a tight tone.

'Is everything all right?'

'Of course,' Wyl reassured, forcing himself to keep his voice even. 'In fact I promised Koreldy that I would visit the Lady Ylena the next time I passed through this region.'

'She is not at Argorn, then?' Jorn asked sadly.

Wyl recalled how Ylena had promised the page that she would send for him once she returned to her family home. He shook his head. 'I can't be sure, Jorn.' Anything to keep the truth from getting out.

'Oh.' The lad looked deflated, then his eyes lit again. 'You might care to try the Duchy of Felrawthy then, madam. My lady married into the Donal family and she might well be visiting them in the far north.'

Damn the lad's excellent memory. Wyl's anxieties increased. How to keep him quiet without provoking suspicion?

'Thank you. I shall make some enquiries.'

Poor Jorn. He was determined that Ylena's promise was not forgotten, even if it meant chewing the ear off a visitor who might meet up with her. 'She said she would send for me, Madam Leyen.'

Wyl put a kind smile on his face despite his fears for Ylena. 'Is being in her service more important than serving the King, Jorn?'

The lad flushed scarlet. 'I would die for her,' he stammered.

This was a shock. Wyl's immediate reaction was to tell Jorn he hardly knew Ylena well enough to pledge such a lofty sacrifice. However, he himself had fallen in love with Valentyna within moments of her turning that direct blue gaze upon him. From then on Wyl Thirsk had become a man of Briavel, her man. Valentyna knew none of this, of course. She loved Koreldy, and she could never possibly love Wyl, and especially Faryl, even though all three were now one.

Wyl sighed, noted Jorn was still blushing and uncomfortable. He found a grin for him. 'Well, let's hope you never have to, Jorn,' he said, praying that his sister was safe. 'But now that you have expressed your loyalty,' he added, taking advantage of the boy's weakness for Ylena, 'I suggest you observe it as sharply as ever. Do you understand?' He could not help but emphasise it further. 'Be discreet to the point of silence.'

Jorn nodded but wore a puzzled expression. Wyl could say nothing more direct; he would have to let the lad figure it out for himself.

'Well, I believe I am expected in the King's suite. Thank you for coming,' Wyl said.

'Call upon me any time, Madam Leyen. Please, give my regards to Romen Koreldy when you see him.'

'And what shall I give to the Lady Ylena should our paths cross?' Wyl said.

He was relieved to see Jorn grin. So the young fellow did have a sense of humour and was not all earnest effort. Wyl smiled his farewell. Jorn may yet prove useful.

It was a mild evening, made milder still by the braziers burning in a circle around yet another private courtyard in Stoneheart. The castle boasted at least a dozen, some of which Wyl had been in at one time or another as he grew up, but this one he did not recognise. It was compact, ringed by beds of herbs including several fine bay trees. There were none of the spectacular flowers for which King Magnus had been known. Nonetheless the area was beautiful in its simple, somewhat stark design.

Its ordered structure was softened by the breathy fragrances of the herbs, which mingled in the warmth to create a sensuous atmosphere. In the centre of the courtyard was a table around which four chairs were placed. The setting was elegant but, again, simple. Wyl was struck by the restraint; he would have expected something more elaborate from Celimus. The King had excellent taste but leaned towards the flashy. What Wyl was looking upon now was understated, more to his own taste in fact, and he felt instantly comfortable in this small square of Stoneheart.

Aremys was already in attendance. He held a cup of wine and was talking softly with the Chancellor, whom Wyl presumed made up tonight's foursome. He saw the mercenary turn, heard the breath catch in the man's throat, and realised in that instant what power a handsome woman held over men.

'Leyen, you look very lovely.' It was Jessom, giving the rare honour of a bow.

Aremys gathered his wits and inclined his head. 'Leyen.'

'Thank you, gentlemen,' Wyl said. 'One of the noble-women took pity on me and insisted on dressing me tonight,' he added, lest they hope this was part of his regular wardrobe.

'She did you proud,' Aremys replied in a tight tone. He coughed softly to clear it then drained his cup.

Jessom held out a goblet. 'May I offer you wine?'

'You may,' Wyl said, graciously taking the cup. 'What shall we drink to? Forgiveness, no doubt?' The dryness of the comment was not lost on his dining companions.

'To duty,' Aremys replied.

Jessom gave a cold smile and raised his glass.

Wyl sipped at the sweetish aperitif and looked around at the garden once again. 'This is certainly a most beautiful courtyard.'

'I'm glad you approve,' the King responded airily as he made a majestic entrance at the top of the shallow flight of stairs.

The men bowed; Wyl was forced to attempt the more traditional curtsy now that he was dressed in a gown. He couldn't imagine how clumsy he must look. Still, Celimus seemed not to notice. Instead he was appraising the woman who stood before him. He remained on the stairs for the moment, preferring not to come down to their level, and in those few seconds Wyl was reminded that Celimus cut the most dashing of figures. He was resplendent in superb garments tailored perfectly to show off his tall, lean physique. Even bathed and groomed Aremys still looked like a scruffy bear by comparison.

Wyl felt the familiar hate curdle within. All the old feelings returned, threatening to unbalance him, but he reminded himself that he was no longer short and stocky with orange hair and freckles. He was tall and lithe, certainly not pretty, but with his own beauty – or rather, Faryl's. He had nothing to feel inferior about. He was the only woman in the company tonight; he must use that power wisely and negotiate a passage as far away from Stoneheart as possible.

Celimus finally descended the stairs. Instead of proffering his own, he took his guest's hand and, leaning over, kissed it, shocking Wyl. The feel of those cruel lips, which ordered the execution of Alyd, against his own flesh made it crawl. Wyl controlled his inclination to shrink away from the touch.

The dark gaze met his own. 'I designed these gardens myself,' the King continued. 'In honour of my bride-to-be, who, I am assured, loves herb gardens and simplicity in all design. Good evening, Leyen.' His eyes sparkled.

'Your highness,' Wyl said, bowing his head, hating the King's confidence that Valentyna was already his.

The others followed suit, bowing low once again.

'What are we drinking, Jessom?' Celimus asked, all ease and charm.

'The Cherenne, sire, your favourite.'

'Ah, indeed. Come, let us sit.' At the King's nod a host of servants descended to lay platters of savouries on the table.

Small talk accompanied the food until a delicate fish course was served, then Celimus banished the servants.

None of his guests needed to be told that what the King had to say from here on was private.

'So, Leyen . . . I understand you are Morgravian?'

Wyl nodded carefully at the King, the sweet sauce that set off the fish so magnificently suddenly souring in his mouth.

'From where exactly?'

Wyl needed to keep the truth from Celimus, but remembered the story he had told his new friend, Lady Helyn. He would have to stick to that. 'Rittylworth, your majesty.' He decided to go on the offensive: 'Although I have heard since arriving here of its demise.'

At this the King stopped in the act of swallowing from a goblet of wine. 'I am sorry to hear that you were raised there. It was a necessary lesson being taught.'

Wyl appreciated Celimus's candour; he had expected lies. 'What lesson is that, your highness?' he asked innocently, taking a small mouthful of the fish and avoiding eye contact with the King.

'That traitors and those who harbour them shall be hounded down and dealt with.'

Wyl simply nodded, his expression blank. Inside, his blood boiled. He felt Aremys watching him carefully. The mercenary knew Faryl was from Coombe not Rittylworth; Wyl had told him as much during their ride.

'Do you know of this village, Aremys?' Celimus said.

'Yes, your highness. I have passed through it on occasion but mostly around it.'

'A sleepy enough place,' Jessom commented, not wishing to be entirely left out of the conversation.

'And one stupid enough to protect those who would betray their sovereign,' Celimus said.

'May I ask who was important enough to have so many good people put to death, sire?' Wyl asked as nonchalantly as he could.

'Ylena Thirsk.'

'A woman?' Aremys blurted. Jessom glared at him.

Celimus did not react. 'Yes,' he said mildly. 'As I even here testifies, women can be so much more subtle than men in their intrigues.'

Wyl smiled at the King, hating him. 'How was this Ylena a problem for you, your highness?'

The King sighed, as though being pressed on the subject was troublesome to him. 'The whole Thirsk family were traitorous, to be truthful. My father, may his soul rest in Shar's safekeeping, protected them for too long. This is all rather tedious but probably worth you knowing,' he said expansively, reaching for his goblet before leaning back in his chair. 'Old Fergys Thirsk was my father's best friend . . . apparently.' The final word was loaded with irony. He grinned, white teeth perfect. 'He was a villain of the highest order and would have stabbed my father in the back at the first chance, although I guess he found it easier to poison him instead – metaphorically speaking, of course,' Celimus added, chuckling softly at his own remark.

Jessom gave his usual cold grimace in response, whilst Aremys remained motionless and watchful, unsure of his place at this table. Wyl only maintained his composure by clasping his hands so tightly his knuckles turned white.

The King continued. 'I was thrilled beyond my wildest dreams when I heard old Thirsk had been cut down. He could not have died quickly enough for me.' Celimus sipped the Cherenne. 'I know what you're all thinking – how could a child hate so much? – but I hated that man for taking all of my father's love and his friendship, not to mention land and wealth, whilst all the time working against the realm.'

'Forgive me, sire,' Wyl said, unable to remain silent any longer, 'I thought I had heard that General Fergys Thirsk took the sword slash meant for King Magnus? It was told in the taverns of the north where I was travelling at the time that Thirsk sacrificed his life willingly for his sovereign.'

The King shrugged, a rueful smile just touching the perfectly shaped lips. 'Who knows what truly happened on that battlefield, Leyen? My father might have protected Thirsk's name to the very last. For all we know it was a conspiracy and someone from our own side killed the General for his devious ways. I would reward that man if I knew him.'

Wyl let out a choked sound which he quickly checked with a swallow of wine. Celimus's contrived story was too ridiculous to feel any further insult. The King had nothing to substantiate his vile and slanderous claims, all but making up the story as he told it. Yet there was nothing Wyl wanted to do more right now than pick up the fruit knife and stab it into the King's throat, for the pure pleasure of the kill.

'You are amused, Leyen,' Celimus said, missing nothing. 'How so?'

'Apologies, sire. It was not amusement – one of these scrumptious dried figs has stuck in my throat.' He swallowed several more mouthfuls of the wine. His glance strayed to Aremys, who was watching him carefully, one eyebrow raised in question. 'Please, your highness,' Wyl said, 'forgive my interruption and continue.'

Celimus did so, outlining the burgeoning of his hatred with the arrival at Stoneheart of Fergys Thirsk's son, Wyl; the two lads' tumultuous childhood; and finally the story of the younger Thirsk's betrayal in Briavel. 'Oh, how I wished we ran our army on the merit system,' Celimus said. 'This tradition of handing down a title through a warrior family may have suited the shrunken men of olden days, but these are modern times and simply because the family produced one hero in an ancient Thirsk it does not necessarily mean it breeds them.'

'Hear, hear, sire,' Jessom muttered, signalling to a watchful servant out of earshot that the plates could now be cleared.

A magnificent spread of cheeses, glacé fruits and sweet fudges were laid out, the serving staff moving deliberately to be away from the table almost as quickly as they arrived.

When it was just the four of them again, Aremys cleared his throat. 'Your majesty, I'm not sure I understand why I have been privy to this intriguing tale, but I'm wondering how a young woman, a nobleman's daughter whose head is no doubt more filled with visions of lace and satin than politics, could be of any threat to your sovereignty.'

The King nodded. 'Indeed, Aremys, well said. It is complicated and I don't wish to bore present company any further with those complexities.' *I bet you don't*, Wyl thought. The King kept talking: 'Suffice to say Ylena Thirsk continues a fine family tradition of treachery towards the Crown. It is my belief that she is currently on her way to the powerful Duke of Felrawthy to stir up trouble.'

Wyl could hardly believe the joy he felt at hearing this statement. 'So you didn't find her at Rittylworth, sire?'

'No, indeed we did not. Which brings me to why we are here tonight,' Celimus said, his tone suggesting he would brook no further interruption. He stood, preferring to deliver his orders from a vantage point.

'I want you, Leyen,' he said, inclining his head, 'and you, Aremys, to travel to Felrawthy. Hopefully you can intercept Ylena Thirsk's journey there.'

'And?' Wyl asked, hardly daring to breathe.

'Kill her,' Celimus replied. 'It's what you do, isn't it?'

Aremys and Wyl nodded, both stunned for different reasons.

'Good,' the King said. 'Jessom, make the usual arrangements. Provide them with horses, coin, whatever they need. No one, and I mean no one, is to know of this mission.' He eyed each of them, a threat behind the look.

Again Aremys cleared his throat softly. He had noticed the shock pass across Faryl's face although she had covered it adroitly. What was going on, he wondered.

'Any questions?' Celimus asked.

Aremys sat forward. 'Your highness, may I ask why the duke would protect her? Surely he would support the Crown rather than risk all for an old friend's daughter?'

'There are reasons. Please trust my judgement on this. I am hiring your services not your understanding, mercenary.'

Aremys nodded politely yet persisted. 'Then may I enquire why the task requires two of us?'

'The duke is well protected with his own men – one of Fergys Thirsk's cronies, I'm afraid, who has grown fat and rich at the Crown's expense. If Ylena Thirsk has succeeded in reaching the duke, things could turn ugly. I'm sending you as a special support, Aremys, although I suspect Leyen is more than capable of pulling this off, considering her last successful task for me.'

Celimus smiled slyly, his glance sliding from Aremys to Leyen, whose face was a blank mask. 'I want proof of her corpse – more than a finger this time, Leyen,' the King cautioned.

Wyl's lips thinned and he stood. 'Then we should leave tomorrow, sire,' he said, no longer able to spend another minute in the King's company. 'I accept the commission, your highness. I shall away to my rooms to make my preparations.'

'So soon, Leyen? I thought we might take some more wine together,' the King replied.

'Er, forgive me, your highness.' Wyl took in Jessom's aghast expression at his audacity at denying the King his company. 'I need a good night's rest and a clear head. My intention is most certainly to intercept the woman before she reaches Felrawthy.' He became businesslike. 'How many days does she have on us, sire?'

'Three, as I understand it.' Celimus looked towards Jessom who confirmed this with a brief nod. 'She escaped on foot – we found this out from one of the villagers who saw her fleeing, accompanied by one of the monks. One so new his pate was yet to be shaved.'

Shar bless you, Pil, Wyl thought, recalling Koreldy's young friend at the monastery.

'Then we should waste no further time,' Aremys said,

pushing back his chair. 'Leyen is right. We must leave at first light to have any chance of catching them.'

Celimus shrugged. 'So be it. Remember now, I want a corpse. For this I will pay you each a fortune in gold. The Chancellor will discuss terms. Perhaps that should be attended to now, Jessom, as our guests seem determined to leave Stoneheart almost as soon as they have arrived.' He held up his hand. 'But I understand and applaud you for it. You shall be well favoured by me if you rid Morgravia of the Thirsk curse.'

Aremys was at Leyen's side. He bowed, putting pressure on her arm to force her to follow suit. Wyl curtsied as best he could.

'Oh, and Leyen,' Celimus said, as an afterthought. 'I have another mission for you when this is done.'

'Yes, sire?' Wyl said, his voice tightly controlled.

'Mmm. If you have a moment?' he said. 'You may go, Aremys, Jessom.'

Wyl watched Aremys leave. There was something in his expression that told Wyl to be careful.

The King returned his gaze to Leyen. 'When you are done with the Thirsk woman I want you to go straight to Briavel.'

Wyl nodded, wondering what terrible deed Celimus was going to ask of him next.

'I want you to take a document to Queen Valentyna which I shall have delivered to you tonight. It is my final proposal of marriage. You will bring back to me her signed agreement that our wedding will take place at the close of spring.'

'And if she should refuse me, sire?' Wyl asked matter-of-factly, careful to keep his voice devoid of all emotion.

The answer was delivered in an identical businesslike tone. 'You will kill her and I will invade Briavel and destroy its Crown once and for all. See that you succeed with both women. You are free to go now.'

As Wyl left the beautiful courtyard, he called on all his training to keep his emotions in check. Aremys and Jessom watched, concerned, as the tall woman in the beautiful gown all but ran past them.

13

WYL HAD NO INTENTION of waiting for Aremys or until dawn. The three women he cared about were under threat from the same man and it was a terrible decision who to try and help.

It had to be Ylena.

If Aremys got to her first then she was as good as dead. He could rely on brave Elspyth to do her best to reach his sister, and if they had not already joined forces then Elspyth had the wherewithal to go on to Felrawthy and deliver the note. He realised she was penniless but he also knew she was resourceful and courageous enough to find her way. As for Valentyna, she was the most protected, at least for now.

With these thoughts cluttering his already swirling mind, Wyl raced back to his rooms and packed what little gear he had. Rousing a sleepy page he asked the lad to find Jorn for him. Whilst he waited impatiently he scribed a note to the Lady Helyn and tucked it with her necklace into a hidden pocket in her daughter's cloak which he had not used that evening. Then he changed out of her daughter's gown into his comfortable travelling clothes.

Jorn arrived with the King's missive which he handed to Faryl whilst he took in her rough riding garb. 'Madam Leyen,' he said astonished, 'surely you're not leaving at this time of night?'

'Hush, Jorn,' Wyl whispered, dragging the lad fully into the room. 'You must never mention to anyone that we had this conversation.'

The boy's eyes widened now, fully awake. 'Heart crossed and hope to die,' he said, making a sign over his chest.

Wyl mustered a smile. 'Good. Now listen to me. Lady Ylena is in trouble. I leave now to find her but I must do so in secret. I need your help.'

He eyed the boy and Jorn nodded mutely.

'You must fetch my horse for me.' Wyl pressed a pouch into Jorn's palm. 'Here's coin to pay off whoever you have to in order to get me safe passage out of Stoneheart.'

Jorn, to his credit, did not even glance at the bag of money. 'But what excuse shall I make?'

'You are the King's messenger – use your status. Tell them I travel on the King's business. Everyone knows I am a guest of Celimus, some sort of courier. Be confident, they will believe you. Use the coin to grease their palms and they will ask few questions. Offer my sincere apologies for disturbing them at this late hour.'

'I'll do it, of course, but it sounds dangerous for some reason, Madam Leyen.'

'No, I promise you it is not. Just irregular. If it was broad daylight no one would think twice.'

'Am I to fetch Master Aremys as well?' Jorn wondered.

'No! He especially must not know that I depart.' Wyl gripped the lad's arm, concerned he even knew about the other guest. 'Promise me.'

Once again Jorn nodded, not understanding but prepared to do what was asked of him.

Wyl pointed towards the bed. 'This gown is to be returned to Lady Helyn Bench.'

Jorn was expecting something more difficult. 'I can arrange that.'

'Thank you.'

'Do you wish to send a note with it?' he asked.

Wyl thought a moment. Truth was danger to this boy. 'No,' he lied. 'Simply return it with my thanks for its use.' He had already tucked the note inside the hidden pocket of the gown, which he had discovered earlier and marvelled at. Women obviously had such things stitched into their garments . . . he had no idea precisely for what, but was grateful for it. He had to hope the Lady Helyn would find the note.

'Do it as quickly as you can for me, would you?' Wyl asked, embellishing his plea further with another lie. 'I believe her daughter would like it returned for her own use tomorrow evening.' It was a thin tale but Jorn was not really paying attention to detail. He had his tasks now and was keen to move.

'I will fix all of this for you. Promise me, Madam Leyen . . .'

Wyl suddenly felt the weight of responsibility he was leaving with this innocent. 'Yes?'

'Please remember me kindly to the Lady Ylena. Let her know I await her summons.'

Wyl felt a sharp pang of grief for Jorn. He would send

for him himself as soon as he reached Felrawthy. 'I shall do that for you.'

Jorn gave a dazzling smile. 'Then I must hurry about my duty, madam.' He bent low over Wyl's hand and, surprisingly, kissed it before turning for the door. 'Leave as soon as you hear the next bell. I will have everything readied by then. Your horse will be at the southern end of the stables.'

'Thank you, Jorn . . . for everything.'

The lad smiled once more and left.

Wyl used the time to tie back his hair tightly and pull on a jacket. He looked around the chamber, checking that all was as it should be. Aremys would surely come looking in the morning and he wanted to leave no clues. He double-checked the note and jewellery were securely tucked inside the pocket of the gown and grimaced. He was risking much in sending that note – its contents would be damning if intercepted – but he hoped his judgement of the noblewoman was on the mark.

The bell sounded not long after and Wyl slipped from his room and stealthily made his way down corridors and through familiar halls. He encountered no one but a maid who took little notice of him anyway – she was in a hurry, rushing from the scullery carrying hot water and towels. Wyl presumed a baby was about to be born somewhere in the many rooms of Stoneheart. He continued on, passing by the kitchens he had so loved as a youngster and out through the small vegetable patch whose produce was reserved especially for the King. Finally he entered the courtyard that led to the stables.

As promised, Jorn met him at the southern end. He led Leyen's horse, already saddled.

'Any trouble?' Wyl asked, his chest tight with tension.

'None. Come, I will walk you out the gate. It will look better.'

Wyl nodded. He put his foot into Jorn's linked hands and stepped up lightly on to the horse. Jorn tied on Leyen's small bag.

'Thank you again for this,' Wyl uttered.

'Don't mention it, Madam Leyen. We work for the same cause.'

Wyl wanted to shake his head. Such loyalty. He felt pride burst in his chest at the lad's dedication. At least the Thirsk family had one friend.

Jorn led the horse slowly towards the main gates. 'Have you already spoken with the guard?' Wyl whispered.

'Yes. Fret not.' Wyl was impressed with Jorn's cool head right now.

They approached a guard, who stopped them. 'This is an odd departure time,' he commented but with idle interest, Wyl noted.

'My apologies. As you know, serving the King is never a predictable duty,' Wyl said and risked a wink.

The man shrugged, understanding the meaning of the woman's words. 'In that you are right,' he admitted. 'Go safely, madam.'

'Are you sure you will be safe in the darkness? Felrawthy is many days away,' Jorn muttered, worried.

Wyl grimaced. He did so wish the boy would learn to keep his tongue curbed. 'The dark is my friend, Jorn. It alone is my safety right now.'

'I don't understand,' the lad said, walking the horse out and away from the gates.

Wyl turned and waved thanks to the guard. He knew

the man might have heard his destination but could only hope he would not have digested it. It was too late to worry; he just had to impress on the boy the importance of keeping quiet over this matter.

'You will. Keep this our secret now, tell no one where I go. May Shar watch over you, Jorn.'

'And you.'

Wyl took the reins, ruffled the lad's hair and clicked his horse into a fast trot. He did not risk looking back.

Aremys paced, unable to sleep. He was quartered near the Legion and he could still hear some of the men singing quietly or talking in muted tones. But it was not the men who kept him awake. It was Leyen . . . or Faryl more to the point. Something was amiss. The speed at which she had left the King's courtyard earlier this evening was a surprise. She looked rattled. The secrets he knew she kept seemed all the more potent tonight. The way she carried herself, her stiffness around the King, and especially the way she reacted to talk of the Thirsk family.

It was obvious — to him, at least — that Faryl was not happy with her task. He wondered why Celimus had held her back. Faryl had been with the King only minutes beyond his own departure, so talk was all that could have occurred and not much of that even. But it was clear that something had passed between the King and Faryl which had disturbed her.

It was none of his business, he knew. And yet he had already lied for her. Why? He liked her, that was true. But there was more. He was not sure yet what it was but he had learned over the years to trust his instincts and they were screaming at him right now that Faryl was in some sort of trouble. Perhaps she could use his help.

Should he go to her? Would she answer his knock at this late hour? Probably not . . . probably never. Her coldness towards him was deep. His betrayal had enraged her.

'I would take it all back if I could, Faryl,' he whispered. 'I'm sorry.'

His mother had always told him never to go to sleep on an argument with a loved one. Well, he could hardly consider himself loved by Faryl, but there had been something of a friendship there before her capture. Perhaps there could be again. Maybe if he explained himself, told her how he regretted his hastiness in turning her over to Jessom, they could start again. They had a long journey ahead and it would be difficult if they were not even talking to one another . . .

Realisation suddenly hit him like a stone.

'You've gone, haven't you?' He spoke out loud, as though Faryl could hear him.

Aremys ran from his chamber, hopping down the hallway as he pulled on his boots. He had to ask directions several times, startling maids and the odd pageboy going about their late-night business. The only reason he knew he had arrived at the right chamber was because he saw a young man emerging carrying a gown he recognised as the one Faryl had worn earlier this evening. He descended on the lad, breathless and angry.

'Where do you go with that gown, boy?' he demanded.

The lad shrieked with fright but composed himself quickly. 'Sir?'

'Answer me!'

'I am running an errand for Madam Leyen. Please excuse me.'

'What is your name?'

The youngster told him, chin held high, adding, 'I am the King's messenger.'

It did not impress as intended. 'Go about your business then, Jorn.'

The lad looked as though he was about to ask Aremys what he was doing there, but he hesitated and obviously decided to hold his tongue. He scurried away, grabbing at the folds of the garment so they would not trail on the flagstones.

Aremys turned to the door, feeling in the pit of his stomach that his hunch was right. He knocked. When no reply came, he turned the huge metal ring, hoping against hope it would be latched and not permit him entry. The door opened easily. He closed his eyes briefly with worry that his instincts were proving correct.

'Leyen?'

Nothing.

'Faryl!' he said, louder now.

No reply.

He stepped inside and closed the door. The chamber and adjoining room were empty. No sign of her. The gown being returned to its owner was the only clue that she had ever been in this room – that and the vague perfume of gardenias which he remembered wafting seductively from her earlier that evening.

He felt devastated. She had gone. Fled from Stoneheart – from the King, no doubt. Or was it from him? He had betrayed her once; she was not giving him another chance. She had a secret and she was taking it with her. Who was she protecting? It was pointless to try and tease out answers from himself. Faryl was an enigma.

Aremys moved swiftly, giving chase to the lad, but he had no hope of finding Jorn amongst the many hallways of huge Stoneheart. Instead he angrily navigated his way back to his room and packed his garb. He would set off after her. It was madness, he knew. The woman was trouble. But he discarded all the sensible objections of why he should not pursue her. He had a hunch where she might be heading.

A light knock came at the door. He flung it open, expecting a messenger. He found Jessom instead.

'Leaving us already?' the Chancellor said, eyeing the bulging saddlebags.

'I can't sleep,' Aremys replied flatly. 'I thought I'd make myself useful – early start and all that.'

'And Leyen?' There was something sly in the tone.

Aremys played it carefully. 'What about her?'

'She's gone – did you know?'

Aremys thought quickly. However he might feel about Faryl, he certainly did not need a king for an enemy. Jessom's arrival and enquiry provided him with the opportunity to appear loyal to both sides.

He frowned deliberately. 'What are you talking about?'

'I've just been to her rooms,' the Chancellor said. 'May I come in?'

Aremys stepped aside and Jessom entered his chamber.

'Close the door,' the Chancellor suggested. After Aremys had done so, he continued. 'I wanted to talk to her about why the King kept her back this evening for a private word. I don't like secrets, and I was intrigued by her hasty departure from the King. Were you not?'

Aremys said nothing, merely raised an eyebrow to show he was paying attention.

'And now I find she has gone. There is no sign of her in her rooms,' Jessom continued smoothly.

'When was this?'

'Moments ago.'

'I see,' Aremys replied, thanking Shar's blessing that he had run out of Faryl's rooms so quickly.

'Any idea why she may have left you behind?'

He shook his head thoughtfully. 'No, indeed. I thought we were supposed to leave at first light.'

'Yes, that was my understanding also. I am wondering if the King gave her another task.'

Aremys shrugged. It was his notion too, but he certainly was not going to share it with the inquisitive Chancellor. 'But why brief us on what seems an important task to the Crown, give us orders to undertake it immediately and then turn around and give a counter order?' he reasoned.

'My thoughts exactly,' Jessom said. 'Although there is never any accounting for the whims or moods of Celimus. He is thoroughly unpredictable.'

'I can't help, I'm sorry.'

'So what will you do?'

'Carry on as instructed. I suppose I shall head off immediately then.'

'Yes, why not. There's no point in you remaining here.' The Chancellor handed Aremys a pouch of coins. 'This should cover you for expenses. I have already made arrangements for payment with regard to your capture and delivery of Leyen. And monies for the execution of the Legionnaires and delivery of their bodies is now paid in full,' he said, handing a bigger sack – of gold this time – to Aremys.

The mercenary grunted his thanks. Money was the last thing on his mind right now. He walked with the Chancellor to the door, eager for the man to leave.

'I shall get to the bottom of Leyen's mysterious departure. I wonder who might have seen her leave?' Jessom mused.

Aremys held the door open. 'Well, start with the lad Jorn, perhaps. Leyen mentioned he was attending to her.'

He knew it was a mistake the moment the words came out. He had meant it as an offhand line, something to move the Chancellor on his way so he could grab his saddlebags and go, but he knew immediately from the clouded look on Jessom's face that he had stirred up more trouble.

'Jorn! The King's messenger?' the man said, aghast.

Aremys needed to recant quickly. 'Oh truly, I have no idea. That's probably not even his name. I thought I heard her mention it tonight but come to think of it she said that some noblewoman had sent a maid . . .' His voice trailed off. It was too late to repair the damage. Jessom's expression had deepened in thought.

'You get going,' the Chancellor said distractedly. 'I must find that boy.'

Aremys shrugged. Jorn probably knew less than he did anyway.

'Report back to me in the usual way as soon as you have news of Ylena Thirsk,' Jessom added. 'We want her corpse in Stoneheart within weeks, although her head will do.' He laughed drily.

Aremys strode away, the sound of Jessom's amusement

diminishing behind him. At the stable he roused the disgruntled horse master, whose temper was only marginally improved by the sight of silver. Aremys learned that Faryl had barely a couple of hours on him.

At the gate he met the same guard. 'Lots of comings and goings tonight,' the man said wearily.

'Yes, I'm afraid we're all on the King's business,' Aremys admitted. 'In fact I've been asked to catch up with the woman who left a little earlier.'

'Ah yes, she took off in a real hurry . . . on royal business,' the man volunteered.

'That's her. Do you know where she was headed?'

'No, sir. Young Jorn might have mentioned something about Felrawthy but I can't be sure. I just open and shut the gate on orders, sir.'

Aremys made an expression of contrived sympathy. 'Thanks, anyway,' he said and tossed the man a silver coin.

The next morning Lady Bench's servant brought her a flask of sweetened wine as asked. He bowed. 'A delivery came for you, my lady,' he said as he poured.

'Oh? When?'

'In the early hours, madam. I thought it best not to disturb you.'

'Really? How very odd. Whatever is it?'

'Garments, my lady, brought by one of the King's pages, returned with thanks.'

Lady Helyn smiled. 'Ah yes. Intrigue over, Arnyld. I lent them to one of the King's guests who was staying unexpectedly at Stoneheart without formal attire. Have the gown cleaned, please, and returned to my daughter's rooms.'

'Yes, my lady.' The man bowed and withdrew.

Lady Helyn was pleasantly engaged in potting the bulbs she had had had sent from her special supplier in Briavel, when the manservant was back and bowing before her.

'What is it, Arnyld?' she said, mildly irritated to be distracted.

'Apologies at disturbing you, my lady. But I checked the pockets of the cloak and discovered this note addressed to you.'

'Oh?' she said, eagerly reaching for the small roll, hoping Leyen might have sent her some titbit for gossip. 'Where is my glass?'

Arnyld lifted a fat disc from a small table nearby and handed it to his mistress.

'Thank you, you may go,' she said.

After the servant's departure, she hurriedly unfurled the slightly crumpled note and placed the disc over the words to magnify them.

She read it several times. When Lady Helyn finally looked up from Leyen's note, her lips were pursed and her eyes reflected alarm. What she read had stunned her.

She ran over its contents again then crushed the note and threw it into the pond. She watched its sodden mass drift gently towards the murky bottom, ensuring no other pair of eyes would ever read.

14

THE PATH SHE HAD been walking for the past two days widened into a proper road and Elspyth's prayers were answered. People moved freely along this road. Two carts, obviously travelling together, almost knocked her down as she emerged somewhat wildly from the adjoining track, desperate to stop them. Stop them she did, nearly falling under the hooves of one of the startled horses.

'Shar's wrath!' someone yelled.

Elspyth fainted with relief or possibly hunger. When she regained her wits, she was lying beneath the canopy of a covered cart with several wide-eyed children staring down at her.

'She's awake!' one of them called.

A woman, obviously the mother of the brood, hove into view. 'Better?'

Elspyth grimaced and nodded. 'I'm sorry.'

'You gave us all a terrible fright,' the woman said. She smiled tentatively. 'I am Ruth. This is my family.' She called to the front, 'Ham, she's awake. Stop now.'

The children grinned shyly then lost interest in the strange woman.

Elspyth sat up as the cart lurched to a halt. 'Thank you for your kindness.'

Ruth smiled, more warmly now. 'Come. It's time we broke our fast.'

The mention of food made Elspyth's belly grind.

Ruth looked at her. 'Time you broke yours too,' she said, frowning.

It was reassuring to be amongst fellow travellers again. Elspyth felt her fears subsiding at the merry voices and the sudden activity to get a fire lit, water heated, food laid out. It was a humble spread but it was a feast to her.

'Eat,' Ruth encouraged. 'How long since your last meal?'

'Days,' Elspyth admitted. 'Is there enough for all?'

'Always,' the woman replied.

The men began to gather. There were two families. The second woman had older children, two boys, old enough to sit up front with their father.

Ham, Ruth's husband, introduced himself first and then the others. Elspyth nodded, smiling at everyone. 'Again, my apologies for startling you. I was so keen to speak to another person. It has been so long.'

'Well, whilst you eat, let us tell you about ourselves,' Ruth said, her kind eyes encouraging Elspyth to slice some meat from the haunch that had been set out. 'We always eat heartily at this time of the day,' she added.

Elspyth did as bade. As she ate she learned that the families were Briavellians – providores returning home after a successful trip into Morgravia.

'What do you sell?' she said through her contented chewing.

One of the lads spoke up, 'Our family are honeymakers.'

She looked confused now as she swallowed. 'But surely Morgravia makes its own honey?'

They all grinned as though this was a regular question. The lad enlightened her, 'Ah, but our bees are special. They have not been cross-bred with any others. They're the Magurian bee, from a tiny island off the southeast coast of Briavel.'

Elspyth was intrigued. 'But how do you stop the bees from breeding with other strains?'

The honeymaker family were impressed that she was taking so much interest. The father answered this time: 'Well, my family has been in honeymaking for generations. I am the third son; there was not enough income for me to make a livelihood in Maguria. So I moved to Briavel as soon as I was old enough to leave the nest and settled on the mainland.' He sucked at a pipe as he recalled those early days. 'I fell in love with a beautiful Briavellian maiden, but I hated the honey on the mainland, preferring the richer lavender and clover flavours of the Magur gold.'

His wife smiled indulgently at his words.

He continued: 'And so rather than the bees themselves, I suggested to my father that I might import some of our honeycomb.'

'I'll bet the Briavellians loved it too!' Elspyth said, enjoying the tale.

'It helped that our dear King Valor, rest his soul, took a fancy to it, having tried it once whilst passing through our region,' the wife said softly.

'And do you supply your lovely young Queen?' Elspyth asked.

Their son was eager to take up the story. 'Yes. Apparently she eats it each day and attaches much to its health properties.'

Elspyth nodded. 'She is very beautiful, I hear.'

The lad blushed. 'She is magnificent. No one can hold a candle to her looks.'

Elspyth grinned. 'Then I must taste this honey of yours for it must be her secret.'

Her companions laughed, offered around more food and tea.

'And you?' Elspyth said to Ruth. 'Tell me about your family.'

'Ham can tell you,' she said, nodding at her husband as she began to clear away some of the debris of their meal.

He obliged. 'Well, our family are grape-growers and wine-makers but not just any old grapes, mind. Our vines produce the prized frostfruit, harvested very late in the year when the first bite of winter is felt. They are exquisitely sweet, very small and produce the most lush, rich wine—'

'Also favoured by royalty, no doubt,' Elspyth chimed in, amusing both families.

'By your own royalty in fact,' Ham admitted, liking her cheek. 'We recently made a delivery to the court of King Celimus and we've been travelling in the north for a while. My son's first vintage and a fine one it is,' the man said proudly, looking towards his boy who shrugged self-consciously. 'Don't be bashful,' he added. 'You've a better palate and nose than any member of our family I can remember.'

'And so Briavellian honey and wine finds its way across the border into Morgravia regularly now?' Elspyth asked and the adults nodded.

'That's wonderful to hear,' she said, meaning it. 'Trade overcoming politics.'

Ham nodded. 'Yes, but only because our two products have found favour with the royals, as you say.'

Ruth sighed. 'It will be a lot easier when your Celimus marries our Valentyna. We can all trade more freely. Worry less.'

'Do you think it will happen?' Elspyth wondered, thinking of Wyl.

'It has to,' said the honeymaker, taking a long puff on his pipe. 'It is the only way our two realms can become profitable. All these wars have achieved is to beggar each realm's producers. If they marry we can forget war and our children can look forward to a better life.'

Sounds of agreement came from those around her and Elspyth felt a surge of sadness for her trapped friend. Wyl loved Valentyna, but it seemed her duty to her realm would weigh heavier than their desire.

'You said you live in the southeast of Briavel. Do you ever get to the capital?' she asked, chewing on a fat fig.

Ham nodded. 'Yes, indeed. My eldest son and I travel there regularly. We were there recently in fact.'

'Oh, so I wonder if you've heard of a nobleman called Romen Koreldy? It's just that I know him quite well and the last time we met he was on his way to Werryl. I heard on the grapevine from fellow travellers that there was some sort of duel between him and King Celimus at the Queen's tourney?' It was true – she had heard as much.

'We were there,' the eldest son said. 'It was more than a duel.'

'It looked like a fight to the death,' Ham admitted. 'Our Queen stepped in to prevent bloodshed.'

Elspyth was shocked. This was fresh news to her, but she knew Wyl had many reasons to hate the King. 'What happened?'

'Nothing much more there,' Ham said, 'but I'm sorry to be the one to tell you this, young Elspyth – Koreldy is no longer with us,' he added as gently as he could.

She shook her head. 'No, I imagine not. He would have to leave Briavel after that, though I wonder where he has headed. I—'

Ruth took her hand. 'No, you don't understand.' Everyone looked suddenly embarrassed.

Elspyth turned to Ham.

'He's dead, child,' the man said.

It felt to Elspyth like several long minutes passed before she took another breath. The silence was painful for all of them.

'You must be mistaken,' she stammered, feeling a chill pass through her.

Ham shook his head. 'It happened at Crowyll – we were there the day after it took place. The town rumour is that a whore killed him, although the Briavellian Guard is saying different. What was her name, son? Someone did tell us.'

The boy stuck his chin in the air and closed his eyes. 'Hilda, was it?'

'No. Hildyth, that's right. According to the gossips she's a striking woman – tall with auburn hair and feline eyes. Unmistakable.'

Elspyth began to tremble; her whole world was crumbling about her. 'Why?'

'No idea,' Ham admitted. 'The story goes that her majesty banished Koreldy from Briavel. He was being escorted to a border of his choice, and he and the guard accompanying him stopped at a place in Crowyll for a smoothing and such-like.' He cleared his throat self-consciously, glad that the youngsters had already gone off to play.

'And?' Elspyth asked, distraught.

Ham shrugged. 'It happened.'

'But there is no reason for it!' she cried. 'Why was he banished? Why killed?'

Ruth put her arms about her. 'Oh, Elspyth, I'm so sorry we were the ones to break the news. He must have been a good friend for you,' she said, holding her close. She scowled at her husband. 'Ham, tell her everything you know.'

Her husband blushed, distressed to be seen as the villain. 'Rumours were rife whilst we were there. Some said the whore worked for Celimus and that the King ordered Koreldy's death. No one knows the truth of it though. And now, with our own soldiers saying it was one of them who killed him, a renegade or something, it's all a bit baffling.'

'The body — who saw it?' Elspyth demanded.

'I'm sorry to say that a close friend of ours helped to clean up Koreldy's corpse. His . . . his heart had been punctured.' Ham stammered over the words, unsure of how much detail his wife meant for him to tell. 'Um . . . my friend is from the morgue and he was called in to deal with the body before it was transported to Werryl. Very trustworthy fellow. He only told me because he was so shocked at the manner of death — he said it looked as if it was carried out by a professional assassin. Apparently, everything was hushed over quickly by the Queen's Guard, and my friend was ordered to remain silent. I'm sure he didn't mean to tell me as much as he did. Now you know as much as I do – and I've told no one bar my wife until this moment.' He glared at the others, daring them to say any different. 'Oh, and she'd cut off his finger too – that's another indication it was a paid killing.'

'What do you mean?' Elspyth said, confounded.

'The finger is proof of death. Apparently Koreldy wore a ring with a blood-red stone and marked with a special family insignia.'

At that Elspyth broke down. It was true then. She knew the ring; knew it was Wyl they spoke of. He was dead. Now Lothryn would never be rescued from the dark magic and the pain.

The others, except Ruth, moved away silently. Ham put his large meaty hand on her shoulder. 'I'm sorry, lass.'

She said nothing but cried harder against Ruth's shoulder.

'Travel with us, Elspyth. You're in no state to move around alone just now,' the woman whispered.

Elspyth did not know how long they sat there together or at what point her sobs subsided and the tears dried on her cheeks. She was only marginally aware of Ruth helping her back into the cart and being laid down, covered with a blanket and encouraged to sleep. She welcomed the escape from her exhaustion and pain.

This time she dreamed of a tall woman with auburn hair and catlike eyes who had destroyed her dream of Lothryn being rescued by Wyl. It was up to her then. She would deliver her message to Felrawthy and keep her promise to the dead friend who had once walked in the guise of Romen Koreldy. And then she would rescue the man she loved.

15

THEY RAN, TERRIFIED, NOT daring to look behind or slow down, until their legs were too weak to carry them any further and their lungs protested, burning for air.

'Please stop, my lady,' Pil gasped, his body bent over. 'We must catch our breath.'

'We cannot rest, Pil!' Ylena's hair was wild from snagging in overhanging branches, her garments muddied and torn. 'I daren't tell you what they were doing.' Her voice broke 'Shar's tears,' she gasped, all strength leaving her as she crumpled to her knees and clasped her face in dirt-smeared hands. She wept, exhausted.

Pil was too shocked himself to offer much comfort. What had happened at Rittylworth could not be comprehended. He knew Ylena was keeping much of the horror from him and he was glad of it. The King's men had planned the attack well, storming the monastery at the break of morning silence to ensure the monks would be in the buildings or working in their gardens. He cast his own teary thanks to whichever angels had been guarding his life and had contrived for him to be looking for the Lady Ylena when the soldiers arrived.

Brother Jakub had asked Pil to remain close to Ylena from the beginning. He recalled Jakub's gentle words. *You are young and she will not feel too threatened by you. She has seen and experienced much sorrow at the whim of powerful men.* Although he did not know the whole story Pil had gathered that Ylena was terrorised at Stoneheart by the King and his minions, which would account for her early distant behaviour. Koreldy had counselled that she was not of sound mind, warning that Ylena had witnessed a horrific murder. In the days he had spent in her company, quietly escorting her, serving her meals, generally being on hand to see to her needs, she had been withdrawn but polite. Her silence or sudden tears were the only external sign of her anguish.

Looking at her now he marvelled at the strength that lay within the fragile-looking noblewoman. She was terrified herself, but had taken command of the situation and rallied his own flagging courage. Such bravery must run in the Thirsk blood, Pil thought; her father and her brother had been revered Generals of the Legion.

The novice was desperate to lay his head down on the grass and drift into oblivion but he dared not for he was sure he would dream of burning bodies. He guessed they had been on the move for roughly an hour, perhaps almost two. He glanced towards the sky – barely mid-morning, he estimated.

'Lady Ylena,' he uttered gently, 'I don't believe we've been followed. I am sure we escaped notice.'

'Everyone's dead,' she muttered, her voice flat. 'And they'll hunt me down until he's satisfied I'm dead too.'

'Don't say that, my lady,' Pil replied, fresh fear coursing through him.

She lifted her head to look at her companion. Her eyes were red from tears and they held a wildness that unsettled Pil further. 'Who do you think they are after?' she demanded.

He shrugged. 'I don't even know why they came.'

Ylena laughed bitterly. 'They were after me, Pil,' she said, shaking her head. 'Me and Koreldy. Where is he? He promised he would not abandon me.'

Pil wanted to interject that she was not abandoned by the monks, they all loved her. Instead he held his tongue.

'My parents are dead, my brother murdered, my guardian sent to his death, my young and beautiful new husband murdered. Doesn't it strike you that this monarch is determined to see the Thirsk name become barely more than a memory?'

So that was the core of her pain. He knew she had seen someone killed but Jakub had refused to say more. He had to presume then that Ylena had witnessed her husband's death. He chose his words carefully, not wanting to deepen her grief. 'I want to be a monk, my lady. I am not a politician. I do not understand the intrigues of the court.'

Her expression became sad. 'It doesn't matter. I am hunted; the last of my line. You would do well to protect yourself by leaving me now.'

Pil was shocked. 'I cannot do that, my lady. I promised Brother Jakub I would take care of you.'

'And who was taking care of Brother Jakub and all the other brothers? You saw some of it, Pil – each one murdered where he stood. Shar alone knows how those senior brothers suffered on the cross. How can a boy protect me when a whole community cannot?'

Pil suddenly felt all of his young years. He understood what people meant when they talked about the blood draining from someone's face. He could feel it now, could feel a weakness moving through his body that seemed determined to shut down his movement, his speech, even his heart, from shock and despair. Not so long ago he had been carefree, laughing with his fellow monks, eager to become a fully fledged member of the Order. And now Ylena had revealed the full horror of the massacre and his mind was filled with visions of gentle holy men being stabbed, their throats slit or swords run through their bellies . . . and nailed to posts.

Every ounce of him wanted to break down and weep. To die where he sat and not have to face this ugliness any more. Instead, it was Jakub's comforting voice he heard in his mind and he adopted a similar tone now.

'We have been spared, my lady. Shar protected us by placing us somewhere unexpected when the soldiers came. And almost no one outside of the monastery knows of the grotto,' he added as gently as he could. 'Brother Jakub was keen for you to have a private place to bathe and rest.'

A wan smile ghosted across her face. 'Go, Pil. By staying with me you put yourself in much danger. I am not sure I can look after both of us. Please, be safe.'

'No,' he said firmly. 'We must stay together as we promised Jakub. That's my job, remember; he told me that now was the time when I would prove my worth.'

A long silence followed and Pil believed Ylena had lost track of their conversation. So it made him jump when she stood and said, 'Only Duke Donal might offer us protection.'

'Then Felrawthy is where we must head, my lady.'

He tried to sound brave despite the sense of dread he felt.

'I don't get your point, Jessom. Frankly, I like her dedication,' Celimus said, kicking away the hand of the stablemaster who was fiddling with his stirrups. 'Leave it!' he scolded. The man flinched and stepped away from the beautiful roan mare the King had just mounted.

'I'll be galloping her,' Celimus warned. 'You're sure her foot is fine?'

The stablemaster nodded. 'Yes, sire, all soreness gone. Enjoy your ride.' He bowed and departed.

'Get on with it, Chancellor!' Celimus barked, irritated by the delay to his dawn ride. 'Tell me what bothers you.'

'It just strikes me as odd, sire, that Leyen would leave under cover of darkness.'

'I would have thought most assassins craved the cloak of night.' The sarcasm bit.

Jessom ignored it, continued smoothly, 'She left without Aremys. No word as to why.'

'And where is he now?'

'No longer at Stoneheart,' Jessom said, deliberately brief. 'Gone about your business, sire.'

'And?'

'Well, I'm just wondering what business Leyen might be about. You specifically gave instructions that they were to track down the person in question together.'

'Do you not trust your own people, Jessom?'

The Chancellor hated the cunning way Celimus always

managed to turn accusation away from himself. He squinted up to where his King sat on his horse, a halo of sunshine about his head. 'I trust no one, my King.'

'Well said.' Celimus relented: 'I gave Leyen some additional instructions to take a message to Valentyna.'

Jessom glanced around to check no one could overhear them. 'I see. Did you ask that she perform this task first?'

'No. It was my understanding that she would handle the business with Aremys before travelling to Briavel.'

'It is strange then that she left so hurriedly and, may I say, she seemed rather disturbed after she left your dinner last night, your highness.'

Further irritation traced across the King's face. 'Your point?'

The Chancellor shrugged. 'Well, perhaps she did not like the message to be passed on to Briavel,' he said carefully, hoping the King would enlighten him as to his instructions to Leyen.

But Celimus was too shrewd. 'It bears thinking about. Do we know anything about her departure?'

'Only that one of your pages, Jorn, was attending to her. He showed her out of the castle gates. He may know something.'

The horse was restless to move, as was the King. He looked puzzled now though. 'Jorn? Perhaps he delivered to Leyen the message I wanted her to take to Valentyna.'

Jessom contrived an expression that suggested it pained him to divulge what he was about to explain. 'Your majesty, my fear is that Jorn, who serves you and attended Leyen – without permission, I might add – also attended Koreldy when he was at Stoneheart.'

That caught the King's attention as Jessom had known

it would. He let the implication hang between them, knowing the subtle mind of Celimus would bring all the strands together.

Anger clouded the olive gaze. 'Find the boy and throw him in the dungeon. Make sure he's frightened enough to tell us everything by the time I get back. And I'm trusting your instinct, Jessom, that there *is* something to tell.'

'As you wish, sire.' Jessom bowed low as Celimus rode his mare out of the courtyard.

16

JORN COWERED IN THE cold damp cell, frightened and confused. Being grabbed by two soldiers in one of the castle glasshouses where he had been collecting some parillion fruit for the King's breakfast had terrified him. Jorn had risen especially early to ensure that when his monarch returned hot and dusty from his morning ride he would have plenty of the refreshing juice he favoured to quench his thirst. Now Jorn mournfully remembered the precious fruit he had dropped and then stepped on in his fright when the soldiers had appeared and manhandled him so roughly towards the dungeon.

He shivered and looked around the cell, his vision dulled from fear at what he could have done to so anger his superiors that they had locked him down here where criminals were kept.

Coincidentally, this was the same chamber from which Myrren had been dragged by her torturers almost a decade earlier. Such information would mean little to Jorn, of course, but if he had studied the last block of stone in the wall behind the cell door he would have noted a curious inscription that might have meant something, considering his adoration of Ylena Thirsk.

On that stone were three words: Avenge me, Wyl.

A boy such as Fynch, susceptible to the ebb and flow of magic in a world that scorned its existence, might touch that inscription and feel the thrum of the enchantment used to make such a mark in stone.

But even if Jorn had such talent, he was incapable right now of focusing on anything beyond his own fear. What had he done to warrant incarceration? He replayed the last few days over and again in his mind, wondering what terrible mistake he had made. He found none, of course – other than his doomed love for Ylena Thirsk. The arrival of the Chancellor did nothing to reassure him. The man's seal of office swayed heavily on its chain as he paced slowly, waiting for the King.

'Please, Chancellor Jessom, tell me what it is I have done,' Jorn begged through the bars.

'I'm sorry, my boy,' Jessom replied, adopting an avuncular approach. 'This is all very confusing. It goes to the highest level, Jorn. Somehow you have attracted the King's attention . . . negative attention, that is.'

'But Chancellor Jessom, sir, it is my pleasure to wait loyally upon the King. I would do nothing to harm him.'

'Would you not?'

The boy shook his head dumbly. Even in his terror he knew he was missing something important. It was written in the Chancellor's heavy-lidded eyes.

'Ah, here is his majesty now, Jorn. Hopefully we can clear this up and you will be back at your duties by the noon bell.'

'Oh yes, sir,' Jorn said, feeling a surge of hope knife through him. 'I'll do anything to set things right.'

'Good boy. Be easy now, your King approaches.'

Jorn could hear the click of his sovereign's boots against the stone of the dungeon floor. He could not make out any words but knew by the eruption of laughter that the King had made some remark which had amused the guards. The swaggering tread resumed and suddenly the tall and resplendent shape of Celimus appeared beside Jessom. His face was shining with tiny beads of perspiration. He had come straight here then from his ride, Jorn thought miserably. Whatever secret he apparently held was considered more important than the sovereign's comfort. The King turned a predatory gaze on Jorn who quailed at the sight.

'Your majesty,' the Chancellor said, bowing low.

Jorn, more terrified than ever, kneeled immediately. 'Your highness,' he whispered, ready to confess to anything.

Celimus glanced towards Jessom, whose slight nod indicated the lad was petrified. Celimus smiled thinly. If Jorn had looked up at that moment he would have known that his life was already forfeit, but he kept his head low to the floor, hands clasping and unclasping nervously as he awaited his King's pleasure.

'Stand up, lad.' It was the dry voice of the Chancellor.

Jorn obeyed, but kept his head bowed. To his shame he realised that he had soiled his trousers in his fright.

The King finally spoke. 'Look at me, boy.' The voice was hard.

Jorn struggled to obey and finally lifted damp eyes towards Celimus. 'I shall ask a few questions,' he continued, 'and what I require from you is complete honesty. You have nothing to fear,' he lied.

Jorn nodded, eyes wide with his intense desire to please. 'Yes, your majesty. I promise to tell you whatever it is you need.'

'Good. Now, do you recall a guest at Stoneheart who dined with me last night? She arrived with a man called Aremys and—'

'Madam Leyen, yes,' Jorn interrupted, anxious to impress his King.

Celimus nodded. Jessom smiled briefly.

'Is it true that you waited on her . . . without permission from either myself or your superiors?'

Jorn frowned. 'I did not wait on her, your majesty.'

'Oh? I hear differently.'

The boy clutched at the bars. 'Oh no, sire. I . . . .' His brow creased as he recalled what had occurred. 'I was on an urgent errand for one of your secretaries, sire, which took me that morning into the wing of the castle where Madam Leyen was accommodated. I couldn't find the person I needed so I was in quite a hurry.' He saw both men nod. 'Um . . . Madam Leyen hailed me as I ran along the corridor.'

'And what did she want?' Celimus prompted.

'Advice, sire.'

Jessom smirked. 'What sort of advice, boy?'

'Well, I didn't find out until later that evening because she could tell how much of a rush I was in to be about my duties. I left straightaway having exchanged only a handful of words with her, sire. She was a stranger to me.'

Celimus was not so easily deterred. 'And later?'

'Yes, later, sire, I did go back to her chamber as she asked me to. I felt obliged, your majesty, because she was your personal guest and had no one attending her.'

The King held on to his patience. 'And?'

'She wanted advice on her gown.'

There was an awkward silence before Celimus said, an edge of threat to his tone, 'You jest, of course?'

'No, sire,' Jorn beseeched. 'I would never do that, my King. Madam Leyen wanted to make the right impression on you, your majesty, for the supper she was sharing. She had no garments of her own and was in a borrowed gown. She sought my approval.'

'A lad's approval?' Jessom's voice was thick with disgust.

Jorn made to shrug, then caught himself and turned it into an obeisance. 'It is the truth, sire. Perhaps she thought I might be of use as I had mentioned that I worked for you as a messenger.'

'That's it?' Celimus said, his own disbelief evident. 'You expect us to accept that this . . . this . . . approval was all she asked of you?'

Jorn bobbed frantically. 'My lord King, that is all she asked of me.' He saw the King's hand turn to a fist as the famous anger was stoked. 'I did go back that night, of course,' he blurted.

'Ah, and why did you do that?'

'To deliver a parchment one of your secretaries bade me take to her. I was told it was urgent, King's business.'

A glance passed between his captors and it was then that Jorn realised where this strange conversation was leading. He had always counted himself as sharp; he made good use of that skill now to make the leap in his mind that it was not him they were after but Leyen. And even she was not the true prey – it was to whom she was loyal that they were most interested in. They were after Ylena Thirsk. Beautiful, sorrowful, tortured Ylena. He would rather die than betray her. And yet betrayal was precisely what they sought from him. He could see it now as clear as daylight. They wanted him to tell them where Madam Leyen was travelling to in such a hurry. They wanted to hurt his beloved Lady Ylena still more.

Well he was only a messenger and thus nothing in the eyes of the King, but he, Jorn, had made a promise to a beautiful woman and she had returned his loyalty with her promise that she would send for him. Any day now he would escape Stoneheart and travel to Argorn where Ylena would welcome him and allow him to serve her as he so dearly wished.

They would not find out her secrets through his lips, Jorn thought. He was not a fiery person; he rarely allowed anything to get under his skin sufficiently to make him cross and his naturally sunny personality helped him to defuse many situations where another's temper might flare. But now a spark of anger had erupted within him and it was fuelled by the accusation in his monarch's expression and the Chancellor's carefully contrived look of sympathy.

The anger took hold and from that moment nothing – not even his fear of the King's reprisal – would provoke him to release Ylena's name to them or her whereabouts. He cared nothing for Leyen but to reveal her direction was to betray Ylena Thirsk and he would never do that.

'Well?' the King demanded.

Jorn spoke with assurance. 'I gave Madam Leyen the parchment and returned her gown, as requested, to Lady Bench's household, your majesty.'

'Leyen left that night, you liar, and you know it!' Celimus spat through the bars.

'I have no reason to lie to you, my lord King. I was coming to that,' Jorn said, pleased he had not flinched at the King's hostility despite the sudden watery feel to his knees. He grasped at the little composure left to him, ignored the damp reminder of his fear and gilded the truth. 'She told me she was leaving. I know not why, sire. She asked me if I would accompany her to the stables because she did not know her way around Stoneheart. It was not my place to question her actions, my King. I am a simple messenger, whose duty is to serve you and your esteemed guests.'

'And so you did,' Celimus said, slyly now.

'Yes, sire.'

'Did she mention where she was going?'

Jorn paused to think how to answer this. 'No,' he said truthfully.

'That's odd, boy, because the guard on duty last night recalls you mentioning the Duchy of Felrawthy.'

Jorn had never given a better performance in his short life. His expression remained impassive even though inside he flared with hate for the man on watch last night. He had given him much coin to keep his mouth closed. 'That's right, sire, I think I might have mentioned it.'

'Why?' Celimus approached the prison bars as a hunter might, closing in for the kill.

'Because that's where I understood Madam Leyen comes from, sire,' he lied.

Celimus looked at Jessom, who blinked slowly. 'I have no information on Leyen's history, sire,' he admitted, somewhat abashed. 'She told us Rittylworth, but she is a mystery and likes to keep it that way. She is usually in disguise, even for our meetings.'

'For all we know she could have been in disguise at supper,' the King growled, not realising how close to the truth he was. 'When did she share this information with you?' Celimus demanded of Jorn.

The lad shook his head, seemingly confused. 'She must have said it in passing for otherwise I can't imagine how I would know such a thing. I am sorry, sire, that I don't remember our brief conversations more clearly. I do not think she told me where exactly she was going – I merely presumed it was to her home,' Jorn replied smoothly. *Forgive me, Shar,* he beseeched inwardly.

The handsome eyes of the King regarded Jorn intently now. His gaze was direct and intimidating and Jorn felt his resolve crack slightly, but he rallied his courage, resisting the temptation to blurt out everything he knew – which, in truth, was little enough – of Leyen and her intentions. He instinctively cast his own eyes down – and this was his final undoing. If Jorn had held his sovereign's cold, compelling look, his unpredictable King might have erred towards leniency in this instance.

Instead Celimus swung towards cruelty, where he felt comfortable. He could tell the youth knew very little and it was unlikely a secretive and highly qualified assassin would share with him her thoughts or intentions, yet it nagged at Celimus that he was being beguiled somehow. As a result he reacted as only one so insensitive to others' suffering could.

'He lies. Wheel him!'

Jorn's ear rang with the hammer of his own heartbeat. He slid towards the floor, dazed with shock at the King's words. He noticed three words scratched into the stone by the cell door before he lost consciousness.

'My King, please . . .' Jessom attempted, alarmed at the idea of the needless torture.

'Do not even think to contradict me, Chancellor,' Celimus warned, his voice hard, eyes glittering. 'I want him wheeled. He's not strong enough to resist the pain. I will know whether Leyen is true to my cause or not.'

Jessom knew Leyen was true to no one but herself yet this was not an occasion to test his majesty's temper. He nodded in acquiescence, keeping his head bowed so he heard rather than saw the King's swaggering departure.

The Chancellor motioned to the dungeon master. Once the man had listened to his grave words, Jessom turned back to Jorn. 'I am sorry, lad,' he said, and meant it.

But Jorn did not hear the apology nor did he feel the rough hands that grabbed his limp body and removed him to a part of Stoneheart he had never seen before — and had never expected to.

It was a genuine surprise to the skilled team of torturers Celimus had assembled that the youngster lasted as long as he did. Many a battle-hardened soldier facing the same honour had begged for the mercy of the sword or simply died from the shock.

First the boy's joints were smashed by a man who asked no questions but simply went about his gruesome business with quiet expertise. Normally he would prolong the session, taking his time at placing the wooden block beneath the sweating shrieking victims before allowing his heavy mallet to descend with its punishment. But the man sensed this young lad was not deserving of the extended version and he pleased the other two torturers by doing his job swiftly.

The second stage was the pulverising of Jorn's skeleton beneath the vast iron wheel. The men rolled it over his body slowly, not because they wanted to increase his suffering but because the wheel was so enormously heavy it took some doing to get it rolling. As it turned the men openly marvelled at the young fellow's capacity to withstand what was regarded by most in the profession as the most intolerable pain a person could suffer.

Jorn was embarrassingly brave to the end and they felt ashamed to be visiting such punishment on a youth. Uncharacteristically, they winced at the loud popping and cracking of the lad's bones until the weight reached his chest and finally stopped his faint erratic heartbeat.

As Jorn died, vague satisfaction skimmed through his blurred mind that he had not let Ylena down despite the chilling shrieks that escaped his throat. Suddenly the three words scratched on the cell wall came back to him. *Avenge me, Wyl*, they read and Jorn made the connection in a fleeting moment of clarity. He sent a dying prayer to Shar to preserve the Thirsk line and ensure his death was not in vain.

The men were expected to use the crushing wheel over the entire length of the victim's body but as soon as Jorn's eyes clouded with death the two men stopped.

'Enough!' one said. He was good at his job but did not like hurting innocents and there had been too many of those in recent times. 'I'm not crushing this one's head for his majesty's pleasure. He's suffered enough – and with courage.'

'It'll be our own guts the King hangs us from if we're not careful,' his companion said.

'Jessom wasn't happy over it. He said to make it swift.'

'Got nothing out of him though, did we?' the other man said.

'Nothing to get, probably. Come on, roll it back. At least if any family come to collect the body they can see his face is whole.'

'Can't say the same about the rest of him,' commented his fellow torturer. He whistled, looking at the shattered bloodied mess before them.

Later that day when Jessom visited the King's chambers, the sovereign's first question was of Jorn.

'Did the page reveal what we wanted to hear?'

'No, my lord King.' Jessom did not have to work at being solemn; he was still in a distracted mood over the morning's horrific events and the altogether unnecessary torture and death of a young man.

Celimus glared at his Chancellor, hand poised over the parchment he was scrawling his mark upon. 'Surely you jest?'

'He took whatever secrets you feel he had to the grave with him, sire.'

Celimus stood, angry at being beaten by a youth. 'He was wheeled as ordered?' he demanded. It was just short of an accusation.

Jessom kept his voice even. 'Yes, sire. Exactly as you instructed,' he lied. 'It seems the boy survived an interminable time. Not until the iron crushed the very beat of his heart did he relinquish his grip on life.' Inwardly the Chancellor felt proud. This was one death he did not agree with.

'He gave us nothing?'

Jessom made a deprecating gesture, suggesting he did not believe there was anything to give.

'He spoke no words at all?' Celimus pushed, determined his oily Chancellor would keep nothing from him.

Jessom kept his expression blank. 'Just the usual assortment of shrieks and groans, sire. No words as such.'

'Admirable,' Celimus said, walking to the window. 'For he was surely withholding something. Where is the body?'

'Ready for burial, I presume, sire.'

'I want you to think hard, Chancellor.'

'I beg your pardon, sire?'

'Think, man! I employ you for your sharp mind. What are we missing? There is something we have overlooked. Ponder upon it – find the solution for me by tomorrow and report back. We shall meet in the morning after my ride.'

Jessom bowed. He felt a pit open in his stomach at the thought of awaking tomorrow with no answers for a King prone to tantrums that usually resulted in someone's death.

'By the way, no burial for Jorn. Impale him and have his body displayed on the main road to Felrawthy . . . just in case.'

'As you wish, sire,' Jessom said, weariness overcoming him. There was probably not much left of Jorn to impale anyway. Was there no end to this man's brutality? He kept his voice steady. 'I shall see to it now.'

'And I shall see you tomorrow, Chancellor, with an answer to my question.'

17

ELSPYTH HAD TAKEN ALL of that day and the following night to surface from her bleak state. When she did she knew it was time to leave the two kind families who had cared for her. She could tell her brooding presence unnerved the youngsters, and the once-lively chatter of the women was now guarded as they were careful not to impose on her sorrowful mood.

The carts rolled to a pause at the Five Ways, where roads led to different regions of the realm, and Elspyth took her leave. She mustered a smile for the families and hugged both the women, especially Ruth.

'I will worry after you,' the kind woman admitted.

'Don't,' Elspyth assured. 'I'm really very capable.'

'You know you are welcome to stay with us,' Meg offered.

Elspyth felt a surge of gratitude and reminded herself that the world was not such an evil place. 'Yes, and I thank you. But I must find Koreldy's sister – that's where I was headed when I stumbled into your path.'

'I'm sorry again, lass,' Ham said, still abashed. He handed her a small sack of food they had put together.

Elspyth took the sack and squeezed his hand to reassure him that she held no grudge. 'You've all been so very good to me. Rather I hear it from kind souls than those who might take pleasure in such news. I'll be fine, I promise. It was just such a shock, but once I deliver a message to the Koreldy family I'll be able to get back to my own life,' she lied.

She hoped no one would ask where this elusive sister might be, or indeed where Elspyth's home was. No one did and after another round of awkward farewells the carts rolled on their way, heading east towards Briavel's border. Once they were out of sight, Elspyth took stock of her situation. She was aware that she could have continued with the families and reached Felrawthy more quickly, but she felt a strange relief to be on her own again. She turned towards the road that led northeast – a more direct route to Felrawthy. She still felt as though her mind was blank; first Lothryn's plea for help and then the news of Wyl's death had left her decidedly empty.

'It's up to me now,' she said aloud on the lonely road.

Hearing her own voice sounding so defiant gave her courage. First she would keep her promise to Wyl, find Ylena and hand her into the protection of the Duke of Felrawthy. That done she would return to Yentro and check on her aunt. Hopefully the old girl was still alive and might be able to offer some advice. Once there she would gather together whatever monies she could find before heading farther north and into the mountains. She did not relish the thought of facing the forbidding Razors at this time of year, but she remembered the terror in Lothryn's voice and knew she could no more sit out the season than fly to Felrawthy.

The only thing that really mattered to her now was discovering Lothryn's fate. If she died in the process, so be it. His love had offered her the first relief from loneliness in a lifetime and she was not about to relinquish it without a fight.

Elspyth squared her petite shoulders, lifted her chin and began her long walk to fulfil a promise.

Ylena and Pil joined the straggling bunch of people and animals roaming through Dorchyster Green's town square. It was market day and the smell of newly baked bread and steaming meat pies sharpened their hunger.

'When did we last eat?' Ylena asked, looking longingly at the wheels of cheese and the potted meats.

Pil's belly was growling. 'I can't remember, my lady,' he said, avoiding the ponderous sway of a cow passing by. 'But we should move on for we have no coin.'

Ylena's despair snapped to anger. 'This is not right. I have money – I just don't have it with me. I'm so sorry, Pil.'

'Hush now,' he soothed, taking her arm. He understood. She was used to fine things in life, not having to wonder where her next meal may come from. In truth, he too had lived a comfortable existence at the monastery where food was plentiful. 'Come, let us continue on our way.'

They had stopped by a stall of fruit and the bright colours arrested their gaze. Now their bellies groaned together as a new smell – roasting meat – mocked them.

'We cannot go another day without eating,' Ylena moaned.

She was right but all he could do in response was shrug.

'Short of stealing, my lady – and I could never do that – I have no solution.'

'Then we shall beg!' She sounded so resolute that Pil's protest died in his mouth. 'Yes!' she continued, 'I shall sing. I have a comely voice, or so I have been told. I shall sing for our food . . . and you . . . you shall dance a jig beside me,' she finished desperately.

'All right,' he said bravely, hoping his voice did not give away his dislike at the thought of her humiliating herself so. 'Anything is worth a try and I am certainly hungry, my lady.'

A vague attempt at a smile appeared on Ylena's mouth but there was no warmth to it. 'Come then, we shall position ourselves over there by the well.'

He followed her, wondering how she thought she would be heard above the din of the market where people called out their wares, beasts mooed and bellowed and children ran helter-skelter.

'Here,' she commanded. 'Lay your hat at our feet.'

Pil did as asked, embarrassed. 'You don't surely expect me to dance, my lady?' he beseeched. 'I find it hard enough to walk without tripping over.'

'You don't have to,' Ylena said, smoothing her tattered skirts and tucking back her untidy hair. 'It was just a thought. But make sure you smile at the passers-by. We need their pity. It's a shame you didn't have your pate shaved – being a monk would have helped our cause,' she said distractedly, going on to clear her throat.

Pil steadied his gaze towards his feet and waited. When the first bright note emanated from Ylena, his eyes widened in amazement and his glance flicked sideways to watch her. Her voice was pure and beautiful, like a bird released to soar towards the sky where it had always longed to be. Pil recognised the song. It was a sorrowful ballad of two youngsters who had grown up together, become lovers and whose rapture for each other was blessed by the gods. But the man is murdered by a jealous admirer of the woman . . . and so the tale continued, pulling at the emotions.

Pil noticed a small crowd had begun to form. Ylena had chosen well, for the song had many verses and was lengthy enough to attract attention. He stepped away from her, realising his presence was no longer needed. The gathering listeners had eyes only for the beautiful, albeit dishevelled woman and her song of grief. Ylena, lost in the telling of her tale and the music, hardly paid them any care and so she did not notice the coins being dropped into the hat or how large and silent the crowd became.

Pil noticed it all, especially the appearance of a man who stepped out from the Dorchyster Arms, the town's inn. He was clearly a wealthy noble from his garb and even in his winter years he remained a handsome, vital man. The once-yellow hair had dulled to a buttery white and was pulled back severely from his face, accentuating the wide square lines of his features. His beard, worn short, was a motley of yellow, silver and even reddish hues. It added to his attractiveness. Deep-set sea-blue eyes regarded Ylena and he held up his gloved hand to the man beside him to stop the fellow talking. This was a man used to giving orders and being obeyed; even the set of his generous mouth suggested he was powerful, a leader of men. He strode from the inn's entrance deeper into the square. People stepped aside, pulling their goats and donkeys out of his way.

Pil saw the noble's eyes narrow in concentration as Ylena reached the peak of the song's tragic consequences. Other men, the noble's own no doubt, began to gather nearby. One risked interrupting his lord's pleasure and was rewarded by the same gloved hand in the air. The man looked around at the others who shrugged. They all understood they must wait now.

Ylena's song came to its heart-wrenching end and cries of appreciation came from the crowd, people surging forward to toss a few coins into the hat. The nobleman shouldered through the crowd and Pil noted that they all moved aside easily, some bowing, the women curtsying. This was no petty lord.

Pil approached carefully and bent to pick up his hat. Ylena had slumped against the well, her eyes closed, her energies spent and her emotions no doubt in turmoil as the song had so obviously been about her and the man she had loved and lost. The nobleman reached for her hand. It occurred to Pil that the man had recognised her status, despite her tattered dusty appearance, for he was touching his lips to her limp knuckles. It must be the clothes, he realised. Only a noblewoman could afford such quality garments.

'My lady,' the older man spoke gently. 'You sing like an angel.' His voice was tender but Pil felt sure his men rarely heard this tone.

Ylena's eyes fluttered open but held no recognition. She affected a brief curtsy of sorts. 'Thank you, sir. I am hoping my voice will feed myself and my companion tonight,' she said, glancing towards Pil and then back into eyes that were now the colour of a stormy sea.

'Shar's wrath!' the man exclaimed. 'But you need not

sing for your supper, madam. Who is your family? I demand to know who leaves you in this state.'

'My family?' Ylena breathed, hardly above a whisper. 'My family,' she repeated, 'are dead, sir. I am all that's left, my lord, and I am on the run from those who would do me harm.'

The noble made a sound of frustration. He signalled to one of his men. 'She's weak, pick her up!' he commanded, taking off his cloak.

The man obeyed and his lord laid his own cloak about Ylena, at which point Pil thought it necessary to step forward.

'My lord,' he said, bowing. 'I am Pil.'

'And?'

'I am a monk,' Pil continued, 'well, a novice in truth – and was instructed to stay close to the Lady Ylena. She is ready to faint from hunger. She has been recuperating with us for some weeks and I fear our journey across country has set her back.'

He hoped he had made a good account of himself. Brother Jakub had always cautioned that brevity was a desirable trait.

The man regarded him before saying, 'Follow me.' Pil found himself all but trotting to keep up with the elderly noble. The hat in his hand jangled with the coins weighing it down. They returned to the inn and were taken straight to its dining room. The noble barked orders and suddenly the room was a frenzy of activity. Men appeared and disappeared, taking their instructions from their chief and going about whatever business he required.

Before long the smell of bacon wafted towards them;

it made Pil dizzy in anticipation. 'Eat first,' the man commanded, 'then we shall talk.'

Ylena was given a posset of sweetly spiced milk which she drank without comment, although her glance towards the girl setting it down was filled with gratitude. Pil was given the same and he gulped the contents of the cup quickly, feeling its healing warmth hit the right spot immediately.

'Thank you, my lord,' he said. The excitement of seeing slices of fresh bread smeared liberally with butter accompanied by thick rashers of sizzling bacon stopped whatever words might have come next. He ate with gusto and in silence, his glance darting towards Ylena who nibbled hungrily on her bread, not yet daring to touch the meat. The noble ignored them for the time being, talking quietly with a man Pil presumed to be his second-in-command. Pil finished his meal and felt immediately drowsy. However, the luxury of sleep was not yet his.

'Now we talk,' the man said and beckoned Pil to a corner of the room where a tray of ales had been set down.

'My lord,' Ylena interjected, 'I can account for myself, sir.'

'Then do so,' the nobleman said brusquely. 'You may speak freely.'

Ylena glanced at Pil and found a brief smile of sympathy for him. Both knew they would have to relive their trauma for this man. Pil nodded encouragingly, noticing the spark was back in her eyes and her expression had lost its despairing look. The food had already worked wonders.

Ylena's voice was steady and firm as she began. 'We

have come from Rittylworth monastery — we were forced to flee.'

The old noble frowned. 'Why?'

Ylena sighed. 'The news has not travelled this far north yet, then?' The man glared from beneath silver-peppered eyebrows, keen for her to get on with it. 'The monastery was burned, my lord. Most of the monks were murdered where they stood, the senior ones were singled out for special torture.'

Two mugs were banged down on the table by shocked listeners, sloshing ale on the fists which had held them. Neither man seemed to notice.

'What?' The noble's voice was hard, disbelieving.

'I speak the truth, sir. I saw it. We were hidden but we saw men flying the King's colours cut down the monks one by one. They crucified and burned the senior brothers.' Scenes flashed into her mind of that terrible morning and she felt sickened. 'It is too terrible to speak of, my lord. They arrived directly as morning silence ended and we have been on the run since.'

'Well timed to ensure they got everyone,' the nobleman's companion commented.

Ylena looked at him for the first time. The easy smile and drape of bright golden hair shocked her — he was so similar to her Alyd it was heartbreaking. He also wore a close beard. She noted his resemblance to the older man. Were these father and son, she thought, not realising she had thought aloud.

'Yes, this is my son Crys. My apologies, my manners have deserted me. I am Jeryb Donal, Duke of Felrawthy.'

Ylena was stunned into silence, could only stare from Alyd's father to his equally handsome brother. Then all the bravery she had found to temper the fear for her own life and despair at losing so many loved ones rose uncontrollably on a wave of emotion which flooded her body. Ylena broke down and sobbed. The two nobles looked at her aghast, entirely unsure of what to do for this weeping woman.

It was Pil who put it into words. 'Good grief, my lord, it is to you that we flee!' he spluttered, looking towards Ylena. 'This is the Lady Ylena Thirsk.'

'Fergys Thirsk's daughter! My son's bride?' the older man roared.

'Yes, my lord,' Ylena said, recovering herself. 'And I bring the gravest of news.'

'I am sorry we meet under these circumstances,' Crys said, extending his hand towards her. The smile froze on his face whilst puzzlement creased his brow. 'So where is Alyd?'

The duke reached for her arm. 'My son Alyd. Why is he not with you?'

Ylena felt her world sway from the euphoria of finding the duke to despair at what she must now share with him. 'No, my lord, he is not with me,' she admitted carefully, the hairs tightening at the back of her head. 'Forgive me, sir . . .' She glanced tearily towards the baffled expression on Crys's kind face. 'It is why I am here . . . to tell you that Alyd is dead.'

The silence that met this statement was vast and of sufficient weight to crush the breath out of Ylena. Her pity for these men of Felrawthy was palpable. As much as she mourned Alyd, she had now accepted his death, knew the only way forward was to seek vengeance. It terrified her, but even more frightening was knowing that Celimus was hunting her down. He would not stop; she knew this. She could run forever and he would not give up — Wyl had said as much when Alyd had spoken of fleeing before the journey. So it was better to turn and fight him as best she could. Nothing could bring back those she loved, but a measure of satisfaction could be gained by helping to bring down their murderer. Alyd's father and brother were yet to grasp the significance of her words let alone know the worst of it.

Jeryb stared at her, his eyes stormier now, brow furrowed and angry. 'Dead you say?' he finally asked.

Ylena nodded, too numb to show her emotion. 'I am so sorry.' She shook her head. 'There is so much to tell, sir. I hardly know where to start, but you must know that you are all that stands between me and certain death too.'

'We cannot speak of this here,' the duke said, closing his eyes in grief. 'I will hear it all but not here. If we ride hard we can make Tenterdyn by nightfall.'

Crys reached over and squeezed Ylena's hand for re-assurance. It was precisely the sort of gesture Alyd would have made, never afraid to touch or show emotion. She hardly dared look at Crys for fear of breaking down. 'Tenterdyn is our family home,' he whispered. 'You will be safe with us.'

Crys turned to the novice. 'Can you ride, Pil?' The young monk nodded. It seemed that Crys Donal had taken control. The duke looked incapable of saying another word. Crys rested a hand on his father's shoulder as he sorted out arrangements.

'Good. Then go outside and tell Parks to find you a mount on my orders. I shall bring the Lady Ylena. Are you happy to ride with me, my lady?'

'Yes . . . yes, of course,' she replied, dreading being close to the man who so resembled her dead husband.

18

WYL KNEW HE HAD pushed the mare hard. He finally slowed her from a gallop to a canter, cooling her down to a trot which the brave horse would hold for a little while yet before permitting herself to walk. He stroked her neck in silent thanks and she tossed her mane as though in response.

The small stream he had expected to find made itself known by a soft gurgling and he angled the chestnut mare off the road, ducking beneath the overhanging trees before emerging into a pretty glade. The horse was happy to stop now. Wyl nimbly alighted and led her to the water where she drank greedily. Fretting for Ylena, Wyl wished he could have continued on, but he knew he was already well ahead of any party sent by the King. He was counting on Celimus not discovering the disappearance of Leyen until later this morning, and even then the King might not sense anything untoward and thus not react at all. Perhaps Jessom and Celimus would simply assume she had set off about her duties. They might think her lack of a formal farewell odd, but would hardly dwell on it.

No, they were not the issue here. The problem was Aremys, but again Wyl comforted himself that he had a lead of the whole of the night and most of the morning on the mercenary. By the time Aremys discovered Faryl's disappearance, Wyl could be halfway to his destination.

With this thought he forced himself to allow the mare some rest time. He unsaddled her and gave her a bag of feed and a quick rubdown before settling himself against a tree to think. He had not counted on falling into a doze quite so readily and so would have heard the approach of the horse much earlier than he did. Leaping to his feet he released the double blades of Romen Koreldy and moved into a fighting stance. A crashing through the undergrowth signalled the approach of man and beast. Wyl had no idea who it was but he was determined they would die. He crouched lower, ready to strike.

Aremys burst through the trees with a roar. Wyl realised who it was and hesitated. The mercenary took that moment to leap from his horse and landed heavily on his prey. Their bodies crunched to the ground, rolled and then Aremys grunted. He lay still for a moment, on top of his victim, crushing the air from Wyl who felt battered from the impact.

'Didn't count on the knives, Faryl,' Aremys sighed and rolled off to show a dark patch of blood already enlarging on his shirt.

'You stupid fool!' Wyl shrieked.

'I asked for it.' Aremys grinned then his face contorted and he closed his eyes. 'Ah, but it hurts.'

'Be still!' Wyl ordered, using the other knife to cut away the shirt. 'You're lucky it's your arm and not your foolhardy chest.'

'And I thought you were accurate.'

'I am.'

'Why did you hesitate?'

'Shut up and tell me what you're doing here,' Wyl said angrily, knowing all too well. He tore a piece from his own shirt and dipped it into the water so he could clean the wound.

'Following you, of course.' Aremys sounded reproachful. Despite the pain he enjoyed Faryl's ministrations and her hands on his body. He especially relished looking up into those fathomless eyes so filled with secrets. 'Why did you leave without me?'

'I don't work with others. You know that.'

'Not even on your King's instructions?'

'Especially then. He wants the job done cleanly and I don't need anyone else making errors.'

'Except you're not going to do it, are you?' Aremys stated, staying her busy hands with his good arm. 'Tell me the truth.'

'About what?' Wyl cried, hating his screechy woman's voice and the closeness of the mercenary.

'About why you have no intention of killing Ylena Thirsk.'

Wyl sat back and tossed the bloodied rag aside. 'It's quite deep and going to need sewing up. You're fortunate nothing serious is severed. Do you want me to bind it for now?'

'Please.'

Wyl tied a tourniquet to stem the bleeding then dressed the wound with a fresh piece of linen. 'It will hold only for a short while. You need to see a physic quickly.'

'Forget my damned arm, woman! I want you to talk to me.'

'Leave me alone.'

'I can't do that. We've been given a task – a paid one – by the King of Morgravia and I see no reason why I shouldn't carry it out.'

'Then you're already a dead man,' Wyl replied in a much softer voice.

Aremys had no doubt Faryl meant what she said. 'Are you planning on using the other knife on me then?'

'If I have to,' Wyl said, removing himself from such close proximity to his companion.

'So her life does mean something to you. Why are you protecting this noblewoman when Celimus assures us she is an enemy of the realm?'

Wyl laughed. It was a bitter sound and made Aremys wince. But it also seemed to open the floodgates and Wyl began talking angrily.

'She is barely seventeen years of age. She lost her mother at birth, her father when she was but an infant, and her brother . . .' His voice broke. Wyl cleared his throat. 'Her brother, Wyl Thirsk, was murdered at the King's command because of Celimus's long-held jealousy over the fact that King Magnus loved Wyl more than his own son.'

He continued, his voice lower and harder with the rage driving it. 'Ylena Thirsk was widowed within hours of her wedding. She witnessed the beheading of her innocent husband, whose only crime was to love her and cheat Celimus of a bedmate. She was made to kneel in her husband's still-warm and gushing blood as her own neck was laid on the block.'

Aremys looked shocked. 'How can you know this?'

'Because I was forced to watch it!' The words rushed out now, angry, bewildering, not permitting Aremys the immediate question which sprang to his lips. 'Her life was saved only because I agreed to blackmail. Either her life was forfeit before my very eyes or I could protect her by undertaking a mission set by the King.'

'Which was?' Aremys muttered, entirely confused now and not sure whether Faryl was speaking of herself or someone else.

'To contrive a meeting with King Valor of Briavel. The name Thirsk meant something to Valor – he respected my father even though they were lifetime enemies. It was the only reason he agreed to allow a Morgravian into his palace.'

Aremys shook his head – why was Faryl speaking as if she was Wyl Thirsk? But she was still talking in that flat monotone and he was loath to interrupt her.

'Celimus used Wyl Thirsk to get an audience with the King to discuss his daughter's marriage to the King of Morgravia and lull the Briavellian Crown into a false sense of security. Meanwhile, he had secretly ordered the death of King Valor, as well as the slaying of myself, both to be performed in the King's study as I negotiated for his daughter's betrothal to Celimus.'

Wyl fell quiet, his head moving in a sad shake as he recalled the events once again. Aremys held his breath, remained silent. He desperately wanted to hear the end of this chilling tale.

'You mentioned a man named Koreldy?' Wyl suddenly said, looking up.

Aremys nodded.

'I lied. I do know him . . . did know him. He was a member of that party to Briavel and saved Thirsk's life you could say. Together he and Thirsk certainly saved the life of Princess Valentyna, now Queen of Briavel.'

Again Aremys was lost. He knew Thirsk was dead so how could his life have been saved? Sensibly he maintained his silence, allowing Faryl to speak on.

'Koreldy took Thirsk's body back to Pearlis to make sure his name was cleared of any traitorous act Celimus might accuse him of to cover up the ambush.

'Because of Koreldy's actions, Celimus was forced to give General Thirsk a full ceremonial burial and his name remains unsullied. And Romen Koreldy had made a promise to the dying Thirsk that he would rescue and protect his sister, Ylena, from Celimus.'

Aremys nodded as the broader picture became clearer, grateful that Faryl had stopped confusing herself with Thirsk. It was such odd behaviour.

'When Koreldy tracked Ylena down she was imprisoned in the dungeons of the castle. This is a noblewoman, Aremys, who grew up in the corridors of Stoneheart, who was ward of King Magnus and had always enjoyed his full protection.' Wyl sighed. 'Magnus loved her as a daughter and she was treated like a princess. What Celimus perpetrated on that young woman during her incarceration is unspeakable. He surely damaged her mind. My sister is no longer the same bright girl I knew.'

There it is again, Aremys thought. What does she mean?

'Koreldy rescued her, under the guise of wanting her for himself. Celimus trusted him as his own man, believing it was Koreldy who had slain Thirsk. I suspect Celimus enjoyed the irony of knowing Thirsk's killer would also rape his sister. It is the kind of cruel twist his mind would love,' Wyl said bitterly.

'So now you are trying to protect her? Why?' Aremys ventured.

'Because she is innocent. Because I hate Celimus. Because she is the last of our line and I have sworn on my own life to protect her.'

Aremys's confusion was complete but still he tried to make some sense of this tale, if just for Faryl's sake. 'Where is Koreldy – is he with her?'

'He's dead,' Wyl said, standing.

'How?'

'I killed him,' Wyl replied, moving towards his horse to resaddle her.

Aremys struggled to sit up. 'Help me, damn it!' he yelled.

'No. You're on your own now. Go get yourself fixed up. I've told you all I'm going to. Now I ask you to leave me in peace. I suggest you head home to Grenadyn as was your original plan. Don't go near Ylena Thirsk or I promise I will finish what I began.'

He stood. 'Then you'll have to kill me, for until I have the truth, Faryl, I have no reason not to pursue my prey. I am not involved in the Thirsk woman's sorrows no matter how sad her tale is.'

'Well, you have been warned. I will not hesitate next time.' Her eyes glittered with menace.

'Then answer me this: why did you say Fergys Thirsk was *your* father?' Aremys saw Faryl become very still. Her back was to him but she was no longer interested in her horse. Her long arms dropped to her side.

'And you said that *you* were blackmailed by the King, that *you* witnessed the death of Ylena's husband — yet it was clear when he met us that Celimus had never clapped eyes on you before! Which one of us is going mad here?'

Now Faryl turned and he felt the full weight of her glare.

He was not to be deterred. 'You make it sound like she is *your* sister — but how can that be, Faryl? How can that be?' he shouted, equally angry now and determined to have an answer.

The movement was so fluid and so fast that he could not have avoided it even if he had full use of his arm and half a day's warning. Within a blink the assassin had a knife at his throat and had twisted his injured arm up behind his back. The pain was agonising — Aremys knew the wound was bleeding again. He was amazed at Faryl's strength. He struggled but it was useless in his state and he felt the blade slice into the skin at his throat — more blood, he assumed, and he fell still in her grip.

She growled into his ear, 'Because, damn you, Aremys of Grenadyn, and your constant interference, I *am* Wyl Thirsk.'

Wyl shoved the burly man away. Aremys staggered forwards, clutching his arm, but managed to turn and face his companion. Faryl looked like a wild animal — he half expected her to pounce again and felt sure that if she did it would be for the last time and he would certainly take his final breath on this earth with a knife slashing across his throat.

She was breathing hard and there were tears in her eyes. 'Leave me, Aremys!'

But he could not. He was too shocked. Stupefied by her angry words, he risked her wrath still further. 'Faryl . . . please?' His voice was gruff with his alarm and emotion.

'My name is Wyl,' came the bitter reply and Faryl turned away to hide her grief.

He left her alone for a few minutes in order that both of them might steady themselves. Finally he walked towards her, clutching at the wound in his arm which was really protesting now.

'Please, explain it to me.' He was begging, he realised, and added, 'I want to help.'

'Help?' she said sadly. 'All I ask is that you leave Ylena be.'

Aremys swallowed. 'I promise you I will not permit a hair on her apparently pretty head to be harmed – not as long as I can draw breath to protect it.'

Faryl or Wyl – whoever it was – turned slowly and he saw a new gleam in the feline eyes. He read it as hope.

'On your honour?'

He nodded wearily. 'I'll make a blood oath if you wish it.'

'And in return?'

'Your whole story.' He held up his hand against the retort that was about to fly back in his face. 'And I will help you to achieve whatever it is you are setting out to do.'

'Why?'

He shrugged, confused. 'Because it was wrong of me to turn you over to Jessom.'

'You owed me nothing. I'm sure he paid well.'

'Not enough for my loyalty. You have that – not that

I really understand who it is I pledge such loyalty to,' he said, rubbing his face.

Wyl reached for the bladder of water and handed it to Aremys. 'Here, drink some. Then you had better sit down and listen well.'

If Aremys thought he was a man who had seen and heard it all, he was sorely mistaken. As the full tale of Wyl Thirsk unfolded, the mercenary's head began to spin with the startling notion that he was now in the company of three people.

When Wyl had finished his story, both men sat in silence and watched the bees buzzing merrily about them, crawling in and out of the bright yellow and orange wild-flowers at the edge of the stream. Sparrows chittered overhead and a frantic blackbird, clearly with a new nest of fledglings to fatten up, busied itself digging for worms nearby.

Spring is almost here, Aremys realised absently. 'Thank you,' he murmured, still not trusting himself to say much more just yet.

'Now I will definitely kill you if you betray me,' Wyl threatened, feeling awkward yet vaguely relieved that the story had been shared.

Aremys breathed deeply. 'I have pledged my loyalty to you. It is not given lightly – no man has ever had it before.'

'I am grateful that you consider me a man,' Wyl said with relief.

The mercenary snorted. 'And I wanted to sleep with you.'

Wyl's shock was evident and they both laughed in embarrassment which, surprisingly, helped to diffuse the awkwardness.

Aremys did not want to let the laughter go. 'You know, you've got the greatest tits.'

Wyl lifted one of Faryl's eyebrows. 'Apparently.'

'I don't suppose—'

'Certainly not!' came the indignant reply and more healing laughter. 'I don't own them – I'm . . . er . . . I'm simply the caretaker.'

'Who else knows?'

'A boy called Fynch whom I trust implicitly. An old woman, a seer, who first sensed this strange magic within me. Her niece, Elspyth, who I hope has already found Ylena,' he said wistfully before adding, 'and a brave warrior from the Razors.'

'A Mountain Dweller?'

'His name is Lothryn and I believe he gave his life to save mine.'

'You believe? You don't know if he's dead?'

Wyl shrugged. 'I hope he is.'

Aremys eyed his companion with surprise.

'I suspect death is far preferable to his probable fate at the hands of Cailech,' Wyl answered, obvious sadness in his voice.

Aremys did not push on that topic. 'So Queen Valentyna thinks you're dead?'

Wyl smiled wryly. 'Well, I am really. Her friendship was with Romen Koreldy. Faryl of Coombe is his murderer, not that I imagine anyone knows that yet, although the suspicion will be there.'

'And the Queen knows nothing of this enchantment which has touched your life?'

Wyl shook his head. 'I believe Fynch has tried to talk to her about it, but Briavellians are even more closed on magic than Morgravians. It was not so long ago that we Morgravians hunted down, tortured and burned suspected witches – magic still frightens us. Briavel has never threatened its people, because they simply do not believe that such power exists. No, I don't think she could comprehend the truth.'

'I'm finding it pretty hard myself,' Aremys admitted. 'But I believe you – there is too much that is odd about you not to believe it.'

He was still trying to come to terms with the fact that the person sitting before him was once the infamous Romen Koreldy from his own island.

'Do you ever feel them?' he asked.

Wyl looked up at him. 'Romen and Faryl?'

'No, your tits.'

At this Wyl exploded into laughter and Aremys loved seeing Faryl's face light up in such a rare showing of pleasure.

'It's amazingly good to hear you laugh,' the big man admitted.

'None of us have had much to laugh about in recent weeks.'

'I'm sorry, I did mean the others,' Aremys admitted sheepishly.

'Yes, they are always present but more as a spiritual remnant of themselves. I can tap into some of their memories, although those fade very fast, but strangely I possess their skills and much of their learned knowledge. Still, there is plenty that is lost to me. Wyl Thirsk just takes over,' he said.

'So what do we do now?'

'Get your arm stitched up.'

'Wait. Before I turned you over to Jessom, you were headed for Baelup. What is there?'

'Ah, yes,' Wyl said, sighing. 'I was trying to track down Myrren's mother. I still will once Ylena is safe. I'm hoping the mother may lead me to where I might find out more.'

'You're hiding something,' Aremys said. 'Remember, *all* the tale – you promised.'

Wyl nodded, struggling against his reluctance. 'I have learned that the man Myrren's mother was married to was not Myrren's true father. I need to find her blood father. The old seer from Yentro I spoke of – Elspyth's aunt – said he would tell me more about this so-called gift I've been given.'

'Is it dangerous for you to travel to Felrawthy?'

Wyl shrugged. 'No more than to Baelup.'

'But you'd prefer to be tracking down Myrren's father rather than chasing across the realm for your sister who, you admit, may already be in safe hands.'

'I can't be sure about that, not with Celimus hunting her down.'

'But he's not. I am. Celimus is under the assumption that he's sent off his agents and I suspect he will not dwell on it further for now.'

Wyl looked puzzled. 'What's your point?'

'I will go after Ylena. You go and find Myrren's father.'

There was a silence. Aremys knew what Wyl was thinking. 'You can trust me. I will protect her with my life, now.' Then unexpectedly he added, 'I had a sister but she died in an accident. She had been left in my care, but I preferred to go hunting. Angry that I was not permitted to do so, I left Serah in what I thought was a safe place in the woods.'

Wyl was listening intently now – so it was not just he who had secrets. 'Go on.'

'She was killed. A wild pig gored her. I'm not sure it wouldn't have killed both of us, but I have still never forgiven myself for deserting her,' he said. 'I'm not sure my family ever did either,' he added quietly.

'Forgive me, Aremys. That is a shocking story but I am still uncertain why you feel obliged to fight my cause,' Wyl said.

'Perhaps if I share the whole truth with you, it might be clearer,' the mercenary replied. 'My father is a noble. We were visiting Pearlis many years ago as a family. I would have been around ten, my sister just four summers old. Celimus was perhaps eight.'

'Celimus?'

'Yes, I am afraid we both have reason to hate the King of Morgravia.'

'And?' Wyl encouraged, mindful of Aremys's blood-saturated sleeve. However, the bleeding seemed to have been staunched.

'My father and brothers were invited to hunt with the royal party. My mother, bless her, was asked to bathe with the court ladies. None of us had seen such resplendence as Stoneheart offered so she asked me to look after Serah for a couple of hours. Play with her, she said. Keep her safe.' Aremys looked to the sky and grunted. 'As soon as mother's back was turned I took Serah to the woods where I wanted to be. I was furious that I couldn't go on the hunt and blamed Serah. Along came Celimus and his friends. They told me they were going to beat sticks in the woods higher up where the wild pigs roamed to see if they couldn't coax out their own game to hunt.' Aremys shook his head. 'It was stupid but we were just boys, eager to be grown-up and keen for our fathers' respect. It didn't occur to me that Serah wasn't safe. I joined the prince and his friends and, suffice to say, we did flush out a pig and made him angry enough to stampede straight into Serah's path.'

'Shar's wrath, man! And Celimus doesn't know who you are?'

Aremys shook his head. 'I wasn't important enough to remember, and besides, at that age my parents called me Remy. He hasn't made the connection. I spent years planning how I would kill him. I blamed him, you see. By the time I was old enough to do it, I realised the folly of youth. I was not going to kill the heir to Morgravia and I am certainly not going to kill its new King. Instead I bleed him of the money he loves so much.'

It all fell into place now for Wyl. 'You!'

Aremys looked abashed. 'I'm afraid so.'

'You told them where the taxes would be coming from,' Wyl stammered. 'You guided Rostyr and his men.'

'It's true. And I shall continue to find ways to make the King's life difficult, whilst simultaneously helping myself to his coffers by doing some of his dirty work.'

'But those seven men?'

'All deserved to die. They were corrupt.'

Wyl could barely mask the sarcasm. 'A selective assassin.'

'You could say.'

Wyl smiled grimly. 'Well, I am not so forgiving as you, Aremys. I aim to bring about the downfall of Celimus.'

Aremys grinned back. 'And I will help you. I hate him as much as you do. Do you believe my loyalty now?'

Wyl nodded. 'Let's get you sewn up and then go find my sister. Together.'

19

THE DONAL ESTATE WAS a series of elegant buildings running off the main two-storey house. It sprawled within a glen, protected on all sides by picturesque hills and flanked by a small forest in the north.

The family had a long and close history with the Crown and a reputation as fearless defenders of the north. In days gone by many Briavellian Kings had thought to storm Morgravia through its north but had met solid, seemingly tireless resistance from Felrawthy. Like the Thirsks to the south, this family boasted an impeccable bloodline of warriors.

Although it was not a family known for its fertility, once Jeryb assumed the mantle as duke he had no intention of following in the tradition of siring a single heir only. His lovely wife had given him one son but he had always hoped for a large brood of children.

It had become a joke in the early days of their marriage. 'It just takes practice, my love,' Jeryb would say, a sparkle in his eye.

The young Aleda would smile forthrightly back and

reply that they would just have to practise each evening then until they became really good at it.

And the twins, Daryn and Jorge, followed this rigorous routine with young Alyd arriving as a special surprise five years later, by which time Aleda had suggested to the man who loved her so much to practise a little less.

'For I think we have the hang of it now,' she had declared, to Jeryb's high amusement.

Jeryb had fought alongside his trusted leader, Fergys Thirsk. Not only had their two wives found enjoyment in each other's company whenever they met, but the two heads of the families knew they could trust one another – and in a battle, trust was the most precious of commodities.

Fergys relied entirely on Jeryb to hold the north against the increasing agitation from the Mountain People. He knew of no noble more loyal to the Crown. Although Jeryb rarely managed to travel south except for highly formal occasions, his relationship with King Magnus was strong. Once, over a warm ale on a frigid night on yet another battlefield, with the smell of blood in their nostrils, they had talked of how their sons would hold the realm as strongly as they had over the years.

Now General Thirsk's daughter was about to experience the generous hospitality that Jeryb Donal had always been pleased to offer her father. Ylena clung to the waist of the kind, bright-eyed man who reminded her too much of someone she had loved. She had not bothered with the more elegant side-saddle position but had lifted her skirts carefully to sit astride the horse. Pil had helped her rearrange them neatly. Crys had left instructions with their men to make their way back to the duchy and then he and Ylena had made haste to follow the duke back to

Tenterdyn. Jeryb had set off first, with just a couple of men as escort, riding at breakneck speed to bring news to Tenterdyn and Aleda Donal of what had befallen their son and his beautiful betrothed.

'Welcome to our home, my lady,' Crys said gently over his shoulder. 'You will be safe here.'

His voice was kind and so reminiscent of another's. Ylena smiled. No one seeing her could have failed to be arrested by her beauty despite the grime of several days' travel.

'Are you all right?' he asked.

'Are you?' she replied.

'Too shocked and distraught at your news to think properly,' he admitted. She appreciated his candour. 'The worst is yet to come, I fear. Telling my mother the full story will not be easy, although my father will have prepared her. Alyd was her favourite, you see.' He looked around and chanced a thin smile. 'Not because he liked it that way. He was the youngest . . . the baby. Everyone spoiled him and adored him. As you know, it was easy to do both.'

She forced back the tears which had sprung to her eyes. 'I am ready. I have not come here to hide, Crys. I have come to ask your father to help me fight the person who carried out this atrocity.'

'You'll find willing warriors here, my lady, for Alyd's sake.'

'Wait until you learn who our enemy is, sir,' she said, more bitterly than she had intended.

Crys kicked the horse into a trot down the hill, raising a hand to his father who had emerged from the house.

*   *   *

Aleda met them alongside her husband. Her face was pale and lined with building grief but she found a brief smile of courtesy for their guest.

'Welcome, child,' she said bravely, reaching to hug Ylena, whom she had only known previously as an infant.

Both women felt the gravity of the moment, the rush of emotion which cared not for circumstance or timing. It boiled over and they gave in to it, sobbing in each other's arms, two strangers linked by the love of the young man they had lost. The men could not bear to watch the upsetting scene and disappeared into the house.

Finally Aleda pulled away. 'I am glad you came here, Ylena.'

'I have nowhere else to go, my lady. Forgive me, but my story is more brutal and upsetting than you can possibly imagine.'

'We shall hear it, child, in all its painful, unmasked truth. But come now, I want you to bathe and rest first.'

Ylena looked at the handsome older woman with disbelief.

'You will tell your tale more succinctly if you are refreshed and rested. I can certainly wait a little longer to hear your news.'

Ylena liked Alyd's mother immediately, admiring the strength she sensed the woman possessed. It had taken much courage to greet her son's bride so graciously knowing what she had come to explain to them.

They walked arm in arm, drying the tears from their cheeks as they entered the double doors of the mansion known as Tenterdyn.

Aleda looked towards her eldest child – Jeryb was

nowhere to be seen. He grinned crookedly and she saw
not only her husband reflected back in the expression but
also the youngest son she suddenly ached to hold again.
She nodded, tight-lipped. 'This girl needs a bath and a
rest and then we will all talk.' Her look brooked no argument. 'Let your father know, please, and call the boys in,'
she added, referring to his brothers. 'We shall sit down
in an hour or so.'

With Ylena settled privately in a chamber and left to
her toilet, Crys followed his aristocratic mother down into
her private reading room, as she liked to call it. It was
actually more her escape from her brood of lively sons and
their booming father. Here she indeed read, but also did
her quiet thinking. It was a brightly washed room of
yellows and greens, hung with tasteful tapestries of her
own design. The furniture was soft and welcoming, the
view from the windows was spectacular, and Crys loved
to share time with her here, although on this occasion he
was not looking forward to their conversation. A servant
stepped in with a tray, poured them each a goblet of sweet
wine and left.

'You look tired, son,' Aleda said, before sipping at her
goblet.

'Has she told you anything yet?'

Aleda shook her head. 'I don't want to hear it anyway.'

Crys saw the pain flicker across his mother's face and
then how it was checked and masked. He knew all too
well that she did not like anyone to read her thoughts.

'Here, my dear. Come and sit down,' Aleda said to Ylena
when she joined the gathered family in their main
chamber. The gown she wore was loose on her — it was

one of Aleda's – but she looked every bit the noblewoman she was.

'Crys, call for some spiced ale.'

Her son, entranced by the woman his brother had chosen to marry, moved swiftly. Aleda motioned her guest towards a comfortable armchair. The room felt suddenly crowded.

'Thank you,' Ylena said, mustering her courage. 'Let me tell you everything.'

'Let us wait for Crys,' the older woman said gently, squeezing Ylena's hand. 'He must hear this too.'

A hint of a smile flickered across Ylena's hauntingly beautiful face. 'Yes, of course,' she said. 'For I fear I will not want to tell it again.'

Crys returned, his expression grim. He glanced towards his father, who caught the look and roused himself from his silent shock in the corner.

'Tell us, my girl,' the duke commanded in his deep voice. 'Tell us everything.'

Ylena spared them none of the horror of their son's death or of her own traumas, including learning of the death of her brother and the sacking of Rittylworth and murder of its brethren. No one interrupted her and by the time she had finished speaking a frigid silence had gripped the room.

'Alyd was executed, you say?' Crys asked, his voice hollow with disbelief.

His father looked suddenly every one of his three score years and ten. His mother, pale and rigid, bit her lip, the only indication that she was fighting her own demons. His brothers stood by, stunned into silence.

Ylena swallowed, fighting the tears for their sake. 'Alyd

was killed before my eyes. They used an axe,' she added bitterly. 'Didn't even give him a noble death.'

Aleda felt sick to the marrow of her bones but she pushed aside her despair. She wanted to hear it all before she began to grieve. 'And you were married?' she said.

Their guest nodded. 'As I explained, it was the only way we could outwit Celimus. He intended to bed me, claiming Virgin's Blood. His intention was always to hurt Alyd and, in doing so, to draw Wyl into the confrontation so he could use that to start dismantling Wyl's power over the Legion and his standing in the realm.'

'Felrawthy will rise!' boomed the duke. He turned to his eldest son in whose handsome face he saw a painful echo of his youngest, now headless and rotting in some unmarked grave in Pearlis. 'We will avenge Alyd and Wyl Thirsk for this atrocity.'

20

AT AROUND THE TIME Ylena and Pil were first entering Dorchyster Green, Jessom was standing in a courtyard sharing with his King what little information he had been able to unearth on Leyen. Deep down he knew he was reaching with this but Celimus had clearly threatened him and it was easier to appease him with some pretence at intrigue than to admit he had no further information. This was all about survival now, and rather a busybody noblewoman's back be flayed than his.

'And you think the Lady Helyn could be a traitor?' Celimus spun around, aghast at the intimation.

'Not at all, sire,' Jessom replied smoothly. 'I think she may be an unwitting accomplice – if indeed there is a crime which Leyen should answer for. We still have no real idea of whether Leyen is guilty of working against the Crown. I have no fear that Lady Helyn does so.'

The King made a clicking noise with his tongue. 'But still I am suspicious. Until we hear differently from Aremys, I am obliged to consider Leyen's actions curious.'

Jessom merely nodded.

'Tell me again. Leave out nothing.'

The Chancellor began over. It was no use protesting. 'On your advice, your majesty,' he said diplomatically, avoiding the fact that he had been threatened, 'I began some enquiries into Jorn's activities on the night in question. It turns out that after escorting Leyen to the gatehouse, he returned to her room and gathered up the garments she had been lent for that night.'

Celimus stopped him with a finger in the air. 'How do you know this?'

'He was seen leaving the castle and heading into Pearlis, your majesty.'

The King's alert mind was in full swing. 'Was he acting in a guarded manner?'

'No, sire. I learned this much from some of our own men who were returning from an evening in the city. They met Jorn, recognised him and teased him – as soldiers are wont to do.'

'And?'

'The lad seemed in no particular hurry. In fact, he mentioned that he was making a delivery to Lady Helyn, so there was nothing secretive in his own mind about his journey, it appears.'

'All right. Go on,' the King replied, showing no remorse at the boy's death.

'I checked with Lady Helyn's manservant, who concurs that delivery of a gown and cloak was certainly made in the early hours of the morning following our supper. The man, Arnyld, said Jorn did not tarry at the house. He handed over the garments with a simple thank you from Leyen then left immediately.'

'No other detours or errands?'

'Not that I can track down, sire.'

'Ah,' Celimus said, leaning forward, 'now we come to it.'

'It seems Leyen did more than finalise her thanks verbally. Arnyld mentioned that a note was found in the pocket of the cloak, almost by chance, much later.'

'You see,' Celimus said, pacing now, 'it is the words "almost by chance" that prick my curiosity. Do you think the note was deliberately hidden?'

Jessom shrugged slightly. 'I cannot guess, sire. Leyen may not have wanted to bother Jorn with trying to remember anything more detailed than a courteous thank you.'

'So what did that note contain?' the King asked eagerly.

The Chancellor shook his head. 'According to Lady Helyn, nothing of consequence. She said it was merely a polite courtesy and she believes she must have sent it out with the day's rubbish.'

'And you believe her?'

'She very kindly spent some time hunting for the note in my presence, just in case her memory was not serving her correctly, sire. She called Arnyld to task over it and he too searched. There was no sign of it.'

'Hmm, perfectly plausible, I suppose.'

'As I thought, sire, which is why I have not pushed any further.'

'How was she when you spoke with her?'

'Charming. As I said, keen to help you if she could and apologetic for her hasty action in ridding herself of the note. I sensed no guile, sire.'

'I'd still like to speak with her.'

'I anticipated as much, my lord. She awaits your pleasure.'

Celimus smiled thinly at Jessom's smooth anticipation. 'Show her in.'

Lady Helyn moved gracefully for her size. She sketched a perfect curtsy to her sovereign. 'Your majesty, this is indeed a rare pleasure,' she said.

'Come, Lady Helyn, walk a short way with me. Let me show you my new floriana garden.'

Clever, she thought. He knows how much I appreciate nature's gifts. 'Of course, your highness, I would be honoured,' she replied, thanking the gods who protected her for keeping any trace of anxiety from showing in her voice.

She took the King's proffered arm and allowed him to guide her out of the courtyard and into an exquisitely perfumed garden, still under construction in places. 'Oh, sire, this is magnificent,' she breathed, genuinely impressed.

Celimus turned on a dazzling smile for this important lady of his court. He knew he must tread carefully. Lady Bench's wealthy influential husband would not take kindly to his King browbeating his wife for seemingly inconsequential information. 'It is not yet nearly finished, of course, but I am glad to show it in its early stages to someone who loves the work of Shar.' He showed her into a superb rotunda containing a small stone table and benches. 'I have ordered some parillion juice which I hope you will enjoy?'

'A favourite of mine, thank you.' She inhaled the perfume about her. 'The floriana display is magical, sire. Such colours! My, my.'

Celimus was nothing but charm. 'Thank you, Lady

Helyn. My gardeners tell me they are the most stubborn of plants. What was it one of them said now . . .'

He cocked his head in thought and she was instantly reminded of his mother. All cold beauty she recalled, not a skerrick of warmth had helped that woman's heart beat. But stunning she had certainly been. No woman in Pearlis, or indeed the realm, could hold a candle to that one. And the son carried all of her grace and poise, the heartstopping looks. Yet it was an eternal pity that he possessed so little of his father.

'Pardon?' Celimus said. 'I missed that.'

Lady Helyn flinched. Had she spoken aloud?

'Your highness, my apology. I was thinking how incredibly like in looks to your beautiful mother you are,' she quickly said and diplomatically followed it up with, 'may Shar bless her.'

He smiled. 'That is generous, my lady. I am reminded often of how special she was.'

His companion nodded her head graciously, relief coursing through her.

The King continued, 'Ah yes, it comes to me now. The head gardener calls these flowers Shar's Folly.'

'Oh, and I can understand why, my lord,' Lady Helyn gushed. 'They are impossible to grow and yet look at your glorious display. I admit I did not realise you cared for such things.'

Now Celimus's expression became soft, almost apologetic. He sighed. 'It is true, my lady, that my passion runs to the hunt, my horses, and my realm of course.'

'And your people, sire,' she added.

'That goes without saying,' he replied evenly. 'But more recently I have developed a new passion . . . for a certain woman, my lady, who makes my heart burn with desire. It is she who has made me appreciate some of the gentler aspects of life,' he admitted. 'This new garden is for her. It is one of several I am creating in her honour.'

There was no avoiding the issue. 'You speak of Queen Valentyna, my lord?'

'Indeed. I hope we will be married by spring's close. I know the union will herald great joy to both realms, Lady Helyn, which brings me to why I wished to see you today.'

Lady Helyn was heartily glad they were interrupted by the arrival of the fruit juice. It was perfectly chilled, the beautifully crafted silver goblet dripping with icy water like dewdrops. 'So cool and refreshing, your highness,' she said, eager for a last chance to think over her options.

Leyen's note had been shocking to say the least. If what the young woman claimed was true, then Lady Bench was sitting with a madman at this moment. A King out of control. His lust for power, for other realms, for yet more riches, had overruled every sensible thought. According to Leyen, Celimus had plotted the assassination of King Valor of Briavel, leaving his daughter vulnerable to hostilities from Morgravia. An even greater shock was learning that Celimus had also contrived the murder of that fine young man Wyl Thirsk. If ever a son was set to follow in his father's footsteps, this was him, she thought. To see his life taken so early, so brutally, was a matter for sincere grief for all Morgravians, but to learn that his death may have been deliberately orchestrated by his own sovereign had left Lady Helyn shaken.

Leyen kept the frightening news coming. Now Celimus was after the sister, the beautiful Ylena. Helyn could barely believe the written accusation that the young woman had not only witnessed her husband's murder but had been herself incarcerated in Stoneheart's dungeon.

Leyen's prose was brief – like a soldier's – yet detailed. She had summarised that it was the King's intention to marry Valentyna and then destroy her and Briavel. Leyen admitted that she was the only one who knew the truth, the only person who stood in the King's way.

It went on to ask her to be watchful and to warn that one day the realm she loved might need her family to make difficult choices.

There were moments since she had read that note when Lady Bench had believed that it was all a terrible hoax. Yet her shrewd judgement of character had told her that the Leyen she met was an honest woman. Either that or she was a supreme actress, but Helyn Bench could not fathom what she might gain by lying.

She swallowed another gulp of the delicious juice, not tasting it.

'Not too sweet?' Celimus enquired, dragging her thoughts back to the present.

'It is perfect, my lord. Where were we?' she asked, in an attempt to sound innocent of a matter she now felt deeply embroiled in.

'Mmm, yes,' the King replied distractedly, as if it was not the major topic on his mind right now. 'I believe we were talking about why I asked you to come today.'

'That is right, you were, my lord. How may I serve you?'

'Well, you see, it is a matter of security.'

'Good grief, I can't imagine any of my petty gossip or court knowledge could assist in matters so lofty, your highness,' she said, laughing gently.

No further parrying; Celimus, she realised, had decided to make his play. 'You lent garments to a guest of the palace,' he began.

She nodded. 'Yes, a lovely woman by the name of Leyen.'

He smiled in agreement. 'That's her. Did you spend any time with her, madam?'

'Indeed, a few hours. We met at the bathing pavilion and I can't resist a new face in the palace, your highness. I pride myself on knowing all newcomers within hours of their arrival,' she tittered, affecting the gossipy voice she used with her ladies.

'What did you learn?' he asked, ignoring the affectation.

She stopped her chuckling and allowed a frown of puzzlement to take its place. 'About Leyen? Not a lot, your highness. She struck me as a particularly private person. I did learn that she was supping with you that evening and had nothing suitable to wear.'

'Yes, the gown you lent was most becoming.'

'My daughter's. I also sent around my maid that evening to dress her hair. A messenger returned the gown and cloak several hours later with thanks.'

She decided to take the risk and lead this conversation towards its end. She was not sure her nerves could withstand his penetrating gaze for much longer. 'I know that Chancellor Jessom was especially interested in a note we found in the cloak much later on the following day.'

'That's right.'

'Do you have reason to suspect Leyen of something, my lord?'

'I do, Lady Helyn. I have reason to believe she may be plotting against the Crown.'

She knew contrived shock would not work now. The

situation required the most delicate of navigation. She looked at Celimus quizzically, deliberately pausing as if to consider before speaking. It all depended on how she carried herself in the next few moments. Either he would accept her explanation or she might find herself a guest of his majesty's dungeon.

'No, sire,' she soothed. 'That young woman had nothing but good to say of you, my lord. She expressed her wish that you would marry Queen Valentyna and admitted to being a courier between the two realms. She would not say more – in fact she admonished my curiosity with a reminder of her loyalty to Morgravia's King and reminded me that as your private agent she was not permitted to reveal anything further.'

'She did?'

'On my word, my King.' *Shar forgive me*, she thought.

The gaze did not falter although she sensed he did not disbelieve her.

'And you trust her?'

'I have no reason not to, sire. I found her to be direct in her manner, determined to serve you well.'

'Did she say farewell?'

'Not in person, sire. It was all in that brief note of thanks – I do wish I'd kept it, just to reassure you that it held nothing more than polite courtesies. If that young woman has any grudge against you . . . well, I did not pick it up and there are few with sharper instincts than I – if you will permit me to say so, your highness.'

Please believe me, she begged inwardly as she waited for his unhurried response.

He took his time, levelling a narrowed gaze at her as if he could see into her soul. She resisted the urge to squirm beneath it. Finally he blinked, graciously took her hand and kissed it. 'Thank you, Lady Helyn. You have put my mind at rest. Jessom here will see you out.'

The Chancellor materialised from behind them, smiling obsequiously in that oily manner of his. Her knees felt weak with relief. She was glad she was still seated. 'I am pleased, your highness, to have eased your mind,' she said, finding the courage to test her knees and stand. 'We all look forward to the nuptials, my lord,' she added.

The King gave her a wolfish grin before permitting her to leave. Lady Helyn fought the urge to run as she left the palace, forcing herself to keep an unhurried pace, smiling at people she knew, even stopping once and annoying the Chancellor whilst she passed on a new titbit of gossip to a person she had not seen in a while.

Now, sitting back in her carriage, she felt her heart-beat finally begin to slow and permitted herself tentative congratulations on the fine performance she had shown her King. It hit her suddenly that she was now a traitor to Morgravia – in lying to her sovereign she was no longer loyal to the Crown.

I may not be loyal to this man's Crown, she thought, but to Morgravia I remain true.

She would need to talk this over with her husband, whenever he deigned to return home. Until then, she would take Leyen's advice and remain watchful.

Lady Helyn Bench was not a lover of travel as her husband was. She felt sure that many of the reasons Eryd found to be gone from Pearlis were contrived, but she did not really mind. She had known from their first meeting that he was a solitary figure at heart who far preferred the open road and his own company to the crush of people and his wife's gossipy intrigues in the capital.

Eryd was wealthy, indeed powerful. His voice counted at court — with both kings, old and new — and when he put his weight behind a particular matter it was considered worth taking note of. Moreover many nobles listened to and took guidance from the steadfast, seemingly incorruptible Lord Bench. He had made his riches through buying and selling exotic spices and magnificent gems from the northern islands. He could, in truth, procure virtually any merchandise from anywhere, ranging from high-quality tobacco to a magnificent horse if that was what was required.

Eryd was the complete opposite of his plump, stay-at-home wife who enjoyed spending his wealth on everything from lavish parties to her prized pond fish. They were an oddly matched yet loving couple whose affection for each other had never waned. Her constant chittering might have driven most men of his ilk to their grave, yet Eryd rather enjoyed Helyn's comforting noise when he returned home, as well as her fussing. Likewise, Helyn did not mind her partner being so elusive; she was more than capable of handling the most formal of occasions without a husband's support and she relished the time alone to pursue her own interests.

And so the Bench household was usually one filled with love and laughter, music and reading, intrigue and storytelling. Power throbbed in the Bench family, which was as generous with its money as it was with its time for friends and acquaintances. The couple seemed to want for nothing and were envied for their secure relationship as much as their wealth.

However, anyone passing beneath Lady Helyn's window on this particular evening might have told a different story at the bathing pavilion the next day. Eryd was not happy and raised voices carried on the still night – thankfully unintelligibly, for the argument had ensued in Helyn's dressing room which was well cocooned by her dozens of gowns and wraps, skirts and coats.

'This is sheer madness,' Eryd roared. 'I have never heard such folly.'

'Haven't you, darling?' Helyn responded in the distracted tone she reserved just for him. Realising he was not to be put off so easily, she stopped her search through her wardrobe and looked at him, exasperated. 'Don't wave that pipe at me, Eryd. I am not one of your workers to do your bidding.'

'No,' he said, less loudly. 'But you are my wife and you *will* listen to me.'

'Of course I shall listen. I don't have to *do* what you want though.' She flounced out of the dressing room into her chamber.

Eryd, still shocked by her news, tried a less dictatorial approach. 'Helyn, my love . . . I beg you not to meddle in the politics of this realm.'

'Why not? You do!'

He looked at her with a pained expression. 'That's not fair, my love.'

She made a sound of disgust, cutting across whatever martyr-like statement was coming.

'This is madness,' he repeated, feeling suddenly helpless.

'I agree. I will do no more than keep my ear to the ground for information that might assist.'

'Towards bringing down your King!' he said, aghast.

'Hush!' she cautioned, speaking more quietly now. 'You of all people should grasp the import of what we have been told.'

'*If* it's true,' he countered, frustrated by her easy acceptance of the word of a stranger.

'Yes,' Helyn answered, 'if it's true. And that's what I'm going to find out, because if it is . . . oh, Eryd, what will become of our realm?'

He sighed and sat on her bed next to her. 'Civil war.'

'That's right. I think Leyen is trying to prevent that, although it all seems so odd.'

'Working against the Crown,' he said sadly. 'It's treachery, Helyn.'

'So is the murder of innocent high-ranking nobles – not to mention the King of Briavel,' she hissed. 'I can't stand by with this information and not do anything.'

'You don't think it could be some sort of horrible mistake?'

She smiled sadly. 'I hope it is.'

'How can you trust a stranger?'

She shrugged. 'Years of experience with liars, my love. Call it intuition – my very own and particular talent. Leyen struck me as very direct; nothing dishonest about her. Secretive, but not dishonest. There was something very vulnerable about that woman. She knows things. Is scared by them. I know she's working for the King, and I also know, following what stopped just short of an interrogation, that the King is determined to find out what she might have told me. Now firstly, why would she tell me anything – a complete stranger, as you say – unless it was true? Why would she risk writing something so damning – it could easily have her executed – if she didn't know it to be true? Secondly, and even more intriguing, why would Celimus have me especially called in on the pretext of a chat when really he was fishing for information on Leyen? What she knew, what she might have shared with me. His behaviour virtually attests to his guilt.'

'Why indeed,' Eryd muttered, beaten by her logic. 'This is dangerous, my love.'

She nodded. 'I do know it.' She leaned over and kissed her husband. 'Thank you for listening.'

'Do you think the King still believes you are involved?'

She shook her head. 'No, I was at my sparkling best. But you are right, I must tread with great care.'

'Let's say you do find it's all true . . .' He stopped. It was a question he was perhaps not ready to ask.

Helyn said nothing, all but holding her breath, wondering if her husband's heart could stand the shock of what she was thinking.

Eryd answered his own question. 'Betray Morgravia?'

His voice was leaden with the fear she also felt. She had no explanation or soft speech of comfort to help him understand. She too was reeling beneath her calm exterior. Lady Bench would far prefer to be focusing her energies on the current rumour of the seduction of one woman's husband by her sister, but Leyen's note, the trust she had placed in her new friend, was irrefutable. She could not ignore it.

'I could never betray Morgravia, my darling,' she said, eyes misting as she stroked his stubbled cheek. 'But this new King of ours . . . I just don't know. If any of what Leyen entrusted to me has an ounce of truth, then he is not a King we would want to be loyal to.'

Eryd took his wife's chubby hands and stared at her intently. 'He may be new and young but he is not to be trifled with. From what I can tell, beneath the vain and seemingly shallow veneer lurks a mind sharp enough to cut and bright enough to blind. You did well to throw him off your scent, but do not be fooled by him . . . not ever.'

21

ELSPYTH ARRIVED ON THE outskirts of the duchy by
dusk. A middle-aged travelling monk called Brother Lewk
with a donkey in tow took pity on the lone, clearly
exhausted woman and suggested she ride the beast along
the road as far as the town of Brynt, the largest in
Felrawthy. Elspyth, believing the monk was indeed a gift
from Shar, gladly accepted his generous offer. She enjoyed
his thoughtful company as he walked alongside and
regretted it when they crested a rise and he pointed out
Brynt below. To the north lay the sprawling pastures of
the duke's private lands.

'That's where you're headed, my girl,' the monk said,
'although you are most welcome to travel into Brynt with
me if you care to.'

Elspyth smiled wearily. 'I must keep moving, father,
but I do thank you for your company and my fine steed.'
She climbed off the beast and patted its coarse hair, marvelling at the serenity in its large dark eyes. *I'd give anything
right now for your simple life, my friend*, she thought.

Turning, she looked into the genial grey eyes in a gently

frowning face. 'I shouldn't miss him for a day or so you know,' her companion said. 'Why don't you take him? I imagine the duke will have opportunity enough to have the little fellow returned to me. I'll be at Brynt for several days yet.'

Elspyth felt her heart fill. Perhaps there was hope for Morgravia with people like this in it. She could hardly refuse, knowing she was in no state to walk many more steps. 'I am surely blessed to have met you, father. Thank you for this. I shall ensure he is well fed, watered and returned tomorrow.'

'Oh, no hurry, child. He certainly doesn't hurry for anyone,' he said, face crinkling into the merriest of smiles. 'Shar guide you in your travels.'

And so it was with some surprise that the noble Donal family welcomed yet another bedraggled and fatigued young woman, this one arriving by donkey. Crys was at the guardhouse, briefing the man on duty regarding new security and the locking of Tenterdyn's gates. As the woman slipped off her mount and landed unceremoniously on her backside outside the gates of Tenterdyn, Crys Donal smiled for the first time since hearing the shocking news of his brother's untimely death.

A gloom had settled over the Donal family home since Ylena's story had been told. Ylena had once again retired for a much-needed rest. With the physician's approval, a mild soporific had been administered and she was released from her memories as a blanketing sleep claimed her. The others had no such relief and were left to pick over the horrific account of Alyd's brutal beheading – without trial, without even so much as the conviction of a crime.

Even more chilling was the revelation that his head had been placed in the dungeon with his wife, and when Ylena had informed them that she had carried the remains of their loved one to Felrawthy, the Donals were shattered. Ylena had left it to Crys to withdraw Alyd's head from the sack, refusing to gaze upon the tragic sight again.

The viewing had left each of the family shaken and withdrawn. Jeryb took his leave to shut himself away in his study where he intended to ponder the right path for revenge. His words left his family in no doubt that Felrawthy would shortly engage in civil war against the Crown. It was an unthinkable scenario. Crys was still churning over the notion in his mind as he helped the young woman up from the ground.

A grin escaped, in spite of his bleak mood. 'A theatrical arrival,' he commented.

'My apologies, sir,' Elspyth replied, a little fractious. 'I have been travelling a long time.' She disengaged herself from his arms.

'So I see,' he said, taking in her ragged appearance but not smiling this time as he could see it had niggled her. 'Please forgive my poor manners. I am Crys Donal, eldest son of the Duke of Felrawthy.'

Elspyth looked at him and felt disarmed as she properly appreciated his looks and quality clothes. More people resembling her companion emerged from the house and crossed the courtyard towards her – they were a handsome family, she noted. But no one looked especially pleased to see her; in fact everyone looked downright miserable.

'Crys,' said the tall, regal-looking woman, 'where are your manners?'

'I was just apologising for the loss of same, mother. I'd introduce you if I knew who was paying us a visit.'

Elspyth blushed and smoothed her grubby garments with dusty hands. 'I'm sorry. My name is Elspyth. I am a friend of . . .' She was momentarily confused: Wyl was the friend but Romen was the man he'd walked as. She chose: '. . . of Wyl Thirsk,' she said firmly and saw alarm spread across the faces before her.

'Have I said something wrong?' she whispered to Crys.

He shook his head sadly. 'No. Just more shock for an already distraught family. Elspyth, may I introduce Aleda, Duchess of Felrawthy, my mother. My father, Duke Jeryb . . .' Elspyth found herself involuntarily curtsying as the duke regarded her '. . . and this is one of my three brothers, Daryn.'

Elspyth smiled tentatively towards the young man.

'The other, Jorge, is with his beloved horses, I presume, and my youngest brother,' Crys added in a different tone, 'we have learned only today is dead. Forgive us our sober welcome.'

The duke took charge. 'But perhaps you already know of this if Wyl Thirsk is your friend?'

Elspyth looked at him directly, sensed his keen pain and softened her tone. 'I do, sir. I am deeply regretful for your family. Alyd was your youngest?'

He nodded.

'Did you know him?' the duchess asked. Elspyth could see her eyes were red but not sore from tears. She fancied this was a strong woman. 'I did not, my lady, only of him.' The duchess nodded, knuckles white where her hands gripped each other.

'Er, may I ask, please, if Ylena Thirsk has made contact with your family?' Elspyth ventured.

It was Crys who answered. 'We met her by chance at a town about half a day's ride from the estate.'

'So . . . she's here?' Elspyth could hardly believe her good fortune.

Aleda nodded. 'Exhausted and mercifully sleeping upstairs. Please, come inside,' Aleda added. 'You look travel-weary, my dear. Let us organise some refreshment for you.'

Crisp orders were given and before Elspyth knew it she was luxuriating in a bath with scented oils. It felt like a healing, an opportunity to clean away the grime but also to cleanse her wrecked emotions and focus her thoughts. On the road, fatigue and hunger had sharpened her sense of rage at all that had happened to her and those she liked and indeed loved. Now, immersed in the fragrant water in the comfortable surrounds of a beautiful chamber, she felt some of that anger float away.

Despite the dozens of questions she sensed they wanted to ask, the duke and his family were extremely gracious to allow her this comfort time as soon as she arrived. In truth, it was the duchess who would not hear of any discussion until Elspyth had enjoyed the opportunity to bathe and feel like a woman again. She liked Aleda very much, even though she hardly knew her, and smiled now, recalling the glare the duchess had given her men when they had tried to interrogate her as soon as she stepped into the house and accepted a cool refreshing drink.

There was a soft knock at the door. Aleda entered. 'Is everything to your satisfaction, my dear?'

'Oh, yes, thank you,' Elspyth said. 'I have never felt more spoiled.'

The older woman gave a sad smile. 'You've probably never felt more tired or tested either,' she said softly, setting down a lamp to brighten the rapidly darkening chamber.

Elspyth nodded, felt the tears burning. 'It hasn't been easy.'

'I gathered as much and I apologise now for my husband's gruff manner. He is suffering, you know . . . we all are.' She snapped herself from her bleak tone. 'Will you be up to talking with us later?'

'Of course, my lady. It is why I've travelled this far.'

'Good girl. I shall make arrangements for dinner. Perhaps you could rest now for a while? Ylena, as I mentioned, has been forced to sleep, but she should be up and around shortly. You'll like her. We all do.'

Elspyth saw the duchess grit her teeth to stop the emotion flowing over.

'How is she coping?'

'She's rather amazing to tell the truth. I can tell she's deeply fearful of Celimus and which of his killers might be tracking her. But she's a Thirsk and that family's blood runs thick with courage.'

Elspyth smiled. 'I know what you mean. If she's anything like her brother, then she'll be looking to make Celimus pay.'

Aleda frowned. 'You speak of Wyl as though he lives. You do know what happened to him, don't you?' she offered hesitantly.

Elspyth felt trapped. She nodded for want of how to answer the duchess without lying. She changed the subject quickly. 'I am so sorry about Alyd, duchess.' She did not know what else to say; even the little she had said was hollow comfort.

The duchess forced a shaky smile. 'I can't bear to think on it just yet.' She rose and went to the door. 'Rest, my dear. We shall see you later. And you must call me Aleda, please.'

Later came all too soon for Elspyth but she felt a lot stronger for the peace and quiet she had enjoyed in a soft bed from where she could gaze out the window to the heather drifts on the surrounding hills. Aleda had arranged for clothes and other toiletry requisites to be brought to her, and for the first time in a very long time Elspyth sensed her old resilient self was in command again.

The three older members of the family were gathered in the reception room. A fire added some much-needed cheer; near to it sat a novice monk named Pil. She learned through Crys, who showed a new appreciation for their freshly bathed and rested guest, that it was Pil who had been Ylena's companion on her journey north.

'And what will you do now, Pil?' Elspyth asked, kindness in her voice as she recognised a fellow sufferer unwittingly trapped in this strange web created by the witch, Myrren. She shuddered inwardly at the anticipation of having to say more about Wyl Thirsk's strange life.

The young monk shrugged. 'I have no idea. I could not think beyond bringing the Lady Ylena to Felrawthy. I should like to return to my Order, but there is nothing at Rittylworth to return to,' he said, his sadness evident.

Elspyth nodded, knowing all too well about the state of Rittylworth. She took the proffered goblet of wine from Crys and smiled at him before turning back to the novice.

'Pil, I hope it's not out of place for me to mention this, but I met a wonderful man on my way here. A monk, like yourself. He travels, spreading the word and doing the work of Shar as best he can from town to village, county to duchy. It was his kindness that saw me reach Tenterdyn as swiftly as I did. I have promised to return the donkey he lent me – perhaps you might take the beast into Brynt where Brother Lewk is staying for a few days? You may find that the two of you have something in common.'

Pil's eyes shone as he understood her meaning instantly. 'Would he allow it?'

She grinned at his pleasure. 'You mean for you to accompany him in his work?' He nodded. 'Why should he refuse you, Pil? He's not a young man, I might add, but he is learned and wise. I suspect both of you could do far worse for a travelling companion.'

The young man beamed. Having viewed the smouldering remains of Rittylworth she imagined he had not had much to be bright about lately. 'Oh, I shall definitely seek him out, Elspyth. I do thank you.'

Elspyth enjoyed the warmth it gave her heart to be able to help someone with a few simple words. She sipped her wine and felt a new sort of warmth slip down her throat. Raising her glass to Crys, she saw his eyes sparkle at her over his own glass and realised he was flirting with her. She hurriedly looked aside. If the younger brother was anything like him, she could see why Ylena had been in such a rush to marry him. As she was thinking this, she noticed all those about her suddenly stiffen. She followed their gaze to the doorway where a glorious young woman stood.

'Ah, Ylena, my dear,' said the duchess. She moved elegantly across the room and, putting an arm around her guest's shoulders, guided her in. 'We want you to meet someone . . . a friend. This is Elspyth. She was a companion of your brother and has travelled a long way to meet you.'

Ylena's gaze settled on Elspyth who felt suddenly plain and awkward amongst such noble company. Ylena was a rare beauty and not at all what she had expected. Wyl had certainly mentioned his sister's prettiness but this poised young woman was exceptional.

'How good of you to come all this way,' Ylena said and bowed to Elspyth.

'My lady.' Elspyth followed suit, not quite so elegantly, feeling the relief of knowing she had kept her promise and found Ylena. 'I am so glad you are safe. Wyl sent me to ensure that you reached Felrawthy.'

Ylena's brow creased with a frown. 'When did he do this?'

Elspyth took a deep breath. Ylena's simple question had cut through all the hesitant politeness and niceties. The time had arrived: she must tell them Wyl's story. Wyl had asked her to keep his secret from Ylena, but Elspyth had decided it was wrong to do so, that his sister needed to hear the truth.

She gathered everyone's attention by her grave look. 'Please,' she said, 'I have a long story to tell you all – and not an easy one. It will shock and perhaps even frighten you, but I must share it so you will understand my reason for being amongst you and why Ylena must remain under your protection.'

She watched them cast alarmed glances to one another, and then the duke nodded. The servant topped up the wine glasses and was then asked to leave.

Pil cleared his throat. 'Should I remain for this?' he asked, uncertain of his place.

'Not if you are horrified by the notion of magic,' Elspyth said cryptically, and began the long story from the moment a young soldier, a General in fact, stepped into a seer's tent one night with his friend, Alyd Donal of Felrawthy.

The duke rose imperiously. 'You expect us to believe that Wyl Thirsk was killed by magic?' he blustered.

'Forgive me, sir,' Elspyth said calmly. 'Perhaps I haven't explained it well. Wyl Thirsk was struck down by a man called Romen Koreldy, who—'

'Yes, yes! Whom Thirsk apparently became — I hear quite well,' the duke retorted, angry and disturbed by this stranger's news.

Elspyth opened her mouth to reply and closed it again. A brittle retort would not aid understanding here.

'Father, please!' Crys said from the fireplace.

'Jeryb . . .' It was Aleda's placating tone. 'I cannot imagine this young woman has trekked from Deakyn to Felrawthy in order to make a jest at your expense.'

The duke muttered something under his breath.

Pil's complexion had paled. 'This is mystifying,' he admitted.

'Yes, it is,' Elspyth replied softly, eyeing each in turn. 'It is, however, the truth.'

Her gaze came to rest on Ylena, who, so far, had made no comment regarding her brother. Now she did. 'My brother is alive?' Everyone could hear the muted shock in her voice.

Elspyth's heart was pounding; she suddenly wondered if it had been a good idea to contradict Wyl's instructions. She nodded slowly.

'And you say your aunt saw this . . . this affliction in him?'

Elspyth nodded again. 'She is a seer. She called it the Quickening,' she said, risking further rebuke from Jeryb. But none was forthcoming.

Ylena looked suddenly thoughtful. 'Do you know, I can remember the night you speak of. It was after the tournament . . . the day following my marriage with Alyd.' Her listeners tensed at the mention of Alyd's name but Ylena's voice was steady. Aleda was proud to see this young woman so in control of her emotions. She alone knew how much her son had loved Ylena, having read his gushing letters many times. He had loved her since they had first met, when he was still a youth and she a child. And Alyd had impressed upon his parents how devoted she was to him. He had plans to set up their estate nearby and had joked that the fine tradition of Thirsks to the south and Donals to the north would continue as Ylena produced more fine sons for Felrawthy. That would not happen now – not through Alyd and Ylena anyway, Aleda thought, sorrow knifing through her again. She returned her mind to Ylena's voice.

'They went into Sideshow Alley. Young men, letting off steam, celebrating. Alyd was drunk.' At this she laughed bitterly. 'Poor fool – I believe he was more intoxicated with life than ale. Wyl brought him back to my chambers and, after settling my brand new husband, we talked late into the night. My brother told me what had occurred in the tent that night. If I recall correctly,' she screwed her face in thought, 'the seer's name was Widow Ilyk.'

Elspyth nodded so that everyone could see their two stories matched.

Ylena continued. 'Wyl was disturbed, very unsettled by what she had said. Neither of us had forgotten the episode with Myrren,' she explained. 'Although I was not present, I heard of it from Gueryn – that's our guardian, the man you mentioned earlier. He told me that Wyl's eyes had changed colour. It had frightened him because it smacked of things magical and sinister, but he forgot about it eventually and frankly so had I until this moment.'

The silence after she had finished was heavy.

Crys, gazing somewhat helplessly towards Ylena, broke it. 'And this Romen Koreldy is now. . . . ?'

'Dead! And dear Wyl with him,' Elspyth answered with feeling. 'A woman, apparently, a hired killer. Goes by the name of Hildyth, although I suspect it's a false one. I have her description.'

'Then detail it and we shall have it circulated,' said Crys, keen to show his determination to help Thirsk's sister. 'All of Felrawthy's loyal should be on alert. We don't know who hired her or if she might strike again.'

'Oh, I think we can safely guess who hired her.' Aleda's tone was acid. Her glance met Ylena's; they both knew who was responsible for killing the man they loved.

Elspyth obliged. 'She is described as not beautiful but an intensely striking woman. Tall with auburn hair and feline eyes apparently.'

'Sounds hard to miss,' Crys commented to no one in particular.

'Koreldy is dead?' Ylena suddenly blurted. 'But he saved my life.'

Elspyth turned sadly towards her and once again took her hands. 'Wyl saved your life, Ylena. He *was* Romen.'

Ylena's eyes filled with tears and no one could blame her. Everyone's heart went out to this courageous woman who was bearing up under so much terror in her young life. 'I can't believe it,' she whispered.

'Brother Jakub said there was something different about Romen this time,' Pil said, eyes shining with awe. 'I noticed it too. If it weren't for the idea of magic, Elspyth, I'd know you were talking truth.'

'I am. You all have to trust me now. Wyl, moving in Romen's body, escaped with me from Cailech's dungeon. It was during our journey through the Razors that he admitted all of this. It was no jest. He spoke like a man beaten.'

The duke looked sharply at Elspyth. 'Wait a minute. What are you talking about, escaping from Cailech? Do you mean the King of the Mountain Kingdom!'

'Yes, my lord. I told you that none of this would be easy to hear. I understand how much of a shock it is. I will explain everything, but it means nothing now that Wyl is dead. Romen is no more.'

'Then we have an axe to grind with both King Celimus and now this Hildyth,' Ylena said angrily. No one in that room denied her words.

Aleda took a breath. 'I think we should eat now, and we'll hear more of what Elspyth has to tell us. Come, Ylena, dear. You look pale, child.'

As the two women left the room, Crys shook his head. 'She is Alyd's widow,' he said, hoping his interest in Ylena did not show. 'We shall look after her now, Elspyth,' he reassured. 'What about you?'

She sighed. 'Oh, I think now that I've fulfilled my promise to Wyl to see his sister to safety, I shall travel home.'

'To Yentro?' he qualified.

She nodded. No one needed to know her intentions from there on. Too many would try and talk her out of it. As it was, she had kept much of the full story to herself. There was little point in relating much more of the strange events for the duke was already sceptical. Crys might be persuaded, but he was anxious to avenge his brother. He would no doubt soon urge his father to ride on Pearlis with their men.

'My lord,' she said, addressing the duke.

The gaze levelled at her was direct and bright. 'Yes?'

'Wyl sent this.' She hesitated momentarily before handing the duke the crushed letter she had dug from her pocket.

He took it. Both she and Crys waited in suspense while he broke the seal and held the parchment to the candle-light to read it more easily.

'Father?' Crys ventured.

The duke looked contemplative. 'He confirms the death of Alyd but speaks of none of this magic. He signs off as Thirsk and asks that we don't rush into revenge. He wants us to hold until he comes. But he's dead – or this Romen fellow is. You told us yourself.' The duke turned on Elspyth.

'But I heard that news from strangers. We can't be absolutely sure it is reliable information. I would urge you to wait.'

'For what?' he asked, his voice struggling against his own emotion. 'My son has been murdered. Do not ask me to stand by and not take action.'

Elspyth held up her hands in a warding motion against his anger. It was a gesture loaded with sorrow to echo his own grief. 'I have passed on Wyl's caution, my lord. It is not my place to suggest anything further.'

He grunted. Crys noted her glance of irritation with a shrug of apology. But none was required. Elspyth, given the chance, would suggest Felrawthy storm Pearlis this very night, if it were possible. She had good reason to hate Celimus herself and could think of nothing better than riding alongside this powerful duke and the loyal men he could muster at a single request to overthrow a hated sovereign. She did not begrudge Jeryb his anger.

Crys did, however. Rage helped nothing, particularly levelled against this plucky woman who had suffered plenty. That said, he knew how deeply the news of Alyd's death had cut his father. 'Mother is waiting,' he said diplomatically.

Elspyth accepted his gracious release and left the duke to brood alone on the letter from a dead man.

22

THE FAMILY AND THEIR guests shared a meal during which Elspyth recounted her story of incarceration in and then escape from Cailech's fortress. The tale was accompanied by much muttering and shaking of his head by the duke. Only Ylena's eyes shone – Elspyth guessed this was with pride for Gueryn's steadfastness and ultimate sacrifice, but especially for Wyl. She did not enlighten them about her feelings towards Lothryn; that was her secret and of no consequence to anyone in the room.

The duchess had suggested the food be kept simple that night. No one's appetite was keen after news of Alyd's death, or learning that Wyl had lived but then died in Romen's body. Duke Jeryb would not be drawn on his plans, not even by his patient wife. Inevitably a bleakness settled once again across the household, sucking Elspyth into its maw as well, driving the conversation towards the inconsequential and ultimately to quiet.

It was no wonder then that when the sound of horses' hooves echoed through the still night the men leapt to their feet. Jeryb silenced the alarmed women and motioned for Crys to find out from the duty guards who now had arrived at Tenterdyn. The Donal men drew their swords — just in case — and Aleda was heard to mutter to her husband that they should have taken the precaution of raising more men at arms when Ylena first arrived.

They waited, the twins watching through the window as their elder brother crossed the main courtyard with long strides. His path was lit by torches. Earlier the duchess had considered it a shame that Tenterdyn's gates should be locked for the first time in the family's history, but now she thanked Shar's wisdom for suggesting to her husband that he do just that.

'He's coming back,' one of the boys said over his shoulder. It seemed that everyone held their breath.

Crys finally re-entered the chamber, a blast of cool air whirling about him. He appeared startled. His attention was riveted on Elspyth. 'You're not going to believe this, but I think the Hildyth you spoke of is at the gate literally begging to be admitted.'

Elspyth could see he was not making a jest.

Crys qualified his claim. 'Shoulder-length golden-brown hair. Tall. Dressed in mannish style. Eyes unmistakably like a cat. It's her all right.'

Elspyth shuddered. She was not the only one to do so. Ylena fairly blazed with a still, silent anger.

'Is she alone?' the duke demanded.

'No, sir,' his son replied. 'She is accompanied by a big man, just short of a giant he looks. He goes by the name of Aremys Farrow.'

'And their reason for coming here?' Aleda asked, her thoughts fleeing to the young woman under threat.

'She says she wants to see Ylena.'

'Of course she does!' Elspyth said, heart pounding. 'She'll have orders to kill her too! Are we safe? Are there enough guards?'

'No one can enter Tenterdyn, child, without my permission. We are safe and well guarded,' the duke replied with calm. 'My love,' he said, looking towards his wife, 'I did take the precaution you spoke of. We have twenty men riding towards us now.'

Aleda felt no little relief. 'What shall we do until then?'

'I shall see her,' Ylena said calmly.

Pil's expression was a mask of terror. 'Sir, I beg you,' he whispered to the duke.

Jeryb came to his rescue in a deep and very firm tone. 'No, Ylena, you will do no such thing. You came here seeking my protection and I am compelled to provide it, not only because of who you married, but because of whose daughter you are. You will do as I say. We need cool heads now. I shall speak with these people myself,' the duke assured her.

'Come, boys,' he said and his three sons fell into step with the man they worshipped, particularly on occasions such as this when he commanded such respect.

'Be careful, husband,' the duchess called after him but there was no response.

The women waited, fidgeting at the window. Pil stood with them and they watched the four remaining men of Felrawthy cross the courtyard with purpose. Aleda was relieved to see her husband lead the boys up into the small tower of the gatehouse.

'Ah, good. He is being careful.'

'Your husband would not risk any of them.' Pil knew

he was reassuring himself; he felt more disturbed than anyone at this turn of events.

There was a protracted wait before they saw the four emerge again from the tower. The duke must have given an order, for the two younger lads hurried to lift the heavy timbers that barred the gate.

'What is he doing?' Elspyth cried.

'Give me a sword!' Ylena cried in her terror. She looked around for a weapon and grabbed a carving knife from the table. She stepped towards the door and hid behind it.

'Shar preserve us!' Pil swore, as they watched the heavy gates being swung back.

'Wait,' Aleda cautioned, fighting back her own fears. 'Jeryb must have learned something. He would not permit them otherwise.'

Twilight had given way to full nightfall and they watched by torchlight as a giant of a man strode into the courtyard. In his wake walked another: man or woman they could not tell right now, but this person was smaller, leaner. Nevertheless the stride was purposeful. This must be the cat-eyed woman of whom Crys spoke. Their horses walked behind and Aleda watched, stunned, as the second figure clasped her husband's hand.

However, she calmed her companions with a look that implied they must trust Jeryb. She nodded encouragingly to Elspyth behind her, who was clearly fretting, but Ylena had disappeared in terror behind the door, unable to see Jeryb's cordiality toward the strangers. They heard voices talking over each other as new guests entered the house. The duchess looked towards the door again at the sound of her husband's tread.

'Aleda,' he said, entering and shaking his head. 'I have the most curious news.'

He could share nothing further as a tall, rather striking woman stepped into the chamber and took off her hat. Auburn hair tumbled to her shoulders.

'Elspyth!' Wyl cried and strode towards his shocked, confused friend. 'It's me!' he laughed.

From behind the door Ylena leaped towards the woman, one intention on her mind: to kill the person who had murdered Koreldy and thereby her brother Wyl also. All she saw in her rage was the wide mouth and feline eyes sparkling.

'Ylena, no!' Elspyth screamed and then there was a riot of movement. Aremys launched himself towards Wyl and even the duke put his arm out to take the blow. All to no avail. Ylena was slight but fast and she had been raised in a warrior family. Although her life at Stoneheart under Magnus's rule had been one of pleasure and indulgence, she had never forgotten the lessons Wyl had taught her as children together in Argorn. She saw them all moving towards her, avoided their reaching arms and struck.

'Murderer!' she shrieked and threw herself forwards with the full force her body could inflict, punching the knife into the neck of the smiling assassin.

'Oh, my darling sister, what have you done?' the woman cried, clutching at her neck from which blood was spraying. Ylena heard the screams and cries of dismay around her but felt only triumph as she looked into the shocked eyes of the dying woman.

Elspyth caught the body as it fell and was instantly drenched in blood; in fact the whole room seemed splattered with it. Crys and Daryn grabbed Ylena's arms but she had tossed the knife aside and crumpled to the ground, her breath coming in deep gasps. She was determined to watch the light die in the woman's hated brown eyes.

Except it did not.

With horror, Elspyth, holding Faryl's head on her lap, saw the eyes flash to an ill-matched sky grey and deep greenish brown. Beautiful hues individually; shocking as a pair. And then she felt the woman's body stiffen in its final death throes, her spine arching impossibly. She guessed what was happening, could almost feel it herself with her sensitivity for magic. She wanted to scream.

Ylena did it for her. Huge, gut-wrenching shrieks escaped Alyd of Felrawthy's wife and her body twisted on the floor. The spirit of her brother fought the transference with all he had, somehow hoping to save his beloved sister — but it was not enough. Myrren's gift was too powerful.

Suddenly it was Wyl giving voice to Ylena's deranged screams as he bellowed his rage at taking the life of his own sister. Crys and Daryn held on to the young woman. Confusion reigned. Jeryb was yelling orders whilst Aleda stared in horror at the brutal death scene, rivulets of Faryl's blood coating her cheeks. Aremys had knelt in disbelief by his friend's body.

'Let her go!' Elspyth shouted above the din. Crys looked even more confused at this order.

'Leave her! It's not Ylena any more!' she screamed, tears streaming down her bloodstained face. 'It's Wyl!'

The brothers stood back, thunderstruck by her words.

Wyl writhed in agony, not from physical pain but from the greatest anguish he would ever feel. He had killed his sister, had taken the life of the very person he had strived so hard to protect. Swirling into her anger which only barely covered her intense fear, he glimpsed Ylena's confusion, tasted her hollow triumph.

He threw his head back and screamed again. The sound chilled everyone to their very core. Wyl pushed away Elspyth's outstretched hands and fled the house.

Once through the gates, he moved blindly – a demented female figure in a blood-spattered silk robe and soft slippers on her feet. Wyl hurled himself up a hill, seeking oblivion in the inky darkness, consumed by hatred and grief. His own wrath mixed with the well of despair Ylena had left for him. He cursed and raged for what seemed an endless time, until he realised his throat was raw. The sobs had ceased; all he could hear now was the haunting call of an owl and the furtive scratching of a mole.

His new body trembled. Wyl didn't know if it was from shock or the cold night. He did not care. Nothing mattered any more. The last of the Thirsks had lost the fight. He wanted to die too, but it would have to be by his own hand. He could not risk another's life.

'I'm sorry,' a voice said gently through the blackness. There was not even the faintest of moonlight this night. Heavy clouds scudded darkly across the heavens obliterating even the stars' illumination. But the voice was known to him; the voice of a friend. 'I just wasn't quick enough,' Aremys added, his words laden with regret. 'I failed you and my promise.'

Apart from the involuntary trembling, Wyl could not move . . . did not want to move ever again. 'She was so bright. Like one of Shar's own stars. She deserved none of this,' he croaked in his new, all-too-achingly familiar voice.

'The innocent never do, Wyl. Yet they always seem to suffer.'

'What was it?'

Aremys knew what he referred to. 'A carving knife, for pity's sake.'

'A lucky thrust,' he said ruefully.

'But just as deadly as Faryl's stiletto.'

There was a bitter laugh as Wyl accepted this notion. 'What possessed her?' he asked, voicing his private thoughts aloud. He required no answer but Aremys still replied.

'Fear that Celimus's assassin had come to kill her, just as she killed Romen.'

'I shouldn't have come. You were right – I should have left Ylena to you, while I went on to find Myrren's mother. I should never have declared myself. How did they know of Faryl?'

'Your friend, Elspyth – she heard of Romen's death on her travels and that a woman of Faryl's description was thought to be the killer. She pieced events together and then told the Donal family and Ylena. She blames herself for not considering Myrren's gift might extend beyond the one transference.'

Again the harsh laugh. Wyl realised he had not sufficiently impressed upon Elspyth the need for secrecy. 'It's no one else's fault,' Wyl said softly. 'The errors are all mine. I was reckless. I should have let you go in first, tell everyone what had occurred . . . prepare them.'

'For whatever it's worth, Wyl, I'm not sure anyone would have believed it.'

'Elspyth would have. Ylena might have . . . given time.'

Wyl heard the big man shift, made out a bulky shadow near a small clump of slender trees.

'You cannot undo what is done,' Aremys offered, his voice as gentle as he could make it. He waited for an angry rebuke.

It came. 'My sister is dead, Aremys!' Wyl yelled. 'And yet she lives. All of my family . . . dead. Alyd, Gueryn, Lothryn . . . even Koreldy – someone I liked – all dead. All because of me.'

The big man grabbed Wyl and pulled him to his feet. He had not counted on Ylena's body being so light and she all but flew up into his arms. He set Wyl down again, knowing he was lucky he could not see the anger he was sure was blazing in her eyes.

Still he pursued it. 'There is nothing you can change about what is done. *Nothing!* But you can track down this manwitch fellow and learn more about his daughter's gift. Perhaps it can be reversed – perhaps it can be stopped?'

'Will it ever stop?' Wyl asked pleadingly in his sister's voice.

'I don't know, my friend. But I make you this promise here and now: I will help you in any way I can. You must help yourself, though. None of us understands this magic in you. The only way forward is to discover its secrets. And the manwitch is the only lead you have right now. Go to him.'

'Where do I look?'

'Find the mother, as you had planned. Start there.'

They heard heavy footsteps and looked around to see the duke, breathing hard from the exertion of climbing the hill. A tiny lantern swung at his side.

'Are you all right?' he wheezed, knowing it was an absurd question under the circumstances. He raked a hand through his silvered hair. 'I am sorry,' he said. 'We're all worried about you. The shock of all that has happened, including this foul magic upon you, is taking its toll. What's more, my good wife has taken charge of proceedings and she can be quite terrifying in full flight. This was my chance to escape.'

Wyl stepped forward and took the old man's hand in the Legion's clasp. 'This is the hardest one, sir. Giving up my own body was a hundred times easier than taking this one.'

'I am sorry, son. I . . . I really am at a loss for words. I must accept this tale because I trust that this is really you, but I understand none of it.'

Wyl shook his head. 'I've had more time to get used to the curse.'

The duke sat heavily on a small mound. 'Forgive me, this has been a trying couple of days.'

'It is I who should seek your forgiveness,' Wyl said, seating himself next to the duke. 'I know your whole family is suffering, sir. Alyd was the best. His loss is a constant pain in my heart.'

The old man nodded in the dark. 'We will grieve later, Wyl, for your sister and for my son. The King is my concern right now. May we speak freely?'

Wyl nodded. 'Aremys is as much a part of this as I, sir.'

Aremys felt relieved to hear it and joined them, seating himself uncomfortably atop the heather.

'Tell me everything,' the duke commanded, 'from the beginning.'

Later, seated at the scrubbed dining table, Wyl faced the rest of the family and their guests. Still shocked, their faces were devoid of expression. Elspyth was trembling. She would not permit Wyl to touch her but her hands instinctively flew to her mouth when she saw him, her eyes betraying all the emotion of these days past and the recognition that Wyl had survived once again. She began to weep and the sound quickly turned to heartfelt sobs, her small frame lurching with each one.

There was a thick silence in the room as everyone felt her grief. Crys would have liked to put his arms around her, but it was Wyl who enclosed Elspyth in an embrace, holding her tight and kissing her hair.

'It's all right, Elspyth,' he said soothingly in Ylena's voice. 'I'll explain everything.'

Aremys bowed in awkward silence to the duchess; she smiled just as awkwardly back. It was the most either could do without formal introduction. He moved to stand beside Pil. 'I'm Aremys,' he whispered for want of anything better to say into the uncomfortable atmosphere.

'Pil,' came the reply. 'I travelled with . . .' He hesitated, not sure if he could still call her Ylena.

'With the sister?'

Pil nodded, too distressed to say any more.

'I'll brew some tea,' Aleda said. 'It's good for shock,' but only got as far as the hearth.

Elspyth finally pulled away to look upon the woman holding her. 'Is it really you? It happened again?' she asked, wanting to cry more.

He nodded. 'Faryl, or Hildyth as you seem to know her, killed Romen as instructed. Little did she know he was cursed.'

'I saw it with my own eyes and yet I don't want to

believe it. Forgive me, but I must insist you prove who you are,' Elspyth said, suddenly cautious.

'He already has, my girl,' the duke said. 'Only a Thirsk would know what he told me at the gatehouse and then on the hill.' He scratched his head. 'I think what we all need is not tea but a sherlac, my dear,' he said to his wife. 'This is all very confusing and too wild for my old mind.'

The duchess smiled indulgently at the man she loved. She felt she could never be happy again, but in looking at him she decided that perhaps love alone would get her through this nightmare of death, deception and magic.

Wyl looked at Elspyth. 'No, you're quite right. What can I tell that only Wyl Thirsk could know?'

She thought a moment. 'When we escaped from the mountains . . .' She had meant to go on but a smile crossed Ylena's face and the soft voice took over.

'. . . we had no money. Or so I thought,' Wyl continued 'But you had a purse which you kept beneath your skirts. We stayed at the Penny Whistle in Deakyn and you bought me a horse with all that was left of your money. I left you to somehow make your way to Rittylworth, your heart bursting with grief for a good man, a brave man, we had to leave behind. I am so, so sorry.'

Her smile of elation dissolved to tears. 'Oh, Wyl – so much to tell.'

Aleda decided it was time to take hold of the emotionally charged situation and spoke to the woman who, a short time before, had been her son's widow, but now it seemed was someone else. 'You are most welcome again . . . er, Wyl Thirsk. I hardly understand any of this. It is too horrific to contemplate, but . . .'

Wyl bowed formally to the duchess, a woman he had

admired since childhood. 'I remember my father telling me how generous you were to my mother when they were first married, my lady. He never forgot how you helped her choose a gown for a summer ball when she was feeling especially young and daunted having married the man our King called his closest friend. She knew how the Queen laughed at her but you reminded her that she was the reason why Fergys Thirsk never lost a battle. You told her, my lady, that he could not bear the thought of not coming home to the most beautiful and cherished woman in the world.'

Wyl cleared his throat of the sorrow in his voice. 'I wish we could have met in less confusing circumstances, my lady, so I could thank you for your kindness.'

Now it was Aleda's turn to feel betrayed by her eyes. She returned a gracious curtsy. 'I would like to have met you as yourself, Wyl Thirsk. Now, I think I need to lie down a time, to think quietly and grasp that this is possible.' She thought she may weep openly at her next thought, but voiced it anyway. 'Our son Alyd worshipped you.'

'He was the best friend anyone could ever have, my lady. I am so much less for losing him,' Wyl replied, softly. 'I shall avenge his death,' he added even more softly, but the coldness in his voice left no one in any doubt.

23

BEFORE TAKING TO HER own bed, Aleda insisted on making her guests comfortable. Wyl's sister's body climbed back into the bed she had left just hours earlier, but it was Wyl not Ylena who agreed to swallow the proffered cup of warmed, sweetened milk.

'What have you put in this?'

'Something to help you sleep,' Aleda said kindly, fluffing the coverlet about him.

It felt similar to how his own mother used to tuck him in at night. 'I wish I could wake up and discover it's all been a nightmare and everything is as it used to be,' he admitted.

She nodded. 'So do I.'

He knew she spoke of her adored son. Wyl took her hand. 'I am sorry I could not save him.'

Aleda's eyes watered but she did not give into the sorrow — not yet. 'He worshipped both you and Ylena. I know his years at Stoneheart were happy because of the Thirsks and I thank you for that. Listen to me, Wyl,' — he noticed she did not hesitate to call him by his real name and he loved her for it — 'we cannot bring them back with our tears, but we can make ourselves worthy of them by avenging their innocent deaths. You may blame this Myrren woman for your despair, but there is one true villain here.' She jabbed her finger in the air.

'Celimus,' he breathed drowsily, beginning to feel the effects of Aleda's drug.

'Let us never forget it,' she said.

'I will kill him, my lady.' His words in Ylena's voice were as cold as the snow that fell on the moors in winter.

'And may you feel the weight of my hand behind the blade you wield — and Alyd's, and Ylena's, and all those other people you have spoken of . . . even that woman, Faryl.'

It was Wyl's turn to feel his eyes brim. Aleda was well aware it was for Ylena Thirsk that these tears welled.

'She was a brave young woman, son. I am not sure she would ever have come back to being the sweet innocent you remember. She had been through so much and that had drawn out a strength in her that might have surprised you. Despite her fear she showed great courage in escaping Rittylworth and getting herself here on foot. She was every bit a Thirsk and a sister to be proud of. I shall mourn her as the daughter I always wanted. Even in the short time we knew each other, we shared enough to form a special bond.'

Wyl did not want to cry. He looked away. 'Do you believe in life after death, my lady?'

She smiled bravely. 'I do. And they are together now, Wyl, in Shar's kingdom. And we shall continue the fight on their behalf.'

'Thank you for all your kindness,' he said, slipping

away towards sleep. 'What about Faryl's body?' he murmured.

'We will take care of it,' she assured. 'Dream peacefully, Wyl Thirsk,' she added and kissed him softly.

Wyl's dreams were anything but peaceful.

He saw a barn. Its doors were closed. From behind them came the fearful noise of a man screaming. His demented shrieks sounded as though they were filled with gut-wrenching pain.

Then the thought *Help me* came crashing into Wyl's mind.

Wyl did not know how to cast a message back. He tried, begging the man to tell him who he was, where he was. But nothing seemed to get through. The terrible wail continued and the more Wyl tried to escape it, the louder it became until it filled every recess of his head, every ounce of his being.

He ran – or thought he did – but it followed. When he stopped and tried to face it, he found he had run nowhere but was still looking at the closed barn. He realised now that dark magic lay behind those barred doors.

A new voice urged at him. It was mellow, kind, and seemed to be coming from far away. *Turn towards me, son.*

I can't, Wyl thought, straining against the first man's screams in his mind.

Be strong. Turn away from it and look towards me.

It took all of his will and courage, but as soon as he tore his eyes away from the barn doors the shrieking ceased.

He felt his body go limp with relief, realised he was breathing hard. *Who are you?*

I am he whom you seek, the voice said, gently.

Myrren's father?

Yes.

Where are you?

Come to me.

How? I don't know where you are.

You will find me. There was a pause. He heard the man mutter something unintelligible, then: *I am where no one else dares go.*

Why can't you just tell me?

Trust the dog, he said, his voice fading.

Come back! Wyl cried but the speaker had gone. Wyl had wanted to ask who had been screaming but it was too late. He had not even asked Myrren's father for his name.

His dreams continued. A new vision swirled before him. He saw Valentyna this time. She was approaching him and his heart leapt. She looked as exquisite as ever in a blood-red gown and yet her expression was haunted. He tried to smile, wanted to reach out his hands towards her, but he could not.

Forgive me, she whispered and then he screamed.

Wyl woke with a start, his mind blank. He could not remember what had frightened him. His nightgown was damp and his eyelids were sticky. He pulled his legs from under the sheets and felt the touch of the rug beneath his feet – his shapely feet. The night's events came back. He was Ylena. He felt a wave of dizziness and disappointment that the truth had not been a nightmare he could escape from. He was living the nightmare.

Shivering, he moved unsteadily towards the basin of water on the dresser and splashed his face, taking care to gently rub his eyes. The feel of Ylena's face beneath his fingertips was so different to Faryl's. Her cheekbones were rounder, her forehead narrower and her hair was long and golden. Wyl moved a nearby burning candle to the mirror then stared at the illuminated reflection. He noticed how similar her mouth was to his own. He could not understand how he had missed this previously. It reassured him.

'I failed you,' he whispered. 'Forgive me.' The echo of the words from the dream made him now recall it. Who had been seeking absolution in that vision? He could not recall now. He thought it might have been a woman . . . perhaps Ylena.

The face looking back at him was sad but beautiful despite the sorrow in it. She looked too thin, so wan. Much of what had made Ylena such a sparkling person, jubilant with the joy of life, had been buried. What remained was barely a shade of the young vibrant woman he had known.

He grasped within for anything of the Ylena he had so loved. It took some time and patience but he finally coaxed her essence free and felt it fill him with its warmth.

'I knew you couldn't leave me completely,' he said to his reflection as memories came roaring back. Childhood memories and a great joy in life. Loving him, Magnus and Gueryn . . . and then later Alyd. Wyl cherished the moment of feeling her love for him, then locked away the swirling thoughts of Alyd. Those were private and belonged to Ylena alone.

Darker images of death and blood, burning and crucifixion coalesced now. He felt savaged by their intensity and gripped the dresser in anger at what his sister had witnessed and endured. Rittylworth was his final punishment, for he had brought destruction to the gentle community.

'I shall kill the King for you alone, beloved,' he whispered to what was left of Ylena. 'Be at peace now.'

He felt stronger for saying his threat aloud. Tying his now grubby robe back around himself, feeling awkward in Ylena's body, he let himself out of the bedroom and crept down the stone stairway.

In the scullery he found a familiar figure hunched over a steaming mug of strong dark tea.

'Can't sleep?' he said, startling Aremys.

The big man looked up. 'No, no chance of that. Want some?' he asked, eyeing the new Wyl carefully.

'I like honey in it,' Wyl replied and, from somewhere, found a thin smile as he sat.

The mercenary nodded, glad for the activity. He moved behind Wyl's new slim back to pour another mug.

'Am I that hard to look upon, Aremys?'

'No,' his friend replied, not turning from his task, 'I just liked Faryl. I have to get used to you as your sister.' Now he did glance around and a look of sympathy passed between them.

'How are the others taking it?'

Aremys shrugged. 'The duchess is extraordinary. I gather they've only today learned about their son's demise and here she is fretting over you. The duke is angry, confused. I don't know about the lads.'

'They do believe me though?'

'Oh, no doubt,' Aremys assured, handing Wyl a mug. 'It takes some getting used to, Wyl.'

'As if I didn't know it,' he shot back.

'I mean, understand their position as they come to

terms with it. Would you have believed this tale if it wasn't happening to you?'

Wyl did not answer immediately. Then he rested his chin in the cup of his hand and shook his head slowly. 'No,' he answered, resigned. 'So how will they?'

'Well, your friend Elspyth believes, and the Mountain man, Lothryn, you said did. Fynch, the seer,' he was holding fingers up in the air as he listed them. 'And you convinced me and I'm a cynic, Wyl. All of us trust you.'

'Why did you believe me?' Wyl persisted.

'Because of the knives – no one throws like Koreldy to my knowledge – and your strange behaviour towards the King. There were other things too . . .' He shrugged and then grinned. 'The mere fact that you could resist me confirmed you were a man.' Wyl guffawed. As always Aremys's timing for jest was perfect. 'So you've just got to trust that they'll believe you. You've already told them too many things that no one else but Wyl Thirsk could know.'

'True,' Wyl said, blowing on his tea to cool it.

'I'm sorry it had to be her, Wyl,' the big man finally found the courage to say.

'Me too,' and a glance to his friend said that he did not wish to talk about it any more.

They brooded over their drinks in a companionable silence both had learned to trust. The soft crackle and spit of the fire which Aremys had rekindled from the embers felt safe and comforting. Wyl warmed Ylena's elegant fingers around the hot mug, fighting the revulsion he felt at seeing them.

'What now?' Aremys finally said.

'Like you said, I must find Myrren's father.'

Aremys sipped and nodded. 'I've been thinking . . .'

'Dangerous,' Wyl commented and returned the relieved grin that played around his friend's mouth. Perhaps they would survive this.

'You cannot travel alone.'

'Oh no, you don't want to sleep with Ylena as well!' he said in mock horror.

The bear-like man's amusement rumbled deep in his throat. It was reassuring to hear mirth after so much ugliness. 'Well, I wouldn't say no, of course, if you're offering . . .' He caught Wyl's glare on Ylena's lovely face. 'I think you need a companion, is what I meant.'

'You don't think I can take care of myself in this guise?'

'I know you can, but you will still be a target. If I were to travel with you, it would prevent the interest that might be levelled at a young noblewoman abroad alone.'

Wyl considered it. Aremys was right, and even though he had already made plans to begin his search alone he might well be vulnerable as Ylena. And in truth, he could use the quiet company of the big man.

'I agree,' he finally replied.

Aremys looked up in surprise from his tea. 'What, not even going to fight me on it? Throw some knives at me or something?'

'No. You're definitely right. I don't have time for the obstacle of unhealthy interest some might take.'

'Well, that's that then,' Aremys growled, relieved. 'Where are we going?'

'I had a dream last night.'

'Oh?' his friend said, lifting an eyebrow.

'A vision perhaps.' Wyl sighed and pulled at his ear. Aremys had seen this identical, almost nervous habit when he was Faryl and assumed he may well have displayed the same habit as Koreldy since it was probably Wyl Thirsk's trait. That felt reassuring for some reason.

'There's been too much talk of magic, I know, but this was real . . . It felt that way, at least.'

'Tell me,' Aremys said.

'A voice – the manwitch – told me to go where no one else dares go.'

'Well, that's certainly specific. We'll find him easily then.'

Wyl gave him a gentle glare. 'It's what I was told.'

'All right, where could that be?'

'Across the ocean?' Wyl hazarded.

'Which one?'

Wyl shrugged. 'All right, the Razors. Most wouldn't think to be heading into the mountains, especially not in this climate with war brewing.'

'And it was definitely a man's voice?'

Wyl nodded. 'His accent didn't suggest he was a northerner, if that's what you're getting around to. He sounded Morgravian if anything – like I used to. A southerner.'

'For a Morgravian, Briavel would be somewhere not to trespass.'

'Except there's been trade between the realms for many years now.' Wyl shook his head. 'No, I don't think it's Briavel.'

Aremys stood and stretched. 'Well, there's always the Wild.'

'The Wild? To the east of Briavel, you mean? There's nothing there, is there?'

'How do you know? None of us have visited.'

'But isn't it supposed to have some curse on it?' Wyl added. 'They say you can't return from it.'

Aremys nodded slyly. 'They say it's enchanted. Sounds exactly like the sort of place cursed people would go.'

'That's not funny,' Wyl bristled.

'It wasn't meant to be,' his companion said evenly. 'Sounds like a neat match to me though – an enchanted place where a manwitch might live.'

Wyl closed his eyes and breathed deeply, trying to find some sense of ease. 'Well, I have no better idea.'

'Then we'll go take a look.'

'How do we get there?'

'You're not going anywhere without me,' Elspyth said from the doorway. She shrugged at them. 'I couldn't sleep. I heard voices.' Then she hesitated, looking at Wyl, emotions marching across her face unconcealed.

Wyl walked around the scrubbed table and hugged his good friend. She wept a little but he had finished with tears; his eyes remained dry.

'Don't cry, Elspyth. We do them no good with tears.'

'I know,' she said. 'This is all my fault though. I hate myself. I should have stayed quiet, should have kept your secret—'

He hushed her mouth with his soft female hand. 'Don't.'

'It's just so much sadness rolling into one huge sorrow,' she admitted.

He hugged her hard again, wanted her to accept his forgiveness. 'Did anyone bother to introduce you to my friend Aremys, by the way? He knows everything.'

'I'm sorry, Aremys, we met under difficult circum-stances,' she said, holding out her hand and remembering it covered with blood only hours earlier.

The big man took her small hand in his and squeezed

gently. 'I understand from Wyl how lucky he is to have you for a friend,' he said, pleasing her with his gentle words, 'even though you are a blabbermouth.' A look of hurt crossed Elspyth's face.

'Take no notice,' Wyl assured. 'Aremys loves to tease.'

She narrowed her eyes towards the big man, saw the levity in his expression and accepted the jest. 'May I have some of that?' she said, nodding towards his tea.

'Surely,' Aremys said, smiling back to reassure her that he had not meant to hurt. He was glad to busy himself once again.

'So where are you going now?' Elspyth asked the angelic-looking woman before her, an accusing tone in her voice.

'I have to find Myrren's real father, Elspyth, before I can tackle anything. I have to know more about this magic within me.'

'I understand,' she replied tightly.

'It does not change the oath I swore to you. I will return to the Razors and find him.'

'He spoke to me, Wyl,' she said, a tremor in her voice from remembering his anguish. 'There was pain and darkness around him. He was frightened. There was someone else too but I couldn't see him – or perhaps her.' She shrugged. 'There was magic somewhere, I'm sure of it.'

'What did he say?' Elspyth's words had jogged Wyl's own memory of the dark dream he had experienced during the night.

'He called to me,' she said, wistfully.

'That's all?'

She frowned in thought. 'No. There was more. He said

something like: *Tell Romen I will wait*. And then he added something strange, cryptic – I can't fathom it.'

'Go on,' Wyl urged.

'He said to tell you that he is no longer as you would expect.' She watched Ylena's face frown, which did nothing to detract from her prettiness.

'That's it?' Wyl said.

'Mmm,' she nodded, smiling fleetingly in thanks to Aremys who set the tea down before her. 'What could that mean?'

Wyl stood gracefully and began to pace. If the two others in the room had known Fergys Thirsk, they would have realised Wyl had caught his father's habit of movement when in thought. 'I have no idea, but strangely I too dreamed tonight . . . well, I think I did. You've just reminded me of it. I don't know who spoke to me but whoever it was seemed to be in terrible pain, screaming for deliverance from it. A man.'

'He's torturing him,' she said bleakly.

They both knew the torturer she referred to.

'If he's trying to reach us, then at least we know he's alive,' Wyl reassured.

Aremys joined them at the table. 'Is this the Lothryn you have spoken of?'

They both nodded.

'I have never given up on the hope that Cailech would keep him alive,' Wyl said.

'But you also believed torture would not be enough for Cailech – not his style, you said,' Elspyth countered.

'That's true. The pain could be something else, of course.'

'Like what?' Aremys queried.

'Magic,' Elspyth murmured.

Wyl shot a glance towards her; he had not wanted to say it himself.

'Why not?' she said, angry now as she allowed the thought to take shape. 'Cailech has that evil Rashlyn hovering around him. Isn't he a practitioner of magic? Just looking at his wild appearance and mad eyes made me go cold.'

'Amongst other nasty things, yes,' Wyl admitted. He drained his mug. 'I don't want you rushing off into the Razors on your own, Elspyth. I know it's crossed your mind,' he added.

She blushed. 'I cannot sit by and do nothing.'

'Cailech will kill you. No parley, no niceties at all. Trust me on this.'

'And you would know?'

Wyl nodded, wondering at the tension between them. It had felt different when he was Koreldy, more comfortable. Elspyth would probably have felt less awkward if he had changed again into a man rather than this fragile beauty who was his sister. 'Yes, I do. Cailech is ruthless. He will have you killed on sight.'

'So what makes you think you can get through his defences, Wyl Thirsk?'

'Because I am no longer Romen Koreldy, that's why. How intimidating do I look, Elspyth, with my long golden tresses, my silk gown and soft hands?'

Understanding dawned on her face and acceptance that she really had to stop seeing the woman and appreciate the man's struggle inside. 'Of course. He will not know you at all.'

'It's our only weapon. Be patient . . . trust Lothryn to hang on.'

Aleda swept into the kitchen. 'I heard voices,' she said matter-of-factly. 'No matter the hour, let's get some food going. How are you, my dear?' she added, looking in her kind way at Wyl.

'Stronger, thank you,' he admitted and she smiled back at him.

'That's the Thirsk in you, child. I told Jeryb you'd find your grit before morning.'

Wyl stood alone with the duke. Ylena's femininity had been diluted with riding trews and her hair pulled back sternly into a single plait. Try though he might, he could not make her feel as masculine as Faryl. It was impossible to hide her ethereal beauty nor make her movements any less elegant. It pained him on a number of levels but he would just have to get used to being Ylena.

Aleda had given Wyl a purse – it was a small fortune. 'Buy yourself some clothes and provisions. You must keep up the noble guise,' she had said. 'Forgive us all that has happened, Wyl. I feel somehow responsible.'

'Don't,' he had assured, wanting to refuse the money. He knew he could visit any one of many hides he remembered from Faryl's memories. However, he realised Aleda was trying to help in the only practical way she could right now and so he had accepted her gift with grace.

'You have been a rock of strength, Aleda,' he had said as he hugged her goodbye. 'Thank you for believing in me amongst all this nonsensical magic.'

'You are living proof of it, son. I shall struggle to make sense of it in weeks to come, I am sure. In the meantime, I trust you now to keep your promise and help us take revenge for Alyd and Ylena.' These were her final words before she left him with her husband. No tears; Aleda was the bedrock of the family and she would not succumb to emotion when there was a fight to be fought.

'Crys will see her safely to the border,' the duke said now, nodding towards Elspyth who sat talking with Pil.

'I know she will be safe once she crosses into Briavel,' Wyl replied.

Crys strolled up. 'Are you sure you don't want me to take Elspyth all the way to Werryl?' he offered.

Wyl shook his head. 'No. Too many spies, Crys. Your family cannot risk being linked to Briavel openly. Just see her safely to the border. The letter I've given her will take care of the rest.'

Crys nodded. 'Shar keep you safe.'

'Perhaps we need a password . . . er, just in case the curse happens again,' Jeryb suggested.

Wyl held the duke's gaze. He was right of course. 'What would suit you, sir?'

The tall man looked towards the sky in thought. 'Carving knife – innocuous enough and I am sure none of us could forget that.'

'I know *I* won't, sir,' Wyl said, eyes darkening at the memory.

The old man shook his head. 'After all these years of fighting . . . now Felrawthy conspires with the enemy.' His voice was thick.

'Briavel is not the enemy, my lord,' Wyl reassured. 'Our own King is the enemy. Valentyna and Briavel are our only allies.'

'Fergys Thirsk would turn in his tomb,' the duke said, disgusted.

'No, sir, he would not. My father would agree with our strategy.'

'Are you quite sure of that?'

'As sure as I stand here.' They both smiled wryly at the comment. 'Everyone has agreed on the story then. Ylena was not here, and although Faryl visited she left immediately. It keeps Tenterdyn free of suspicion. In the meantime, you must not give Celimus any hint that you are no longer loyal to him. I know you are expecting your mustered men soon, and no doubt others from the border, but make an excuse if questions are asked. Whatever lies he tells you, sir, accept them for what they are. Show him nothing – no emotion. He will surely concoct some fabrication for the disappearance of your son.'

'Why can't I just kill him?' The duke's voice cracked with the emotion powering his question.

'Because you or whoever you give the job to, sir, will never get out of Stoneheart alive. Legionnaires are sworn to die for their King . . . and they will. You and your family will be tracked down and slaughtered, and then he will go after your men. Please believe me when I say he is ruthless. You have no idea of his ambition, sir – you have been away from the capital for too long.'

'Fighting the Crown's battles!' the duke growled but his voice had no bite to it.

Wyl continued. 'He has amassed a private guard of mercenaries too – he is well protected. No, duke, trust my counsel that it is far better you play Celimus at his own game. I have much less to lose than you: leave the killing to me.'

'So I must sit tight and not raise my hand.'

'As we agreed this morning, sir. Assemble a guard

around Tenterdyn by all means but keep it as innocent-looking as possible. Parley with the King. See what he has to say. And if you can infiltrate the Legion in the meantime and spread the word, all the better. Work out who is loyal to our cause. And, sir, beware of Cailech. He is unpredictable and far stronger than most of us have realised.'

'You really believe he will raid Morgravia?'

'Not yet. But he is capable of anything. Be warned: he is cunning and highly intelligent. He will not do anything obvious – perhaps he may not do anything at all – but you need to keep your men alert. In fact, you might use Cailech as your excuse for assembling men at Felrawthy. Celimus will agree with that.'

'And I should offer my services to the King?' Jeryb said as though tasting something bitter.

'Reinforce your services to him. It will throw him off your scent, sir.'

The old man sighed, heavy with his troubles. 'What happened to good old-fashioned war?'

Wyl extended his sister's milky white hand. 'We fight a different war now, sir. We do it with intrigue . . . and magic.'

Jeryb grimaced. 'Shar's guidance over you and your strange, impossible life, Wyl,' the duke said. 'I shall wait for word.'

'Be strong, sir,' Wyl said, feeling the old man's need for revenge. 'You shall hear from me.'

Wyl crossed the elegant courtyard with its large pots of winterberry bushes making bright splashes of colour against the deep-coloured stone. It reminded him of Stoneheart. He went to where Elspyth stood by her horse.

The duke had provided all of his guests with good horses for their various journeys.

'Are you all right?' he asked as he drew close.

She nodded. 'Angry.'

'I will get word to you.'

'You know I want to head back to Yentro.'

'Don't lie to me. I know you want to go straight into the Razors.'

She pursed her lips. 'You don't own me, Wyl. I shall do as I please if it comes to it. I feel sick over what's happened to you, but you are going your own way – where you know you must. What about me?'

He bowed his head. 'I'm sorry, Elspyth, you're right. I don't want to talk about last night again. I can't fix what's happened – not yet anyway – and I lay no blame. But I cannot lose you too. Don't you see: this is about keeping you safe, not ignoring your needs.'

'And Briavel is all you can offer?'

'For now, yes. It's important. Important for your safety and important for our cause. You want Celimus to pay – so do this. Go to Valentyna and live under her protection. I will come to you there and then we can work out what we're going to do about Lothryn.'

Elspyth glared, knowing what he said made sense but hating him momentarily for being right and for caring about her. Too few people had cared for her as much as he did. 'And I can tell the Queen nothing of you?'

'Nothing! And you need to keep my secret this time. She won't understand anyway. Just be her friend, if she permits it. You know what to say. You'll be safe there, until I come for you.'

'You will come?' She took his arm to reinforce her query.

Wyl nodded, feeling Ylena's plait bounce at his back. 'I promise you. It seems I cannot die, no matter how hard I try,' he said half jokingly, but there was too much grief in his tone for Elspyth to smile. 'Not yet anyway,' he added and squeezed her shoulder.

He looked now to Pil. 'In all the whirl and drama of last night I did not get the chance to thank you for all you have done for our family.'

Pil regarded him shyly. 'I wish I had done so much more, kept her safe.'

Wyl took the young novice's hand. 'You did plenty. I was the one who failed her, not you.'

'I still don't understand,' Pil admitted. '*You* were Koreldy when he came to Rittylworth?' he asked, unable to let the topic rest.

'I'm afraid so. Forgive me for the duplicity.'

Pil shook his head. 'I thought he was different. I was much younger of course when he first came to us so I put it down to me being more grown-up, seeing him through adult eyes.'

'I would appreciate it, Pil, if you would keep this to yourself.'

'I think I'd be locked up as a halfwit if I told this tale,' the novice admitted. 'Your secret is safe with me.'

Wyl changed the subject. 'You are clear on the story we are all sticking to?'

Pil looked unhappy but nodded. 'The woman, Faryl, visited but left soon after when she found Ylena had not been here.'

'Good.' Wyl could see the youngster was not comfortable with the falsehood and may fail to keep to the story.

'We lie for good reason, Pil. And now you go to seek the monk in Brynt?'

'To return his donkey, yes. His name is Brother Lewk. If you ever have need of my help, it is yours, although I don't know how we will find one another.'

'Who knows, our paths may yet cross again,' Wyl said. 'Be safe, Pil. May Shar's light shine upon you always.'

The young novice paid his respects to the family and other guests, then climbed on to the patient beast and rode out of the gates.

Elspyth also prepared to leave. 'So we must part again, Wyl,' she said, determined not to show her fear or grief at the separation.

'Once again I ask another journey of you, another favour,' he said, putting his arms around her. 'Thank you for believing in me.'

She pulled out of his embrace to regard him in his new, far prettier body. 'I am trusting you. Do not let me down.'

'I won't. Oh, we have a code by the way. It was the duke's idea.'

Elspyth nodded. 'I see, so we know it's really you and don't try to kill you should you approach us in the guise of our enemy.'

'Precisely. The code is "carving knife". I think the duke retains a sense of humour in spite of himself.'

Elspyth gave him a thin smile. 'Take care, Wyl. I shall look after your Queen for you.' She liked that her comment made him look sharply at her. His Queen. Even as a woman his care and love for Valentyna was written all over his face.

Aremys arrived. 'We'd best be going,' he said.

'Where are you heading?' Elspyth asked.

'Where most do not dare to go, apparently,' Aremys admitted, giving her a look which suggested he had no idea. He reached around her tiny frame and dared a hug. 'Be safe, blabbermouth.'

They had decided to travel as the Lady Rachyl Farrow from Grenadyn and hope to Shar that King Celimus did no thorough investigation should the name ever bubble to the surface of his memory.

'Farrow is your family name, right?' Wyl asked as Aremys sipped a decent ale and he had to make do with a watery version. They had stopped at an inn in Brynt, as befitting a noble lady.

Aremys nodded. 'At least I can give you all the background information you need.'

'You're sure Celimus would not remember?'

'Our families go back, but he was young, as was I. You could simply be a baby sister.'

'Born after your own true one, you mean?'

The big man sipped. 'Or another one. Stop worrying, the Crown has had little to do with Grenadyn really. It's just that our fathers fought together, got to know one another. To Celimus, Grenadyn is a backwater where they breed good horses — that's about all he'll know of it.'

'So, do I look all right then?' Wyl asked, straightening the bodice of the gown he'd changed into at the inn.

'Every bit the noblewoman,' Aremys said, looking at Wyl's new clothes. 'I think you should be married actually.'

'I can't wait to get out of these skirts and into my riding trousers tomorrow.'

'Well, suffer now for all our sakes.'

'What happened to Faryl's body by the way?'

'The boys buried it somewhere remote.'

'Good, so if the King's men come looking . . .'

'They'll find no trace and suspect she's on her way to Briavel or wherever. Who cares?'

Wyl stared into his mug. 'Pil might yet undo us.'

'You think so?'

'He is a man of Shar. The lie about Ylena and Faryl does not sit easily with him.'

'I wonder how easily he'd sit in the King's dungeon.'

Wyl grimaced. 'No point worrying, I suppose. It's out of our control now. I wonder why the manwitch wouldn't tell me where we have to go.'

'Perhaps he couldn't,' Aremys said.

Wyl frowned. 'I don't see why not, but now I recall, he wasn't exactly forthcoming with much information, not even his name. I've been thinking it has to be the Wild.'

'That's certainly a place where no one goes.'

'Do you know much about it?'

Aremys sighed. 'Not really. They say it's haunted – alive in some way. You know how superstitious Morgravians and Briavellians have been in the past.'

'Ah, the old stories. And you believe this?'

'Enchanted is probably the better word.'

'They say no one returns from it.'

'I've heard that. I believe it could be true, don't you?'

Wyl shook his head sadly. 'Until I became Koreldy I would have scoffed at the notion. But I have to believe in magic now. I always thought the Wild was just a fable built around an uninhabitable wilderness.'

Aremys drained his cup and stretched. 'If it was

harmless, it would already be part of Briavel or similar. Whatever it is, it's managed to keep all the hungry land ravagers at bay.'

'There's something else,' Wyl said, draining his own cup more delicately.

'Tell me.'

'Knave.'

'The dog you spoke of . . . so?'

'Well, apparently he will find me, and guide us, I guess.'

'Stranger and stranger,' Aremys admitted, wiping his mouth dry of ale. 'Do we just wait then?'

'No, we keep moving. He'll find us, I suspect.'

'Can you trust Elspyth?'

'Yes,' Wyl said emphatically.

'I didn't mean it that way. I meant, will her love for this Lothryn get in the way?'

Wyl shook his head. 'The worst of this is having to rely on others, Aremys. I am relying on Elspyth to get word to the Queen; and for the duke, in all of his pain and anger, to stay firm and hold the north, and act loyal to the King when all he wants to do is gallop with his army towards Pearlis; and I am relying on Valentyna to keep her nerve and not capitulate to Celimus, whilst hoping Cailech does nothing rash.' He made a sound of agony.

'Then don't,' the mercenary said, his gaze firm. 'Rely on no one, Wyl. That's my creed. You cannot orchestrate the lives of others like some sort of omnipotent being. Do what you must do and deal with the problems as they unfold. I don't trust that Elspyth will be able to wait if you take too long; I don't trust your Queen will be able to stave off Celimus for very much longer or that Cailech won't take matters into his own hands. And who could blame Felrawthy for taking vengeance? All you can do for now is concentrate on one priority – you can't be everywhere at once. You want answers to this curse of yours, then let us find those answers. Let us seek out this manwitch.'

'Why are you doing this for me, Aremys?'

'Because frankly, I have nothing better to do.'

24

KING CAILECH TOOK THE baby in his arms. He felt a
rush of such affection in his heart that his breath caught.
He hushed the child's soft whimpering, admiring his
healthy long-limbed body. He had seen the child kick his
legs furiously when happy or distressed and had laughed
joyously at his son's lusty cry. He would be a strong king
one day, his father thought with pride.

Cailech stroked the child's downy golden hair and
smiled indulgently at the dimple in his cheek that marked
him so clearly as the son of a king, for Cailech's own
dimple had been cherished when he himself was an infant.
His mother had told him it was a sign that Haldor had
blessed him and he would lead a special life.

'Aydrech,' he cooed. Cailech had never felt such intense
love. This sense of ownership, this bonding with a helpless infant created from his own seed was so powerful it
threatened to overcome him. 'My son,' he whispered and
kissed the baby softly, his heart smitten. He knew in that
instant of tenderness that he would never love anyone as
much as Aydrech. His heir.

Voices pulled him from his adoration and he reluctantly handed the baby back to its wetnurse as the wild-looking Rashlyn approached.

'Ready?' the King asked.

The barshi simply nodded.

'Bring the boy,' Cailech ordered the woman and she fell in behind the two men.

They reached a dusty area surrounded by wooden palings known as the breaking ring. Cailech climbed the stairs to a raised platform. His son was carried up behind and promptly set to suckling contentedly at the woman's concealed breast.

The King's attention was diverted now; his eyes hungrily sought his prized new beast whose brilliantly shiny black coat twitched in the harsh sunlight. The wild stallion snorted, nostrils flaring in warning, and stamped its feet angrily.

'He is magnificent,' Cailech breathed, inspired at the sight. 'Truly magnificent.' It was far more than he had dared imagine.

A special horse-breaker, the best in the mountains, bowed. 'Sire, would you like me to begin?'

'No. He's all mine,' Cailech said, leaping down lightly from the platform and glancing towards Rashlyn who barely smiled.

'As you wish,' the horse-handler replied. 'A word of warning, my lord,' he risked, 'this is a very aggressive beast. He will take some special handling.'

Cailech nodded and took the proffered gloves and rope. 'We won't be using the hobbling method, Maegryn.'

The man immediately looked worried. 'Please, my lord King, it is all this one would understand.' When he saw the immovable set of his leader's jaw, he nodded. 'At least allow me to take the first session.'

Cailech put his hand on the man's shoulder. He towered over him. 'Be easy. This one will not hurt me. And I do not wish to win him through pain. We will break him the old way – by trust. He and I must trust one another. He must know what it is to fear me but without pain. That is the greatest conquering of all, don't you think?'

It made no sense to the man. 'Sire, you—'

'Hush, Maegryn. I know best,' Cailech assured as he entered the breaking ring.

Onlookers gathered as word spread that the King was personally breaking in a new stallion, a fiery one. Cailech slapped the rope against his thigh and the horse glanced towards him with a wild and angry look in its dark eyes. It had been kept isolated for days and now it was outside in the fresh mountain air it was brimming with unspent energy and fury. The King could see the whites of the beast's eyes – a sure sign that the creature was just short of demented at being penned in.

It snorted. Cailech knew this was a threat, knew he must answer it.

'Hah!' he yelled and slapped the rope again, making a loud crack against his soft leather riding trews.

The horse began to paw the ground. Another sign. Dangerous this time.

Maegryn tipped his head towards some helpers. They were ready to leap into the ring and distract the angry animal should it charge their King.

They watched Cailech stand to his full height and raise his chin high. He had inherited the talents of his father who had been a skilled breaker of horses. Those who

understood the process knew that with this simple movement Cailech was throwing down the gauntlet to the
horse, inviting it to test its nerve and resilience against
him. This would be a fight of stamina and mental strength
– male against male – the different species hardly
mattered. The horse knew exactly what was being offered
and knew only one of them could win leadership.

The King took a short aggressive step towards the stallion, holding the rope aloft. It held its ground but flinched
momentarily, which to Maegryn's experienced eye was an
indication that it was unsure about this challenge. The
beast would proceed with caution, he realised with relief.

Cailech whipped the rope outwards this time, towards
the horse's rump. Incensed, it began blowing fiercely
through its nostrils and pawed the ground. Cailech
shouted, distracting it with his voice and diverting its
attention with the rope which licked at its back now.

The animal screamed, not from pain but anger. It
moved towards the King – the last warning before it
might decide to pummel him with its hooves. The other
handlers tensed. One even raised a bow, its arrow tipped
with the sap of the falava bush. A skilled shot in the rump
would sedate the horse, although it would not act
instantly. They would need to get the King out of that
ring immediately if the scene turned ugly.

Once more Cailech stood his ground and repeated the
process.

This time the horse reared. Although Cailech stepped
back he yelled more loudly this time, whacking the animal
hard with the rope. Stung, the beast backed off. Man and
horse regarded each other. It was as if no one else was
present. Cailech could hear nothing but the angry

breathing of the beast. He slapped his thigh with the rope once more. The horse reluctantly began to move around the ring.

Those watching let out their collectively held breath. It was a start.

The breaking continued relentlessly over the next few days. Four suns later the stallion stood sweating and trembling from its exertions. The wildness was still in its eyes but now it respected the man who stood tall before it. He too was perspiring but his cold green gaze never left the horse's majestic face.

Now, sire! Maegryn thought, filled with admiration for his King's performance. And as if Cailech could hear his private thoughts, he watched him suddenly round his shoulders and body in a manner which, in the language of horses, conveyed safety and companionship. The stallion whinnied softly in answer. Until now Cailech had forced his domination and the horse had faced away from its adversary, preferring little or no eye contact. Now it turned directly towards him and eyed him. Its magnificent glare was still defiant, but its body language told Maegryn that the King was no longer rejected. In fact, he was accepted.

Another long day of this routine continued before finally the stallion, nicknamed Proud by the Mountain Dwellers who had watched the exciting drama unfold, lowered its defiant head in deference to its breaker, walked over to Cailech and nuzzled at his shoulder.

As soon as this happened, Cailech straightened. 'Tie him to the snubbing post,' he said, not prepared to lose the moment.

'Perhaps we should wait, my lord,' Maegryn ventured.

'Now!' Cailech replied. He left no room for argument.

Rashlyn approached the King as the men moved in cautiously to halter the horse. He handed Cailech a skin of water. 'Well?'

'Impressive.'

'Thank you.'

'Now we make him fully trusting,' Cailech said, taking a long swig and handing back the skin. 'I shall be riding him by this afternoon,' he said fiercely.

Rashlyn nodded, his sly grin evident beneath the flurry of hair.

'Ready, my lord,' Maegryn called.

Cailech stepped back to the black horse. It was blowing and trembling, angry and confused again, this time at being tied to the fence.

'Put on the saddle,' Cailech said.

This was easier said than achieved but the men working the horse were swift and experienced. After this was done, Cailech carefully approached the stallion which was still hitched to the post. He kept a continuous murmur of soothing words flowing towards the beast so it would feel comfortable about the person coming close. And then, in one smooth movement, Cailech leapt nimbly onto the horse's back. Alarmed, it instantly tried to buck and jump, squealing with rage and as determined to unseat its rider as Cailech was to remain in place.

The stallion finally calmed, but only through exhaustion, too spent for even one more effort. The King could feel its entire body shaking with despair as well as fatigue. It had done its utmost. It had failed.

As Cailech slid from the saddle, the horse turned its

head. He was ready for the bite — a last-ditch effort to inflict pain on the victor. The King back-handed the horse in the face with all the strength he had left and the beast squealed in obvious shock and agony.

'Unsaddle him!' Cailech commanded, rubbing the pain from his hand. He had not wanted to do that, but it was necessary. Only he and Rashlyn knew how much emotion had driven that blow.

Maegryn was shocked at his sovereign's aggressiveness towards an animal he had claimed he did not want to hurt, but he was also relieved. King and horse had been trying to outdo each other for too many days. The horse had lost that battle, which was as it should be, but the handler was keen for the beast to have some rest from its exertions. In truth, he believed this strange horse would prefer death to subservience.

'I will ride him this afternoon,' Cailech said. 'Have him readied.'

'Sire?' Maegryn asked, shocked for the second time in as many minutes.

'His name is Galapek. I will ride him without a saddle.'

Maegryn dared not contradict the madness that had the King in its grip. 'As you command,' was all he permitted himself to say.

Cailech strode away, Rashlyn at his side. 'I will be taking my son out alone this afternoon,' the King said.

'On the stallion?' Rashlyn asked, surprised.

'Have Aydrech brought to me at the edge of the lake directly after the midday meal. I want him to know this horse.'

'Is this wise, my lord?'

'He'll be fine,' Cailech replied, his stride lengthening, forcing the barshi to all but skip alongside.

Rashlyn was not sure whether the King referred to son or horse. 'I do not recognise the name you have given the beast.' The sorcerer was not of the mountains.

'It is in the old language of our forefathers.'

'Oh? What does it mean?'

'Traitor,' the King snarled and left the practitioner of magic in his wake.

Maegryn brought the stallion to the King. 'My lord, please let me saddle him,' he beseeched, fearful at what the proud beast might do if it sensed how dangerous this situation was for Cailech.

'Take off the halter. I ride alone and bareback.'

Maegryn blinked. He could not contradict the King even though he knew his leader was wrong. This huge horse was more than capable of killing. But the handler wisely understood that so was his King, and it would be his own neck being snapped at the end of a noose if he risked angering Cailech.

'I will mount him first, then you are to remove all restraints,' Cailech instructed.

Maegryn gave the King a leg-up and was relieved that the horse protested only slightly by moving its back end around. He held his breath and looked towards his sovereign, who nodded. The handler removed the halter and the stallion shook its head at the sense of freedom.

'Leave us,' the King said and Maegryn departed reluctantly, still fearful that anything that might go wrong would come back to haunt him.

Once he was alone, Cailech laid his head against the

stallion's strong neck and, as he stroked it, he whispered. 'Now you are mine for good. Come, my friend, let us ride together once again.'

And the man once known as Lothryn, now called Galapek the traitor, took his first unhappy steps as King Cailech's four-legged servant.

Watching from a distance Rashlyn smiled thinly, admiring his work.

Gueryn lay on the pallet in the dungeon, to where he had been returned once his wound had healed. He had spoken to no one since then. The dungeon-keeper was a nice enough fellow who regularly changed the straw and brought fresh food and water. He had tried talking with the prisoner but Gueryn had pointedly refused to respond. Nowadays that same man entered and left the cell in silence.

Today was different though. When the man arrived he walked straight over to Gueryn and prodded him. 'Come on, we've got orders to exercise you.'

Gueryn stirred. No amount of pride would permit him to refuse the opportunity to walk in daylight and breathe fresh air. Cailech had promised neither, so this was quite a development. Obviously the King had paid attention to Gueryn's threat and was as determined to preserve his life as he himself was to end it.

It was more logical then to try a different tactic, for it was obvious that Cailech wanted him kept alive for a reason. So his protest now was silence. They would get nothing from him. More recently Gueryn had realised that deep down he wanted to live too . . . if just to hear news of Wyl – if he still lived – and Ylena. He would stay alive and alert until he could somehow contribute towards bringing this Mountain Kingdom down.

After so long without exercise, walking sounded easier than it was and it took two men to support him. When they emerged from the dungeon it was not into broad daylight as Gueryn had expected but into the inkiness of night. An unbelievably beautiful starry sky greeted Gueryn back to real life. He inhaled the piercingly cold but most welcome night air and immediately began to cough.

'Take it easy, old man,' one of his aides murmured.

Gueryn growled something unintelligible through the cough.

'What was that?' the Mountain man enquired, amused.

'I think he's telling you your fortune, Myrt,' the man on the other side of Gueryn said and laughed.

Gueryn cleared his throat now that his initial attack had settled. 'I said I'll knock you senseless next time you call me old.'

Both men laughed and Gueryn chuckled too. It felt suddenly permissible and even rather empowering to share a jest with others, even if they were the enemy.

'How old are you?' Myrt asked.

'Two score and five,' he replied, shuffling awkwardly between them.

'Then you'd better start acting like it,' Myrt said. 'The King wants you fit and healthy, not dying in his dungeon.'

'I gathered. How thoughtful of him.'

'Well, now that your wound has fully healed, it's time you got your body well.'

'I'll do it, just so I can enjoy fighting some of you when my chance comes again.'

Myrt chuckled. 'That's the spirit. Can you manage on your own now?'

'Let me try,' Gueryn replied gruffly.

He doubled up to cough again but soon enough was able to totter more freely, if laboriously.

'Don't worry, I'm not going anywhere,' he said to his captors who smiled back.

'Dyx up there will see to it you have another nasty wound if you try,' Myrt warned, nodding up to where an archer watched from a higher vantage point.

Gueryn nodded. He hardly had the strength to hold himself upright but in that moment he decided he would work his body hard from now on and regain its former strength. He had to make himself useful to Morgravia . . . if just as a rather pathetic and captive spy.

As he began on another pitifully slow circle around the two men who hardly seemed to notice the cold that bit so cruelly into his bones, he heard the name of Lothryn and his attention was immediately caught. He moved more slowly still, veering slightly closer so he could eavesdrop on the conversation without appearing to be listening. He turned his head away, maintained a blank expression and relied entirely on his good hearing.

'. . . so have you seen him?'

'No,' Myrt replied. 'And he's not in the dungeon, I've checked.'

'So where is he?'

Gueryn, facing away from the men, assumed Myrt must have shrugged.

'Not dead, surely?' the other man queried, bewilderment in his tone.

'Loth always warned us the King is unpredictable. No

one, not even Loth himself, can gauge his moods but he was the only one who seemed able to talk with Cailech when he was dark of spirit.'

'But they were so close, as good as brothers,' the man said, aghast.

'Loth betrayed us, Byl. Don't you understand? That's about the worst sin that he could have perpetrated on the King, next to murdering one of our own. Cailech demands loyalty above all else.'

His younger, less experienced companion grunted. 'Seems odd then that he's permitted to summarily execute one of our best.'

'They're the rules. Loth would have known the penalty when he broke them,' Myrt said unhappily.

Gueryn thanked Shar for his keen hearing and had to stop himself swivelling around when a third voice came out of nowhere.

'He is not dead,' the voice said. Gueryn continued his revolution of the space, working hard to keep his face devoid of all recognition as a figure melted out of the shadows. It was the hideous medicine man who had saved his life but watched with bright eyes as they took Elspyth's.

'He is amongst you,' Rashlyn said with a trace of glee.

Out of the corner of his eye Gueryn saw both Mountain men bristle at the approach of the wild-looking man. It seemed only Cailech suffered the fellow gladly.

'I haven't noticed him,' Myrt replied carefully.

'Oh, indeed you have, you just haven't realised it,' Rashlyn said. He glanced Gueryn's way and changed the subject. 'I see he can walk unaided now.'

Gueryn turned his back; he imagined the two men nodding.

'This is good. We need him healthy,' Rashlyn said.

'Why?' Myrt asked, desperately wanting to know more about Lothryn.

'Ah, that I cannot divulge. But your King has plans for him.'

Gueryn felt his stomach clench. He despised the evil nature of this man.

'Can you get a message to Loth for me?' Myrt asked, ignoring the sorcerer's evasiveness.

Rashlyn laughed; a snigger filled with guile and knowing. 'No, I can't do that. Have you admired the King's magnificent new stallion by the way?'

'The best I've ever seen,' Myrt agreed, frustrated by the barshi's irritating leaps from topic to topic.

'And do you know what Galapek means in the old language?'

'No.'

'Well, you should try and learn more of your ancestors' tongue,' Rashlyn answered and walked away smiling.

'Now what's that all supposed to mean?' Byl asked.

'Search me,' Myrt replied. 'His mind is as frenzied and unreliable as his appearance. He gives me the creeps. Superstitious or not, I don't know how Cailech can stand him near.'

'Looks like our prisoner has had enough,' Byl suggested, noticing that Gueryn had stopped his pacing.

'Come on then,' Myrt called to Gueryn. 'Let's get you back to your cosy guest room.'

Gueryn said nothing more, other than to thank the men for the rare treat of being outside.

'Don't mention it,' Myrt replied. 'We'll force you to do it each evening until you feel fit again.'

After the men had left, Gueryn allowed his mind to embrace the disturbing nature of what he had overheard from Rashlyn. Myrt and his friend might not have understood the sly message underlying the medicine man's words, but Gueryn was classically trained. His great-grandmother, originally from the Outer Isles of the north, had been married off (more like traded, his grandmother had told him) to a noble in Morgravia. She had accepted her new life but never fully relinquished her cultural background, particularly its language, which she had religiously taught to her daughter, who had in turn instructed her own grandson.

Gueryn knew all too well what the word 'galapek' meant in the old language of the north. Traitor. An odd name for a stallion.

He shivered in the damp cell and pulled a blanket about him. What was the medicine man inferring – that Cailech had named his new stallion after his best friend? Or was it more convoluted than that?

Rashlyn had said Lothryn was alive and amongst them. Yet neither of those men, presumably friends of Lothryn and close enough to the King to be familiar with him, had seen the courageous Mountain man. Further, Rashlyn had insinuated there were things none of them could understand. What was the link between the horse and Lothryn?

Gueryn drifted off into unhappy sleep as he pondered this, promising himself he would make more effort to talk with his guards tomorrow night during the walk. Now he too wanted to know where Lothryn was.

Meanwhile, in the stable, a man trapped by the powerful shapechanging magic of Rashlyn threw his magnificently sculpted new body angrily against the timber and screamed for deliverance.

25

KNAVE COULD FEEL THE pull of Wyl's thoughts. He already knew the Quickening had happened again and had startled his companion the previous night with a terrible howling.

Fynch was far too sharp not to recognise this keening from the last time Knave had made this sound; then it was undoubtedly to signify that Romen had been killed and that Wyl had become Faryl. He had to assume now that Wyl had died once more and come back to life again – that he was now walking in a new body. The fear of not recognising Wyl in a different form gnawed at Fynch, but he was too distracted by his own fear to allow that notion to gain too much space in his mind right now.

He and Knave were sitting at the edge of dense brush on the northern border of Briavel, known aptly as the Thicket. For those unfamiliar with its more mysterious purpose, it was simply a barrier to discourage any unsuspecting traveller from heading into the famed and sinister Wild. Beyond the Thicket line was a small tributary that

eventually joined the major River Eyle which bisected
Briavel and Morgravia. This body of water, ominously
known as the Darkstream, was the only access into the
Wild.

'Are you sure, Knave?' Fynch whispered once again.

The dog nuzzled his face. It was answer enough. Knave
would not let anything bad happen to him. As it was,
the dog had somehow managed to get them from Baelup
to the north of Briavel with dazzling speed. Fynch knew
Knave used magic; had accepted it now.

'How do you do it?' he asked his friend, who stared
back at him with dark liquid eyes. 'I mean, I curl up with
you in one spot and I wake up in another. Do you carry
me?' he wondered aloud, scratching gently at the dog's
ears, which was hugely appreciated by his companion. 'Or
do you just "send" us from one place to another, like I
"sent" to Myrren's father?'

Knave groaned with pleasure. It was the only answer
Fynch was going to get to his musings. 'I guess I shouldn't
put it off any longer,' Fynch said, hoping to find some
comfort in the rallying words. Knave nudged him this
time. He wanted Fynch to move. 'I'm frightened,' the boy
admitted.

He knew of the Wild from his mother's stories around
the fire at night. She had terrified him with dark tales of
what must happen to the intrepid explorers who took fate
in their hands and put their names down to enter the
Wild. That's right, he remembered — all travellers
choosing to use this tributary had to register. It was how
the authorities monitored who had gone missing over the
years. Fynch felt his legs go watery at the thought. What
if they were never seen or heard of again? How would

Wyl know where to find his body? What would happen to Valentyna?

Knave growled softly, urging him to move. Fynch unravelled the thong of Romen's he had taken to wearing about his own tiny wrist. He tied it now to a branch, casting a prayer to Shar that someone might find it – that someone being Wyl, if Wyl should even know to come looking here!

Fynch took a steadying breath, summoned his courage and stepped into the Thicket. It was dusk outside but beneath the tangle of yews it was all brooding shadows, making it look and feel as dark as the night. Was it his imagination that the branches bent as if to touch him? He tried to assure himself it was a fanciful thought. He decided to keep his eyes fixed on Knave, who now led the way through the foliage with seeming ease. There were no bird calls, no animal sounds. Not even an insect chirped. The heavy silence made Fynch curve his shoulders inward and wrap his thin arms about his body. Then he heard the rush of water nearby, close to their path, it felt like. He broke into a trot to keep up with Knave who was pushing more quickly now.

Fynch suddenly realised he was unconsciously casting a repetitive thought. *I mean no harm*, he was saying over and again in his mind. Perhaps it was his susceptibility to magic that convinced Fynch the Thicket answered him, although he could no more articulate what was said than he could sprout wings and fly.

After some time casting his mantra, the Thicket no longer felt threatening. The whispers – which was the only way Fynch could describe them – became increasingly gentle and warm. What had initially struck him as sinister now felt oddly friendly and, he had not imagined it, leaves were softly trailing against his face no matter how agilely he ducked and weaved. And with each brush of a leaf or a twig, he felt a tingle pass through him. There was no time to stop and consider it though. He was all but running after Knave now.

Finally they emerged on the other side. It had felt like an age had passed during their passage through the dark, gloomy Thicket, but as they reached open air once more and the weight of its presence had lifted somewhat Fynch realised the journey had taken barely minutes.

The Darkstream had indeed kept them company through the trees and now they saw it properly. It did not flow as quickly as Fynch had expected nor was it nearly as wide as it sounded. It was sinister, though, its waters dark and intimidating. Across a small wooden bridge, surrounded by the first rocky mounds which would become the Razors, there stood a hut. A cheerful column of smoke drifted from its chimney. A path led from its door to a jetty nearby, where a trio of small rowboats bobbed in the water, neatly tied to wooden poles. It was an unexpected homely scene and yet the gurgle of the deep waters that passed by warned Fynch that this was not a safe place.

Knave walked a few paces across the bridge then looked back at Fynch. The boy gathered he was supposed to follow. Again he felt he might be imagining the tingle that passed through his body as he stepped on to the timbers of the bridge. It passed as quickly as it arrived and Fynch was left wondering what his fears were doing to him. He found grim amusement in the thought that the bridge should yell out 'Friend or foe?' as it might have done in the old fairy tales. And then behind the door of the hut should be a troll.

He knocked at that door now. No troll. It was the normal voice of a man, friendly enough, calling that he was coming as fast as he could.

'Now then,' the man said, pulling open the door at last. 'Shar strike me down, look at the size of that thing!' he said, his hand going to his chest.

'He won't hurt you, sir. He's just big,' Fynch reassured, relieved the person looked nothing like a troll.

The man looked at him somewhat quizzically and his pudgy face puckered in a genial manner. His ruddy complexion added to Fynch's notion that this was a good-natured soul, who might enjoy a tipple and perhaps some company on the rare occasion it presented itself.

'Come in then, boy. My name is Samm. Your . . . beast, or whatever it is, can wait outside.'

'He is a dog, sir.'

'Whatever, don't dawdle and let the cold air in, child.'

Fynch glanced towards Knave, who had already settled on his haunches. The dog knew what to do, so Fynch followed the man's large backside into the hut. The smell of soup reminded him he had not eaten in a long time, despite his canine companion bringing him freshly killed rabbits most evenings. He imagined it was about now that this seemingly friendly soul would throw him into a cage and fatten him up for cooking in the soup pot later – then shook his head free of the silly stories from childhood.

'Well now, lad, what brings you through the Thicket?'

Another deep breath. 'I must travel into the Wild, sir. I need to hire one of your boats.'

'I see. And why do you need to do this?'

'No offence, sir, but is it required that I have to answer your questions, sir?' Fynch asked earnestly.

'That you do, son. Without my approval, you'll be heading straight back through those trees.'

'It was my impression, sir,' Fynch began carefully and seriously, as was his way, 'that the boatkeeper may not refuse anyone to journey on the Darkstream.'

The man sighed and his grey eyes gleamed deep within his fat face. 'This is true. You are well informed.'

'So you cannot deny me passage?' Fynch qualified.

'Not if you have coin to pay, no. I can, however, do whatever I might think of to dissuade you from the journey, young man. You are so young to be here.'

'I seek someone,' Fynch replied in answer to the original question.

'Someone who is lost?'

Fynch nodded. This was not strictly true and he hated to tell lies. Somehow not speaking made it easier.

'Family?'

'Possibly.'

'How old are you?'

'Old enough.'

It was obvious the man did not believe him. 'You understand how perilous this place is, boy?'

'I do. I have my dog to protect me.'

At this the man laughed. 'Priceless. Come and sit by the fire, lad. Let me fetch my ledger.'

Fynch did as he was told, relishing the warmth. 'Do you live here alone?' he called to the man who was rifling through a chest.

'Yes. Have done all my life.'

'No family?'

'No.'

The man mumbled as he looked beneath books and clothes, 'Raised myself in the foothills . . . a travelling monk taught me my letters. He stayed a while and left when he felt I knew enough to get by.'

'How long have you been the boatkeeper?'

'I've always been the boatkeeper. Ah, here it is,' he said, blowing dust off the large black book he had pulled from the bottom of the chest. He carried it to a desk. 'Can I interest you in a bowl of soup, child? I've more than enough for myself.'

Fynch grinned awkwardly. He could use some hot food and he could tell Samm did not want to give any explanations. 'Thank you, sir.' He wondered if it was poisoned; that might be how the seemingly friendly man entrapped his unwitting guests. He had to stop this.

'Polite one, aren't you? There's a bowl on that shelf. Help yourself whilst I find my place in this book.'

The soup was simple vegetable broth but it pleased Fynch greatly and was far from poisonous. He ladled out a small bowlful and sat at the rickety table to enjoy it.

'Bread?' the man asked, not looking up.

'This is more than enough.'

The boatkeeper grunted as if to suggest it was hardly anything.

'Right then, lad . . .' He cleared his throat as he began his official speech, fixing Fynch with a steely gaze. 'I am obliged to tell you that the Law of the Wild was set two centuries or so back. Both Morgravia and Briavel agreed upon it. All of their peoples have access to the Darkstream but no rescue parties have ever or will ever be sent in search of the missing. They are always presumed dead. Do you understand?'

Fynch looked up from his food, his brow furrowed. 'I understand, sir, but if no one ever returns from the Wild how come you always have boats? They don't look new to me.'

'A sharp lad you are too — what's your name?'

It could not hurt, he figured. Celimus was hardly going to check the records out here. 'Fynch.'

'Pleased to meet you, young Fynch.' Fynch nodded, unable to do much else with a spoonful of soup in his mouth. 'Now, to answer your clever question — the boats always find their way back.' He regarded his guest and smiled. 'Upstream and against the current.'

Fynch was wide-eyed now. 'Magic,' he said with reverence.

'I'm not saying one way or another,' the boatkeeper replied. 'My job is just to record whoever sets off from here and charge the fee.'

'Taxes on death,' Fynch mused, taking the last spoonful.

'Hardly; more a formality really. Not much money to be made from here. The last person who took the Darkstream registered more than two decades ago — probably closer to a quarter of a century if my memory serves me correctly. A woman it was and her fee is the same as yours.'

It fired Fynch's imagination to think of some brave woman facing the Wild alone. 'I wonder what or whom she sought.'

Samm cocked his head to one side in thought. 'They never say — just like you. Oh, but she was lovely as I

recall. Such a waste. I nearly talked myself hoarse trying
to convince her to stay. But she would not be persuaded
otherwise.'

'She obviously badly needed to go there.'

'Broken heart perhaps.'

'What happened?'

Samm sighed. 'The pretty lady never returned, of
course, but her boat did. Ah, here's her name: Emil, that's
right. Never heard that name before. Her hair was as dark
as the stream and she had a milky complexion.'

Fynch felt as if the soup soured instantly in his belly.
'Did you say Emil?'

The boatkeeper nodded. 'Aye. Odd one, isn't it?' He
looked up. 'Why?'

'Oh, nothing,' Fynch said hastily. He felt lightheaded.
Emil was the name of Myrren's mother. It could be a co-
incidence, even though it was a far from common name.

'Was she from Morgravia?' he asked as casually as he
could, setting down his spoon.

'Er . . . yes, Pearlis it says here.'

Too much of a coincidence then. Myrren's mother was
also originally from Pearlis and the timing fitted too neatly
in Fynch's sharp mind. Myrren was around eighteen years
of age when she died. Her death occurred six years ago.
No, much too coincidental. So at least one person had
returned from the Wild: Emil had made it back and raised
her child. There was hope for him yet.

'Is something wrong, lad?'

'No. Your soup is delicious, sir. I was contemplating a
second bowl,' Fynch said honestly. 'But I won't, thank
you.'

'You eat like a bird!'

He was glad to have thrown Samm off the scent. 'So I'm told.' He grinned. 'Can I travel at night?'

'I wouldn't advise it. Best leave at first light. It also gives you the night to think on it.'

'I won't change my mind.'

Samm smiled kindly. 'I understand. Have a good night's rest. You're most welcome to bunk down here with me. It will be dark in moments anyway.'

'Can I pay you now?'

'Tomorrow's soon enough.'

'I will be going, Samm,' Fynch said firmly.

He grinned. 'Is your dog all right out there?'

'Nothing bothers Knave. Thank you for your hospitality.'

'Don't mention it. I don't get conversation often – no human company around here,' he admitted. 'Settle yourself in then, lad.'

Fynch did not sleep well. He mainly dozed, feeling the touch of Knave on his mind. That was reassuring, just in case Samm did turn out to be some sort of ghoul who ate people who crossed his bridge. He woke at first light, glad to be up and moving, although his mind felt dull. His body fidgeted in nervous anticipation of the journey ahead.

He roused Samm, put on a pot of water and politely shared some porridge with his host. In answer to Samm's gentle questions, none of which Fynch considered too pointed, he slid around the truth and gave the impression he was from Briavel and had on occasion worked at the castle.

'Will you give me no reason for your journey, son? It seems such a waste.'

'Maybe I shall return, Samm,' Fynch said brightly, trying to avoid the question.

'I must ask again whether you understand the terms of your departure. There is no rescue party once you step into the boat and leave the jetty.'

'Truly, I understand,' Fynch said, very seriously.

'Then you owe me a crown.'

Fynch handed over the coin. 'I'm ready, thank you again.'

Samm took it and neatly recorded the details in his ledger. 'I've put your home as Werryl – would that be right?'

Once again Fynch nodded, loath to speak a lie.

'I've put together a small sack of food for you and a rug for the cold. You look too scrawny to last a day,' Samm grunted, embarrassed. He pointed towards a small table by the door.

'Can I pay—'

'No, it's nothing. I have plenty. Go on with you then, boy. And may Shar and that black beast protect you.'

Samm stood and Fynch followed suit, eager to be gone now. He took the sack and opened the door to where Knave awaited, stretching. Together the three of them walked to the jetty.

'Take your pick,' Samm said, gesturing at the boats.

Fynch climbed into the nearest one, Knave following. 'Bye, Samm. I won't forget your kindness.'

'Be safe, Fynch, lad,' the man said sadly, knowing the child would be carried into the wilderness and would not return. He untied the rope. 'May Shar watch over you.'

And they were gone, the stream's current pulling them towards two huge willow trees whose overhanging canopy formed what looked like an archway into a dark tunnel. Fynch turned to wave as the willows gobbled the boat into their shadows but Samm had already gone.

26

AS FYNCH WAS TURNING back towards the willows, his fear of the unknown intensifying, Elspyth was doing her utmost to convince herself that Wyl had made the right decision. She was not happy at heading off once again on a journey towards a woman she did not know – a Queen no less this time. She was glad for the company of Crys, despite his sorrow.

'Your mother is marvellous, so resilient,' she ventured when she could no longer stand the awkward silence between them. Too much had occurred in the day and night previous for them to talk much, and they would hit the Briavellian border within an hour.

'I never really think about it,' he replied. 'I think we all take her strength for granted, particularly my father.'

She took the opportunity to touch on the hardest topic of all. 'Crys, I haven't had the chance to tell you how sorry I am about your brother. I feel so awkward, not knowing him and yet feeling like I do somehow, through all of you.'

He smiled sadly at her. 'Thank you. He was just such a good lad – one of those rare people who can always see the positive side of life. Father had high hopes for him at Stoneheart too; once Wyl made him his deputy, his future was secured.'

Elspyth understood. 'The fourth son, you mean?' Crys nodded. 'How did it happen that he left your home and was sent to the capital?'

'Bit of a long tale, really. Let me see if I can simplify it. Father and Fergys Thirsk go back a long way; they always had a lot in common in terms of position and shared similar outlooks on life. Also my father was intensely loyal to King Magnus, so the family connection to Stoneheart and the Crown was already strong. The King made a trip north not long after General Fergys died and naturally he stopped at Tenterdyn. I think my father must have mentioned he was not sure what to do for Alyd and the King suggested he send him south – apparently he said he knew another young lad around the same age who could use the company.'

'Wyl?'

'That's right. My father was happy to keep the families close through another generation – although we didn't bank on Alyd falling in love with Ylena.'

'I gather they were the perfect couple.'

He nodded. 'My parents only knew of Ylena as a small child, but her reputation as a young woman sparkled before her.'

'I'm surprised your family did not visit Stoneheart more frequently,' she mused.

'Well, Magnus and my parents hadn't seen each other in a long time. He was a little in love with my mother in their early years, I think. Perhaps my father never trusted the King around my mother.' Crys winked.

'Truly?'

'No, I'm teasing. It's true that the King had a terribly soft spot for my mother when they were all very young, and to his death he considered her with great affection, but he knew how much she loved my father. I think the reason for the long length of time between their visits is that Felrawthy really holds the north for the Crown. Traditionally, Father has always overseen the Legionnaires who guard the Razors.'

'I see. So that's why Jeryb wasn't at Stoneheart for the tournament.'

'Yes. We were all furious not to make it — Mother desperately wanted to see Alyd and the tourney was a great excuse to pay a visit south. But the border has become more threatened in recent years and Father would not risk it.'

'You know Cailech and his men slip into western Morgravia regularly?'

He glanced at her. 'We have suspected as much.'

'I've seen them. No one minds them much in Yentro. They keep themselves to themselves; trade a bit and disappear almost as fast as they arrived.'

He nodded thoughtfully. 'They have excellent scouts. We can't even catch them in Morgravia, let alone track them into the mountains.'

'You wouldn't want to — they know them too well.' Elspyth frowned. 'But why did our soldiers kill those children? It enraged Cailech and he's vowed revenge of the most horrible kind. That is why Gueryn le Gant was captured and tortured.'

Crys slowed his horse. 'Elspyth, it wasn't our men who killed those children, nor was it our men who travelled with le Gant.'

She pursed her lips. 'It's always Celimus behind it,' she said bitterly.

'The King orchestrated all of it – through his own henchmen, of course. I've never seen my father so angry as the day he received orders to send le Gant in with that scrawny bunch of men. They weren't even proper soldiers. Le Gant insisted my father stay out of it or risk disloyalty to the Crown. He said in as many words that Celimus had planned to separate him from Wyl and that he suspected treachery somewhere.'

'So I heard.'

'Do you think he's still alive?'

She shook her head. 'Gueryn was nearly dead when we left him. If a Mountain Dweller's arrow didn't find its mark that night then his fever would surely have killed him.'

'I gather Wyl doesn't want to believe it?'

'It's the fear that Cailech might have kept Gueryn alive as bait which makes Wyl determined to go back to the Mountain fortress – that and for another brave man called Lothryn.'

'I've heard you mention him before. You always say his name tenderly.' Crys glanced towards Elspyth, who blushed.

'Do I?'

'Mmm.'

They rode in silence for a few moments.

Elspyth broke the quiet first. 'I am in love with Lothryn.'

'I worked it out.'

'Oh?'

'Most women can't resist me,' he said mock archly and grinned.

'It must be your modesty,' she replied, but liked him all the same for it.

'He's a lucky man, Elspyth.'

'He's very special,' she admitted softly. 'It is taking all my courage to ride south and away from him.'

'And all of ours not to wage war on the Crown,' Crys added, bitterness strong in his tone.

'What will happen do you think?'

'Wyl's beseeched my father to keep up the pretence. I hope he knows what he's doing.'

'You must trust him . . . as I do,' she replied. 'He needs to be able to rely on us.'

'But what is his plan?'

'Your guess is as good as mine. He is trying to find the father of the woman who cursed him with this magical life.'

'It is all too strange – I can hardly bear thinking on it to tell the truth. How bizarre to become a woman.'

'Imagine how he feels! He was Romen Koreldy when I met him. Since then he has become this Faryl woman, and now look at him.' She shook her head. 'That poor sister of his.'

'What can he hope to achieve as a woman?' Crys wondered aloud.

'Don't be so quick to doubt!' she cautioned. 'Women are far more cunning than you give us credit for. Wyl's new facade means different doors may well open to him that were closed to himself or Koreldy.'

'You forget that Celimus knows Ylena. If he has been hunting her, then he will have her killed on sight.'

'I'm sure Wyl's aware of that, which would explain why he's so determined to find Myrren's father. Perhaps he can give some answers to this gift.'

Crys interrupted their conversation by holding his hand up. 'We've reached the border,' he said, pointing towards a sign.

'So I just ride my horse across the imaginary line?'

'Yes. Security between the realms has been stepped up since the death of Valor – they'll soon pick you up. There are guards everywhere.'

'What about before?' she queried, referring to a time prior to Valor's demise.

'Well, merchants could come and go fairly freely. But these days you need a permit for trade, or good reason for the crossing if you're not a merchant.'

'And what's my reason?' she asked, worried now.

He grinned. 'I can always get you past the guard from Morgravia's side. You just have to hope that letter from Wyl gets you through Briavel's scrutiny.'

'Or?'

'You'll be coming back with me – and nothing would give me greater pleasure.' He grinned at the innuendo in his words.

Elspyth found his wit infectious. If not for Lothryn, she might well have fallen prey to this man's obvious charm. 'You have been very kind to me, Crys. I hope I can repay you some day.'

'Well, marry me then,' he jested and pulled a face at her scolding expression. 'All right, my apologies. Come now, let me get you safely across.'

As he gestured for Elspyth to follow, he heard the sound of a rider coming at a breakneck gallop. 'Wait!' he hissed to her. 'I can see my father's standard, something is wrong.'

The rider came into view. They could see the lather

flying off the animal which had been all but run to death. 'It's Pil!' Crys exclaimed.

Elspyth felt the chill of fear crawl up her spine and ooze throughout her body until every hair seemed as though it were standing on end. No one rode this fast unless pursued or outrunning danger. She could see the wild look in both man's and beast's eyes as they approached.

Pil pulled the horse up too sharply and in its pain and panic it reared throwing him to the ground. It ran away into the nearby trees, terrified and exhausted.

Elspyth and Crys leapt from their own mounts. 'Shall I go after the horse?' Elspyth said, knowing how the Donal family prized their animals.

'Leave it,' Crys ordered through gritted teeth. 'Pil, what madness is this?'

Elspyth could see the strength and leadership of the duke now in his eldest son. It was an attractive quality he had not formerly revealed, deferring to his father. Its reassurance cut through her fear. 'Take a deep breath, Pil,' she urged.

The novice's eyes were wide and scared. He rubbed at his newly bruised elbow. 'Shar's blessing, I found you.'

'What's happened?' Crys demanded.

'They're all dead,' Pil blurted. 'Your family.'

Elspyth felt Crys's body go rigid next to hers. 'What are you talking about?' he growled.

Pil looked towards Elspyth; his words came out in a rush, tripping over one another in his terrified eagerness to explain. 'Brother Lewk wanted to pay his respects to the duke and duchess. I said I'd take him back to the estate. When we arrived . . .' His voice broke.

'Tell me all,' Crys said, pain spreading to all reaches of his body from the ball of emotion which unfurled in his heart.

According to the novice, it was Aleda who first heard the sound of galloping horses. She wondered aloud to Pil and his companion Brother Lewk if it could be the men at arms arriving, but as the troop entered the courtyard it was clear they were not of the Legion although they bore the King's standard.

'The duchess sent us into the house to hide,' Pil said. 'She told us to go up into the attic so there would be no trace of the presence of any guests at all. Daryn had come to warn her that the men were looking for the woman, Faryl, or any woman fitting the description of Ylena.'

Angered by the soldiers' audacity Aleda had swept across the courtyard to join her husband where he was talking with the leader.

The young novice told them how, from their hiding spot in the attic, he and Brother Lewk had watched as heated words were exchanged by the two men.

'The man didn't even climb down from his mount,' Pil recalled. 'He just addressed your father from the saddle.

'The rider kept pointing at the duke, issuing orders it seemed, but the duke stayed calm. He must have offered an invitation for them to search the house but that's when it all went wrong. I have no idea what happened but I suspect the man said something to your father which your brother, Daryn, could not tolerate,' Pil said to Crys, whose stony expression did not flinch. 'He bravely – or perhaps unwisely – grabbed the leader and pulled him down off the horse.'

'Stupid boy!' Crys cried. 'Daryn never could keep a cool head.'

'Pandemonium broke out, my lord,' Pil said. The new title was not lost on his audience. 'One of the riders fired an arrow into Daryn's chest. He dropped like a stone. Your mother screamed and fell to the ground beside him to cradle him. He may still have lived for a few moments, my lord; I could not tell for your father had already drawn his sword. He didn't stand a chance. He fought bravely but they brought him to his knees.'

'Stop!' Elspyth interrupted, tears blinding her. 'Crys, I—'

'I will hear it all!' Crys yelled, ignoring his own free-flowing tears. 'Say it!' he commanded.

Pil shivered and nodded. Jakub had always warned him to stick plainly to the facts when conjuring an important event. He told precisely how it had unfolded, hating every painful word and its effect on Crys.

'They beheaded him, my lord duke. It was not clean. I had to look away. They held your mother, made her watch When it was done, they took her and tore off her clothes. They raped her one after another in the court-yard. Your other brother, Jorge, suddenly appeared from the stables, but he died also, fighting for her dignity.'

At this, Crys fell to his knees and screamed out, beseeching the heavens for deliverance from this nightmare.

Elspyth threw herself on top of him, arms around him, weeping as hard as he was. She could understand his pain, wanted to absorb it for him. He cried in her embrace for a lengthy time whilst Pil sat in horrified silence, head bowed between his knees.

Finally they heard Crys's voice, croaked and muffled.

'Pardon, my lord?' Pil said gently.

'I said, how? How could they know?' the new Duke of Felrawthy screamed. He moved so swiftly that Elspyth fell backwards as he grabbed the monk in a vice-like grip, their faces barely inches apart.

Pil stammered out the final crushing item of information. 'Brother Lewk, my lord – he's a spy.' He began to weep now. 'I led him to your family, asked them to make him welcome. I tried to keep up the pretence, to stick to the story we'd all agreed on. But, my lord, I could not lie to a man of the cloth. I didn't mention about Wyl being Faryl of course, but I admitted that I had escorted Ylena to your family.'

Crys looked as wild and angry as an injured beast. He shook off Elspyth's touch and pushed Pil away then ran blindly towards the shadow of a few trees.

'Leave him,' Elspyth said. She could feel the tension in her jaw, causing her temples to throb as she asked, 'And the duchess?'

'I don't know. I have no idea whether she lives or died.'

She felt sickened. 'Everyone else is dead, you are sure?'

He nodded, although a sob escaped. 'I don't know what happened to the twenty men, but they didn't arrive in time to help anyone.' 'The duke is definitely dead. Jorge was hacked down and Daryn's body did not move after Aleda was pulled from him. The arrow had hit in the region of his heart.'

'Shar's despair . . . all of them, all of them gone,' she whispered, shaking from the trauma of realisation. 'I led you to Brother Lewk. It is all my fault. Again. I did it! I am a curse!' she wept, feeling herself losing control.

'No, Elspyth. How could you know he was an impostor? I fell for it too. Anyone would have.'

'How did you get away?'

'I fought him. I sensed him watching me closely when the first of the deaths occurred. Something about him suddenly felt wrong. It all began to add up – the fact that I sang a well-known hymn on the way to Tenterdyn with him and he didn't know the words. Plus he said he'd visited Rittylworth, yet couldn't remember Brother Bors – everyone knows Brother Bors, he was over ninety years old.' Pil shook his head. 'I suddenly realised I'd been duped. When I saw them hurting Aleda, I began looking around for a weapon. I knew it was stupid – how could I fight them? Yet I needed to do something. But he grabbed me, and that confirmed his betrayal. So I fought him, fought him with everything I had. I knocked him unconscious, more through luck than anything, and then I fled. I climbed out of the window and ran across the rooftop as I had once before with brave Ylena. The soldiers never knew I was there of course so I was able to get to the stables, steal a horse and come after you and Crys.'

'Did you kill him?'

'Brother Lewk?'

She nodded.

'I . . . I think he was just stunned.'

'Then he will tell them about you and they will come after us,' she said, newly panicked. She leapt to her feet and ran after Crys.

'Go away, leave me!' Crys roared, rounding on her.

'Listen to me,' she begged. 'They will be coming after us, Crys, I'm sure of it, and they will slaughter what remains of Felrawthy. You are its duke now. You are all that's left. We will avenge them, but not unless we get you to safety.'

He laughed bitterly. It was a horrible sound. 'Duke of Felrawthy, you say?'

Elspyth looked around at Pil. 'Get the horses readied. Yours is over there,' she said, taking charge. 'Crys, look at me. We have no time for recriminations, not yet anyway. We must flee and save our lives.'

He groaned. 'Elspyth!'

His broken expression tore at her heart. 'I know,' she wept, reaching for him. 'I know. But you have to be strong now. You will get your war with Celimus, but you have to—'

She never finished what she was about to say. He took her into his arms and sobbed into her hair. She shook her head towards Pil and he obediently led the stray horse back towards the others, leaving them alone. It felt frightening to hold this man so close. Their emotions were strung out and tragedy and pain can bind as much as cleave souls. Elspyth felt a dangerous stirring in them both but particularly Crys. She pulled away, shocking him with her sudden movement of rejection.

Gazing directly into his hurt handsome face, she spoke softly. 'Come now – we must get you to safety.' She hoped he would recognise her affection for him – perhaps not right now whilst he hurt, but later when he was rational and understood her heart was already claimed.

'Where?' He looked lost.

'Briavel. They wouldn't dare follow us there.'

He nodded, capitulating to her strength and suddenly

glad to be led. He understood how Ylena must have felt not so long ago. 'Let's go,' he said, a grimness in his voice that had not been there before.

27

CELIMUS SAT ATOP A white mare. His new prize in the royal stables. He called her Grace which was befitting: she was light, elegant and the swiftest horse he had ever ridden. He was still breathing hard from the gallop during which he had given her the rein and allowed her to show her superb speed. Cooling her carefully now he walked her towards the shade of a tree where they would wait for Jessom and his falconer who would be a while yet catching up. He bent to stroke her and she tossed her mane, keen to be off again. 'Not so fast, bright one. There is business to be done yet,' he cooed.

The King took a draught of water from his flask and surveyed the beautiful landscape about him.

'I must have an heir for all of this, Grace,' he said, tapping her beautifully muscled neck. 'I want him to have two thrones.' He laughed. 'Why not three even?' he added, throwing the Mountain Kingdom into the ring. 'He shall be called Emperor — after me, of course. Empress Valentyna shall be his mother and I shall teach him to mock the pretender, Cailech, whose head I shall have preserved and spiked outside Stoneheart for eternity.'

He drank again, noticing the two riders finally appearing over the crest of a small rise. They arrived, panting.

'Sire,' the falconer said, 'we are ready. I have your three favourite birds and we are positioned down there, your majesty.' He pointed into the distance where two men could be picked out.

'I won't be long,' Celimus said to the falconer, who dismissed himself with a nod to his King and a glance towards Jessom who was still catching his breath.

'I think we should introduce a new rule, sire,' Jessom commented once the man had departed and he felt more composed, 'that you should not ride without at least one guard.'

'Bah! This is Morgravia, man. I have my bow with me,' the King said contemptuously.

'Nevertheless,' Jessom replied somewhat imperially. It was his favourite retort.

'I won't be babysat. I am a King.'

'My very reason for suggesting the higher security, your majesty. Your status demands it.'

Celimus nodded reluctantly. He knew his Chancellor was right.

'Did you want me to watch you work your birds or shoot arrows at deer, my lord, or is there another reason I am abroad in this thoroughly fascinating landscape and freezing my balls off?'

The King laughed. Jessom's timing on when to jest with his sovereign was always masterful.

'I am meeting someone. Not for castle ears.'

'Ah,' his man replied knowingly. 'Do you want me involved in the conversation or hidden, sire?'

'You may remain. Here he comes now,' he said, nodding towards a lone rider.

'Excellent timing,' Jessom said, shivering at the bite of the spring morning. 'Who is he, my lord?'

'His name is Shirk. He ran an errand for me.'

It was all Jessom needed to know. Shirk was clearly one of the King's newest henchmen, sent off to tackle unsavoury tasks which could not be given to the Legion.

They watched him approach. 'Lady Bench?' Celimus enquired of his Chancellor whilst they waited, his glance not moving from Shirk.

'Having a large party in a few days, I gather, sire. Her husband is on one of his rare visits to Pearlis, though I imagine he won't remain long.'

'He's a wanderer that one. However, my father suggested I should listen to his advice. Much as I detested my father his strategy was sound. I have found Eryd Bench, so far, to be reliable counsel.'

Jessom nodded and remained quiet, waiting for the next question.

'So nothing out of the ordinary for Lady Bench, then?'

'Not that I can tell, your highness. I am having her household watched day and night as you requested, sire. There have been no odd comings or goings.'

'Good. Keep her under watch.'

'Another week, sir?'

'That should do it. Ah, Shirk.'

'Your highness.' The newly arrived man bowed in his saddle.

'This is Chancellor Jessom. You may speak freely.'

The man nodded at Jessom. 'Thank you, sire. Shall I report?'

'Go ahead,' Celimus said, looking down towards the falconers as if it did not matter one way or the other to him.

Jessom noticed the man's clothes were of sufficient quality to need reasonable coin. A well-paid mercenary then, he presumed.

'We found no sign of the Lady Ylena Thirsk, your Majesty, nor the woman, Leyen, who you described.'

The Chancellor saw the King's jaw clench in disappointment. He wished that his King had asked him to handle this particularly delicate mission. It needed finesse. He could only imagine the damage he suspected he would be left to mend.

'But?' the King asked, his tone still deliberately casual.

'The family – that is, the Duke of Felrawthy's son – was not co-operative.'

'I see,' Celimus said. 'Something to hide then. And did you handle it as I recommended?' he asked, choosing his words with care. Jessom feared what was coming. Surely nothing had befallen the aristocratic duke and duchess?

'Yes, your majesty. Precisely as you required. The duke, duchess and their sons are dead.'

Jessom flinched. He tried to set a blank expression on his face but was sure he was unsuccessful. This was a dire revelation and he had no doubt whose hand had pulled the strings of the puppets who had done the deed. His normally controlled thoughts spun frantically. How would they cover this new atrocity? This was well beyond even his slippery and dark notions of manipulation. Jessom enjoyed power but he was not a bloodthirsty man and would not order anyone injured or killed unless he could justify it in his mind. He could not come up with one scenario which justified the slaughter of the loyalists in the north who had single-handedly shielded the realm from invasion.

In Jessom's short experience Duke Jeryb had shown himself to be steadfast and true to the Crown with a bright intelligence and an information channel to the King which could only be admired. He ran his Legionnaires with a firm but fair hand and even Jessom, from his much removed position, sensed that the Legion admired the duke and his fine family in the same manner that they had admired the Thirsks. Killing the youngest son had been a horrific mistake. Fortunately it had been covered well, but here they were still dealing with the repercussions of that murder. The remains of the Donal boy could reappear to undo them all. He could not imagine how they might now explain away five more deaths in the same family, and yet already his mind was racing towards how they might do just that.

'You are quite sure?' Celimus said, fixing the man now with his unnerving gaze.

Jessom noticed the man hesitate and blink. It was a telltale sign that perhaps all had not gone according to plan.

'Well, the duke's head is no longer attached to his body,' the man replied, with an unsure grin, which quickly vanished. 'His wife — well, she's dead, I'm sure of that. I know one of the men checked and the—'

'How did you deal with her?' Celimus asked, his voice seemingly innocent but his intense stare suggesting otherwise.

'As you required, sire. We humiliated her.'

'You raped her.' Celimus said the words for him.

He nodded. 'Yes, your majesty. Each of the men took a turn with her.'

Celimus was unfazed. 'But someone checked her pulse,' he said.

Again the man nodded, dumbly this time, Jessom noted. The man was clearly not so sure of the duchess's current state of health.

The King let it be for now. 'The sons — all three of them dead?'

The mercenary looked up sharply now, turning from his King to Jessom with a beseeching expression.

Jessom helped him out. 'There are three sons. The heir is Crys — you could not miss him. Golden-haired, tall. Handsome, they say. The other two are darker, more like the mother. One is Daryn, the other Jorge.' This was the Chancellor's first and only contribution to the conversation but his words made the mercenary visibly pale.

'I see,' the King said, understanding all too well. 'Which one didn't you deal with?'

'The handsome one, your highness,' he stuttered. 'There was no sign of him.'

'Is there anything else?' Celimus kept his disgust in check. Jessom felt a little sorry for the well-dressed man before them for it was now very clear — to the Chancellor anyway — that the mercenary's days were sadly numbered.

'Yes, my King.' The man tried for crispness but failed, perhaps already sensing his own demise. 'Our spy, posing as a monk, managed to corner a stranger. His name was Pil, a novice. But the youngster escaped over the rooftops.'

'You've caught him though?' Celimus enquired. Jessom

felt genuine pity for the cornered mercenary. The King's voice, so well controlled, managed to imbue a horrific sense of threat all the same. He was a master at it.

'We have given chase, your highness. We should have him by now.'

'A novice you say? What was he doing with your spy?'

The man began to shrug but shook his head instead to avoid offence to a sovereign known for his erratic moods. 'I don't know the answer to that, sire, but he introduced Lewk into the family. Lewk – that's our spy – felt he could learn more about whether the two women had been at Tenterdyn.'

'And did he?'

'Yes,' the man uttered triumphantly. 'The women had been there. It was the novice who brought the noble-woman to the family.'

Oh, you poor fool, Jessom thought. This should have been the first item on the report. He feared for the man's next few minutes.

'Shar's wrath, man!' Celimus bellowed, leaning forward in his saddle to strike the man hard across his face. The mercenary toppled from his horse. The King leapt down from his own mount, all feline grace, and in one smooth movement kicked Shirk so hard he could not get to his feet. He lay there coughing, groaning in pain.

'Where are they?'

In obvious agony the man spluttered his answer. 'The woman, Leyen, goes by the name of Faryl, sire. According to the novice's information, she did not tarry long at Tenterdyn. There was no trace of the noblewoman. The young monk said he had delivered her and departed the duke's hospitality almost immediately.'

'Lies!' Celimus roared. 'Felrawthy protects her! I was right to suspect the duke. He was not loyal to me,' he raved.

Jessom thought otherwise. The duke had given no reason to date to be considered anything but loyal to the Crown. The truth of the death of his son might have changed that, but so far all that had been kept secret. 'Sire—' he attempted but was rewarded with a glare so fierce he closed his mouth and sensibly opted to remain silent.

'Get away from me,' Celimus spat at the injured man. 'Crawl away from me, down the hill. Do not let me look upon your face again.'

Shirk did as commanded, leaving his horse, no doubt eager to be away from the King's wrath. Unhurried, Celimus reached behind and unstrapped his bow.

Jessom felt pity for the man on all fours retreating down the incline. He had not been disloyal, simply careless. But then Celimus suffered no fools about him.

He sighed. 'Would you like to see me in your study, sire, after I clear up here?' Jessom enquired, knowing the answer, his mind already racing towards how he would tackle the damage in the north.

Celimus nocked his arrow and took aim. 'Immediately,' he said and loosed his anger towards the man who had failed him.

Jessom watched his quarry alight from their carriage. He had decided to handle this particular item of business himself. Crossing the road, lifting his robe slightly so it would not trail in the general muck and damp of the busy market cobblestones, he angled his direction perfectly and artfully bumped the shoulder of the man.

'Do forgive—' Jessom began a solicitous apology then feigned an expression of delighted surprise. 'Lord Bench, what a pleasure. I'm so sorry for knocking you just now. I was in a hurry to cross the street.'

'No harm done, Jessom.' Eryd Bench waved off the apology.

'Lady Bench,' Jessom acknowledged with a short bow.

'Chancellor,' she said, nodding, her hand tightening ever so slightly on her husband's arm. 'I'm so sorry you couldn't attend our recent supper.'

'Not as sorry as I, my lady,' Jessom replied. 'I am afraid our King keeps me on a hectic schedule,' he admitted, permitting a rare smile.

She felt its insincere touch, knew he suspected something. Also knew that so far he had nothing to level their way. 'Oh, such a shame, Chancellor. I know how you like lamprey too – it was on the menu.'

He made a soft noise of despair at missing out. 'Are you home for long, Lord Bench?'

'No, not this time. We are about to take a family trip actually.'

'Oh?' Jessom enquired, already knowing the general gossip. 'Where are you off to – somewhere warmer I hope?' and he chuckled, pulling his cape closer around his thin shoulders.

'No, indeed.' Bench smiled ruefully. 'I am headed north in fact to meet a wonderful shipment of exotic goods coming into Brightstone. Helyn and Georgyana thought they might accompany me this time.'

'Yes, I've decided it's high time I saw what my husband does on these trips,' Helyn offered with one of the chortles she reserved for intrigue.

'And where will you stay?' Jessom asked, all politeness.

'Normally I'd stay at an inn, but with the ladies along we have a small holding up north, not far from Yentro and Deakyn in fact. Been in the family for donkeys years. I thought we might make them more comfortable in the house.'

'Indeed,' Jessom soothed. 'A lengthy trip?'

Eryd knew he was being interrogated, as his wife had been not long ago. 'Not sure yet. With my family in tow, I suppose we can take our time. I thought we might travel up via the east. Perhaps catch up with that old rogue Jeryb and his marvellous brood before my shipment comes in.'

Jessom was alarmed but did not show it. 'Brr, it is cold out today. Can I offer you both a nip of shorron to warm our insides?'

Neither of his companions cared to spend a moment longer with him.

'Of course,' Eryd answered. 'I am never one to say no to a glass.'

'We shall have to be swift, my love,' Helyn warned, wishing Eryd had declined. 'I have lots to purchase today for our trip.'

Eryd patted her hand in reassurance and the trio headed towards the nearest shorron counter where the hot, bitter liquor was served in warmed glasses with a dollop of honey to sweeten its passage. Shorron was a local specialty of Pearlis so there were bars and counters aplenty. In summer the drink was serve chilled but its warming, softly aphrodisiac effect was best felt on a crisp, cold day.

Jessom ordered three shots. 'Would you mind, Eryd,

if I suggest you don't travel to Felrawthy,' he said quietly
as they waited. Helyn had already fallen into conversation with a friend at the counter.

'Why ever not?' Lord Bench asked, wondering at the
Chancellor's sudden familiarity.

'Bad news up north, I'm afraid. Our King will announce
it to the court tomorrow in fact. We only heard this
morning.'

'And what is it?' Eryd felt a chill crawl through him.

'We have received sketchy reports that the duke might
have been killed.'

'Shar save us!'

Helyn turned at the exclamation and excused herself
from her friend. 'Eryd?' she said, coming over.

'That is not all,' Jessom said sorrowfully. 'We have had
no confirmation yet but the same source reports that all
in the family are presumed dead.'

'This cannot be right,' Eryd blustered, the chill
extending to all parts of his body.

Jessom shook his head. 'We are not sure, as I say,' he
said carefully. 'I have sent some reliable men to check. It
is shocking, I know. The King is devastated, as you can
imagine. He relied heavily on the duke's counsel regarding
the north.'

'Not to mention his protection. But how could such a
thing happen?' Eryd said.

'Drink this,' Helyn said, piecing together the
disturbing news. She handed her husband his shot.

Jessom tipped back his head and downed the liquor,
feeling its burning warmth. Eryd followed suit, genuinely
appalled at the news. Helyn toyed with hers. She suspected
– as did her husband – that they were being fed untruths,

and yet the story was so shocking it would have to be based in reality, which meant that marvellous family up north probably had suffered.

'Everyone dead, you say?' Eryd asked.

Jessom nodded. 'We await confirmation. The barbarian King's men apparently. The family was expecting re-inforcements of their own and had left the gates open at Tenterdyn. It was so easy. We shall know more in a couple of days. I just think it's best you don't take your family to the scene of carnage in case it is true. The region is clearly dangerous now.'

'Cailech! Why would the Mountain King be bothered with Jeryb?' Eryd spluttered, signalling for a second shot.

'I think the self-crowned madman of the north must have decided that the duke was his main obstacle. By dealing with Felrawthy he probably believes he has effectively crushed Morgravia's northern defences.'

Helyn could hardly help her snort. 'You believe that the Mountain King has actually invaded and might head south?'

Jessom put his hand to his lips to signify that they must be careful what they said. 'King Celimus suspects as much. The duke had confirmed many sightings of Cailech's men in our northern lands. I fear, madam, that it is only a matter of time before the Mountain King feels confident enough to try for an invasion.'

'Well, thank you for the warning, Chancellor,' Eryd said, holding out his hand in farewell. 'This is dire news indeed. We shall certainly steer clear of that region.'

Jessom blinked slowly and nodded before he shook Eryd's hand. Helyn decided he reminded her of a vulture. 'I am glad, Lord Bench. Be safe on your travels.' He bowed and turned to Helyn. 'Lady Bench, my respects to your lovely daughter. May Shar guide you all on your journey.'

'Thank you,' she said sweetly, pulling her hand away as quickly as she dared from the vulture's touch.

They left, Eryd's second glass of shorron untouched. Jessom drank it himself, pleased with his morning's work. He felt quietly confident that he could call off permanent observation of the Bench family now. He would have their party followed on their departure for the north, and if they took the westernmost road towards the port of Brightstone rather than the road which veered east towards Felrawthy, it would satisfy him – and no doubt his King – that this family was no threat.

Outside, Lady Bench hurried to keep up with her husband's long and presently angry stride. 'Do you believe him?' she asked breathlessly.

'That Felrawthy has fallen? Yes. Not how it fell, though. Cailech is not that bold. Jessom forgets I know the north better than most. No, this is darker work. I think Leyen's warning, and your suspicion about our King, is right.'

'What do we do?'

'Nothing! Just observe for now – it's what you're best at.'

King Celimus pondered all that Jessom had told him. 'I am inclined to agree: the Bench family is no threat. Their watchers can be released. Now, I want you to have a letter couriered to Valentyna for me. It is obvious that Leyen or Faryl, whatever her name is, has not succeeded in dealing with Ylena and perhaps may not follow my other instructions to head to Briavel. We shall have to rely on

Aremys to deal with the Thirsk woman. I'd prefer it if you copied this one yourself.'

'Of course, sire.' Jessom fiddled with parchment and quills, searching for the right one. 'Ready, my lord.'

Celimus strolled to his study window and glanced down into the courtyard. 'My dear Valentyna,' he began. 'No, wait! Make that, Valentyna, my dearest,' the King corrected. He listened as Jessom scratched away at the paper then continued slowly: 'I do hope this finds you in good health, although no doubt as busy with matters of the realm as I find myself. Perhaps you have made some time to get to know the exquisite filly I gifted you? I gather she arrived in fine spirits at her new home and I know she has found the most generous and caring of owners. I would be interested to hear whether you liked the name I chose for her – she is the latest offspring of one of my finest brood mares. I am sure that you and she will enjoy sharing good times in that beautiful woodland surrounding Werryl.'

He paused, waiting for Jessom to catch up.

'Darling Valentyna – I hope that's not too forward?'

'No, sire, it's perfect,' Jessom replied, faithfully recording his monarch's love letter.

'Darling Valentyna,' Celimus repeated, 'I hope you know that it is my heart's desire to formalise our union without unnecessary delay. Since meeting you I have thought of nothing else but our marriage and the bringing together of our realms in peace and harmony.'

Jessom scratched furiously. 'And now a gentle threat, sire?' he prompted softly.

Celimus chuckled. 'You know my mind too well, Chancellor,' he said. 'Indeed, we must spice this note with a warning. Let me see now,' he pondered, watching the comings and goings in the yard below. 'Ah, yes. Time threatens our peace, my dear one. The upstart of the north – King Cailech, as he hails himself – has spilled the blue blood of Morgravia with his slaughter of the Duke of Felrawthy and his entire family. I am sure you will grieve with all Morgravians at the tragic loss of this fine and noble line. We are taking steps to shore up our defences in the north, but I sense that Cailech grows confident and with the smell of Morgravian blood in his nostrils will now push south. My fear is that when he meets our resistance – and it will be fierce, I promise – he will turn his attention to Briavel. I cannot – nay, will not – permit this savage to threaten you, my darling, or your land. Once sworn enemies, we must now cleave together. Let me help to keep you and Briavel safe. I will pledge my entire Legion to the defence of both our realms as soon as you confirm our marriage.'

He turned and beamed at Jessom. The Chancellor wondered how Valentyna could ever resist that radiant smile. 'Brilliant, sire. Perhaps we should suggest a date?'

'Yes! Read back the last line.'

Jessom did so.

'Good. Go on and say, I have set a date of the last day of spring. I see you as a spring bride when the land is bursting with life again. It is how you make me feel, Valentyna, filled with a sense of new beginnings.' He paused again to consider how to finish his letter.

'My man carries accompanying paperwork for your signature and, once returned, I will begin to make preparations for our splendid wedding day, a day when all Morgravians and Briavellians will rejoice together. And our enemies will fear us, my beautiful one. No one will ever threaten our new empire.'

He clapped his hands gleefully. 'And then you can finish as you see fit.'

'I shall get this away immediately, sire.'

'Have the courier await the reply. A few days' turnaround no doubt?'

'Weather permitting, my King.'

'See to it, Jessom.'

The Chancellor began clearing his papers.

'What's happening at Felrawthy by the way?' the King asked.

'I have sent some reliable men to clear away all evidence.'

'The bodies?'

'Will be burned.'

'Excellent. But you will leave some signs to suggest this was the work of the Mountain Dwellers?'

'Already taken care of, sire.'

'Thank you, Jessom. And I want news of your assassins soonest.'

Celimus felt happy and in control. In this mood he felt it was appropriate to take his pleasure with a woman.

'Have the Lady Amelia sent up.'

'As you wish, sire. I believe her bruises have healed,' Jessom murmured as he bowed and departed.

28

THE MEN STOOD AROUND the pit looking deeply disturbed. Some scratched their heads nervously, others fidgeted and tried to hold their breath. No one was sure what to say. There were supposed to be four bodies but they counted only three stinking corpses.

'Fetch someone who was here,' their leader growled. A man was brought before him several minutes later. 'How many corpses were there?'

The man looked surprised. 'Four – three men, one woman.'

'Well, we've got only the three men. The duke and the two sons you managed to deal with.'

The sarcasm was not lost on the man and he responded with defiance, not cowed by this second group who suddenly appeared today with new orders from the Chancellor. 'The third son was not at Tenterdyn. The woman definitely was.'

'Well, she's not now!' the leader roared. 'Do you want to explain that to the man who is paying us a lot of gold to do this?'

'What are you suggesting?'

The leader sneered. 'I'm suggesting, you idiot, that the woman was never fully dead. She might have looked it but she's got away . . . or someone helped her.'

The other man bristled at the insult, remembering how revolting it had felt to rape the dead woman. It was clear then she had taken her last breath. 'She was dead I tell you,' he snarled back.

'Well, you find her corpse and let the paymaster know when you do. I shall be reporting that we disposed of three male bodies only. And I reckon it's not just your purses you men should be worried about.' He winked at the first man, who understood perfectly the underlying threat. 'Burn the three men,' he added, 'and I suggest your people start searching Brynt and its surrounds for a dazed woman. Try the chapels, the hospices, anywhere they offer succour without questions. She will go to ground.'

Not far away Aleda grimaced as she heard this conversation come to a close. If only they knew that she was barely a few yards from where they had done their ugly work.

She had regained consciousness during the early evening of the day of the attack. With her wits had come memory and all the horror of what had passed. It was only then that she became fully oriented and realised she was lying on top of one of her sons in a pit covered by branches. Dusk allowed some dying light to filter through the leaves and twigs overhead and she screamed to discover Jorge beneath her. His eyes were open and it seemed to his mother that he wore an expression of anger, even though she knew that in death it was not possible to hold any look. He had died fighting for her honour. She began to weep and scrabbling further discovered her other boy, Daryn, as cold and lifeless to the touch as his brother. She remembered now how he had been cut down before her.

To her despair her darling husband's headless body lay at the bottom of this pit of death. She saw his head tossed carelessly at his feet. Her sobs grew louder. They would have laughed as they threw it in, she imagined. She had cradled the bloodied head of her husband in her lap and cried for hours as she stroked his dearly loved face.

When her sobs finally subsided realisation had hit and she looked around frantically. 'Crys!' she shrieked. It was the absence of her eldest son that gave her the courage to claw her way out of the pit. She fell several times, sobbing and scrabbling at the earth that caved in on her and covered her beloved menfolk. Finally she made it and lay at the lip of the pit, keening with sorrow and trembling from her exertions. She did not notice her bleeding knees or torn fingernails.

Perhaps Crys still lives, she comforted herself, desperately pushing away the fear that he might have been taken and tortured by their attackers. And then she remembered Pil and Brother Lewk and wondered why their bodies were not here amongst the dead. Aleda ran her hands through her hair, streaking it with more mud, and slowly permitted herself the knowledge that her body was badly hurt. The pain was not easily described. It felt deep within and, with a woman's instinct, she knew the injuries may yet kill her. It was almost night now, so she could only see the blood on her skirts as a dark stain but she knew it was there, remembered all too well how it was earned. Death was not her fear now. Time was. She was happy to die, would welcome the sight of Shar's Gatherers, if not for the painful hope that Crys may still live . . . may still need her.

She could hear Jeryb in her mind, encouraging her to flee. 'Get away from here,' he said to her. 'Hide!'

Exhausted, she re-covered the pit and, weeping more lightly now, remembered a hide that Crys had once made just slightly uphill. He had boasted that he could see the northern route from there, just in case the Mountain People ever came raiding. He was much younger then and she had laughed indulgently at him but his father had praised him for his endeavour and foresight. 'You can never be too well prepared for raiders, son,' he had said and ruffled the youngster's hair.

Her eldest son still used the hide occasionally when tracking animals and had kept it clean and dry. He had invited her to sit in it once and Aleda had marvelled at the cosy comfort. It was sheltered and relatively warm for their harsh climate, and he always kept it stocked which amused her. Food had always been high in her growing son's mind.

She had crawled towards that haven and lay in its safe womb for two days, trying to heal, thanking Crys silently for the waterskin there. There was no food, but the water had kept her alive. Aleda had heard the men come back, heard their banter and ugly jokes at her family's expense. And now she could see them as they dragged the bodies of her beloved menfolk towards a fire and, without cere-mony, threw them on to the flames to burn. They could not burn her memories, though, Aleda thought, fanning her fury in tandem with the fire as its flames licked higher into the air. She knew who was responsible for this – a king, yes, but not the Mountain King. Celimus would be sorry his cold and beautiful mother ever conceived him, Aleda promised herself as she watched her family burn.

She waited another half day in the hide, just to be sure the men had gone. It was too late to retrieve anything from the pyre. They had scattered it, destroying as much evidence of the fire and its contents as possible. All her men were dead – bar one, she prayed. She clung to the hope that Crys lived and, as she crept back to the family house to find warm travelling clothes and medicines to help kill the pain of her injuries, Aleda tried to imagine where her son might find sanctuary. He was no longer safe in Morgravia; neither was she for that matter. He had been escorting Elspyth to the border with Briavel. Perhaps he had returned to Tenterdyn but seen the devastation in time and fled. But where to?

There was nothing for it. She would have to travel to Briavel and find Elspyth. Perhaps the young woman's final encounter with Crys might reveal something. Hopefully Elspyth had succeeded in gaining the protection of Queen Valentyna. Aleda, in her befuddled state, even began to beg Shar that Crys had seduced Elspyth – it was obvious to all that he had been entranced by the woman from Yentro – and that they had travelled on together into Briavel. But Crys would not desert his family. It suddenly dawned on her she was not just chasing the last remaining heir of Felrawthy but also its new duke. Did Crys even know?

With only a small bag to carry, it was not worth looking in the stable for a horse. The attackers had stolen everything; the house itself had been ransacked of all valuables. None of it mattered. Grazing in a nearby field was the same donkey that had brought Elspyth to them. She would take that. She assumed Brother Lewk had fled in such a hurry that he would not be back for the animal.

She led the animal to the stables, found a saddle that would do and, as fast as her aching body allowed, got the animal ready for the long trip to the famed city of Werryl.

If Wyl Thirsk believed in the Briavellian Queen, then so must she.

Aleda lost track of time on her journey. She could no longer remember when the attack had occurred, how many days it had been since death came to Tenterdyn. All that mattered now was staying alive long enough to make it to the famed palace at Werryl and keeping the donkey fed, rested and watered so she could achieve her goal.

She had been clear-thinking enough to pack oats and water. She knew the animal could forage along the way for grass and foliage that had survived the winter frosts. She herself was warmly dressed; besides, her anger and fierce single-minded determination prevented her feeling the cold's pinch on her face. She intended to ride the donkey for as many hours a day as she could before her body fell from the saddle.

She had bled again but ignored it. She did her best to keep her strength up and forced herself to eat. Sometimes she managed only a few mouthfuls but persevered. Her body – if it was going to heal, which she doubted – needed nourishment. She had also had the foresight to grab some family documents and a small portrait of herself and Jeryb. These would be required, she assumed, in order to prove her identity, for right now she looked anything but the wife of the second wealthiest man in the kingdom of

Morgravia. She also carried the sack with its gruesome contents that Ylena had brought with her to Tenterdyn.

Once Aleda had crossed the River Tague, she felt a small measure of her burden lift. She knew she was on enemy territory now, yet it was to this enemy she was turning for safety. She moved towards the east for some hours, knowing she would be picked up by the Briavellian Guard soon. She hoped so for her strength was rapidly dwindling; even her sight felt as though it was narrowing. But she had to hold on, had to find word of Crys.

29

THE CURIOUS-LOOKING TRIO of travellers waited at the Werryl Bridge while word was sent to the Briavellian Commander of the arrival of a novice monk, a noble from Morgravia and a young woman from Yentro claiming to have a special missive for Queen Valentyna.

Liryk recognised the noble's family name; it was not one to be ignored. All the same, he shook his head. 'Ask them to give us the document and we will consider their request.'

'I've tried that, sir,' his captain replied. 'They are quite firm.'

Liryk considered. The Queen's mood had plummeted into nothing short of despair since the death of Romen Koreldy. She masked it well for strangers but those close to her knew their sovereign was emotionally scarred. She carried on her duties with vigour and dedication but she was withdrawn and strangely detached from all of them.

'Tell them it is impossible. The Queen is indisposed and they can either pass over the letter and await instructions or they can leave.'

His captain clicked a bow and, rather than leave it to one of his minions, went out to meet with the Morgravians himself.

'I'm sorry, I've been advised to tell you that Commander Liryk will not permit you entry. He insists on seeing the paperwork you speak of and then your request will be considered.' The soldier saw the woman's shoulders slump. All three looked exhausted and disappointed.

As fate would have it, Valentyna chose that moment to emerge from her private study and stroll out on to the battlements. She noticed the trio on the bridge speaking with her captain. The woman seemed to be looking at him imploringly.

'Who are those people?' she enquired absently of Liryk who had welcomed her with a broad smile.

'Morgravians, apparently, your highness, requesting entry to Werryl. Captain Orlyd will bring news of them shortly.'

She looked down again. Their clear fatigue piqued her interest. 'Do we have their names?'

'The young noble's name is known to me. A proud Morgravian family, but for all we know this man could be an impostor.'

Valentyna frowned. 'Why are they here?'

'Our patrol picked them up at Greenfield. They impressed our men as honest, offering the information that they were from Morgravia with a missive for you, your highness.'

This struck the Queen as odd but she held her tongue and waited until Captain Orlyd had reappeared.

'Ah, Orlyd,' Liryk said.

The man's eyes flicked warily towards the Commander as he bowed to his sovereign.

'What news of those people, captain?' Valentyna asked, the kindness in her tone encouraging the young officer.

'Your highness, they beseeched me to tell you that they are friends of General Wyl Thirsk. They . . . they mentioned Romen Koreldy,' he stammered, embarrassed. He was one of those entrusted with the secret of Koreldy's death and subsequent burial at Werryl.

Both men saw Valentyna's eyes widen and the flash of colour that suddenly erupted on her cheeks at the mention of Romen's name.

'Bring them to me,' she ordered, flustered. 'I shall be in my solar.'

Liryk sighed and nodded. 'Search them carefully,' he ordered Orlyd.

Two soldiers escorted the travellers across the famous Werryl Bridge. Former Briavellian Kings watched them pass by, their carved stone forms towering over them. Crys, despite his bitter sorrow, could not help commenting on the city's spectacular setting, with meadows all around and the river rushing beneath them. He told their guides how he had heard about Werryl from occasional travellers who passed through Morgravia's north, but no one had ever done its beauty justice. The men smiled, enjoying his sincere appreciation of their city.

On the other side of the bridge their horses were led away and Elspyth, Crys and Pil were asked to follow the captain through the huge gate that yawned before them, giving entry to the famed city of Werryl. Elspyth marvelled at its sparkling beauty and soaring towers of whitestone, exclusive to this region. It struck her that where Stoneheart was all dark and brooding majesty, this palace was bathed in a light of its own, reaching towards the skies. She did not remark on it though; instead she lowered her head and gratefully followed the soldier to their audience with Wyl's Queen. She could think of Valentyna no other way.

'Let me do the talking, Crys,' she cautioned in a whisper. He nodded. Pil trotted silently alongside, dazzled by the beauty around him.

They ascended an ornately fashioned staircase. An older man met them at the top. 'Thank you, Captain,' he said and dismissed Orlyd.

The old man bowed slightly. Elspyth appreciated his graciousness towards them. 'I am Chancellor Krell. I will escort you to meet her majesty,' he said. 'Perhaps we should hold off further introductions until you have been presented to our Queen and Commander Liryk. Come now, you all look terribly tired. Let me organise some refreshments.'

He signalled to a page and quietly issued some orders. The boy hurried away. Krell gave the trio a reassuring nod. 'I have decided you look famished too – we'll rustle up some food so none of you collapse at her majesty's feet.'

Elspyth grinned. She liked him straightaway.

'Why did her majesty suddenly agree to see us?' Crys asked.

Krell smiled benignly. 'Perhaps her highness should answer that herself. We are here.' He knocked at the door, then opened it for them.

Elspyth knew for certain why the Queen had invited them in – it was the mention of either Wyl's or Romen's name. She knew Valentyna was attractive because she had pushed Wyl for a description during their long walk from

Straplyn to Deakyn, which felt like a lifetime ago now. But expecting the description to reflect the embellishments of a man in love, she was completely unprepared for the tall, statuesque beauty who turned as they entered. Wyl had not exaggerated in the slightest.

'Your highness,' Krell said, 'this is Elspyth of Yentro, Crys Donal of Felrawthy, and Pil, novice of Shar and lately of Rittylworth Monastery.'

Valentyna nodded thanks to her Chancellor. 'Be welcome, all of you. Krell, have we organised some refreshments?' She knew he would have but the polite enquiry would help to ease introductions.

'On its way, your majesty.'

'Thank you. Come in, all of you,' she motioned as they straightened from their various bows. 'Do sit, please. I understand you have made a long and tiring journey.'

A little stunned to be in the same room as this dazzling woman, they sat silently.

'Now, forgive my informal welcome,' Valentyna said, smiling wryly at her garments. 'These are the Queen of Briavel's working clothes,' she added, arching an eyebrow and making Pil chortle briefly, which was precisely the effect she was hoping for. They all looked so tense, she could hardly imagine what news was about to be delivered. 'This is Commander Liryk,' she said.

Their gazes turned towards the man standing near the solar window. He nodded at Crys. 'I know your father,' he commented. 'A fierce soldier, a good man.'

'Knew him, sir,' Crys said. He had not meant it to come out so viciously but his emotions were not in control right now. 'He was murdered a few days ago, along with my mother and my two brothers.'

Elspyth's heart sank. She had hoped to handle the news with a bit more diplomacy but it was out now. She risked a glance at the Queen who threw a look of sympathy towards her, as though she sensed this was not how Elspyth had planned their meeting.

'What?' Liryk roared. 'Felrawthy dead?'

Elspyth knew she had to take control; she could not let Wyl down again and allow Crys's mouth to run away with details the Briavellians would not accept. This had to be told properly in order to win their help. She stood.

'Crys, please. Your highness, we have a shocking tale to tell you. Perhaps if you'll allow me. . . . ?'

Valentyna nodded. 'Of course,' she said, waving away Crys's attempt to begin an apology. The Queen, Elspyth could see, was very concerned for the young noble. Elspyth glared at him to stop him saying anything else damaging.

'My companion is having to deal with much heartache,' she said. 'Please forgive us this sudden intrusion and how odd this must all look. Commander Liryk, Crys Donal is the new Duke of Felrawthy.'

The Queen sat down, sensing the import of what she was about to hear. 'Tell us everything,' she said, as Krell ushered in serving staff with trays of food and drinks, both hot and cold. 'But first you must eat.'

She smiled encouragingly at Crys, but it was Pil, smitten by this utterly gorgeous woman who was a Queen but sat before him in the plainest of garb, who beamed back at her.

In between mouthfuls, Elspyth told her audience their sorry story. When she had finished speaking she could not help but lean over and squeeze Crys's hand. He had not eaten or drunk anything.

'All dead,' Liryk muttered angrily. 'You're quite sure?'

'Pil witnessed all that I have spoken of. He can confirm that the duke and his twin sons are dead.'

The young monk nodded bleakly.

'They would not have permitted my mother to live,' Crys said, emerging from his silence.

'And you are absolutely certain that these men were hired by King Celimus?' Valentyna asked, her voice as cold as the grave.

Liryk squirmed. This was everything they did not need as negotiations progressed towards the marriage of Morgravia's and Briavel's monarchs. 'Your highness,' he began but Valentyna held up her hand and returned her penetrating dark blue gaze to Elspyth.

It was unsettling to have such intense attention levelled at her. Elspyth suddenly felt as though no one else's opinion mattered to the Queen but hers. She recalled how Wyl had mentioned how Valentyna could make you feel as though you were the only person in the room.

'From what I gather, your majesty,' she said carefully, 'Celimus is capable of anything.'

'That's not absolute certainty, though, is it?' the Queen replied, her gaze steady.

Elspyth blinked. She could tell Wyl's whole story and shock these Briavellians but she had sworn not to break the promise, had seen the damaging effects of having done so once before. 'No, but Aremys and Faryl, both assassins in the employ of Celimus, confirmed it was his doing. They were ordered to kill Ylena Thirsk.'

'Your majesty, we cannot go on the word of hired

mercenaries. They would say anything, do anything, for gold,' Liryk warned.

Elspyth bristled. 'We did not pay them!' she said angrily to the soldier, then pulled back her claws. 'Forgive me, your highness. Aremys can be trusted.' She delved into her pocket. 'I have a letter for you. It is from . . .' and she hesitated, almost saying Wyl. 'From Ylena.'

'Wyl Thirsk's sister?' The Queen frowned, taking it from her.

'Yes, your highness. Aremys took her to safety,' she said, despairing at her own ability to lie so easily. She eyed the others, daring them to contradict her.

Krell stepped back into the room and glided towards the Queen at her nod. He bent to whisper something to her.

'Excuse me,' she said distractedly to her audience. 'Apparently there is an urgent messenger from Morgravia.' She tucked Wyl's letter away. 'I shall return shortly. Please make yourselves comfortable and eat more. We won't keep you long from your beds,' she finished kindly.

In her absence Liryk felt obliged to continue the discussion, despite his shock at learning of the death of Jeryb Donal, a formidable enemy who had respected the laws of war. Like his former General, Fergys Thirsk, the duke was not one to pursue a battle for the sake of it.

'I am very sorry to hear of your loss, son,' he said into the awkward silence.

Elspyth was glad that Crys was gracious enough to acknowledge the Commander's commiserations.

'Can you enlighten me as to how you know for sure these were men sent by your King?' Liryk pressed, hoping they could not.

Crys glanced towards Elspyth and caught her glare. 'Well, because they apparently said as much. They were trying to track down Ylena Thirsk, who had been removed from Stoneheart by Romen Koreldy.'

Pil nodded. 'That's right. Koreldy brought her to the monastery seeking shelter and sanctuary. She had been abused by the Crown, and I don't put that lightly, sir,' he qualified. He flushed at everyone's attention suddenly locked on to him. He too had been sworn to secrecy about Wyl and was terrified he might slip up. 'Romen left her with us.'

'And then the King's men burned Rittylworth you say – its monastery too. Whatever for?' Liryk asked.

Pil's eyes misted as he thought of his destroyed home. 'They were Legionnaires, sir, under orders to raze the village and teach it a lesson for harbouring a traitor. It was Ylena they were calling a traitor, although they would have to be especially brainwashed soldiers to believe that of Thirsk. Ylena was sure they were mercenaries masquerading as Legionnaires for this reason.'

'None of whom were traitorous to my knowledge,' Elspyth said, realising too late that it was a mistake to say this because she apparently had not known Wyl Thirsk. However, the Commander was sufficiently confused not to pin her down on this point. She suspected Valentyna might have and knew she would have to be still more careful when the Queen returned. She wished she could just come clean but they might throw them all out for being halfwits if she were to suggest that Wyl Thirsk now walked in the body of his sister.

'The men were also looking for the woman known as Faryl of Coombe,' Crys added. 'She had been at Tenterdyn, but did not stay once we told her we had not seen Ylena,' he said carefully. 'Faryl had most recently come from the King and she too was tracking Ylena Thirsk with a view to killing her. We learned this through Aremys who arrived shortly after her departure, also looking for Ylena but to protect her not kill her. It is too much of a co-incidence that these assassins, paid by the King, should be followed by more men bent on finding Ylena Thirsk.'

'And this Aremys you speak of – if he is a hired mercenary why does he want to help Ylena?'

'He is a friend of Romen's,' Elspyth cut in before either of her companions could respond. 'I . . . er . . . gather they were both of Grenadyn,' she added, recalling something Wyl had mentioned.

The Queen re-entered, her expression grim enough to be set in stone. Both Liryk and Crys stood immediately and bowed. Pil leapt to his feet too late. Elspyth was not sure what the correct protocol was, having never been in a sovereign's presence.

'Relax, everyone,' Valentyna said, pushing away some stray strands of hair. 'We have much to discuss. You need a rest first, though. Please follow Stewyt who will show you to some rooms where you can sleep for a few hours and refresh yourselves. Commander, I have called a meeting of our senior nobles. Krell is gathering them now. We meet this evening. The news from Morgravia is extraordinary.'

Elspyth lay restless on the bed in a small chamber that smelled of fresh herbs and offered a beautiful view of orchards. She knew she would not sleep. She felt as she had that day in Cailech's fortress, when her emotions had churned inside her. Although she was desperately tired, she could not drift off as she so wanted to. The refreshing bath and the generously provided clean garments made her feel even more awake in fact and so she welcomed the soft tap at her door an hour or so after she had been shown to her room.

It was Stewyt again. 'Her highness wonders if you would care for some company, Miss Elspyth,' he said with a small bow.

Elspyth was both surprised and delighted by the invitation. 'Of course,' she murmured. 'I'll just fetch my shawl.'

She followed the lad along the corridors and stairways of the palace. This time she did notice its elegance, so different to the duller grey of Stoneheart. It was built of the cool whitestone of Briavel which seemed to pulse with its own inner light, reflecting and intensifying the glow of flames from the sconces and cressets. Its architects were aiming for beauty alone in this palace of exquisite archways and wide, sweeping flights of stairs. Colour was everywhere in tapestries and carpets, paintings of previous kings and floral decorations. Elspyth had never been in a palace before but she knew from conversations with people who had visited Stoneheart that Morgravia's royals lived in a far more sombre place than this.

A sound of pleasure escaped Elspyth as they entered an area which contained a series of recesses which had been artfully painted to show glorious scenes, presumably from Briavel's folklore. 'Aren't they brilliant!' she exclaimed. 'I feel as though I can see forever into the landscapes.'

Stewyt beamed. 'This is a special kind of art, peculiar to Briavel, Miss Elspyth. It's called Pretence.'

She glanced at him quizzically. He continued. 'These are more than a century old. There was a movement of art in our realm called the Pretenders. They created scenes from our old stories and legends which is why they have this fantastical quality. And you mentioned the perspective.' He nodded at her. 'Their work tricks the eye into believing you are looking through a window on to a spectacular outdoor scene.'

'I adore them.'

'Thank you. It will please her majesty to hear this,' he said graciously, then added as they turned a corner, 'Our Queen loves music . . . and dancing.' They passed a chamber through whose slightly ajar door Elspyth glimpsed a quintet of musicians practising. It was a wondrous sound of strings which echoed down the new wing they were currently travelling. Elspyth realised that they were not heading deeper into the palace.

'The Queen will meet you in the herb gardens,' Stewyt said and held open a door for her that led outside.

They found Valentyna picking lavender. She had changed into a deep purple gown and again wore no adornments. She needs none, Elspyth decided, admiring the Queen's natural beauty.

Valentyna looked up at the sound of their arrival. 'Oh, I'm so glad you came,' she said to Elspyth, smiling warmly as if welcoming an old friend. She handed the lavender stems to the page. 'Thank you, Stewyt. Would you have these sent up to my chambers, please.' She turned back to her guest. 'Walk with me, would you? It is a beautiful afternoon and these gardens do wonders for my spirits.'

Elspyth hardly knew what to say as she fell in with the Queen's graceful step.

'I thought you might find it easier to speak freely without the men,' Valentyna admitted conspiratorially.

'Thank you, your majesty. Crys is having to face so much – it's certainly difficult talking about it all.'

'I can't imagine what he's going through, losing his family in such horrific circumstances.'

'Do you believe us, your majesty?' Elspyth asked in her direct way.

The Queen paused beneath a lemon tree. She inhaled its fragrance. 'Yes,' she replied softly.

Elspyth let out her breath. She felt like crying with relief.

'Do you know that Romen Koreldy is dead?' Valentyna asked, just as directly.

Her companion nodded. 'Word travels fast.' Her mind raced as to how she could know this. Before she could find an explanation the Queen spoke again.

'From whom did you learn this news?'

Elspyth felt trapped. This was a test clearly. She wanted to be as honest as she could with this woman whose sanctuary they sought, but she could not betray Wyl's wishes once again.

'Originally some Briavellian merchants told me. I was travelling with them. But it was confirmed by a woman called Faryl,' she said, making her decision, trying to be as truthful as she would with Valentyna.

'And how did she hear of it?' the Queen asked, bending down to smell some basil. It seemed a reasonable question but there was a tension there that told Elspyth how loaded it was.

'I gather she was in Briavel when it happened, your highness.'

'I see. That's interesting. Would you describe her to me? I do have good reason for asking.' The Queen handed Elspyth a sprig of mint to smell and smiled disarmingly.

Elspyth took a deep breath. 'She is tall and strong-looking, a handsome woman. She has a very direct golden-brown gaze,' she said, recalling Faryl in better detail as she concentrated on remembering those terrible few minutes after Wyl had entered the room at Tenterdyn.

Valentyna put her hand on Elspyth's arm. 'Ah yes, her eyes have a feline quality, don't they? And her hair is an auburn colour, not unattractive but unfashionably short for a woman at shoulder-length.'

Elspyth blushed as the Queen turned her now-hard blue gaze on her. 'Yes,' she stammered. 'That sums her up rather well.'

Valentyna's look darkened. 'I believe, Elspyth, that this Faryl you speak of is the Hildyth who murdered Romen. No one else believes me here. It is not something that matters to them, but it matters very much to me to know who perpetrated this.'

'She . . . she is in Celimus's employ. Aremys confirmed that she is an assassin, your majesty, paid for by the King of Morgravia.'

Valentyna raised her face to the sky in obvious despair. 'I knew it,' she muttered. 'She killed him as he made love to her,' she added in a choked voice.

'Please, your highness, let us sit,' Elspyth suggested, taking the Queen's arm and encouraging her towards a low stone bench surrounded by sweet-smelling bushes.

'Thank you,' Valentyna said when they were seated. There was a slightly awkward pause as she pushed away the one stray tear that threatened to roll down her cheek. 'May I tell you a secret, Elspyth?'

'Yes, your highness.'

'I was in love with Romen Koreldy but we never made love, not like he did with that murderous whore, Hildyth.'

'He was an easy man to fall in love with,' Elspyth admitted, unsure what was expected of her during this moment of candidness from the sovereign.

'How well did you know him?'

'We met each other in Yentro. We were captured together by men from the mountains.'

'I know.'

'You do?'

'He told me everything of his time in the north.'

Not everything, Elspyth suspected. 'Then you have heard him speak of me, your highness?'

'Yes, I know of you, Elspyth. This is why I do believe you about this terrible business at Felrawthy. But you see, all of my advisers and the nobility of Briavel so badly want me to marry Celimus. I need to give them proof that he is as sinister and treacherous as you tell us.'

'And the death of your father is not sufficient, I presume?' Elspyth said bitterly, then grabbed the Queen's hands and swung to her knees before her. 'Oh, your highness, forgive me,' she begged. 'That was cruel. You have been very fair with us – I just feel so frightened and desperate.'

Valentyna smiled softly at the bowed head of Romen's friend, wondering how he had not fallen for this pretty, feisty woman who had come into his life before she had.

'You are forgiven, for it is a fair accusation,' Valentyna replied. 'But you need to understand that we cannot risk war with Morgravia, Elspyth. This is diplomacy at its most frustrating. It seems my father's death must be overlooked in order to win peace for Briavel.' She paused before adding, 'Romen mentioned a Mountain man called Lothryn.'

Elspyth flinched at the name and saw recognition of that reaction in the Queen's imposing gaze. Honesty was required here. She nodded. 'A very brave man who put our lives before his own because he did not believe we deserved to die. He defied his King, probably paid for it with his life.'

'Romen said that you and Lothryn are in love.'

'I . . . we were . . . are, your highness,' Elspyth admitted, deeply disconcerted that Valentyna knew so much about her. 'I will never love another.'

Valentyna's expression showed a ghost of a sad agreement. 'Then you will know how hard this is for me. I too can never love anyone as much as I loved Romen Koreldy in the short time we knew each other, but I am being forced to marry the man who organised the slaughter of Romen, the assassination of my father, and the murder of Wyl Thirsk who tried to warn me about Celimus.'

'Don't marry him, your highness,' Elspyth warned. 'Do everything in your power to avoid it. Did you read Ylena's letter?'

'I did. She wants me to wait for her and says that she will help me.' The Queen gave a short hollow laugh. 'What can a young helpless noblewoman from Morgravia on the run from her own King – who wants her dead – do to help the cause of the Briavellian Crown?'

Elspyth agreed, it did sound futile. She desperately wished she could tell the Queen the truth that Ylena was brave Wyl, had been Romen. 'Trust her is all I ask. She begged me to implore this of you and to offer my service to you.'

'Yes, she mentioned that too. I am glad of your friendship, Elspyth, really I am, but can you appreciate how odd all this is?'

Elspyth nodded, returning to sit beside Valentyna.

The Queen sighed. 'The worst of it is that I do want to trust her! She sounds like a man writing to me if you can believe that – as though her own brother, the General, is talking as he did during our only meeting. Romen made me feel safe and secure; Wyl Thirsk did too when he ordered me to accompany Fynch to make our escape from the mercenaries who killed my father. And now his sister conveys the same sense of strength.' She shook her head. 'I miss Fynch. He has gone away too, you know. Did you ever meet him?'

Elspyth held her breath at what Valentyna had just said. Without knowing it the Queen had already hit on the truth. Her senses served her well. 'No, but Romen did speak of him.'

'He is a very special person. Odd, most might think, and incredibly serious, but there is something about him I can't really explain. It is as if he is all-knowing, or at least more enlightened than I often feel.' She turned to look at Elspyth directly. 'Do you know what Fynch believes?'

Elspyth shook her head slowly, could guess what was coming.

Valentyna raised her shoulders in a gesture of helplessness. 'He believes that Wyl Thirsk and Romen Koreldy are somehow linked. I don't mean through friendship either. He claims there is a spiritual link, as though they may be one. *Are* one, in fact, though he stops short of saying it. Now what do you say to that?'

Elspyth squirmed, the truth aching to escape from her lips. She fought the temptation. 'Queen Valentyna, I hope you won't be offended if I admit that I believe very strongly in spiritual connections. I do not doubt that souls who belong together will always find one another again, even after death. They will be reborn and search for each other.'

'Do you really?'

She nodded. 'I do, your highness. And that is why I believe you and Romen will find each other again,' she added, coming as close to the truth as she dare.

'But not in this life,' Valentyna said sadly.

'You never know, your highness. There are those who believe that sometimes if a life is taken early – before it is ready to be gathered by Shar – it stays close to the ones it loves.'

Valentyna smiled at her. 'That's a rather lovely way of looking at life. It lifts my heart just to hear you say it, even if I can't believe it.'

'Oh, you can believe it, your majesty. Allow yourself . . . take a risk and believe it.' Elspyth seized her opportunity. She owed Wyl Thirsk this much. 'I believe that some people are reincarnated. Perhaps you should listen more carefully to your friend Fynch. It is to this which he refers, I am sure. And you must promise me that should another person look at you and perhaps touch you emotionally as Romen did, reminding you uncannily of the man you loved, that you will permit it.'

'Permit them to love me, you mean?' Valentyna said, her voice laced with gentle amusement.

Elspyth nodded. 'Perhaps even a woman,' she dared.

'Because it might be him?' Valentyna's dark eyes flashed with both embarrassment and bemusement.

'Yes.' It was a risk but Elspyth was glad she had taken it.

The Queen surprised her by giving her a hug. 'I shall remember that. Now come, I have avoided it long enough.' Elspyth looked at her quizzically. 'I have called a meeting of the nobility. It's serious and that is why I am out here.'

'Thinking time?'

Valentyna nodded, knew Elspyth would understand. 'I feel as though I am about to enter a chamber to bargain for my life.'

Pil preferred to remove himself from the world of politics and asked to be excused to spend time in the palace chapel with Father Paryn, a man he took to immediately. Crys and Elspyth were invited to attend the meeting which brought together the nobles of Briavel. Respecting the sensitivity of the issue, Chancellor Krell would take notes from the meeting himself and dutifully make a copy each for two important nobles who were not able to reach the capital at short notice. Couriers would take the notes of the meeting to their respective destinations across the realm.

The Queen sombrely entered the chamber where the nobles were gathered. They had arrived a little earlier and were sipping on wine, which most barely tasted. The feeling of tension at being called to this unexpected meeting was overwhelming. Krell dismissed all the servants and, when privacy was assured, Valentyna introduced first Elspyth and then the new Duke of Felrawthy.

Shocked whispers ran around the room; most there were familiar with the towering reputation of Jeryb Donal.

'Gentlemen, these Morgravians are our guests and enjoy the full protection of Briavel,' the Queen continued. 'They risked their lives to bring us grave information, riding here in urgency and outrunning their pursuers, who we are presuming were sent to execute them.' She allowed this fact to sink in. Then outlined succinctly the terrible events that had taken place in Felrawthy.

'We are not just talking about a very high-ranking noble, gentlemen, but two of his heirs and his wife – all innocents. If it was not for the foresight of Elspyth here, there may well be no heir left to Felrawthy at all,' the Queen finished.

'There were four sons if I am not mistaken,' someone said.

Crys cast a glance at the Queen before answering. 'Indeed, sir, there were four of us. My youngest brother was murdered at the King's pleasure in Stoneheart. Reliable witnesses have attested to this fact.'

Excited talk broke out and anything further Crys had planned to say was drowned out. Elspyth noted that Crys had benefited from his rest and refreshment. He looked composed and very focused. Perhaps the gravity of this meeting had reminded him of who he was now and his importance in the political landscape of his realm and indeed of Briavel's. She chanced a small smile towards him and was thrilled when he cast a tiny wink her way and lifted his strong chin. She knew how deeply he must have dug within himself to find this strength and composure in front of these important strangers. *The Duchy of Felrawthy is in safe hands, Jeryb*, she thought.

'Your majesty,' said a deep and distinguished voice from the centre of the room.

'Lord Vaughan,' Valentyna replied.

'With the greatest of respect to our noble guest, I must ask what the internal politics of Morgravia have to do with Briavel? Until you are married to King Celimus and formally link our two realms, I believe it may be unwise for us to meddle in or even concern ourselves with Morgravia's domestic matters. Who the King's men execute on his soil is surely his business alone, providing it is only Morgravian blood that is spilled.'

'I appreciate your thoughts, Lord Vaughan,' the Queen said. 'The problem is that Morgravia has brought this problem to us . . . in more ways than one. I have only outlined one part of this tale, my lords. As I mentioned, a man of Shar, a novice but nonetheless a devout believer and practitioner, witnessed the shocking slaughter at both Rittylworth Monastery and at Felrawthy. He now seeks peace from these nightmares from our own Father Paryn. I do not for one minute doubt this young man's word about what he saw. Peaceful men of Shar were cut down as they tended the monastery gardens; the senior monks were crucified and burned.

'Pil escaped and with him took a woman called Ylena Thirsk, who will attest not only to the bloodbath at Rittylworth but to the execution of Alyd Donal of Felrawthy, her husband of one day. I am sure the significance of her family name is not lost on any of you.'

Angry mutterings broke out which she hushed. 'Ylena Thirsk was taken to Rittylworth for sanctuary and safekeeping by none other than Romen Koreldy. I already knew of this because he told me about it during his stay with us. When the executioners came they were Legionnaires under the King of Morgravia's express order to raze the village and its monastery and to kill the holy men.'

'How can we trust this information, your highness?' Lord Vaughan asked, sounding exasperated.

Valentyna ignored his tone and looked towards Elspyth who had half hoped she would be spared such scrutiny. She took a deep breath and begged her voice to hold firm.

'My lords, I happened upon Rittylworth soon after the devastation. I saw the chaos the raiders had left behind, the cruelty of their work. I spoke with the dying head monk as he hung, still smoking, from his cross.' Elspyth was pleased to see how many of the nobles looked away in pain at her words. 'He could barely talk through his scorched throat but he confirmed to me that these were the King's men, that they were searching for Ylena Thirsk and would kill her if they found her.'

'It seems the King could not risk an all out revolt by the Legion which remains loyal to the Thirsk name. Instead, assassins were set upon Ylena Thirsk's trail, gentlemen,' the Queen continued. 'Once again it seems she has escaped – this time with a man known as Aremys Farrow of Grenadyn. But the noble family who offered her safety did not escape the King's attention and were punished in the most dire manner.'

She glanced towards Crys who took up the tale.

'My youngest brother, Alyd, was beheaded as punishment for marrying Ylena Thirsk. The other members of my family were murdered because they offered her a haven. This is all at the hands of a mad King,' Crys said, eyes burning passionately with hate for his sovereign.

Angry exclamations from the stunned audience prompted Krell to cast a warning glance to his Queen.

'Gentlemen, please.' She held her hand up. 'Let us take some wine together and calm ourselves.'

The mood did not change, despite Valentyna's best intentions, but at least the gathered nobles were prepared to hear her out and quietened as they drank fresh goblets of the fine wine.

Valentyna motioned to Krell who handed her a parchment. 'This arrived today from Morgravia,' she said. 'It is a firm offer of marriage from King Celimus. He has set a date of the last day of spring.'

She could feel their joy at the reality of the wedding like a separate pulse in the room. It nauseated her.

'He continues by warning me of a very real threat from King Cailech of the Mountain Kingdom.'

'Briavel and Morgravia are stronger united, your majesty. Celimus is right,' said a man from the northern province, who felt Cailech's threat more keenly.

The Queen nodded without commitment to his sentiment. 'Celimus goes on to explain that he has proof of this threat, claiming that the Donal family of Felrawthy were slaughtered mercilessly by Cailech's men.'

Crys stepped forward angrily. 'That's a lie!' Elspyth reached towards him but he shook her arm away. 'Cailech is too wise to risk his people now. It's easier to let Morgravia and Briavel tear each other apart . . . can't you see?' he roared, looking around the room. 'The Mountain King has never set foot in Felrawthy. Our men would have known about even the slightest incursion into the east and we would have been well warned of any raiding party. The northern defences established by my father were second to none. Believe me when I say that this is Celimus contriving excuses, poisoning Briavel's collective mind to alleviate himself of suspicion so that the marriage will go ahead.'

The Queen nodded; Crys had summed it up perfectly. She looked around the room, trying to gauge the mood.

'My lords, Wyl Thirsk warned me of Celimus's more sinister intentions when he brought the marriage proposal to my father. He counselled that Celimus may not be as interested in peace as he is in acquiring the rich and fertile lands of Briavel. It is my belief that he wishes to rule us, gentlemen, merely paying lip service to our own proud sovereignty. He is empire building, sirs. Why else would King Valor have met such an ugly death? Celimus wanted us vulnerable and desperate for peace.'

She hoped this subtle mention of her father might win the support she wanted but instead all eyes averted their gaze from her own. There was uncertainty in the air.

'We must not turn from the prospect of peace, your majesty,' one of the oldest nobles declared plaintively. Valentyna's heart sank. She knew in that instant that she would not escape marriage to the King of Morgravia. These nobles would prefer to accept rule from the usurper if it meant no more of their brave bright sons had to march towards a hopeless war. She felt the tears of realisation prick at her eyes and blinked them away. How could she blame them? Her father had refused to risk her life, had given his own to save hers. Wyl Thirsk too had died saving her life. Why should these fathers feel any differently and give up their beloved children for such a pointless cause? Her marriage to Celimus would bring the peace they craved and give their children prosperity.

So what if that meant giving up King and Queen to the rule of an Emperor?

She felt her gut twist at the thought.

'Peace at what price, my lords?' she asked the room, eyeing each of them with her hard blue gaze. 'Is this what you have fought for all of your lives, and your fathers and grandfathers before you? Is this what my father raised me to believe? To marry for peace and squander Briavel's name and pride?'

She felt her heart hammering at the passionate words she spoke. It won the nobles' attention – the men she thought she might have lost shifted uncomfortably at her accusation.

But it was the powerful Lord Vaughan who spoke for them all it seemed. 'We need more proof, your highness,' he said firmly into the silence.

'What proof would satisfy you, my lords?' she asked, her tone as sharp as a blade.

Lord Vaughan shrugged. 'So far, your majesty, with respect it is hearsay and unreliable accounts. I acknowledge what Elspyth of Yentro told us of what she saw at Rittylworth but we need more. Bring us Ylena Thirsk. She more than anyone might convince us that Celimus's intentions are as dark as you suggest.'

Valentyna saw heads nodding, knew her fate was sealed. Ylena Thirsk could not save her. No one could. She would be wed to the King of Morgravia in the same helpless manner that a baby lamb is led to its slaughter.

30

WYL AND AREMYS ARRIVED at the Thicket from the village of Timpkenny on the northeastern edge of Briavel. The village had struck them as an odd, almost nervous place that suffered from being the closest clump of humanity to where the Darkstream presumably joined the River Eyle. Much quiet superstition surrounded the Darkstream. It was not a fear of magic so much as a privately held belief amongst these northerners that the Wild beyond was enchanted and not a place for sensible people to roam.

No one could tell Wyl and Aremys where its ultimate source or indeed destination might be, but everyone they spoke to confirmed that the Darkstream was the only way to cross over into the Wild, once you had negotiated the Thicket. Aremys asked one man why he lived so close to a place that held such superstition. The man had shrugged, answering that the land of this region was uncannily fertile and the weather, though cold, was reliable. The rains always came and the summer never failed. 'Our animals and crops thrive,' he had said, shrugging again. 'My family eats.'

Wyl and Aremys knew they should count themselves lucky for having experienced an uneventful journey north. They had travelled relatively swiftly from Brynt across the border, always heading towards the mighty Razors, then cutting east once the famed mountains began to rise up menacingly before them. Briavellian guards had picked them up not far over the border, but did little more than smirk when the travellers admitted they were hoping to find a quiet pass into the Razors to avoid Cailech's fortress. This was the cover story they had agreed on.

The captain of the guard was not so easy to convince, however, when his men escorted them to his checkpoint.

'There are several entries into the Razors from this part of Briavel but you say you are headed for Grenadyn. Surely it would have been easier for you to access the mountains from western Morgravia?'

'Too much trouble brewing on the border over there, sir,' Aremys had said. 'It might be dangerous to take my lady via those routes.'

The officer had nodded thoughtfully. 'You have made your journey three times as long, though.'

'Sir,' Wyl had interrupted, noting how the man instantly regarded him with softer eyes. He wondered if he himself had done this when addressing a good-looking woman. In truth he found it insulting that a woman should be considered with such instant sympathy – or was it desire? He had tried not to let his irritation show in his tone. 'It is imperative that I return to my home in Grenadyn.' The lie came surprisingly easily. 'However, I wish to draw as little attention to myself as possible so am prepared to lose the additional week or so that this more circuitous route will take.'

'And whose attention are you trying to avoid?'

'Why, Cailech's of course,' Wyl had replied, with a hint of irritation now. 'We have learned on our travels that the Mountain King is threatening summary execution for strangers.'

'Morgravians only as I understand it, my lady.' The captain eyed her and stifled a smug expression. 'You could have sailed more easily to Grenadyn, surely?'

'But we were nowhere near the coast, sir. I am sure you do not need to know my life story, Captain er . . . ?'

'Dirk, my lady.'

'Captain Dirk,' Wyl had said. 'I appreciate your concern for our long journey, but I have employed Aremys as my guide and he knows the mountain routes well. We shall be fine,' he had finished, hoping to bring an end to the man's inquisitiveness.

'Well, Lady Farrow, it is none of my business where or how you choose to go but—'

'That is right, Captain,' Wyl had interjected gently, as he thought Ylena might have admonished someone. 'I understand that you are responsible for the security of this part of Briavel but as you can surely tell, we are no threat to the realm nor indeed to anyone within its borders. We are simply travellers passing through. I gather there is no law against that. I appreciate your concern for my safety but Aremys will see to it.'

The man had shown amusement for the first time. 'I was only going to say that I thought you were not dressed sufficiently warmly for the Razors, my lady. It will be rough sleeping in the mountains. Are you really up to such a challenge?'

'No need to worry,' Aremys had chimed in. 'It is my

intention to make a stop at Banktown and buy what we need.'

Wyl knew there was little more the captain could do unless he decided to detain them, but he would need good grounds to prevent a noble passing through. Besides, it was now obvious that Aremys did know the region; perhaps the captain had not expected him to know the local towns and villages and was testing them. As it turned out he had nodded, wished them well and allowed them to move on.

Aremys had seen to it that they left the patrol in a northerly direction, as though heading deeper into the foothills and ultimately up into the Razors. He knew the terrain well enough and soon had them back on track, heading east across the relative obscurity of the lightly wooded hillsides. They had arrived at Timpkenny – their real destination – just before dark, taken a couple of rooms in a very ordinary inn and, in the morning, had sold the horses. Wyl knew the price they had managed to nego- tiate was just short of theft but they had no choice. It was on foot from here on as the famed Thicket would not permit horses to enter. After purchasing a few minor provisions they had set off.

Aremys and Wyl stared now at the dense Thicket without knowing that not so long ago a small boy and a large dog had sat and regarded this strange freak of nature from virtually the same position.

'It suits its name,' Wyl said. 'Have you been here before?'

'No. I've skirted around this region but never actually seen it.'

'How do we get in?'

'Push in, I suppose, although the old stories say it lets you in once you've made up your mind to enter.'

'Lets you in, but not out?'

Aremys grinned at the beautiful woman who crouched next to him with a scowling expression. Strange as it was, he had thought of her as Wyl ever since Tenterdyn – not that he had ever known Wyl Thirsk. He had witnessed the magic of Myrren's gift with his own eyes and suddenly anything and everything seemed possible. He had never considered whether he believed in magical powers or not – it was simply not an issue which had come up during his childhood in Grenadyn. That far north the old stories prevailed and were accepted as folklore. It was only when he found himself in the south of Morgravia that he noticed how wary of magic the people seemed to be.

Now he did believe in it, having seen Faryl change into Ylena. Stories about the Thicket and the Wild were suddenly plausible, not just horror tales to frighten youngsters. It was at this moment that he realised how vulnerable Wyl was as Ylena. Who knew what lay on the other side of the Thicket or what was to come? Would she be able to cope?

As if reading his thoughts Wyl nudged him. 'Don't stare at me like that. I know what you're thinking and, big as you are, you're no match for me, Aremys. I may look fragile in Ylena's body but I assure you I am not.'

'Did Myrren make you a mind-reader as well?' Aremys asked, turning back to regard the thick mass of trees and bushes that confronted them.

'No. You're as easily read as an open book. Didn't your mother teach you to mask your emotions?'

'I thought I had,' Aremys said, feigning hurt. They

grinned at each other, although with little mirth, only anxiety. 'To answer your question: no, apparently the Thicket only lets you travel from this side to whatever lies on the other side. That's my understanding anyway. I believe legend has it that you cannot turn around halfway through and change your mind. Once committed and once permitted entry, you have to continue.'

'Extraordinary,' Wyl breathed. 'And we're not supposed to believe in magic,' he added, somewhat sarcastically.

Aremys did laugh out loud now. 'I think you and I know better after what you're going through. Come on, if we're going to do this we should start now. There are rainclouds set to burst.'

'I'll go first,' Wyl offered.

'Are you scared?'

'Yes.'

'Good,' Aremys sighed. 'I thought it was just me.'

Wyl grinned. 'Shall we hold hands then?' he suggested with only a hint of sarcasm.

'Oh no. Ladies first,' Aremys offered in an overly polite tone.

Their banter was just another way of avoiding making the move. Wyl forced himself to step closer; as he did, he noticed something dangling from one of the low branches. His gaze slid past it momentarily as he scanned for the best entry point before recognition hauled his attention back. 'Look at that!' he said. He untied the item, elation burning through him. 'This is Romen's bracelet.'

Aremys shook his head. 'I don't understand.'

'I do!' Wyl said fiercely, tying the thong around his now-dainty wrist. 'Only one of two people could have brought this here and I suspect it wasn't Queen Valentyna.'

'Who then?'

'Fynch!'

'The gong boy you've spoken of? But he's a child.'

'Never dismiss him as just a gong boy . . . or a child. He is a gifted youngster and with enough courage for both of us. If we look hard enough I reckon we shall find paw prints close by. Fynch and Knave have already come this way and left this as a sign.'

'Brave lad,' Aremys murmured. 'Well, if a boy can do this, so can we.'

Wyl nodded and bent to push his way into the Thicket. Before he entered fully he called over his shoulder to his companion, 'Can you whistle?'

'I guess that's a fairly important question that needs answering right now?' Aremys said, all but bent double to follow directly after Wyl.

'It's just that Ylena can't. One thing I couldn't teach her.'

'Well, I really appreciate that critical information,' his friend grunted behind him.

'Aremys, whistle, damn you! I can't, so you'll have to do it for both of us!' Wyl snapped.

'Happy to indulge you, my lady. Just not sure why?' came the response.

'Because we don't know what might happen in here. I don't want us to be separated.'

'Oh,' Aremys said, understanding now. 'All right. Any requests? I do a fine "Under the Gooseberry Bush".'

'Just get on with it, you fool!' Wyl said, daring a laugh through his fear. The Thicket's presence was ominous and he could not shake the feeling that danger was ahead.

'Can I just mention, as we're on the topic of Ylena's

strengths and weaknesses, that she's got the best arse I've had the pleasure of being close to.' Aremys's muffled voice came from very close behind.

'Whistle!' Wyl ordered in his girlish voice. He knew what Aremys was doing. He was forcing the light-heartedness to combat their fear but it was not working; they were both frightened enough to feel their own hearts pumping hard in their chests. It felt as if the Thicket was drawing them in . . . but to what?

He marvelled at how Fynch had found the courage to take this path and then remembered that Knave almost certainly would have been with him to lead the charge.

Entering the gloom of the Thicket Wyl was immediately struck by its eerie silence which was sufficiently heavy to cause a sense of suffocation. He could not stand upright, for the branches were so low and tangled. He breathed hard and loosened a button at his throat. He knew it was afternoon outside yet it was dark enough beneath the yews that he could swear night was coming on. Nothing moved but them.

At that moment he felt a terrible pressure on his chest, as if all his breath was being sucked away. He could hear Aremys crashing into the Thicket behind and momentarily heard his bright whistling before the sound was suddenly cut off. And then he could breathe again.

Wyl swung around, presuming his friend's quiet was due to shock at the silence and dark but he could not see his companion.

'Aremys?' He listened. Nothing.

'Aremys!' he yelled.

Only dread silence responded.

*   *   *

Valentyna finished dictating her response to King Celimus, the couched threat in his letter burning in her mind. It had taken much soul-searching on her part to reach the decision, but now it was finally made she knew it was the only one she could have taken under the circumstances. The nobles were not going to support her without Ylena Thirsk, and even then she could not imagine what the young noblewoman could say or do which might change their minds. Yes, she may argue convincingly that Celimus was every bit the snake Wyl Thirsk had once described him as, but Valentyna had seen the truth in their faces this afternoon, read it in their pained expressions, heard it in their voices made awkward by the tension: the Briavellian nobles wanted peace with Morgravia above everything. Even above her.

She was a pawn; the valuable key that might unlock the barrier between Morgravia and Briavel and enable them to live side by side as friendly neighbours, as allies.

Valentyna clearly understood that whatever lip service they had paid her this afternoon with regard to finding more proof, the fact of the matter was that they did not care. They did not want further proof. Whatever Celimus was and whatever his intentions, it apparently mattered not. If she were married to him then no more of their proud sons need die. Even if – Shar forbid – Celimus somehow contrived to make himself Emperor of both realms, he would no longer wage war on Briavel which meant their children were safe. And, after decades of warring, peace was what the Briavellians wanted more than anything.

It finally occurred to her that despite all the adoration she was expendable. The realisation was a deep pain in her heart and she felt breathless as its truth sank into her very soul. She was a figurehead Queen. Her own people might well accept Celimus as their sovereign once the marriage was realised. All the talk of finding Ylena, considering new strategies, even stalling the marriage any further, seemed so very futile all of a sudden. She must marry Celimus on behalf of Briavel and sacrifice her peace for its peace.

As these thoughts raged in her mind, Krell finished his scratchings on the paper and blew on it to dry the ink.

'I shall add the royal seal, your highness, once you have signed it.'

He handed her the quill. She did not take it.

'I am doing the right thing, aren't I, Krell?'

He searched the anguished face that so echoed the beautiful woman who had birthed her, and he thought of her father and how proud Valor would be of his daughter right now. She was putting her realm before her own inclination and thereby ensuring its prosperity in the future. 'Your majesty,' he said gravely, 'Briavel will flourish because of this important decision you have made today.'

Her smile was thin and wavered beneath the force of her will as she pushed away tears or sentiment. 'I don't want to marry him, Krell, but I know I must.'

'If you will permit me, your highness . . . ?'

Valentyna nodded. She trusted Krell implicitly and needed his assurances now more than ever before, because he had been so close to her father and because she knew how much he cared.

The Chancellor's rheumy gaze fixed upon her. 'If you are strong from the outset, child, Celimus will never make

Briavel bow to Morgravia. You are a Queen in your own right; you must not lose sight of this. We need his peace, yes, but oh, your highness, he needs your sons! The bluest of royal bloods mingling. It is a royal fantasy, your highness, which both our dear King Valor and the great King Magnus probably dared only conjure in their wildest daydreams. Imagine your own blood reigning over two realms in years to come.'

She nodded again, tears rising now. 'I agree. If my reign is remembered for nothing else, I will secure peace for Briavel and birth the heirs it needs to sustain peace in the region.'

'That's the spirit, your highness. Very few royal marriages are made by Shar — most are pragmatic and highly strategic. This is no different. Your father, may his soul rest quietly, would advise the same.'

The Queen smiled sadly. Krell knew what she was thinking. She had hoped to marry for love. What woman did not?

She could not help herself; it needed to be said. 'And I must forget that Celimus designed the death of my father, the death of Wyl Thirsk, the murder of Romen Koreldy, the slaughter of those monks at Rittylworth and the noble family of Felrawthy . . . and no doubt countless others?' Her chest rose and fell with the anger she was holding at bay.

'My Queen, we have no proof that his hand was behind the weapons in any of those deaths.'

'But we know it, Krell!'

'Yes, your majesty,' he admitted truthfully. 'But as diplomats we must pursue this peace he offers or more of our young men are going to die. We stand to lose a whole generation if we go against him. Celimus, I fear, does not possess the qualities of Magnus; he will fight us until the last man of Briavel falls and then he will likely dissolve the realm as we know it, wipe out its name and make it an annexe of Morgravia.'

Valentyna did not want to say that she felt in her heart that he would annex Briavel anyway. 'And still you would urge this marriage, knowing that I sacrifice myself to a man I could never love?'

'Love is not the issue here, my Queen,' Krell said firmly. 'This is politics and your emotions must be set aside. Your decision is purely a diplomatic one . . . a sound one. You will be Queen of Morgravia as well as Briavel and you must use that status to great effect. This is not Celimus, King of Morgravia and Briavel with his Queen consort. You are both equal sovereigns with equal say in the running of both realms. You alone can carve a path for this marriage to work. Put aside what you feel you are losing and consider only what you are gaining, your highness.' He surprised Valentyna by suddenly kneeling before her. 'You must leave behind whatever has gone before. Cut yourself free of those bonds and those sentiments. Start a new life with Celimus and see if you cannot be the one who makes the difference.'

'To him, you mean?'

'To him, to Morgravia and Briavel. Both realms crave this union and the harmony it will bring. Work hard for peace in the marriage, your highness, and you may well bring about surprising changes.'

Valentyna felt entirely trapped. There was nothing more she could do. All of the warnings she had heard from Wyl, from Romen, from Fynch and even more lately from Elspyth, haunted her, yet Celimus's messenger had been ordered to wait for her response. Time was the enemy. The King was both impatient and impetuous – who knew what he might do if she did not answer in the positive. How long could she wait for Ylena and *why* would she? What difference would Ylena Thirsk make anyway, she asked herself, filled with frustration.

She made a small sound of despair before grabbing the quill and quickly signing her name to the acceptance of marriage to Celimus.

'There,' she said, unable to disguise the disgust in her voice. 'Get it away with the messenger.'

'Yes, your highness,' Krell said, rising. He felt a sense of loss at his part in forcing this young woman to act against her instincts, but the alliance was necessary for the wellbeing of Briavel. He and King Valor had discussed on many occasions how insecure Briavel would be if faced with a battle on two fronts and Krell firmly believed that the threat from Cailech in the near future was real.

Wyl felt a cold tremor pass through him. Aremys had gone; disappeared. There was no sign that he had even followed Wyl fully into the Thicket except Wyl's memory of his friend whistling the first few bars of 'Under the Gooseberry Bush'. Somehow he knew it would be pointless to search. If the Thicket was as enchanted as he had been led to believe then it had made the decision to separate them.

He shivered. *Magic.*

And as that thought passed through him, a black dog melted out of the darkness and sat huge and still before him.

'Knave.'

The dog leapt and Wyl felt a moment of exquisite fear that it was attacking. He should have known better; he found himself on his back and winded amongst the leaf mould with the dog towering above him, licking him.

'Where's Aremys?' Wyl asked, pushing him away. He wondered how Knave felt seeing him as Ylena whom the dog had always favoured.

Knave growled low. It was an answer but not one Wyl could understand.

'Is he all right?'

This time Knave barked once. Wyl convinced himself the animal had answered affirmatively. He had to believe that Aremys was somewhere safe and not wandering aimlessly through the Thicket.

Knave growled again and turned. Wyl knew the dog wanted to lead him somewhere. They set off, the black beast at a trot and Wyl behind, crouching, blindly following. There were moments when he felt convinced that the branches were reaching out to touch him but none actually did. The silence was oppressive with only Knave's presence and his own pounding pulse to reassure him that life existed in this strangest of places. It felt to Wyl that they had been moving for a long time and he could hear the rushing of water nearby.

With that sound, images echoing his fears engulfed Wyl. Aremys lost in the Thicket, calling to him. Valentyna being raped by Celimus. Elspyth screaming for Lothryn whilst the man she loved begged Wyl for help. Romen, Faryl and Ylena walked towards him, arms outstretched like supplicants, their expressions as lifeless as he remembered from when he stole each of their bodies.

He shied backwards from their touch. And then, worst of all, blood and gore surrounding Tenterdyn. He could almost smell the carnage. Just when he thought he would have to scream out for the dog to stop, that he had to go back, they burst through the other side, emerging into grey daylight and a soft drizzle of rain.

Wyl dragged in a lungful of the damp air, not caring that his cheeks were wet from his own tears rather than the misty rain. Knave was gone. Instead, through the murkiness he saw a small cottage on the other side of a short bridge. Its chimney smoked cheerfully through the gloomy afternoon and light glowed at the windows. Like a magnet the dwelling drew him to its warmth.

31

ALEDA WAS DYING. SHE knew it, but somehow it was all right, providing she could cling to life long enough to learn the whereabouts of her eldest son or at least that he was alive. That knowledge would allow her to pass over with grim happiness that the Donal name had not been completely stamped out. But right now each heavy step of the faithful donkey hurt her and her mind and body focused on simply remaining on its back. If she fell off now, she was sure she would have to lie there and wait in hope that the Briavellian Guard would find her before she took her last breath.

Shar was guiding her passage that day. A tinker, selling pots and sharpening knives from village to village, came across the blood-spattered, bedraggled woman with the torn fingernails. He could see she was just about ready for the Gatherers to take her to her god. He leapt from his small cart, calling to the horse to be still as he reached for a water skin.

'Drink,' he said, offering it.

Aleda did so. She had not taken water in hours. Perhaps

she had forgotten to – she could no longer remember. 'Thank you,' she croaked.

The tinker looked around anxiously. There would be no help here; they were in the middle of nowhere it seemed. He himself had crossed the border at around midday yesterday. Mind you, Brackstead was not far away, he was sure.

There seemed little point in taxing the woman with questions. She looked too ill to speak anyway. 'Come on,' he encouraged. 'We have to get you to Brackstead.'

Aleda did not complain; she too wanted to keep moving. Who this kind stranger was mattered not – if he was going to help her to get another step closer to Crys, she would take it. 'Thank you,' she whispered again.

'Don't talk. Save your strength.'

They set off, Aleda feeling stronger just for the presence of another person. They had travelled less than a mile before they rounded a bend in the road to see the cheering scene of a large village laid out before them.

The sight of Aleda brought several people running to help.

'I don't know her,' the tinker replied to their queries. 'I found her just a mile back. Can we get her to a doctor?'

Someone sent a young boy running for the travelling physic. 'You're lucky he's in our village today,' the woman said.

'Is there an inn?' the tinker asked.

A man nodded. 'Yes, The Lucky Bowman. Shall we go there?'

'Please. She says she has money.'

It was a woman who ran the place. 'Shar's mercy,' she

cried as three burly men carried in what looked like a corpse.

'The physic's coming,' one said and nodded to the others to head upstairs.

'Room four,' she called to their backs, before turning to the tinker, who looked thoroughly uncomfortable, and the older woman who had stayed with him.

'They've just arrived, Nan, in terrible shape,' the woman said, clearly excited by all the activity. 'I've sent Rory after that travelling physic who was here today. There's coin to pay for the room.'

'I don't even know her name. I . . . I just stumbled across her on my way here,' the tinker admitted.

Nan nodded towards the door. 'Here's the physic – we can sort out her food and board later,' she said kindly. 'Take them up, Bel, I have to keep a watch on things down here.'

Bel was only too glad to remain involved in the day's intrigue and she called to the physic, a middle-aged man with grey at his temples and a soft-spoken voice, to follow her. He stopped to confer briefly with the tinker who then took his leave, glad to be gone from all the attention and bustle.

Alone with his patient, the physic learned the full horror of what this severely injured woman had gone through and, even more distressing, who she was.

He gave Aleda a draught of a crimson fluid. 'Rest now, Lady Donal,' he said, taking her hand. 'We will get word to Werryl for you.'

At those reassuring words, Aleda gave in to the drug's sedative quality.

The physic went downstairs to speak with Nan who in turn called for Bel.

'She needs a carer,' he explained. 'You will be paid.'

Bel nodded. 'You want me to stay with her until you return, right?'

'She will not recover from her internal injuries,' he said. 'But yes, I need someone by her side. I have staunched the bleeding for now and she will sleep for several hours. When she wakes, I want you to brew up these leaves,' he said, handing her a pouch. 'They will give her strength.'

'Food?'

He shook his head. 'Furthest thing from her mind. Keep her water up, though. She will die of her injuries before she dies of starvation.'

'How long can she hang on?' Nan asked, not at all happy at the thought of a potential corpse cooling in one of her beds.

'She's got courage. That alone will keep her going twice as long as someone with a weaker disposition. A day or so perhaps.'

'And where are you going for help, Physic Geryld?' asked Bel, ever curious.

'I will ride back to Werryl and bring help swiftly,' he answered, determined to keep the patient's identity a secret. He knew they had guessed her status as a noble-woman but he did not wish to give away private details to these village folk. 'Your job is to keep her alive until then with the tea and your voice.'

Bel frowned. 'My voice?'

'Talk to her. Keep her alert when she's awake. She will need her wits about her. I shall leave immediately.'

'How long will you need?'

'I hope to have help back here by tomorrow if I ride through the night.'

He returned to the room and was surprised to see that the Lady Donal was not sleeping, was agitated in fact.

'I told you to rest,' he said sternly.

Her eyes were glazing from the effects of the sleeping draught but she was fighting it. 'Not until I give you something to take to Werryl. You must show it to the Queen, sir,' she said emphatically, pointing to the sack which had been attached to the donkey.

He frowned. 'What is it?'

'The proof that she is contemplating marrying a madman.'

32

AREMYS CAME TO SLOWLY. Was someone kicking him? He could not be sure just yet. In fact he was not sure of anything other than the reality that he breathed. Everywhere else there was pain. There were also voices, men's voices, and then he made out the familiar sounds of horses. He risked opening his eyes, trying for the life of him to remember why he was lying down in the open in such a freezing temperature.

'Ah, so you're alive then?' someone said.

He grunted. 'Just.'

'Get Myrt,' the voice said and Aremys heard footsteps retreat, crunching across fresh snow. It was a lovely sound; one he thought he remembered from childhood. 'Can you move?' the man asked.

'Let me just open my eyes properly,' he replied, squinting at the sharp brightness. A big scowling man, tall enough to match even his substantial height, came into view. He closed them again hurriedly.

More footsteps. A new voice, deeper this time. 'Well, help him up, Firl.'

Aremys felt himself hauled roughly to his feet. His legs were unsteady and leaden, his mind clouded. He forced himself to open his eyes again but he ignored the man called Firl and regarded the older fellow with knowing grey eyes. The pain that sliced through his head was significant. 'I'm sorry.' He smiled crookedly. 'My head aches.'

'You must have fallen and hit it,' the man suggested, presumably Myrt of the deep voice. 'What is your name?'

Aremys reached up to scratch his head. Everything hurt. 'I'd tell you if I could. I can't remember a damn thing right now.'

Myrt sighed. 'Get a blanket around him, someone. You, Firl, double with him,' he said. 'Let's go.'

Bruised and feeling sorry for himself, Aremys was helped none too gently on to a horse with the surly man called Firl – who clearly did not want to double with him – and began a journey to he knew not where, why or even where from.

Firl ignored him for the first hour or so. This did not bother Aremys; he was too concerned with keeping his balance and trying to remember his name. He was grateful for the blanket though.

'Where are we?' he finally asked.

'Razors,' the man responded bluntly.

Aremys never could suffer fools graciously. 'Yes, I think I've worked that out. But where exactly?'

The sarcasm seemed to have little effect on the young brute. 'East.'

He could tell he was not going to get much more out of this chatty fellow so he delved back into his own mind, which presently felt like tangled skeins of wool. Ignoring the growing headache he forced himself to concentrate in order to recall anything about himself. Nothing surfaced and he growled in his frustration.

'Who are you?' he asked.

His companion spoke again with the same uninterested tone. 'Firl. I thought we'd already established that.'

'And the others?' Aremys asked, struggling to keep his irritation in check.

'Do you want me to list their names?'

'Not if they're all as uninteresting as yours.' He felt the man's body stiffen and was glad he had struck a blow. 'I meant what are you doing out here?'

'We're a scouting party.'

'For Cailech?'

'Who else?' the man said and Aremys, sitting behind, imagined him scowling.

'Am I a prisoner?'

The man snorted. 'Why don't you make a run for it and see what happens? I'm a great shot.'

'Look, Firl, I don't even know what my name is let alone why I was lying flat on my back in the Razors. Why don't you just shut your stupid mouth or I'll shut it for you!'

Myrt overheard the raised voices and steered his horse over. He lifted his chin in enquiry. 'Anything wrong?'

'No,' Firl mumbled.

'Actually, yes,' Aremys countered. 'I want to know if I'm a prisoner and why. I'd like to know where we're headed and why. I'd appreciate knowing why I've seemingly been captured by a scouting party, why I'm sitting with this oaf of few syllables and I'd love to know my own name!' he roared, his headache pounding in tandem with his rising blood pressure and anger.

'Hop up with me. Firl, you go on ahead,' Myrt ordered. There was something of an admonishment in his expression towards his subordinate and it was not lost on the sulking Firl.

Aremys was more than glad to clamber up behind the superior. 'Thank you,' he mumbled. 'And for the blanket I'm sorry for the outburst. I seem to have lost my manners as well as my memory.'

'Either that or you're a clever spy,' Myrt said, clicking to his horse and moving forwards again.

'Shar strike me! Is that what you all think?'

'Why wouldn't we? You are Morgravian, aren't you?'

'I . . . well . . . I don't know,' Aremys blustered.

'You dress like one and curse like one.'

'Then perhaps I am. I have no idea who I am. Mind you, I understand the Northernish you were muttering with your men earlier. Does that mean anything?'

'Is that so? And what were we saying?'

Aremys told him.

'All right, stranger, I'm impressed,' Myrt admitted. 'Most Morgravians wouldn't understand a word of it, which is why we used it in front of you. Anything else?'

'No, not really,' Aremys said. 'The mountains are familiar, although I can't tell you why. No horse, no belongings save my sword.' He shook his head. 'No memory,' he added mournfully.

'Well, perhaps pulling out your toenails will help your memory,' Myrt said and felt Aremys start behind him. He let out a deep rumbling laugh, enjoying his own jest.

'Shar's wrath, man! Will it come to that?'

'Be easy. Did Firl tell you our business?'

'Oh yes, we enjoyed a long and cordial chat.' Myrt

waited, unaffected by the biting wit of their new guest. 'Only that you're a scouting party,' Aremys grumbled.

'That's right. Do you know Morgravia has all but declared war on the Mountain People?'

'If I do I don't remember.'

'Then you'll forgive us our suspicions,' Myrt said. 'Well, if you're from Morgravia – which you probably aren't – you'd know about our problems with King Celimus.'

The name was familiar and its mention sounded a distant series of alarm bells in his mind. Aremys pushed at them but had no success. 'Why do you think I'm not from Morgravia?'

'Because we picked you up on the Briavellian side of the Razors and your accent isn't right. It's Morgravian, all right, but it's covering something else. If I didn't know better I'd think you were from the northern islands.'

Again, a prick of familiarity but it was evasive. 'I see. Maybe I am. I wish I could dredge up something to help my cause.'

Myrt nodded. 'It will come. To answer your question: yes, you are our prisoner, but we shall treat you honourably until the King has decided what to do with you. I'm afraid relations with Morgravia are strained but your odd accent may save you yet. What shall we call you until then?'

Aremys pondered, unhappy at his situation but realising he had no option but to co-operate. He had no mount, no food, no memory and being alone in the Razors could kill him in a single night. 'What's a good Mountain name?' he asked, following his better judgement.

'How about Cullyn? It's one of the oldest.'

He shrugged. 'Fine.'

'No such thing as a free meal in this troop, Cullyn. We'll be on the ridges for a few days yet. What can you do to earn your keep?'

Aremys shook his head, feeling suddenly grateful to the big Mountain man. 'I have no idea. You tell me.'

'All right, then. We're about to make camp here. You can provide the entertainment for tonight. How about you take on sulky Firl with the sword? I think he'd quite like a go at you.'

'And me at him, I assure you.'

Myrt laughed. 'I like your arrogance. Hope you haven't forgotten your skills, Cullyn. Our Firl is one of the best in the Razors with a sword.'

'Just promise me some ale and worry about your Mountain boy over there,' Aremys said, grinning despite his pounding head.

A camp was settled and the horses corralled in a small copse of fir trees which would also provide the wood for the men's fire. Myrt ran a tight troop and gave orders briskly. Some men were designated to prepare the food, others to gather the wood, some to take care of the animals and the younger ones to restock the water skins. He took Aremys and another man to hunt down some meat. Aremys pleased his host by shooting four hares without wasting a single arrow. Each man returned with a brace of small game which was quickly skinned and gutted, and before long was roasting over the coals.

They no longer spoke in Northernish, a language only used these days for secrecy. If Aremys's memory was intact he would know that the language only survived because of King Cailech and his love for the Mountain culture. He had made an edict that it would be taught from elder to grandchild and keep itself alive. In daily life, however, the Mountain Dwellers spoke the language of the region, a common tongue from Briavel in the east to as far west as Tallinor. Aremys had recognised the Northernish because his wetnurse, an old woman of the isles, had sung to him in the old language, but that was a memory closed to him right now – he could not even remember as far back as the previous day when he was clambering through the Thicket. One moment he had been following the shapely bottom of Ylena Thirsk; the next a wave of magic had roiled about him thickening the air to a dull, almost solid wall. Then an even more powerful blast of the magic opening a cleft through which his unconscious body was pushed . . . and dropped on a northeastern ridge of the Razors.

Whilst the meat cooked and a hearty vegetable broth simmered in the pot, Myrt posted lookouts then called the remaining eleven men around the fireside for the evening's early entertainment. There were fifteen of them in total, all strong-looking fellows but only Firl was tall enough to go eye to eye with the giant stranger.

'How do you feel, Cullyn?'

'Like hurting someone,' he mumbled. A roar went up from the delighted audience, ready for sport.

'All right, then. Do we have a sparring partner to go up against our huge guest here?'

Firl stood, cutting the air with his heavy sword. He held it two-fisted and snarled, 'He's mine.'

Aremys shook off the blue blanket which had been lent to him and drew his own sword. As he did so, the dyed wool reflected off the blade and he momentarily staggered under the fleeting blaze of memory. 'Koreldy,' he whispered, with no idea who the person was who owned the name, and for no reason he could explain he associated that name with a blue-tinged sword.

Only Myrt caught the word and he too paused in recognition of a name known all too well to Cailech's trusted senior men. This was not the time to raise it with the stranger, he decided, and instead stored it away. It would be brought to light when it counted, before the King. Suddenly this man amongst them was important.

He cleared his throat. 'Firl, Cullyn, this is not to the death. If either of you mortally harm the other, I shall kill the perpetrator myself. Do you understand?' Aremys nodded. Firl just snarled. 'Firl?'

'I understand, sir.'

'Good. This is sport, for our entertainment, don't forget it, either of you. First blood declares the victor – then we shall eat in his honour.'

Both men touched their blades together then Firl adopted the two-fisted stance of the Mountain race, one leg placed wide diagonally behind the other, knees bent, ready to strike. But it was Aremys who surprised them all, including himself, by holding his sword upright before his face, fist upon fist on the hilt. This was a stance unique to one region alone. Everyone recognised the formal Grenadyn salute before combat.

Myrt, more taken aback than any, wanted to halt the proceedings but it was too late. Each combatant hurled himself at the other.

Firl gave away much in bulk but he fought like a savage. Myrt could see straightaway, however, that his own man was no match for the stranger. Cullyn, or whoever he was, was clearly a superior swordsman with moves and speed that came only with a soldier's experience. Firl was young and headstrong. He might feel invincible but his skills had been tested only amongst the Mountain men and, courageous though he was, he knew none of the finesse of the southerners who prided themselves on grace and speed rather than brute force.

Myrt could see that Cullyn was merely blocking rather than attacking. He was allowing Firl to wear himself out and, too immature to realise it, this was precisely what the youngblood was doing. His heart was generous and his spirit keen but the older soldier was virtually playing with him.

Aremys looked over at Myrt and winked. It was all Myrt could do not to laugh, particularly as Cullyn began to back away, supposedly defending his life, as the enraged Firl stomped forwards, blustering and roaring his anger, slashing with the heavy sword he used like a battering ram at times.

Despite his dislike of Firl, Aremys felt sorry for the youngster. He was brave, but would almost certainly lose his life young if caught in any serious fight with a Legionnaire. He could tell the man wanted to impress his companions against the arrogant stranger and, with years on his side, was ready to let him do so. It would not do to humiliate Firl – he would make no friends amongst the Mountain men then, and oddly he felt he could quite easily fit in with these soldiers.

After all, Myrt had been fair. With Morgravia an enemy, they could just have easily run him through as he lay in the snow, but instead they had given him warmth and transport, food and company, as well as safety. Not humiliating Firl – as much as he would have liked to – was the least he could do, if just for the leader, Myrt. And so he winked and the message was understood.

The fight continued until Aremys felt the pain of his headache begin to weigh heavily. He had been able to set it aside but hunger and the exertion of the contest brought it pounding to the fore again. Seeking the right opening, he feinted all too obviously. Even the less agile Firl could see it coming and he slashed. Aremys felt the welcome, if painful wound open up on the top of his non-fighting arm. He yelled appropriately and the audience roared appreciative applause for the youngblood, who grinned awkwardly but regarded his fighting partner with unease. Both stood before each other breathing deeply.

'Good fight, Firl,' Myrt said. 'We eat in your honour tonight.'

Aremys nodded at Firl. 'Well done,' he said but the younger man just stared. Others rose to thump him on the back which meant Aremys could turn away from the unhappy stare. The lad was no idiot; he knew he had been allowed to win.

'Come, let me bind that for you,' Myrt said to Aremys 'And don't say no, it's too awkward for you to do yourself.'

Aremys gladly followed the leader towards a tiny spring that skirted the copse.

'That was bravely done,' Myrt said, kneeling beside his guest. 'A lesser man would have felt the need to impose his superior skill.'

'Nothing to be gained by that but an enemy.'

Myrt nodded. 'A soldier with wisdom.'

Aremys looked at him. 'What makes you say soldier?'

'You fight like one. You've had experience – even you must have felt that.'

It was so frustrating not to know. 'A soldier?' he mused. 'The sword felt comfortable in my hand, I'll admit it. He's your best, you say?'

'I said it for his benefit. Firl's a good man but he's young and hot-headed.'

'He'll die quickly in battle, Myrt.'

'Then teach him.'

'What?'

'You've got nothing else to do right now. Teach him, teach the others.'

'How to kill Morgravians, you mean?'

Myrt grimaced as he cleaned the wound. It was a surface cut, nothing serious, and even the victim wasn't complaining. 'Your loyalty does not lie there.'

'And you know this?' Aremys muttered.

'Cullyn, I think I am right in saying that you are from Grenadyn originally.'

Aremys shot him an angry look. The naming of that place seemed to jolt some memory from long ago. It made him think of children . . . a young girl in particular. He could see her. All curls and chubby smiles. She threw herself into his arms and kissed him. 'Serah,' he breathed, the sorrowful memory of a sister slotting into place.

'What?'

'I am from Grenadyn,' he declared, knew it was right.

'You remember?'

Aremys nodded. 'I think so, yes. It would explain why I understand Northernish.'

'And why you hold your sword in the formal Grenadyne manner.'

'Hmm . . . now you're just showing off.'

'I miss little. Who is Serah?'

Aremys was not ready for this man — albeit someone he could not help but like and trust — to know too much. He suspected his lost memory possessed secrets and although he could not remember them just yet, if his memory was going to come back in dribs and drabs he would rather be in control of what he revealed in case it was dangerous knowledge. 'I don't know,' he lied effectively. 'Her name just drifted across my mind.'

'You see, I said your memory would come back in time,' Myrt said, pleased. 'There, it's just a nick. My thanks for your indulgence with the lad.'

'He needs encouragement,' Aremys admitted.

'And training,' Myrt said. 'Perhaps we all do,' he added sagely before returning the wink.

The meal out in the open and the cold, huddled around a campfire, was the best Aremys felt he had eaten ever. Although these were hardly friends, the men were convivial enough. Even Firl had relaxed and was treating him with a new cordiality, remarking on some of Cullyn's moves and how he might like to learn them. It was the closest the younger man got to admitting he was no match for Aremys, but even that was not needed. The songs they sang he knew somehow, reinforcing to him that he was from Grenadyne stock and not Morgravian. That was reassuring; yet why did he feel the pull towards Morgravia and, more keenly, towards Briavel where he was now sure he must have been relatively recently? He had no explanation for why he had been in the Razors alone and without a horse.

The men explained it away by saying the horse had probably bolted; all were sure they would come across it dead soon enough. But Aremys had felt over all of his head and there was no bruising and no lump. Still, it hurt bad enough at times to make him feel nauseous. This was no fall from a horse. This was internal pain, but he could not explain it.

Another worrying fact was the tingling sensation in his fingertips. That was odd. He had felt it immediately on regaining his wits but had paid no attention initially. It was not painful, not even that uncomfortable, but it was not in his imagination – it was definitely there yet he had no idea what it was, why it occurred or even if it had been there before the unconscious spell.

The night closed in around them and they sang more mournful ballads now, suiting his mood. Serah haunted his thoughts. Serah and the name Koreldy, prompted by the blue glint of his blade. Was this the key to who he was? For now, though, he was Cullyn. It would have to do, he thought, as he drifted off to sleep.

33

WYL HESITATED IN HIS path towards the cheerful hut. He felt empty and angry, suddenly lost without Aremys who had disappeared without a trace. And now Knave had gone too. Late afternoon was reaching across the small clearing and Wyl shivered. There seemed to be no others around; just this cottage on the outskirts of a place of fear. He cast a glance behind at the black smudge which was the Thicket. It did not look so menacing from this side but he knew it held secrets. He had felt the thrum of its magic in that moment when his breathing had become so difficult and he had wondered if he might die.

Where could Aremys be? It was no good, he would have to satisfy his anxiety by at least trying to find his friend. He could not just leave him. He turned back the way he had come.

'No, don't do that, my lady,' called a voice.

Wyl swung around to see a large man coming towards him across the bridge.

'I'm Samm, the boatkeeper. I saw you hesitating just now and thought I should come out and provide a welcome. It must be hard for a lady travelling alone,' he said looking about him. 'You are alone, aren't you?'

'I . . .' Wyl wavered between the truth and a lie. He opted for the latter. The fewer people who knew the better. 'Yes, yes I am. My apologies, I am Lady Rachyl Farrow.'

'Would you like to come in?' Samm said kindly, gesturing towards his cottage.

'Um, well, I think what I need is a boat to tell the truth,' Wyl said, feeling his way now, unsure of the usual practice here.

'I understand. Come in. Let me at least fix a pot of tea and then we can discuss your requirements.'

After a last searching glance at the Thicket and another roving look for Knave, Wyl accepted that he was alone on this journey now. He nodded to Samm to lead the way.

'Why did you say that I shouldn't go back into the Thicket, Samm?'

'I felt something a few moments ago. Just thought it best to let it be. The Thicket can be contrary I've realised over my time and I've got used to its strange sighs and movements. There are occasions when it feels quite alive.'

'And this was one of them?' Wyl queried, crossing the bridge behind Samm.

'Yes,' the man replied simply.

Inside, Samm went about the business of making tea. 'Why are you here, my lady?' he asked gently.

Wyl opted for honesty. 'I'm following someone. A boy.'

'Ah, the lad Fynch.'

'That's right!'

'And his strange black beast.'

'Knave. He's my dog actually.' Wyl felt a surge of relief that Fynch had passed through safely.

'Is the lad in trouble?'

'No, not at all.' He thought quickly. 'He's my brother.'

'So you're from Briavel too?'

'Yes, that's right,' he answered, desperately wondering how much deeper the lying would get. Already he was no longer from Grenadyn which was the original plan.

'Your brother was seeking someone?'

'Mmm, yes.' He did not want to answer these questions. 'Do you need any help with that?'

'No, my lady. Here we go,' Samm said, putting down a mug of tea. 'Honey?'

'Please.'

'Family?' Samm was not going to be put off, Wyl could tell.

'That's right,' he answered, sipping the tea, desperately hoping to escape further interrogation. 'How much for the boat?'

'One crown. Is there anything I can do to dissuade you from going, my lady? Your brother will not return from the Wild. No one does.'

'I must try though, Samm. He's so young,' Wyl said as plaintively as possible.

'It is a one-way journey, my lady. People leave and empty boats return. His has already found its way back to its mooring. To lose two fine people such as yourselves so fast . . . well, it disturbs me. I always hope I can stop someone going.'

'Not this time.'

'That's what Fynch said.'

'I must leave before I lose the light. Thank you for your tea.' Wyl stood and held out his small and pretty hand.

'Why not go in the morning? Sleep on it?'

'No, Samm. I really must get going.'

Samm sighed heavily and went foraging for his great black book. Following the same routine as with Fynch he intoned the terms and conditions of his visitor's departure, his genial face heavy with regret that another young life was to be lost.

'Thank you,' Wyl said, having clearly spelled out his name to record in the book. 'Just out of interest, Samm, who was the previous person to enter the Wild before Fynch?'

'Funny, we had the same conversation, miss. It was a young lady like you. Her name was Emil Lightford, a scholar from Pearlis.'

The name meant nothing to Wyl but he nodded and smiled.

'That was so many years ago,' Samm said. 'And now two of you in such a short time.'

'Here's my money,' Wyl said, holding out the coin. 'Do I take any boat?'

'Whichever you like, my lady. Let me escort you. And don't worry about steering. It navigates itself.'

Wyl smiled in nervous thanks and followed Samm down to the jetty. He selected the nearest boat.

'That was your brother's choice too,' Samm said. 'All I can offer you now is good luck.'

Wyl waved once then turned to face two huge overhanging willows whose drooping branches looked like tentacles waiting to grab him and pull him into their darkness. The absence of Aremys played heavily on his mind – another person who trusted him, loved him even, now gone. Wyl could only hope he was not dead, but perhaps he was. Why would the Thicket be selective, he wondered, then forgot the thought as the thick canopy of overhanging trees enveloped him. His eyes slowly adjusted to the murky darkness and he even risked sitting down on the small plank across the boat. There were no oars.

It was cold; Wyl hugged Ylena's arms about himself. Just as he was starting to feel slightly less threatened by this journey a sheer rock face came into view around a slight curve in the Darkstream. It was huge – most likely part of the Razors, he thought, by the granite. A low arch was hewn out of it, very narrow, just sufficient to allow a single boat through. He held his breath, wished goodbye to all that he recognised as familiar and reflexively shut his eyes as the mountain closed its lips around the little boat and swallowed him up.

Initially there was only depthless black when he opened his eyes. It was disorienting and he held the sides of the boat to give him a sense of up and down in this dread place. If he'd thought it was cold before, it was freezing beneath the weight of the granite and his teeth began to chatter. Ylena just did not have sufficient flesh on her body to keep warm in such conditions. Shivering uncontrollably now, Wyl wondered whether Samm had been right: this was a one-way journey; no one ever returned. The tunnel would go on forever and its travellers would die of the trauma of being alone in the dark or freeze to death.

These macabre thoughts were his only companions as the journey through darkness lengthened until any sane person would have felt the first flutterings of panic. Wyl could not tell whether he was imagining it but the ceiling of the narrow tunnel seemed to lower. He felt too frightened to let go of his grip on the boat to confirm it. There was a curious battle going on inside him. Wyl was not one to be afraid of the dark or enclosed spaces, but through his increasing agitation he recalled that Ylena had liked neither. Even as an adult she had always kept a single candle burning through the night, and as a child her worst nightmare was of being locked in a cupboard. Was some residue of Ylena's fear surfacing now? Whatever it was, it was getting worse. His pulse had quickened to panic point and his breathing was coming in shallow gasps. He did his best to quell the fear, to rationalise it, but the tunnel was surely closing in and the thick silence was working against him.

Ylena's fear took full flight and Wyl began to scream. He stupidly tried to stand and instantly lost his balance. His hysterical shrieks were cut short by a new darkness, wet and drowning. He gulped for air as the Darkstream drew him into its fathomless depths, down towards death where perhaps he would come to rest next to Fynch and Emil . . . or whatever her name was . . . he could no longer remember. All he could focus on now was the ebbing of his life.

Perhaps it was for the best. His life – if he could call it that – was too dangerous, a weapon in itself. Who needed a sword or a bow when the mere act of succumbing to your opponent's weapon was enough to kill? Wyl hated the curse that lay upon his life. He would welcome death now, a death that claimed no life but his own.

He let go of the last bit of breath in his lungs and his hold on life, and allowed himself sink into oblivion.

A savage yank bit through his shoulder and reawakened him to his struggle. His lungs were bursting for air, he had no idea which way was up and was too dizzy to think straight. Death was indeed close. Just moments ago he had anticipated seeing the friendly, welcoming faces of Shar's Gatherers, assuring him that all would be well once their outstretched hands fell upon him.

But now there were no faces, no welcome. Just a fight for air and a monster, big with teeth, and strength that dragged at him. *Survive, damn you!* a voice cried in his head. They burst through the Darkstream's surface.

'Here, Knave!' a voice called. It was Fynch and next to him another figure. 'Quickly,' Fynch urged. 'Drag him over here.'

Wyl was pulled, near unconscious, from the black icy water.

'Let me see him,' the other person said.

'Her,' Fynch corrected, shocked. It was Ylena's body which lay inert and pale before them. He helped Knave from the water and gritted his teeth as the huge dog shook his shining black fur free of the Darkstream. 'This is Ylena Thirsk,' Fynch admitted sadly.

His companion shook his head. 'Let me help him.'

Moments later Ylena's body shuddered and spluttered with a heaving cough, brought up the water swallowed and sucked in lungfuls of lifegiving air. Her eyes flew open. 'Fynch?' The coughing began again.

The boy nodded. 'Hello, Wyl. We thought we'd lost you.'

Ylena's expression was confused. She was shivering uncontrollably amidst the coughing. 'Who . . . ?'

'It was Knave – he dived so low for you and was gone so long I worried for his safety too.'

Knave took this moment to loom into view and lick

Ylena's face. Fynch took Ylena's slim, delicate hand. 'Wyl, this is Elysius . . . Myrren's father.'

Wyl, glad to have finally rid himself of the dregs of the Darkstream, regarded the strangest-looking person he had ever seen.

'Don't talk yet,' Elysius said softly. 'You're shivering. We need to get you warm and dry very quickly.'

'Where are we?' Wyl asked. He must have been sleeping, he realised.

'We're with Elysius, where he lives . . . in the Wild,' Fynch said. Wyl could see he was struggling with his emotions.

'Well, it's certainly good to see you again, Fynch,' he said warmly. Sitting up, he opened his arms for the boy to fall into them.

'What happened?' Fynch wept. 'How come you're Ylena?'

'Oh, a long and horrid story. I can scarcely believe it myself and hate even thinking about it. It only happened a few days back so I'm not very used to being her.' He smiled awkwardly with her beautiful face and held Fynch away so he could look at him. 'You're amazing, do you know that, to get yourself all the way here?'

Fynch risked one of his rare smiles. 'I got a fair bit of help from my four-legged friend over there.'

Wyl looked over to see Knave settled by the side of the bed and regarding him with those dark knowing eyes. Knave barked once and Wyl grinned. 'Thank you for coming after me, Knave, I was all but finished down there,' he said, flinching at the memory of the Darkstream.

He turned back to Fynch. 'I'm glad he keeps you safe. Where is Elysius?'

'Preparing food.' Fynch chuckled. 'He's a terrible cook.'

Wyl shook his head. 'I'm not sure I really caught sight of him properly back there.'

Fynch grew serious again. 'You did. He's . . . well, he's strange to look at.'

'What do you mean?'

'See for yourself,' a voice said. Elysius had returned.

Wyl thought the man looked like one of Shar's jests, the sort of creature one might see in Master Jensyn's Freak Spectacular which roamed the realms, terrifying and amusing people with the tallest man, the ugliest woman, the boy with no face and suchlike. Elysius, however, struck him as being one of those freaks who would normally not be permitted to take a second breath beyond birth.

'Which explains why I live in the Wild,' Elysius continued, breaking the awkward silence.

'Wyl!' Fynch admonished under his breath.

'You are not what I was expecting,' Wyl finally said, lost for the right words.

'Neither are you,' Elysius admitted, a crooked smile splitting his strange face. 'I had heard from your friend here that you were a hired assassin called Faryl of Coombe.'

Wyl was fascinated. Elysius's head was too large for his dwarflike body which was big through the abdomen and sat atop ridiculously short legs. It struck Wyl that his arms were not the right length either; in fact everything about Elysius was out of proportion. Wyl recalled how he had once worried about being deeply unattractive with his red hair and freckles – here was someone to make him feel ashamed of such sentiment. Elysius was ugly beyond imagining. A massive forehead swept down towards a heavy jutting brow and a wide flat nose. When he smiled, as he did now, his mouth seemed to stretch forever, revealing huge horselike teeth. If this was not enough, his face was covered in unsightly lumps and both his eyes were milky white – to all intents, blind. Lank dark hair was carelessly tied back behind his enormous troll-like head. The only attractive feature of this person was his voice. It was all warmth and mellowness – that same voice which had soothed Wyl when he needed an anchor to stop his fears taking full flight.

'It is not polite to stare, you know,' Elysius said in his lovely voice.

'I . . . I'm so sorry,' Wyl said, wondering how the blind man had known.

Elysius felt for and took Ylena's tiny fingers in his own oversized hand. 'No, I think I am the one who should be sorry, Wyl. You have suffered greatly at my whim.'

There was another awkward silence as the gravity of what had just been said sat between them. It was Elysius's fault that Wyl now lived in his own sister's body, and before that had walked as Faryl and Romen.

Wyl took a slow breath. It *was* all in the past. They were dead. Even he knew that the magic of Elysius could not bring those people back. Keeping Valentyna safe and securing her realm was the only thing that mattered to Wyl now – that, and keeping his promise to Elspyth to track down Lothryn. His own life was inconsequential. He cared nothing for it.

'Tell me about yourself . . . please,' Wyl finally said.

'Over some food. Come, join me at my table. Do you feel better?'

Wyl nodded. 'Did you make me sleep?'

'I did. Your body needed a rest after its shock. I'm afraid you have been out for many hours. It is night outside – too dark to see anything.'

Fynch led the way.

'I'm not much of a cook,' Elysius admitted, waddling after Fynch on his short legs. He really was something out of a horror tale.

'So I have heard,' Wyl said and then gave Ylena's warm, reassuring smile when Elysius feigned hurt at the comment.

'Fynch is plain ungrateful,' he grumbled. 'Starling-and-fish pie is delicious.'

Wyl threw a troubled glance towards Fynch who could only shrug.

The so called starling pie was not nearly as bad as Wyl had imagined. He munched hungrily on the breads and delicious cheeses Elysius had also laid out.

'Drowning must give you an appetite,' Elysius remarked, enjoying seeing his guest eat so heartily.

Wyl grinned, feeling immeasurably better for the rest, food and convivial atmosphere. 'I shall have to stop soon. Ylena will never forgive me if I ruin her figure.'

His jest was mild but it struck a blow at Elysius once again at the havoc his actions had wrought on Wyl's life. 'I owe you an explanation,' Elysius admitted as he reached to refill the mugs.

'Start from the beginning,' Wyl said, swallowing a mouthful of the refreshing ale. 'I want to know everything.'

Elysius sighed, sat back in his comfortable chair and began his story.

34

VALENTYNA WAS PICKING AT a late supper with her Morgravian guests and her two most trusted counsellors, Commander Liryk and Chancellor Krell.

The new Duke of Felrawthy had, to all outward eyes, battled through the worst of his horror and grief. The wound no longer showed so openly on his face, although Elspyth, who had known him briefly before the trauma, could see he was a changed man. The pain would never leave his heart. He would hide it, because that was how he had been raised, but Elspyth felt her own grief that the bright expression which had come so naturally to Crys's face now held a haunted quality. Another reason for her to hate Celimus. Still, for the Briavellians who were just getting to know the new duke, the intelligence, integrity and humour this young man embodied were testimony to his fine parents.

The supper conversation had been driven deliberately by Krell to steer clear of the subject of his young Queen's impending marriage, even though it was clearly on everyone's mind. He knew she had enough misgivings and fears of her own without being subjected to the weight of the Morgravians' despair when they learned of her decision. Krell had taken it upon himself to speak quietly with the young woman from Yentro, who was the most vocal, and had tried to make her understand the fragile and highly complex position the monarch of Briavel found herself in. Elspyth had listened but he saw the pity and disgust she felt on behalf of her new friend, and knew he must do everything he could to dissuade this fiery girl from convincing the Queen that her marriage was doomed.

Supper had been his idea. Since the Morgravians' arrival the atmosphere around the Queen had become tense. He felt that a light meal late at night in Valentyna's private solar might help to alleviate some of the tension and would be an ideal opportunity for himself and Liryk to help these guests understand how important it was for Briavel to start living without the proverbial sword hanging over its head. It was his hope that talk might even touch on their departure, for as long as they remained with Valentyna, their discussions of Celimus would poison any chance Briavel had of achieving peace.

The novice monk, Krell noted, had closeted himself away with Father Paryn, choosing to share his meals and his time with the elder man of Shar. Perhaps Pil might choose to remain in Briavel; this was less disconcerting for Krell.

All was going well until Liryk was called away by the head guard on duty for the night. The Commander returned to whisper something in Krell's ear and both men disappeared.

'Chancellor?' Valentyna enquired when Krell reentered looking decidedly sombre.

'An exhausted and disturbed Physic Geryld, your majesty, asking for an audience.'

'Good grief,' she said, standing. 'He attended my father on occasion. Permit him to enter immediately.'

'Perhaps, your highness, I might bring him to your study,' Krell said cautiously, glancing towards the Morgravians.

Her gaze narrowed. 'This is urgent, I gather?' He nodded.

She thought of the study — there was no fire burning there this evening. 'I think you should bring him here. If he is exhausted the man needs warmth and food. I cannot imagine why he would ride in so late.'

Krell did not look happy at her decision and disappeared.

'We can leave if you wish, your highness,' Crys suggested.

'Please stay,' she said. 'I imagine this is some small domestic matter which we can sort out quickly. No need to disrupt everyone's supper.' She cast a smile his way.

Elspyth in turn gave him a wry look. It was clear to her that Crys was entirely captivated by the Queen. Who could resist her, Elspyth had to admit, looking at the statuesque monarch who would surely dazzle even if she wore hessian rags.

Krell and Liryk re appeared, escorting the fatigued physic who carried a leather sack. Valentyna wondered why no one had offered to take it for him. 'Physic Geryld,' Krell announced unnecessarily, a stickler for detail.

Elspyth and Crys had already withdrawn to the back of the room to stand in the shadows. They felt like intruders even though Valentyna had gone to such lengths to make them welcome.

'Your majesty,' the doctor murmured, struggling to bow in a genteel fashion. 'Forgive my intrusion.'

Valentyna threw a glance of concern towards Krell who hurried to help the man to a chair. 'Please, Physic Geryld,' she said, 'sit by the fire and warm yourself. You look half frozen, sir.'

He shook his head and remained standing. 'No time, your highness. I bring grave tidings. May I speak freely?'

'You may,' she said, holding her breath now. This felt ominous.

'A woman is dying in the village of Brackstead, your majesty. She has but hours to live. This is no ordinary soul — she is of noble rank, a Morgravian no less, who begs your help. She tells a tale so horrid, my Queen, that I could not trust anyone else but myself to deliver it.'

Elspyth and Crys both stepped forward from the shadows. A Morgravian! This concerned them as much as the Queen.

Liryk muttered something under his breath about how many more Morgravians were going to seek shelter in Briavel but cut it short when he caught the warning glance from his Queen. 'Go on, sir, please,' Valentyna said.

The physic shivered. 'Actually, I will take that seat, your highness, if I may. I am not used to such wild rides at night.' He smiled nervously and sat, feeling the fire's heat.

'And you will take a cup of something, physic, please,' the Queen said, motioning towards Krell who obliged.

The doctor took the cup and swallowed its contents; the powerful liquor offered an almost instant revival. He cleared his throat and looked at his sovereign.

'The woman is the Lady Aleda Donal of Felrawthy

and she is gravely injured from a terrible attack on her family.'

A stunned silence claimed the chamber then Physic Geryld felt himself lifted in a firm, unshakeable grip.

'Where is Brackstead?' a young man implored him, his tone just short of threatening.

'Who, sir, are you?' the doctor asked, confused.

'I am the Duke of Felrawthy, the dying woman's son.'

Valentyna restored some measure of calm. 'Let him finish, Crys, please,' she cautioned.

Crys knelt by the doctor, murmuring an apology.

'It's all right,' Physic Geryld assured, taking the young duke's hand. 'Son, it is for you alone that she clings to life. She needs to know that you are alive and safe. We must go to her, but first there is more to tell.'

Valentyna steeled herself. She was not sure how many more shocks she could cope with after the last few days. All of them led back to the hateful man she was to marry. Anger threatened to overwhelm her again – as it did every time she permitted the marriage space in her thoughts. She fought it back. There was time still . . . for what she did not know, but time anyway before she would have to face him again, say his name, make her vows.

'Tell us, sir, and then we must make immediate arrangements for Brackstead.'

Physic Geryld nodded. He was beginning to think more clearly now that the liquor had worked its special enchantment to warm him.

'Celimus will know she has survived,' Elspyth muttered before the doctor could speak again.

Both Liryk and Krell wished they could shut up the woman of Yentro. She was too poisonous to be around the

Queen. This whole situation was turning more dangerous by the minute.

'Your majesty, please,' Krell counselled softly.

Valentyna looked towards the doctor. 'Please speak, sir,' she said kindly, not wanting to push him too hard.

'There is something, your majesty, which I was charged by the Lady Donal to bring to you.'

Valentyna nodded, deliberately expressionless so her anxieties did not betray her. 'What is it, physic?'

'I do know not, your highness, she would not say. She merely asked me to tell you that what she has sent is proof that you are marrying a madman – or words to that effect,' he said awkwardly, embarrassed now.

Liryk rolled his eyes and Krell shut his with despair.

'Where is this proof?' Valentyna asked, angry herself as the physic's harsh message touched a nerve.

Physic Geryld picked up the leather sack he had carried in. 'This is what she gave me, your majesty. I have not looked inside.'

Crys gasped as he recognised the sack Ylena had brought with her to Tenterdyn. Valentyna stilled him with a glare.

Liryk could not help himself. 'Well, tip it out, man.'

Crys felt sorry for the doctor who was having to absorb everyone's shock and frustration. He knew precisely what was in that leather sack. They had not had time to deal with it in the chaos that had occurred at Felrawthy.

'Allow me, sir,' Crys said. 'Although I could tell you what it is without looking.'

The Duke of Felrawthy reached inside and pulled out the head of his most beloved brother. 'This is Alyd Donal, your highness. What is left of him anyway after Celimus had his pleasure.'

Pandemonium broke out.

Valentyna had organised their immediate departure for Brackstead. She insisted on meeting with the Lady Donal herself. After the shock of seeing Alyd Donal's remains she felt compelled to offer her sympathies and promise this family that she would give protection to the Donals' remaining son and whatever help she could.

She sat now on her favourite horse, dressed in simple riding clothes. She wished the horse had not been a gift from Celimus but it seemed he knew how to navigate his way with a woman. No fabulous jewels or sumptuous ermine cloak for Valentyna. He had worked out quickly that she was not a woman to be won with ornaments or finery. She had clapped eyes on the filly and fallen in love. The King had even had the audacity to name the horse on her behalf. She wished she hated Bonny's name but she could not. It suited her. Feisty and intelligent, the filly was bonny indeed and very much to her liking.

Chancellor Krell had beseeched her to leave the matter to her guard, but the Queen had refused.

'Krell, this woman has almost certainly given her life in order to reach me,' Valentyna argued. 'She had no idea her son was here so her intention was purely to speak with me. I am not, as perhaps you suspect, scavenging for excuses to renege on my decision. But let me tell you this: I will reconsider my position if I find firm proof that King Celimus is directly responsible for all of these deaths.'

Krell had noted the set of her jaw; precisely the same

as her father. Nothing was going to change this decision and he was better off leaving it as an unfinished battle to fight another day rather than lose now, as he surely would if he persisted.

'As you wish, your highness.'

She had softened her manner. 'I am a sovereign, Krell. I must not be wrapped in fine linen simply because I am a woman and, for some bizarre reason, considered more fragile than a male. My father raised me to rule and rule I will, as I see fit. It would be imprudent of me to leave this woman to die without making an effort to grant her the audience she has given her life for.'

He had nodded. 'Be safe, my Queen.'

'Liryk is bringing enough manpower to take on the Morgravian army it seems,' she said, trying to lighten his mood.

There was no smile in return. 'Do not jest, your highness. I hope you never have to face such a thing,' and he bowed and removed himself.

Valentyna recalled his words now and his rare anger, albeit couched in polite words. He was most unhappy with her. So be it. *Be true to yourself first*, her father had always said. *Follow your instincts even if counsel wishes otherwise.*

And that is what I am doing, she reminded herself. Following my instincts.

One small consolation for Krell and Liryk was that the Yentro woman was not riding out with them. She had taken herself off to check on Pil, muttering something about waiting for Ylena.

'I don't care what she does,' Liryk had admitted

privately to the Chancellor, 'so long as she's not around to whisper in the ear of our Queen.'

'I can't agree more,' Krell said. 'I don't doubt she has been through much but none of it is our concern. We must keep the Queen focused on her marriage and this Elspyth is a serious threat to it.'

Liryk snorted. 'And you don't think riding off to Brackstead to hear more about his unsavoury activities isn't?' he scoffed.

Krell ignored the sarcasm, accepting that both his and Liryk's nerves were frayed. 'I cannot stop her in this, Commander. Just keep her safe and bring our Queen home as fast as you can.'

The soldier nodded. 'Hopefully the Morgravian noble's already dead,' he whispered. 'Nothing more for her majesty to learn.'

'Yes, but we still have the business with the head and no doubt the Thirsk woman will arrive at some point with another sordid story,' he said, disgusted. 'This is *none* of our business,' he added, more to himself than to Liryk.

Liryk sighed. 'Time to go.'

'May Shar guide you,' Krell said.

He did not mention to the Commander the idea which was forming in his sharp mind. It was laced with its own perils but the Chancellor was feeling uncharacteristically ruffled by events. He was a man used to being in total control, both of his own emotions and his office. Suddenly all of the activities of recent days had sent events spinning beyond his reach. The Queen was making firm, independent decisions and, although she still looked to him for his counsel and indeed his friendship, here she was riding off impetuously on behalf of Morgravians.

When the very first messenger from Celimus had brought news of Wyl Thirsk's imminent arrival, King Valor had wondered aloud to Krell what in Shar's name the enemy was doing in sending a diplomatic envoy. Krell had not forgotten the look of awe on his majesty's face at the notion that the special emissary being sent from Morgravia might well be coming to bring a marriage proposal. That Briavellian sons might live to old age without facing battle and that their sons could be raised never knowing the threat of war or its loss seemed impossible and yet wonderful in theory. All it would take was the joining of the two realms in marriage. And Krell wanted to see Valor's hope come true. He did not like Celimus; for all his easy charm and grace, his honeyed words and grand style, the man was sly. His eyes were cold and calculating, Krell felt, and something dark lurked within. But in spite of this, and as much as he too loved Valentyna, he knew she must make this sacrifice for her people. Unlike Thirsk and the other critics, Krell did not believe Celimus would seek to destroy her majesty or her realm. He truly believed Valentyna had the capacity to affect Celimus for the better, to change him. Together they would begin a mighty dynasty to rule over both realms, not unlike the famed union of the great western realm of Tallinor with the marriage of King Lorys to his beloved first wife, Nyria.

The fact that Krell had won the Queen's acceptance that this marriage was her duty and had seen her signature on the parchment now on its way back to Morgravia was balm to his troubled soul. But these new events unfurling threatened to damage irrevocably the pledge of marriage. He could not let it happen. He, Krell, would have to do something to save the situation.

His mind was made up. Another messenger would be sent, a private one. Two heads are better than one, he told himself, and the recipient would surely assist in easing the passage towards this marriage, perhaps help him to put out the fires that kept erupting and threatening to destroy the two realms' plans for peace.

As the Queen and her entourage thundered across the Werryl Bridge in a bid to reach Brackstead before the Lady Aleda breathed her last, Krell was summoning a page.

'Have a courier readied at once.'

'Yes, Chancellor Krell,' the lad said. 'What message shall I give him, sir?'

'Tell him it is a letter to Chancellor Jessom of Morgravia.'

35

FYNCH WAS JUST AS fascinated to hear Elysius's tale as Wyl was and even though he had faded quietly into the shadows whilst the conversation between his two companions continued, he continued to drink in the details as if he was parched.

'I am Myrren's father,' Elysius said, 'but my story begins much further back, when I was a youngster growing up in the far province of Parrgamyn.'

'Where Queen Adana was born?'

'That's right. And a similar cruel streak to that which ran in that woman also ran in the veins of my younger brother. I do not know where he is now, somewhere in Morgravia, I suspect, but I sense the malevolent swell of his dark magic and his dangerous activities.'

'How did you both come to be in this part of the world?'

'Our parents were part of Adana's retinue when she was sent to Pearlis to marry King Magnus. My father was one of her father's most trusted advisors and was asked by the King of Parrgamyn to accompany the young Adana on her journey to Morgravia. He fought the duty because my father despised the woman for her determination to wipe out all those gifted with magic. His family was his secret burden.'

'Because you were empowered,' Wyl finished.

Elysius nodded. 'Yes. It came from my mother's side and was very strong in us boys, which is odd. It normally transfers through women rather than males, but my mother told me once that there was a wildness to our magic which she could not account for.'

'So you came to Stoneheart.'

'We didn't live there. Adana set up a household for her own people in Soulstone.'

'Oh, of course,' Wyl said, remembering the story now. 'Did she prefer the country palace?'

Elysius snorted. 'No. She never had a kind word for anything Morgravian. But she preferred to keep her own people away from Stoneheart itself. She hated Pearlis and Morgravia's King. She had grand ideas of running a separate court; it was obvious to all that she could hardly bear to spend any time near the King. Then Celimus came along and that changed her life dramatically. Even though King Magnus didn't have much time for the boy, he certainly wouldn't agree to his heir being carted off to Soulstone. He wanted him in the capital. From what I gathered from my father, this enraged Adana and life between the two royals became strained enough that its chill reached all the way south.'

'And how old were you by now?' Wyl asked, trying to work out Elysius's age which was unreadable in his strange face.

'We were lads. I was sixteen, my brother fourteen.' He

sighed softly as he was transported back to those early days. 'Myrren's mother was so much older than I. I could almost wish I had never set eyes on her during one of the rare visits we made to Pearlis with our father. He was often called upon to advise Adana but he did not like taking us boys into the city with him.'

'Was he worried about your magic?'

'Not me, Rashlyn.'

Wyl felt his mouth dry in an instant. Elysius sensed the change in his guest's demeanour. 'What's wrong?'

'You said Rashlyn?'

The man nodded.

'I have met him.'

It was Elysius's turn to be surprised. 'I lost trace of him when I was banished.'

'He works for the King of the Razors.'

The man's eyes narrowed. 'Cailech!' Elysius declared, quietly shocked. 'So that's where he is. What use is he to the Mountain King?'

'Plenty, apparently. He bears the title of barshi, which means wise or magic man in the old tongue of the north. They are close. But more than that, I sense your brother has a somewhat unhealthy hold over the King.'

Elysius bared his horse teeth in a grimace. 'Rashlyn is very dangerous. He is the reason I appear to you in this guise.'

'Guise?'

The manwitch smiled ruefully. 'There is so much to tell you,' he said, realising his tale was disjointed, leaping from one amazing fact to another. Still, he knew it would all come out in the end and Wyl would make sense of it. 'I was actually quite a handsome sort once, tall and strong.

Myrren's mother, Emil, was a fine-looking woman whom I met whilst running a couple of messages to her husband, who was physic to Adana. He was older than her by a number of years and I think she found herself lacking in amorous activity, you could say.' He grinned. 'She was attracted to me from the moment we met.' He shrugged. 'What young man with urges beyond his control would say no? She possessed a brilliant scholar's mind too.'

Wyl's eyes widened with understanding and he glanced towards Fynch whose attention was riveted on their host. Whether he understood the nuance of this particular thread of Elysius's tale Wyl could not tell, but he had no time to linger on sensibilities right now. 'And she became pregnant,' he stated.

'Immediately. We were together only once,' Elysius admitted, 'but then she became obsessed with me. It was sad. I do believe she did actually love me, and in a way I loved her, but there was no future for us. My father discovered the truth and was horrified — not just because of my indiscretion but there was the threat of passing on my abilities to a child, you see.'

'Which you did.'

'Only marginally. Myrren was not a witch in the true sense, Wyl. She had some powers, but mainly of the healing sort. If she'd had the chance to follow in her father's footsteps — I mean, the man she called father — she would have been very talented at medicine.'

Wyl was astonished. 'Not a witch! But the gift . . . ?'

'Is all my doing. I channelled through Myrren.'

'As you channel through Knave?' Fynch chimed in, his first words in such a long time that his host had all but forgotten the quiet lad sitting in the corner.

Elysius nodded. 'Yes, son. That's right; as I use Knave to be my eyes and body elsewhere.'

Wyl sat back speechless. He had truly believed Myrren to be a witch, and ever since Knave had revealed mysterious powers, he had been sure that Myrren had possessed magics which she had managed to keep secret for many years. He said as much.

Her father shook his head sadly. 'She was innocent, poor child.'

Still trying to absorb this revelation, Wyl pressed on. 'But why me?'

Elysius shrugged. 'You were the only one who showed her any pity that day. She did not deserve to die, especially in the way she did, for that young woman never exercised her weak powers on anything but doing good for others. If not for her eyes, which she unluckily inherited from her great-grandmother, no one would have been any the wiser. I was angry, Wyl. She wanted revenge on those who were hurting her and I wanted to give her that.'

'So you used me.'

He nodded. 'I could tell you were the only person in that chamber who possessed nobility in the true sense of the word. I could count on you.'

'To do what?' Wyl asked, his voice rising in anger.

'To kill the man who crafted her death,' Elysius answered quietly.

'Lymbert?' he said, aghast.

Elysius shook his head. 'Lymbert was only the instrument.'

'As I understand it then, Lord Rokan called for her death,' Wyl continued, his anger still high. 'And King Magnus permitted it.'

'No, neither of them. Yes, they were partly responsible but they were not the key to Myrren's suffering. One person alone encouraged the King to sign her death warrant. One person alone truly enjoyed her agony.'

'Celimus,' Fynch whispered.

They both looked towards the boy and Elysius nodded. 'Yes, Celimus. Through Myrren I heard him boasting about how he had coerced his father into allowing the torture. You were there also, Wyl, but I think you were too young, too alarmed, to concentrate on the prince's bragging.'

'No . . . no, I do remember now. The priest was saying a final prayer and above it Celimus was boasting that the trial had been his idea,' Wyl recalled, frowning.

'That's right. And then Myrren singled him out, demanding to know why a prince of the realm would be present for such mummery.'

'And he said it was in the name of education, using me as his excuse,' Wyl followed up despairingly, remembering it all again as if it was yesterday.

'Myrren sensed your hatred for the prince, Wyl. She was not able to call upon pure magic but her power gave her a highly developed perception of others. It allowed her to look into you, you could say. My daughter knew that you were true and that you despised the young man who had forced you to be present to watch the ugly proceedings. She learned who you were that day and that you had the ear of the King and the status to wield power. She chose you. But it was I who used you, son. Forgive me. If I could take it back, I would.'

'You mean you can't?' Wyl asked plaintively. He had secretly harboured the hope that if he could find the manwitch, then he could reverse the gift.

Elysius shook his large head with deep regret. 'No. It must run its course.' Their host pursed his wide lips and stood, clearly upset. He began clearing the table. Wyl's temper flared and boiled over.

'Leave it, damn it!' he cried, reaching for the man's elongated arm. 'I must know!'

Elysius looked down to where Ylena's fingers dug cruelly into his thin arm, the pressure of her anger chasing away the blood to leave blanched spots.

Wyl pulled away as if stung. 'Forgive me, Elysius. This is a terrible burden . . . a curse,' he moaned, remembering all those who had died or been lost as a result of Myrren's gift.

The little man returned to his clearing-up and silence spread uneasily through the large room, punctuated only by the clatter of dishes. Wyl sat glumly whilst Elysius busied himself making a pot of tea. Soon the silence eased itself into something less awkward, with Knave's odd grunts and sighs a welcome interruption. Elysius sat himself closer to Wyl when he returned to the table and surprised him by taking Ylena's uncared-for yet still elegant hands between his two enormous palms. His milky eyes seemed to regard Wyl despite their limited sight.

'There is nothing to forgive, son. The apology is all mine. I deeply regret all the terrible events that have occurred in your lifetime and wish I could change the magic which is within you, but I can't. Once cast, it is its own master. No one can control it.'

'But how do I stop it?' This time Wyl's voice held nothing but helplessness. Fynch had to look away, unable to bear the look of defeat on Ylena's face or his own sense of loss at this news.

'It will stop,' Elysius answered gravely.

Fynch held his breath at the words and saw Wyl search his host's face. 'Tell me how,' he whispered.

'It will stop when you become the person you are meant to be, the person Myrren wanted you to be.' Wyl swallowed. He thought he already knew the answer; did not want to believe it. Elysius spoke the very words Wyl did not want to hear: 'The sovereign of Morgravia.'

Wyl's emotions were not his to command at this moment and he let out a long cry of such deepest despair that Fynch began to softly weep in his corner.

'No,' Wyl begged. 'Please, Elysius . . .'

The manwitch bent his large head low. 'I am sorry.'

When Wyl pushed the chair away and disappeared out the door, Elysius told Fynch to let him be.

'The dog will go with him. Wyl can come to no harm in the Wild with Knave nearby.'

It was hours before Wyl returned, subdued but composed. Elysius knew he had not gone far, barely steps in fact from the small dwelling he had built himself many years ago. He understood Wyl's need to be alone, to deal with the confusion and the terror.

Elysius had long since carried Fynch, sleeping, to the same pallet Wyl had used earlier. It was still not dawn.

'I imagine you have questions for me,' he said gently to Wyl. 'Put on the pot, we'll have another jar of tea each, I think.' As Wyl silently moved to oblige, Elysius added, 'I'll tease up the fire again.'

Knave padded up quietly to sneak a warm spot at the hearth. Water was set to heat whilst the embers were prodded and encouraged to flame again. New kindling erupted into larger flames and a fresh log was thrown on to catch. Satisfied, the manwitch made himself comfortable in the creaking rocking chair he had also crafted.

'Now, ask me whatever you will,' Elysius said. He could feel the barrage of queries shored up in Wyl's mind.

'How do you see?'

'I am virtually blind. I use others. Knave is my favourite, but I can use birds or other beasts.'

'People?'

'Only if I am prepared to open my magic to them.'

'Which you don't, I gather.'

'No. It is too dangerous. Animals take nothing from me.'

'But you used Myrren for this purpose,' Wyl accused.

'Only during her incarceration, and yes, I had to relinquish some of my powers to her. She took just enough to dull the pain of her torture.'

Wyl nodded, seemingly satisfied with that line of questioning. 'Your brother – I gather from what you've said it was he who made you look this way?' he said, trying hard not to give offence.

'Yes.'

'Why?'

'Because he hated me. I was just slow to understand.'

'Why did he hate you?'

'I would not share with him the secret of communicating with beasts and birds. It was evident to me from a very young age that Rashlyn was unstable.' Elysius scratched his large chin. 'More than that, in truth: I knew Rashlyn was mad. He was cruel beyond imagining for a child. As he matured, he became worse.'

His curiosity piqued, Wyl could not help but ask more

about the strange dark man in the mountains. 'How come he didn't possess the magic you do?'

'We have different skills. My magic is based in nature and living things. Rashlyn has . . . well, other talents. His magic is frightening and, with his twisted mind wielding it, it becomes the darkest of weapons.'

'But he could learn your magic?'

'Oh, yes,' the manwitch answered. 'As I could his, and he offered me all of it, every answer to every question, if I would give him the secret of the beasts.'

'I wonder why he wanted it so badly.'

'To command them, I suspect.'

'To what end?'

Elysius smiled but there was no mirth in it at all. 'He would rule the entire land if he could.'

Wyl looked at him incredulously. 'You mean as a sovereign . . . a usurper?'

'Why stop there? Why not Emperor? Why not Lord High King of the three realms for just a start? He would look to Parrgamyn and further. With all that power at his disposal he could control all of us.'

'Why hasn't he tried to do something like this already? Surely if he can call up storms, he can wreak all sorts of havoc.'

Elysius nodded thoughtfully. 'I think my brother is losing his wits. I sense that his periods of lucidity are becoming shorter. He will seek to influence instead, and this is perhaps why we find him in the Razors working with Cailech. Rashlyn always did crave power. Youngest son, you see. And as much as my father was uncomfortable with my magic, he loved me and I him. His relationship with Rashlyn was strained from early childhood. My father sensed the darkness in his youngest son, often talked to me about it and asked whether I could somehow work my powers to stem my brother's.'

'Why didn't you?'

Elysius flinched. 'It seemed cruel at the time I was asked. He had so little going for him and I seemed to have it all, I didn't want him as my enemy. As we got older I realised my mistake but by then it was too late. He was far too suspicious of me. I am surprised he took as long as he did to exercise his power over me, to tell the truth. We had little love for one another.'

'Could you not,' Wyl searched for the right words, 'prevent him from using his magic on you?'

'Shield myself from his powers, you mean?'

'I don't know what would be the right expression,' Wyl admitted.

'It has taken me years to learn his "scent". That is probably the easiest way to describe magic, as a sensation of the wielder's characteristics.'

'And so you can what . . . feel him using his powers?'

'You could describe it that way, yes,' Elysius replied. 'He is up to dark mischief, Wyl, and it bodes badly for all of us – for Morgravia and Briavel, even for the Mountain Kingdom he apparently serves.'

'Can he sense you?'

'Perhaps. I don't know. I use my magic fleetingly these days. I also suspect that the Thicket filters sentient activity in one direction. I can sense him, in other words, but he can't sense me.'

'Why would he not have recognised the enchantment when I walked in Koreldy's form?'

'Because of the Thicket – it has subtle powers, most

of which even I am not privy to. It is my belief that it has protected you.'

Wyl had the feeling that Elysius was not being entirely forthright here. If his sense of perception served him right, he would say that the sorcerer was holding back information. He could continue probing but decided it was more important right now to focus on the important details of Elysius's story, which would affect his decisions for the future. Rashlyn was not important to Wyl now — or so it seemed to him — and he returned to the tale of how Elysius ended up in the Wild. 'So tell me, what happened after your father asked you to hinder your brother's magic?'

'I lied that I could not. I was too young and stupid to realise that decision would come back and bite me. My father's relationship with Rashlyn was non-existent by the end.'

'The end?'

'Yes, I'm sorry, we've been jumping about, haven't we? After my father discovered my affair with Emil, he banished me to Parrgamyn to live without my family. Leaving Morgravia was punishment enough, but to be without my family — he knew how much it would hurt. My parents did not know that Emil was pregnant, of course, but Rashlyn suspected as much. He also guessed that I would not return permanently to our place of birth. I rather liked Morgravia and I especially enjoyed the south where it is green and filled with meadows and woodland. Parrgamyn is more arid, you see.'

Wyl nodded.

'Anyway, in my anger I carelessly boasted to Rashlyn I would jump ship and escape back into Morgravia. I thought he might help me. Quite the opposite: he began to blackmail me. Told me I must give him the secret to the beasts or he would tell our father of my intention.' Elysius laughed but again there was little amusement in it. 'I refused to relinquish the secret, no matter what his threat.'

'So what happened?' Wyl prompted, absorbed by this tale.

'He weaved a dark and evil concoction of spells which capsized the ship I was on. I imagine he hoped I would drown with the rest of the unfortunates on that voyage, but his mind works in a cunning fashion, Wyl. Rashlyn took the precaution that, should I survive, I would never be able to live in normal society again. Death would have been easier and my brother knew this; he understood my love of poetry and literature, knew I would suffer without the social contact I thrived on.'

'And this is the result of his work . . . this guise you wear?'

Elysius nodded. 'We had barely got out of the port into deeper waters to sail around the Razors towards Grenadyn when the vessel began to break up and sink. There were ninety souls lost that day. I miraculously remained afloat on a spar, although the freezing waters of the north would have surely killed me. With my last remaining strength I summoned a wind and cast my luck with it.

'I remember very little of that wild night but when I regained consciousness I had washed up on a tiny beach in the far north . . . and I looked like this and had lost most of my senses of sight, taste, smell.'

'Have you somehow seen yourself,' Wyl wondered aloud.

The man nodded. 'The creatures explained in great detail. I knew I was different from the moment I regained consciousness, but their descriptions pained me nonetheless,' he said softly.

Elysius fixed his non-seeing gaze on a far away spot and recalled that difficult time. 'With a sea eagle's help I navigated my way into the foothills of the Razors and then, using a variety of animals as my lost senses, I skirted the mountains for several weeks. I was in such shock. I had nowhere to go and was so terrified of being seen that I had to avoid all humanity. My friends, the animals, whispered to me of a place – an enchanted place – called the Wild, where no human dared go. "Take me there," I begged them . . . and so they did. I have lived here since.'

'The spell cannot be lifted?'

'Not with any magic I own,' he answered ruefully. 'Though I have tried, Wyl, I have tried.'

'We are both cursed then.'

'You speak true,' Elysius admitted. 'You are only the third person I have seen since I came here.'

'And Fynch is the second, so that means . . . ah yes, of course, Emil. I remember now, the boatkeeper gave me her name but I didn't make the connection. So Myrren's mother came to you?'

'Yes. She braved the Thicket and the Darkstream to find me.'

'How did she know where to find you if everyone thought you were lost?'

'I shouldn't have, but I used a seer I knew to seek her out.'

'Widow Ilyk!' Wyl cried, immediately hushing himself for fear of waking Fynch.

The manwitch nodded. 'I knew she was safe to use because her powers were weak. Whatever enhancement I added by opening myself up to her would not make her dangerous – I believed she would take only what she needed to make herself more skilled in her craft, but then I was still rather young and desperate to make contact with Emil so you could say my power of reasoning and subsequent decisions were juvenile.'

Wyl wrapped Ylena's thin arms about her body and shivered. 'Tell me about the widow.'

'Well, she and I had met on several occasions during her visits through the southern region and once in Pearlis. I had always liked her and so I took the chance. I cast myself wide and was able to reach out and find her. I could not do the same for my brother who was well shielded by then. Naturally she was amazed to hear my voice in her head, but she was a believer in magic so I suppose she overcame her fright rapidly. She agreed to find Emil and give her a message. In return she took some of my power – not very much, she too was not greedy – which allowed her to become gifted with her sight into people's lives.'

Wyl sipped the strongly brewed tea. 'Extraordinary.'

'Emil came when she received the message. She was shocked and terrified, of course, by the state I was in. I learned of my daughter, and she learned that the child she had borne might be cursed with the same magic. She could not bear to look upon me and all my hopes of finding some love or companionship again evaporated the moment I felt her revulsion. With some help from me she was able to navigate her way back through the Thicket without the boatkeeper noting her return and we have had no further contact. I am presuming she never told anyone that I am still alive.'

Wyl shook his head. 'I imagine not. How did Myrren react to learning her father was not her real one?'

Elysius grimaced. 'It was as if she had suspected as much all her life   and yet how could she? Nevertheless, she took the news calmly when I finally found the courage to speak with her in the dungeon – it felt almost like relief that she knew the truth. The next time we spoke it was very brief and after her torture, so she was near enough dead. She told me she wanted vengeance on the prince through you. I think she believed you might relish the opportunity. I could not refuse her.'

'Her gift seems to be more suited to her uncle's magic if you don't mind me saying so, although perhaps you both share some powers?'

'You are right on both counts. There are certain skills we can both wield. And it might be that Myrren did inherit some of our combined magic, and when she took my power perhaps she corrupted it with the sort of dark twist Rashlyn would use. She made the conditions of the gift, not I. I simply channelled her the power to achieve her desire.'

'And so I have no choice in this? My destiny is mapped out as to who I must become,' Wyl said into the gloom. A slash of brightness through the window suggested dawn was not far away.

'You also have no choice in how the gift plays out. An accident could kill you once and for all, Wyl, so chance comes into it. Remember this: you cannot force or invite death. It does not work that way. Myrren's gift has its own momentum, its own force you could say. You do not control it; it controls you.'

'So if I threaten Celimus, invite him to stick his blade into my belly, the gift won't work?'

Elysius shook his head slowly. 'What is more, it will make you pay a penalty, because I could not risk you running around inviting people to kill you. Now that I know you, I realise you would never do such a thing. Power is not what you crave. Still, you cannot welcome death through someone else and thus manoeuvre it to your own ends; that was my condition to Myrren — that and the fact that the gift is subject to the whims of the world around it.'

'What do you mean?'

'I am not someone to use his power for dark purposes and this vengeance had a blackness that goes against the spirit of my magic. So I maintained that, although you could not control the gift yourself, it was subject to choice.'

'Other people's choices, you mean?'

'Exactly. Death must visit you because the perpetrator decides it, not because you or the gift do. Other people will influence how the magic applies itself, in other words.'

'And that made it all right in your mind?' Wyl asked, aghast, his tone leaden with disgust.

Elysius felt the anger and frustration of his victim. 'It made it easier, Wyl, that's all. I thought that if others had some choice in the matter, you might be spared.'

Wyl laughed humourlessly. 'And as you can see, I *have* been spared.'

Elysius remained quiet. There were no words of comfort to offer.

'And it will stop when I rule Morgravia?' Wyl said into the thick silence.

'Yes. This I do know. It was Myrren's greatest desire that Wyl Thirsk rule the realm that caused her death.'

'Because she knew I would stop the persecution of witches once and for all?'

'Because she knew you would stop the torturing of any souls and, especially, stamp out the persecution of empowered people,' Elysius said softly.

Wyl sighed. 'Of course she wasn't to know that the same King who permitted her death would campaign to stop all further persecution. She could have saved me a lot of trauma.'

Elysius nodded. 'Magnus was a good King, despite allowing my daughter to die.'

'Elysius, is there anything remotely positive about your daughter's gift to me?'

'Only one factor – an odd one. Myrren was determined that any child of yours would truly be yours.'

Wyl frowned with confusion. 'But what does she mean by that?'

Elysius shrugged. 'If I understand her correctly, it means that when you father an heir to the throne of Morgravia, no matter whose body encloses you the child will truly have Thirsk blood running in its veins.'

It was cold comfort for Wyl but comfort nonetheless in an otherwise cheerless tale.

36

ALEDA HAD SLEPT AS deeply as the doctor had predicted.
When she surfaced it was into a dulled confusion; she did
not recognise where she was but there was a woman staring
at her. She felt weak, knew her time was upon her.

'Welcome back,' the woman murmured, her expression
one of relief.

'Where am I?'

'Safe. In a town called Brackstead.'

'In Briavel?' Aleda asked anxiously.

The woman soothed her. 'Yes. My name is Bel. Let me
help you to sit up. You need to drink this – all of it.' She
held out a mug.

'What's this?'

'A special tea. Physic Geryld insists. I'll tell you about
him.'

Images flooded back as her mind cleared. 'Did he go
to Werryl?'

'Hush,' Bel said. 'Physic Geryld rode to Werryl for
help.'

'I have to find my son,' Aleda whimpered.

'You're in no state to do anything.' Bel did not want to tell her that she would probably never leave this bed. 'Let's wait for news from the capital.'

Aleda already knew her fate. She was too weak to sit up. 'If I can last that long. I can feel the bleeding has begun again.'

'You must hold on,' Bel urged. 'Please . . . drink.'

Aleda struggled with a few sips then let her head fall back on to the pillow.

'You must keep drinking the tea if you want to live,' Bel urged, terrified of losing the woman and being blamed.

'I have nothing to live for. My family is dead, murdered. You can't know what that feels like,' she groaned.

Bel fell into an awkward silence and hoped the noble-woman slept. She might even have dozed herself until a noise disturbed her.

'Riders!' she said, sitting up.

There was a cacophony of excited voices from below. Then footsteps, a man's tread, heavy and eager, thundering up the stairs. The door burst open.

'Mother!' Crys cried, his voice thick with emotion, and then he was across the room in a few strides, his head buried in his mother's arms. A smile of pure joy stretched across the older woman's face. 'My boy.' She was so weak she could only whisper. 'You made it.'

The Queen was not far behind Crys. Bel, in her excite-ment and confusion at being burst in upon, did not realise who the tall woman was as she was summarily escorted from the room by Liryk.

Crys wept into Aleda's chest only momentarily, sensing that he would lose her very soon. He looked up into the

face which had always made him feel safe and loved. 'Pil
found us, told us . . . Elspyth made me ride to Briavel
rather than home.'

She could see his despair at having made that decision,
knew he wondered whether he could have saved his family
if he had ridden in the other direction. 'You chose right
– thank Shar for Elspyth's clear head. You live, Crys, and
you are now Duke of Felrawthy. Make that count.' Aleda
refused to dissolve into the tears she felt were just as determined to fall. 'They never gave us a chance. They were
sent by Celimus to slaughter us and you would be dead
too if you had returned. But you must fight back now,
son. Rally an army, as Ylena advised, and make that treacherous sovereign of ours pay for what he has done to our
family and to the Thirsks.'

Crys marvelled through his grief that his mother could
set aside her pain and loss in her final moments of life to
talk to him about duty. He could almost hear his father's
voice joining with hers, urging him to live up to the
family name, but this time to fight against rather than
for the Crown. It was a chilling thought.

'I love you,' was all he could say to his mother in
the moment before she died with bittersweet joy in her
heart that her son lived and Celimus might yet face
retribution.

At first the commotion was only about the sudden arrival
of Briavellian soldiers. The folk of Brackstead were thrilled
to see the purple and emerald colours so rich and bright
on a cold spring morning. Then word got around that
Commander Liryk himself was in town. Whatever was
happening at The Lucky Bowman was obviously of great

import for the highest-ranking soldier in the realm to descend upon the inn without warning.

'It's to do with the stranger,' Bel offered knowingly to any who would give her an ear. She had been thanked for her time and paid handsomely, then asked to leave. 'I should know, I was asked to look after her. She's noble for sure and with a Morgravian accent. What she's doing travelling alone is anyone's guess, and that youngblood who suddenly appeared was apparently her son,' she said, nodding as if she had solved the puzzle. When pushed it was obvious Bel knew very little more; nonetheless she enjoyed far closer attention than she was used to as the locals clamoured for news.

When an observant onlooker suggested he was sure it had been their young Queen riding into town and leaping off her horse with long-legged agility and a toss of her ponytail, the tempo of the conversation increased to near boiling point. Such high excitement had not been experienced in Brackstead since King Valor himself had dropped in for an ale on his way back to Werryl from the north three years back.

Confirmation had to be sought. Bel considered it was her duty, now that she had been elevated to such stellar heights, and she accosted the irritated innkeeper whose rooms had been suddenly cleared of patrons by the Briavellian soldiers on account of the official-looking people in room four.

'Just tell us, Nan,' Bel urged. 'Or I'll never be able to get them to leave the place,' she added conspiratorially, as if she held such sway over the townsfolk.

Nan remained tight-lipped for a moment longer before realising that her friend was right. A crowd would just keep gathering and hindering proceedings if she did not come clean. 'Yes, yes, all right. It is her.'

Bel swung around to the waiting people. 'It's true! Our Queen is here!'

A roar went up and Nan understood all too clearly her mistake. The frenzy was too high, no one would leave. Her admission had only made it worse as runners were sent off to take messages to more of the townsfolk.

She sighed. 'Reduced-price ale for everyone but it's served outside,' she said to Bel. 'Anyone not drinking will have to leave,' she warned. 'I might as well make myself a penny or two if you're all going to clog my footpath.' More cheers as Bel passed on this news. 'But, Bel, you'd better keep them quiet for now. They've asked for hush and that's from the top.'

The woman's eyes widened with excitement. As she turned to relay the instructions to an eager audience, Nan stomped back inside and dropped a curtsy to Commander Liryk who happened to be blocking her way.

'Sir, I've done my best but they're not leaving until they see her . . . er, the Queen. I've offered cheap ale and they in turn have promised quiet.'

'Thank you,' he said gruffly.

He had no doubt Valentyna would oblige her people eventually and took one more look around the inn to check all entrances were guarded and all windows blocked by burly men. Once satisfied he gave the word for the Queen and her companions to come down to the common room. She was resting her hand on the Morgravian duke's arm, no doubt offering condolences. He appeared composed – stoic, in fact, Liryk noticed – which was to be expected of a duke of the realm.

'Please, Crys, be at ease. The regret is mine that I did not have the chance to meet her and offer my thanks,' Liryk heard Valentyna say. 'She brought proof, that's enough,' she added. The Commander of Briavel had to wonder what this new turn of events would mean for their realm and its hopes of uniting with Morgravia.

Crys Donal, still struggling to come to terms with the death of his family, let alone having his mother die in his arms after such a courageous and tragic journey into enemy territory, was hiding his grief admirably. His father would be proud. Hearing himself addressed as Duke of Felrawthy was still a bitter sound to his ear and he had asked the Queen to call him by his given name rather than his title, even in this company.

He was glad she had obliged so readily and could hardly believe how adeptly Valentyna had turned the awkward situation into something more bearable. Her ability to put people at ease was a true skill. She had used it well with himself, Pil and Elspyth when they had turned up so unexpectedly with such shattering news, and she was using it again now to ensure that everyone remained calm.

He watched her stretching out her stiff limbs and yawning, issuing requests for food and warm drinks, making everyone relax. It was a deliberate and calculated move and he admired her judgement and stored it away as something he must learn himself. His father had tended towards a more authoritarian style of managing his people but Crys appreciated the pragmatic way Valentyna dealt with those around her. She remained very much in control – she was their sovereign, after all – but she listened to people, and even in the short time he had known her Crys could see that she strived to ensure everyone's needs were acknowledged.

As he was thinking this he saw Liryk step up and mention to her majesty that the townsfolk were eager to see her. She nodded and said something back and Crys knew that she had agreed to do what would please her people without considering her own fatigue.

She turned towards Crys now and he snapped himself out of his thoughts.

'I haven't yet formally offered my sympathies,' she said and took his hand.

'At least I saw her . . . had the chance to hold her as she died,' he said bravely. 'Which is more than I could do for my father or brothers.'

'Do not torture yourself,' the Queen said. 'I speak from experience. It makes no difference and will not bring them back. You must take up where your fine father left off and fill his boots.'

He smiled. 'As you had to.'

He sensed the sadness behind the soft smile she gave back. He felt as if he was the only person in the room with her right now. 'Yes. And his boots felt very large indeed at first. Allow yourself to make mistakes; forgive yourself when you do. And follow your instincts, Crys. I have no doubt that your parents have groomed you your entire life to take on this challenge, as my father did for me. The know-how does not come easily but we are both more ready than either of us trust, I am sure.'

It seemed that Valentyna knew precisely what to say at the right time. She made him feel strong when the detracting voices inside were doing their best to weaken him.

'Thank you,' he said, wishing he could kiss her and not just out of gratitude. The same voices told him immediately to get that idea out of his head.

'You are welcome,' she replied. 'And no matter what happens, Briavel will always be a friend to the Duchy of Felrawthy.'

And with that final comment which lifted his spirits and filled his heart with hope, the Queen of Briavel released his hand and called for a hearty breakfast to be served once she had had the opportunity to say hello to the people of Brackstead and apologise for the lack of warning in descending upon them.

Her comment regarding the need for food made people nearby grin. It was a well-known fact in Briavel that their Queen, despite her lean figure, possessed a fierce appetite. The guards loved her for it, all the more so on the nights she strolled on to the battlements and never failed to show interest in what was on for supper, more than happy to crouch with them and share a small bite of whatever they were eating or drink a mug of ale with them. Somehow it never felt unseemly; she had the knack of making everyone feel comfortable in her presence whilst never relinquishing her grace or regal bearing.

Later, over that same breakfast, Valentyna and Crys spoke of the tale Physic Geryld had related on Aleda's behalf.

Crys shook his head. 'The hide, the timing . . . it all fits. That area would also be the logical place to do their ugly work of burying and later burning the bodies.' He did not want to say that not so far away was also buried the corpse of Faryl of Coombe, a spot chosen for its remoteness. It seemed Celimus's mercenaries had selected well.

Valentyna put her face in her hands and sighed. 'You are quite sure it was the King?'

'I wasn't there, your highness, so I cannot be absolutely sure. However, all the shocking events which led up to this seem to be coming together into one nasty campaign from a new King determined to stamp out anyone else's threat to his power. He must be demented if he feared my father – there was no more loyal duchy to the Crown than Felrawthy, other than Argorn perhaps. And yet Celimus has done his utmost to destroy both the great loyalists to the north and south. He thinks he has achieved it, but I live to fight on and this time it won't be for him. It will be against him.'

And against me, Valentyna thought miserably, should I marry Celimus. 'So your mother brought the – pardon me for mentioning it again – the remains of your brother to me,' she said aloud. 'Who brought them to your family?'

'Ylena, my lady, from Rittylworth. The head was left with the monks by a man called Romen Koreldy.' Crys saw the Queen react to the name. 'Do you know him?'

Valentyna nodded. 'I did. He is dead, no use to any of us now.' She tried to make her words sound offhand but they came out forlornly. 'I am pleased he rescued Ylena Thirsk.'

Crys dared not explain Ylena's fate.

'Where is she now, do you think? You said she was at Tenterdyn with your family.'

The lie came easily as Wyl had instructed. 'She was taken away at the same time Elspyth and I departed, by a man called Aremys Farrow. He is a Grenadyne, knew Koreldy apparently.' He saw the Queen's brow furrow in thought and knew her next question before she asked it, so kept talking. 'Apparently Koreldy asked that Aremys look in on her at Rittylworth.' Crys shrugged, hoping he was being convincing. 'I suppose when he saw what had happened there he came looking for her at Tenterdyn. Presumably Koreldy had mentioned that she had married one of the Donals.'

'So where would this Aremys have taken her?'

'He cautioned that if any of us knew where they headed we could be in danger from Celimus, who might target yet more death and destruction.'

The Queen nodded. 'It seems he was right.' She was thinking of the note Elspyth had brought, but her thoughts were disrupted by a new voice joining the conversation.

Liryk cleared his throat. 'I don't think we should jump to any conclusions, your highness.'

'No?' the Queen said. 'How can you look me square in the eye, Commander, and tell me it is otherwise regarding the man I'm supposed to marry?'

She instantly regretted her barb, knowing it was wrong of her to belittle this good man who had only her well-being at heart, and in front of strangers, Morgravians especially. 'I am sorry, Commander Liryk,' she hurriedly continued. 'You are right, of course. I must think on what I have heard.'

The damage was done though. The old soldier looked mortified and did not acknowledge her contrition. Valentyna could do nothing to repair his injured ego at present. Instead she stood.

'Well, there is nothing more we can do here. We travel for Werryl immediately. Liryk, please make arrangements for the Lady Aleda to be transported to the palace chapel where Crys will have the opportunity to pray to Shar for his mother's soul.'

'Thank you, your highness,' Crys murmured.

'I wish I could do more,' Valentyna said, taking her leave.

37

AREMYS WAITED OUTSIDE THE great doors into Cailech's private rooms. He had not recovered himself fully, although tantalising glimmers of information teased at his mind and he believed it was only a matter of time before his memory was restored. One stroke of luck was that he had finally remembered his identity, but he had no intention of revealing it just yet to the Mountain People. Much as he liked Myrt and his men, he remained suspicious of their intentions for him. Until he knew more, he would keep his secrets.

With the arrival of his name a flurry of other memories had flooded into his consciousness, mostly from earlier years. More recent events remained vague; he now knew he had been on a journey with someone when his memory was lost, but he could not remember either the person or their destination. Aremys decided he would just have to trust now that his mind was intact and when it had fully recovered from the blow or whatever had so damaged his recall, it would return his memories to him.

For now he was Cullyn and he would need his wits

about him. Myrt had cautioned him not to play the innocent victim with the King. Aremys's damaged memory
had reminded him that Cailech was known as the Fox on
Grenadyn . . . for good reason. He would heed his new
friend's warning.

Myrt emerged. 'The King will see you now. Remember
what I said.'

Aremys nodded and followed the Mountain man into
a vast light-filled chamber warmed by an open fire at
one end. He was entranced by the view from the tall
windows.

'This is Cullyn, my lord, although that is not his real
name,' Myrt said to the yellow-haired man who sat at one
end of a table, eating.

Aremys bowed low. Royalty made him feel anxious but
this King looked anything but regal. He wore no outward
signs of his status and stood to greet the stranger, wiping
his hands on his breeches. 'Welcome, Cullyn . . . or whatever your name is,' he said.

'King Cailech, I am honoured,' Aremys replied,
straightening from his bow.

He had height and width on the King but then Aremys
did on most men. This one, however, was not in any way
cowed by his size, more amazed if anything.

'Haldor's arse, but you're huge, man,' Cailech said,
good-naturedly. 'A Grenadyne, I hear?'

'Yes, my lord. We think so.' Aremys grinned.
'Apparently my accent gives me away. Plus I held my
sword in Grenadyne fashion. It seems I understand
Northernish and . . . well, I just know I'm not from
Morgravia or Briavel.'

'So what were you doing in the Razors just north of

the Briavellian border?' Cailech enquired, straight to the point.

Aremys shrugged, genuinely baffled. 'I cannot tell you, my lord. Not yet anyway. I am hoping my memories will not stay blurred for long.'

Cailech held his gaze, granite-faced. It was a test, Aremys knew it, and much as he felt inclined to look away from that searching scrutiny he forced himself to hold the penetrating stare from a King used to finding out what he needed to.

'And you fight like an experienced soldier, I hear.'

Aremys was not sure how to answer. 'I don't remember any training, my lord, although I suspect there must have been some in my past. Yes, sire, I am good.'

'A mercenary perhaps?'

He nodded this time. 'That's probably true,' he agreed. 'I have been thinking as much myself.'

'Join me,' the King said.

Aremys was taken aback. One moment Cailech was interrogating him, the next inviting him to eat with him. He sat. 'Thank you,' he replied, confused. 'But I am not hungry.'

The King gestured that it was of no matter. He resumed his meal and nodded to a man who immediately poured Aremys some wine. 'Try this, it's my favourite,' Cailech encouraged.

Aremys did and it was delicious. He told the King so.

'It was also Romen Koreldy's favourite when he was here,' Cailech said conversationally.

'Koreldy?' Aremys frowned. 'Who is he, my lord?'

'I thought you knew him,' Cailech replied, not looking up from his baked waterfowl. 'Myrt tells me you mentioned his name.'

'Did I?' Aremys asked, looking around for Myrt. Even Cailech believed him – if this man was shamming then he was one of the better actors. 'When?'

Cailech nodded towards Myrt who was standing near the window.

'Wait!' Aremys interrupted deciding to come clean. 'I do remember now. I said Koreldy's name when I was preparing to spar with Firl.'

Myrt nodded.

'So you do know him?' the King continued, pleased that this newcomer was apparently being honest.

'I must do, but I can't dredge up from where. It was . . .' he searched for the answer '. . . that's right, it was something to do with the sword that reminded me of him. Is he a Grenadyne?'

'He is,' came the reply.

Aremys shrugged. 'That's how I know his name then. I have no other recollection, other than the prompt from the sword of all things.'

'He carries a sword of bluish hue, my King,' Myrt said softly.

Cailech said nothing in response.

Aremys nodded, recalling a blue sword. 'Yes, that is so. But I don't know if I know this or am recalling something I've been told, as I remember nothing about the man, sire. Is he important?'

'To me, yes.'

'May I ask why?'

'Koreldy and I have unfinished business to settle,' Cailech said, his unfathomable eyes glinting over the rim of his goblet. 'To your full health returning, Cullyn,' he said, raising that goblet now.

'I'll drink to that, your majesty,' Aremys replied. 'What is your plan for me?'

Cailech resumed his eating. 'Well, with no memory to draw upon I presume you are in no hurry to be anywhere right now, so why not remain with us? Myrt tells me you can help by teaching my men some sword skills.'

Aremys could see no harm in it. He rather liked the Mountain Dwellers and could not help but like the direct man who ruled them. 'I shall be glad to. Do I remain as your prisoner?'

Cailech smiled now. 'I think guest is a nicer word,' he suggested.

Aremys understood. It was true: he had no idea where he should be or why, so he might as well accept the hospitable imprisonment of the Mountain King and make the best of it until his memory returned fully.

'Oh, and Cullyn, with regard to the Morgravian King. Do you have any thoughts on him . . . any memories coming to mind?'

It could not hurt to be honest with this question, Aremys decided. He knew within himself that he hated the man called Celimus but could not remember why. 'I hate him, sire . . . I think. When Myrt mentioned his name, my hackles rose. It must mean something, though I am yet to learn what.'

The King nodded thoughtfully. 'That makes two of us. I hate him enough to do battle with him. But I fear a war right now would be wasting my men.'

Aremys looked startled. 'I am sure my limited recall serves me faithfully when I suggest that to take on the Morgravian Legion would be suicide for your men. The Legion are well-drilled soldiers. I know your people are tough and do not lack for courage, but I would avoid out and out war with Morgravia.'

'Unless of course we could bring them into the Razors. If we fought on our own territory, we would win.'

'Undoubtedly,' Aremys agreed and believed it. 'But Celimus would not be lured, sire. He's too smart.'

'Then you have met the man to have this opinion, I presume?'

Aremys scratched his head and frowned. 'You must be right – I suppose I have met him to feel so assured of his ability.' There were thoughts niggling at the fringe of his mind; they were just out of reach for now which was frustrating, but Aremys reminded himself to hold faith, his memory would return.

'Do you have another suggestion?' the King asked, more as conversation than genuine expectancy that the injured man could offer advice.

'Yes! Parley. As long as you're talking, no Mountain Dweller is losing his life.'

Cailech fixed Aremys with his hard gaze again. There was humour in it this time though, because the stranger had taken him by surprise. 'Go on.'

'Why fight – for what reason? Do you truly want Morgravia?'

'I might,' Cailech said, not prepared to share his thoughts.

'No, sire. Why would you want Morgravia? Your people belong here in the mountains. But what if trade was free and your people could come and go across the border without fearing an arrow? That would be worth striving for – not dying for though.'

Myrt smiled to himself in the background. Cullyn was turning Cailech's own creed back on the King. He had preached a policy of negotiation for all of his early life and thus had united the tribes of the mountains.

Aremys pressed on. 'And by the same token, sire, Celimus might think he wants the Razors, but in truth why would he want the Mountain Kingdom? What is he going to do with it? No Morgravian would survive easily up here, save a few hardy northerners perhaps. And he certainly isn't going to move his palace here, my lord. It's pointless. From talking with Myrt — and I mean no offence, sire — I believe this is two obstinate kings, neither prepared to give ground. Why not get together and work out a solution? Spill no blood. Who knows what good might come of it?'

It was a long speech for Aremys, but as much as he knew he hated Celimus, he did not for a moment believe the Mountain Dwellers were a match for the Legion. A new thought struck him. 'And should you escalate these skirmishes I've been told of, my lord King, then if I was Celimus I would unite with Briavel to crush you. Between the Morgravian Legion and the Briavellian Guard, your people will die, sire, and in numbers no matter how brave they are. You are a nuisance, for want of a better word, and Morgravia might well put aside its differences with Briavel if it meant getting rid of the nuisance from the north.' He had no idea where this assurance had come from and could only assume that his knowledge was returning at a rapid rate now.

He expected a harsh reaction from Cailech, but the King nodded. 'You speak sense, Cullyn. I just want to teach the upstart King a lesson, let him know we are not the simpleton barbarians he believes us to be. In truth, I could not leave my beloved mountains.'

'But that's precisely what you would have to do, sire, to conquer him. And anyway, there are many ways to skin a rat, my lord.'

At this old northern adage the King laughed, green eyes twinkling with his mirth. 'You mean there are other ways to teach the southerner a lesson.'

Aremys nodded. 'Precisely. It doesn't have to be by proving you are mightier. Intelligence is the key here, sire. Prove you are the King with the vision for peace.'

'Do you think Morgravia and Briavel will unite?' Cailech asked suddenly.

Aremys could not guess at this. 'It was a theory, your majesty, but one with merit.' He shrugged. 'If I were the Morgravian King and facing war with you, I would seek to do the same. I think I'm right in saying that the Briavellians are a more tolerant people but they have their own suspicions about the Mountain Dwellers. Faced with fighting you, yes, I think they might strike up a tentative bargain with Morgravia to work to defeat you.'

'And that's precisely what the King is doing, Cullyn. Your instincts are sharp but your faded memory has not reminded you that Celimus is petitioning Queen Valentyna of Briavel in marriage.'

At his words, old memories resurfaced and slotted into place. A man called Wyl suddenly came to Aremys's mind. He could not see him in his mind's eye but he was thinking orange-hair . . . a General. Morgravian no less, but try though he might he could not put a face to the memory. He kept seeing a woman's eyes . . . feline and sensual. The naming of the Queen had prompted this memory of the Morgravian, as if the two were connected. He shook his head to rid it of the disjointed thoughts – he would have to consider them later.

'All the more reason to parley, King Cailech. Seek friendship, seek trade, seek peace. You will be the winner; it is your people who would benefit more than the Morgravians, in truth.'

'I like your style,' Cailech said, after draining his goblet. 'What do you suggest?'

Aremys thought about it and the King did not seem to mind the pause. 'Do not be too proud,' he said finally. 'Lead the talks; show his people and your own that it was you who had the vision rather than he. Celimus is not trustworthy so you must tread carefully. And should the talks fail, then no one can accuse the Mountain King of acting in anything but a chivalrous manner. They will know you held out the hand of peace.'

Cailech stood, impressed and a little startled. He needed to think this audacious idea through, perhaps have the Stones read.

'I like you, Cullyn of Grenadyn. We shall talk more. Join me later for a ride. You must see Galapek, my new stallion.'

Rashlyn moved the Stones about before him. He was alone and he was baffled. They spoke to him of *change*. Big change, but he could make no sense of it. He cast again, looking specifically for any indication of his greatest fear – the death of King Cailech. He had saved Cailech's life once previously, when Koreldy had threatened it all those years ago, now he regularly searched the Stones for answers to Cailech's longevity.

Alas, *change* once more was all the Stones would yield.

What did it mean? Without Cailech he had no power. He must not allow the King to be threatened in any way and yet here was Cailech murmuring about escalating his dislike for the Morgravian King to war.

Rashlyn moved restlessly to the window of the chamber he liked to work in, well removed from the hustle and bustle of daily life in the cave. In his increasingly rare lucid moments, such as now, Rashlyn knew he was losing his mind. It was a slow and tormenting process and he hoped this inability to get more out of the Stones was not part of that disintegration. He pulled angrily at the wild beard he hid behind and admitted to himself that spells that once were so easy for him to devise were now challenging. Oh, he was still brilliantly skilled but the talent was beginning to elude him and he alone knew it. Stranger still, he was beginning to recall in vivid detail memories of playing with his brother in childhood.

Elysius! Curse him! Rashlyn felt sure he must be dead. He felt no remorse for causing his brother's death. Emil had met Rashlyn first and had flirted recklessly with the plain young man, picking her target perfectly for it was obvious he was starved of female attention. As much as Rashlyn desperately wanted to touch, to kiss, to lie with a woman, none would have him willingly so Emil was a revelation for him. Even the whores of Pearlis thought twice about taking Rashlyn's money. There was something about his wild eyes and disturbing manner that frightened them. And they were right to be scared. Rashlyn's insecurity had caused the death of two prostitutes on separate occasions when he was unable to see their brief paid coupling through to the normal close. Embarrassed to the point of anguish, he had lashed out with his powers and murdered both cruelly and painfully.

Since tasting the power of killing he had wanted more, needed more. He wished he had killed his brother sooner, then Elysius would never have met Emil. As soon as she clapped eyes on his handsome brother, the humiliation for Rashlyn was complete – her passing interest in him was done. So be it, he had decided, I will find my pleasures in other, darker ways. And he had.

More recently, he had come to the startling realisation that death was easy to inflict; it was the crafting of a spell to prolong an agonising life that was the challenge. It gave him even greater power to control someone through his magic and manipulate them in unthinkable ways.

The transformation of Lothryn from man to horse was the culmination of years of practice in his wing of the mountain fortress where no one could hear the screams of the rabbits and squirrels he selected for his experiments.

He had hated his brother for his looks and his easy manner with others, but mostly he had hated him for his ability to work magic with animals. For as helpless as they seemed to Rashlyn when he had them pinned down or trapped, he had no control over them in any other way, no relationship with the natural world at all.

He hoped Elysius had fought death hard before the sea consumed him. And if by chance he had cheated the waters, then he hoped his brother had died a pitiful death as a freak in some far corner of the realm. Perhaps he had been set upon by a gang of frightened people – he hoped so, for Rashlyn had certainly seen to it that Elysius could not risk appearing in public.

Rashlyn had not felt his brother's magic since that dark

day of death, but then he could not be confident that his waning power could detect a magic as subtle as Elysius's at work. It was an artful and delicate power, and so potent it took his breath away. He had feared that as Elysius matured he would have learned the key to cloaking his magics – and perhaps he had . . . perhaps he was alive and practising his art right now?

Since his brother's presumed demise and his own defection to the Mountain Kingdom, Rashlyn had devoted his energies towards unlocking the secret of power over the animals and birds, the mountains and the trees. One could rule the world with that sort of power at your call. His own skills simply made him a sorcerer, which was why he had attached himself to the far-thinking, highly intelligent King of the Mountains. Using him as his cover and, indeed, his tool, Rashlyn envisaged himself manipulating great power . . . and not just in the Razors. But right now Cailech was being rash. He was howling for Morgravian blood – too soon in Rashlyn's opinion. The King had this notion that Rashlyn's magic would serve to keep him utterly secure and prevent casualties amongst the Mountain Dwellers.

Rashlyn needed more time to shore up his defences, to work new spells. He could hardly explain to the King that his magic was failing him. He remembered how he had only just managed to maintain that glamour of the woman from Yentro. A few moments more and the vision would have crumpled, revealing its deceit to the Morgravian soldier. And the breathtaking spell on Lothryn which so impressed his King – that had been achieved brutally. There was nothing subtle or beautiful about that enchantment, even though the result seemed so miraculous. It was an abomination. Elysius would never have created something so tainted, but he was not Elysius, he was Rashlyn, the unloved, unwanted madman of the family.

He considered Lothryn now, wondering at the pain he was probably suffering. If Elysius had constructed the shapechanging spell, Rashlyn knew in his heart he would have done so effortlessly, without the smashing and distortion of limbs, breaking of the mind or any of the torturous pain Rashlyn had forced upon the courageous man. It was not that Rashlyn regretted Lothryn's pain. No, his despair was all selfish: he wanted his magic to be subtle, like the magic of Elysius. Instead, it was messy and clumsy.

Would Lothryn die? Rashlyn had no idea if the man's spirit would survive the trauma and keep the beast alive, or whether it would wither and kill Cailech's beautiful new stallion.

Rashlyn comforted himself that this time of anxiety and soul-searching would be brief. The madness would descend any moment now and his mind would once again swirl back into its dark and twisting pathways where there was no remorse, no sympathy, no love for anything but power and corruption.

Next to shapechanging Lothryn, tapping into Cailech's mind was Rashlyn's most recent diabolical act. He had learned how to manipulate the King's thoughts and influence his decisions to suit his own base ends. But he could not wield this magic unless the King stood near him and was receptive to that manipulation. There were times when Cailech was utterly closed to him. That was his weakness.

The door opened and Cailech entered as if at a silent signal. No one else but the King ever came to his rooms and he was the only person anyway who would never feel the obligation to announce himself with a knock. The sorcerer felt the familiar drag downwards from rationality into his other, deranged self.

'My King,' he said, not turning yet, using the moments to compose himself. 'I was just admiring the day.'

'We must speak,' Cailech said, clearly agitated. 'I want you to do a reading for me.'

'I just have, my lord King.'

'And?'

'The Stones predict change.'

'Oh? What sort of change?' Cailech's body language was suddenly intent and eager.

Rashlyn noticed the flush at his King's cheeks. Something had created high excitement in him, he realised. 'This they do not tell me. I have cast the Stones several times, your highness, and each time they simply prophesy change.'

Cailech surprised his barshi by clapping his hands and laughing. It was a cheerful response to something which would normally disturb him. Rashlyn frowned, unsettled by this reaction.

'Perfect!' the King muttered. 'Do you have any wine here?'

'Er . . . why yes, of course. Let me pour you some,' Rashlyn offered, intrigued. He poured for both of them and waited for the inevitable toast.

'To change,' Cailech obliged, holding up his cup before swallowing the contents.

Rashlyn copied his King and put his cup down. 'So you are happy with my prediction, your highness?'

'Yes. It confirms what I must do.'

'And what must you do, my lord?'

'Go to Morgravia,' the King said, as if the barshi should have known something so obvious 'for a parley with King Celimus.'

'This is a jest, surely? The Stones suggest no such thing,' Rashlyn spluttered, all politeness deserting him.

Cailech hardly noticed. He put a gleeful finger in the air. 'Ah, wait, hear me out,' and he told him of the capture of and his subsequent meeting with the man known as Cullyn.

'And you trust this man? This stranger!'

'Oddly, yes,' Cailech replied, unpredictable as always.

'Wait,' Rashlyn cautioned. 'Say no more until I have consulted the Stones about him.'

Cailech nodded and settled back with a second cup of wine whilst his barshi set about casting the smoothed rocks with their odd engravings. He remained silent as Rashlyn threw the eleven stones across the floor and squatted to read them. He stood up again after a long time.

'Well?'

Rashlyn shook his head slowly. 'The Stones are confused. They tell me that he speaks the truth but—'

'Ha!' Cailech interrupted, delighted.

'But . . . he holds back on things. I cannot tell what these are.'

'He has lost his memory, man, that would explain it. And anyway, we all have secrets — even you, Rashlyn,' Cailech said, sounding even happier if such a thing were possible.

Not you, sire. I can read your mind as if it were an open page, the man of magic thought sourly, knowing this was not wholly true. 'I would recommend caution, my lord.'

'The Stones themselves predict change. Change of scenery, change of heart, change of ideals, change of plan. Not war with Celimus, Rashlyn, but trade as equals, prosperity together. I am ashamed I wasn't the one to think of it first. It is inspired – I can't wait to tell Lothryn about it. Do you think he hears me, understands me?'

Rashlyn sighed inwardly. The King's mind was made up. He would go right into the dragon's den. So be it. 'I think there is enough of his spirit still left in the horse, though I cannot promise it will remain so.'

'Excellent,' Cailech replied, 'for he would approve of this plan.'

'My lord King, may I ask how you intend to orchestrate such a delicate parley?'

'Not me – Cullyn, or whoever he really is. He will make it happen.'

Rashlyn nodded and changed the subject to something he could control. 'About the prisoner, my lord, the Morgravian soldier . . .'

'I'm not planning to give him back as a peace offering, if that's what you're leading up to.'

'No, sire. But may I have him? For my experiments,' the barshi said, reaching out with his probing spell and entering Cailech's mind.

Later that afternoon Aremys, with Myrt, Firl and a couple of other Mountain men, including Maegryn, in attendance, met with the King on horseback.

'Isn't he magnificent?' Cailech said to his guest.

Aremys had to admit that, intact memory or not, he

did not believe he had ever set eyes on a finer horse. 'Fit only for a king, my lord,' he said and could see the comment pleased Cailech. 'May I?' he asked, wanting to touch the sleek black coat of the stallion.

'Of course,' the King replied and Aremys hopped down from his own chestnut mount. He walked around the black horse which tossed its head. Aremys whistled. 'I have never seen a prouder stallion,' he said, stepping gently towards the animal in order not to startle it.

'Here, Cullyn, give him this,' Maegryn said, tossing an apple towards Aremys, who deftly caught it. 'He's picky, he doesn't like the green ones, they make him sicken.' The men laughed.

Aremys held the apple in his flat palm and raised it towards the horse's mouth. He was captivated by the animal and enjoyed watching it snaffle the fruit greedily. But as its velvety lips brushed against his hand, Aremys felt a tremor of shock pass through him. It felt like a dam had burst in his mind and a river of information – his memories – flooded in. He staggered backwards, holding his head.

It was Cailech who reached him first, leaping down from Galapek. Again Aremys was struck by the man's lack of pretension. He could just imagine Celimus caring enough to even look his way!

'Cullyn, man! Are you ill? What's happening?' the King said, reaching for Aremys whilst holding the reins of his horse.

Aremys was not ready to reveal too much. His cautious nature forced him to take stock of his situation first and consider his position fully. 'I . . . I'm sorry, sire, my head suddenly hurts.' In this he was not lying; it throbbed.

'Take him back,' Cailech said to one of his men. 'If he's well enough, he can ride with us tomorrow.'

'I'm sorry,' Aremys repeated, stunned with shock, not just by the return of his memory but something else, something frightening. He straightened, deciding to give the worried men something. 'My name is Aremys Farrow,' he said, hoping it was not an error to admit as much.

Cailech scrutinised him, then nodded. 'We know of your family then. You are from the northern isle of Grenadyn. Anything else?'

Aremys shook his head miserably. 'Only that. It came to me just as this pain did,' he lied. 'I'm sorry about the ride.'

'No harm done,' the King said affably. 'I am pleased your memory returns. Are you able to ride back on your own horse?'

'Yes, of course.' Aremys reached again towards the King's stallion, bracing himself this time. He needed to be sure of something. He touched the animal's neck as if in farewell to the riders. The tremor that passed between him and the horse was genuine. Magic! How he knew this, he had no idea; he just knew it existed. The stallion was riddled with a huge and tainted spell – he could feel it passing into his hand and resonating throughout his body. It made him feel like retching. 'I shall rest, my lord, thank you,' he said as evenly as he could.

'We shall see you later, Aremys Farrow,' Cailech said, an unreadable expression on his face.

Alone at last in his chamber Aremys remembered everything and it was terrifying. It was the Thicket which had risen up against him and, using its magic, had hurled him into the Razors. As it occurred, he had understood that the Thicket did not want him to pass through with Wyl. One moment he had been whistling and admiring Ylena's rump, the next he found himself separated from Wyl. He remembered now how the air had become suddenly chill – freezing, in fact – and then he had felt it gathering about him. It was as if invisible hands had shoved him through that thickened air to blast him into a different place.

It was the Thicket's magic which had knocked out his memories for a while. No blow to his head, he realised, it had all happened internally. He felt his insides twist with fear for Wyl, travelling alone as a helpless young woman, although in truth he knew Wyl could easily hold his own against others. Perhaps not against magic though. What if the Thicket had done the same to Wyl? Perhaps it had not wanted either of them there and now Wyl was lying in some corner of the realm also trying to piece his strange life back together.

Aremys's thoughts began to travel rapidly now. He needed to get out of the Razors and back south to Wyl. He must find him, help him. If, by some stroke of luck, Wyl *had* found Elysius then no matter what occurred between them Wyl would still head towards Briavel and Valentyna, of this Aremys was sure. However, if Wyl had not made it to Elysius and the Thicket had treated him with similar disdain, then he might be in Morgravia. It was unlikely he was in the mountains, for Cailech's scouts would have surely spotted him by now.

Thoughts and plans raged around his mind but once the initial panic had settled Aremys began to think more clearly. Perhaps he could be of some use to Wyl whilst he was kept here. His friend had spoken of the soldier, Gueryn. In his heart, Aremys believed Wyl's mentor was dead — there was just no reason to keep the man alive and, going by what Wyl had told him, Gueryn had been a thorough nuisance to the Mountain King. However, Wyl believed the man was alive and would be kept alive as bait to lure Romen Koreldy back into the Mountain King's fortress. Aremys grimaced. He wondered what Cailech would make of it if he told him that Koreldy was long dead and that Ylena of Argorn was now host to Wyl Thirsk. What would he think of Ylena arriving to rescue Gueryn, if he lived? Plus there was the other man — Cailech's man — who had turned traitor to help Wyl and Elspyth escape the Mountain fortress. Wyl had told Aremys often enough that he would return, come what may, to discover the fate of brave Lothryn.

'I must find them for Wyl,' Aremys muttered, swinging his legs over to sit on the edge of the bed. 'As long as I'm captive here, I might as well make myself useful,' he whispered to himself.

Then he turned his mind to the strangest of all experiences: the fact that he could suddenly detect magic. It pulsed through the stallion, Galapek, and his own head still pounded from the ferocity with which that magic had spoken to him. He could only assume that the huge jolt of magic from the Thicket had somehow made him sensitive to sentient matter around him. He had not imagined it either; he had touched the horse a second time to check.

Aremys shook his head. He understood none of it, but one thing was for sure: he had to get into the dungeons. If Wyl's friends were alive, that was as good a place as any to start searching for information about them.

A knock at the door disturbed his thoughts. Aremys looked out of the window and noticed the sun lowering. He must have been wrestling for a long time with his confused thoughts.

'Who is it?'

'Messenger. The King wishes to see you.'

38

WYL WAS ADMIRING ELYSIUS'S handiwork. 'You made all this?' he said, his gaze sweeping across the breathtaking landscape. They were standing on a rise amidst a copse of tall trees whose leaves shone a fantastical bright green as the sun slanted through their translucent canopy to the gently moving stream below. Beyond the copse was a rugged cliff face over which water plunged direct from the Razors, Wyl presumed. They had walked here through sweet-smelling meadows from the modest dwelling Elysius had built for himself on a hill overlooking an equally panoramic view. Wyl could hardly believe how incredibly beautiful the Wild was.

The little man took a few moments to reply. 'In Parrgamyn we believe in Mor. In Morgravia and Briavel it is Shar who holds the spiritual power. In the kingdom of the Razors, the Mountain Dwellers pray to Haldor. My belief, Wyl, is that we are all praying to the same god. And I think that god is Nature. More powerful than we can imagine. Anything which can create such beauty as this,' he said, sweeping an elongated arm across the vista, 'or craft such sophistication as you and I, or such grace as a deer or such majesty as an eagle, then this is the god of all for me. This god created what you see before you . . . I have simply embellished some of it,' Elysius said. 'I may not have my own sight but I see perfectly well through the creatures to appreciate the beauty of this place. My skills relate to all things natural. The waterfall's theatrics is my work but in truth the framework had been in place for centuries. Shar had seen to it.'

'So this wild beauty was already here? Harmless and gorgeous . . . and feared.'

Elysius nodded. 'And I seem to be the only one who enjoys it. It suited my purposes in the early years to live a hermit's existence, but loneliness is a curse. It would be a pity for Briavel to discover how harmless the Wild is — it would quickly become an annexe of that realm. Just imagine its trees cut down, its streams dammed and diverted, its sheer wildness harnessed. On the other hand, I do miss people. Sometimes I fly with the birds so I can look through their eyes over Briavel or Morgravia and get a sense of being back amongst a community.'

'Then go. Can't you cast a glamour about yourself and leave?'

The manwitch smiled. 'I cannot work magic on myself of that nature, no. Irritating but true.'

Wyl frowned. 'So if the Wild is not enchanted, why did people of old fear it?'

'There is magic here, Wyl, be very sure of that. I can't explain it; I simply accept it. The Thicket, for example, is something rather extraordinary which, from what I can tell, exists purely to keep people away from the Wild. Perhaps if we delved back into history, scholars might throw some light on why no one has explored the region, what exactly they feared so irrationally or perhaps knew to be true.'

'Old superstitions, I'd guess.'

'More than that. The Thicket is real and thinks for itself. It allowed me to pass through all those years ago, then Emil, and then you and Fynch, but I suspect it actually does frighten away many who might attempt to enter. It certainly dealt with your friend.' He saw Wyl's expression fall at this comment. 'I'm sorry, that was clumsy of me. I don't believe your friend has been hurt – I feel sure the Thicket has never injured anyone – but it has the power of choice and it chose for him to be repelled.'

'What has it done with him?'

Elysius sighed. 'You are the first person I have shared this with. You will not be the last though – one other must know,' he said cryptically. 'The Thicket is more than just a barrier – it is a gate.'

'To what?'

'I don't know. Other regions, I imagine,' Elysius mused. 'Perhaps other worlds.'

Now Wyl was astonished. 'What?'

'I don't know enough about it. I have never made use of it, nor will I.'

'So Aremys might be in a different world, you're saying?' Wyl said, aghast.

'No, I'm not saying that. I understand it so little that I would never suggest such a thing. The Thicket acts as an entry to other places, to cause travel, is all I'm hazarding.'

'And Aremys has been pushed through that gate?'

'I'm sorry, Wyl, that I can't enlighten you further. For

all we know he could be on the other side, taking an ale in Timpkenny. It is not important.'

'Not to you perhaps,' Wyl said tersely, moving to check on Fynch who was playing in the nearby stream with Knave.

'And that was clumsy of me again. What I mean to say is that I believe he is safe, wherever he is, and that what is of importance right now is you and the decisions you make.'

'I came here for an answer, Elysius, and I have it now.' Wyl scowled, spoiling Ylena's pretty face. 'There are no further decisions to make. I must leave for Briavel.'

'You know Valentyna must marry Celimus, don't you?'

'It doesn't have to be so,' Wyl countered. 'And how could you know that so surely whilst you're stuck out here?'

'I know many things, Wyl, and I have explained that I travel with the animals — I see and hear much.'

Elysius's calm countenance could be frustrating. 'How? How can you know with such certainty that she must marry the madman of Morgravia?'

'It is prophesied.'

'By whom?' Wyl demanded, his tone slightly mocking.

'The Stones tell me so. They always speak the truth.'

'The Stones! The same pebbles your brother uses to advise Cailech on how to roast people alive?' He was yelling now.

Elysius was wise enough to understand Wyl's sense of helplessness and his fears. He did not react to his wrath. 'The Stones do not advise, they simply give answers to questions. Their answers are not always clear, I grant you, but in this they are firm. Queen Valentyna of Briavel will marry King Celimus of Morgravia, come what may.'

'Then we had better hope he kills me first,' Wyl said bitterly, 'for I won't allow it. I will use everything I have within myself to prevent such a marriage taking place.'

He hated the sympathy on the manwitch's face, as if he already knew this to be a hopeless cause.

'I'll take my leave now, Elysius. I thank you for your hospitality and your explanations.'

'I am deeply saddened, Wyl. I wish I could offer more comfort, at least more guidance, but the way ahead for you is not clear – other than Myrren's choice for your final destination. Your journey there is shrouded.'

Wyl nodded, too depressed to respond, and walked away.

Elysius called to him. Reluctantly Wyl halted and looked back. 'We will not meet again, Wyl Thirsk. The Thicket will permit you through. Take food from the cottage and leave before dark. Remember my warning: Myrren's gift cannot be manipulated or it will punish you in ways you cannot imagine. She insisted you rule Morgravia. Rule you must.'

Wyl felt a tremor run through Ylena's thin body at such prophetic words. He could not speak, simply raised a resigned hand in farewell.

'Trust Fynch, although he too has his own path now,' Elysius called after him somewhat cryptically. He wanted to say more but he feared it might persuade Wyl that the Quickening could be foiled. Elysius knew better. He watched the retreating back of the only person in the land who could save Morgravia, Briavel and the Mountain Kingdom. He watched until Wyl was long gone and his own ugly wet cheeks had dried from the tears he had shed.

*　　*　　*

Fynch sat in Ylena's lap, her thin arms hugging him to her chest. Knave had positioned himself so close that he was touching both of them.

'I don't mind that you'd like to remain here a while. It's so beautiful, I could live here forever,' Wyl admitted.

'But why can't you stay longer?' the small boy asked.

'I must go to Valentyna, Fynch. I have to get a grasp on what's been happening.' He scratched his head. 'I don't even know if time passes the same in the Wild – who knows what might have occurred since we were last in Briavel?'

'Time is the same,' Fynch assured. 'And you're sure you don't mind if I stay here a little longer?'

'I promise,' Wyl said, meaning it. 'Is there a reason beyond the peace and solitude, though?'

Fynch nodded. 'I can't explain it, but I feel compelled to remain.'

Wyl noticed Knave was staring at him. He wondered if Elysius was with them, seeing through the animal. The dark eyes seemed to be imploring Wyl to trust the boy.

'Come straight to Werryl once you leave here. I hope I'll be there, but you know you have friends at the palace, no matter what.'

Again Fynch nodded, his mind already turning to more practical matters. 'How will you travel?'

'I'll buy a horse at Timpkenny.'

'I have plenty of coin if you need it.'

Wyl laughed. It was the first time in a while that he had heard Ylena's tinkling laughter. 'You're an extraordinary child, Fynch, do you know that?' he said, ruffling the lad's hair. 'And I suppose you have Knave so you don't need to worry about transport.'

'That's right,' Fynch said, turning in Ylena's arms. 'Be careful, Wyl . . . please.'

Wyl nodded. 'I promise to try and remain Ylena,' he said and was rewarded with a smile from his friend. 'Although you know this thing isn't over yet. Elysius says it will continue—'

'Until you rule Morgravia,' Fynch interrupted. 'Yes, I know. But who knows what might happen yet.'

'He says that is the outcome.'

'Then he's ignoring the notion of free will. Remember, Myrren's gift is still bound by the will of others, if not your own.'

Wyl hugged the boy again. How odd that no adult could bring the comfort that this child could. Fynch always seemed to say the right thing at the right time.

'I must go.'

They stood and Wyl leaned down and kissed Fynch. He looked towards Knave. 'Bring him safely to me.'

The dog growled softly in answer.

Wyl wasted no further time. He packed a small sack of bread and dried meat, together with some hard biscuit and a bladder of water. It would do. He left the cottage with a single backward glance, in case Elysius had come to add something heartening. Only Fynch stood there, one hand on Knave, his other in the air waving.

Leave soon, Fynch, Wyl suddenly thought, even though an hour earlier, with the boy hugged close, he had felt the lad was safer in the Wild than in any of the neighbouring realms. He could not put his finger on the reason for this about-face but he had a sense that Fynch would be changed the next time they met. As he raised his hand in farewell, he took a moment to fix in his mind the picture of the innocent, serious little boy and the large, mysterious dog. He felt an urge to warn Fynch but he was already too far away. It would mean climbing back up the hill and the small boat was bobbing invitingly just steps away on the Darkstream. The craft must know he was preparing to leave, he realised, for it to be waiting so patiently for him.

Against his inclination, he made the decision to press on. As much as he felt a fear for Fynch he knew it was irrational, and Wyl would be the first to admit that both of them were caught up in something so dark and strange that no one could predict the outcome. He wanted to believe he could stop Valentyna uniting Briavel with Morgravia through marriage but there was something about Elysius's sorrowful look that told him the prophecy was true and he was fighting a hopeless cause. Still, he must die trying, and he smiled grimly, for death was all that was ahead for him until he became the person he was destined to be.

As for Fynch, he was on his own path of destiny and although their paths were firmly linked at certain points, for the most part they ran parallel. He would just have to hope nothing untoward leapt into Fynch's way. With Knave at his side, Wyl doubted that anything – even magic – could deter Fynch from his journey, whatever that was.

He lowered himself into the boat and undid the small rope. Immediately the craft set off against the current, which was fascinating in itself. It moved effortlessly through the dark waters towards the great mouth of the mountain which had swallowed him once already.

He sent a prayer to Shar that he would hold his

nerve this time and make it through to the other side without succumbing to the Darkstream's invitation to drown.

39

FYNCH SAT QUIETLY WITH Elysius outside his dwelling watching the birds darting in and out of the trees and swooping across the picturesque meadows. He made a chain of daisies and looped it around Knave's neck. The dog did not seem to mind – he was more intent on snuffling around for a smooth round stone he could persuade Fynch to throw for him in the absence of a ball. In the comfortable quiet Elysius considered with a heavy heart how to approach the frightening topic that needed to be discussed.

'How long will you stay here, Fynch?' he asked finally.

'As long as it takes,' the boy replied, stringing a second daisy chain over Knave's head.

'For what?'

'For you to tell me what it is that burns at your lips and makes you so anxious.'

Elysius was stunned. He was right about the child. 'How do you know?'

Fynch shrugged. 'I sense it. Near to you, it's easier for my senses to tap into your mood. And Knave's magic is strong because you are so close. I think he helps me to understand all sorts of things. And then there's the Thicket. Even through the rockface it seems to whisper to me.'

Elysius nodded, amazed. 'You sense right, child.'

Fynch scattered the flowers he held. 'Then tell me. Don't be scared.'

'Have your senses told you what it is that sits between us?'

The boy shook his head. 'It's important, though, isn't it?'

'It is also a secret.'

'You didn't tell Wyl?' This obviously surprised Fynch because he frowned, then sighed as if accepting something unpleasant.

'No. Trust me when I say it would endanger him if I had.'

Fynch accepted this without further question. 'Should I be scared?' he asked, eyeing his companion.

Elysius did not know how to answer this. Fynch was such a sharp child, it would not be right to give him anything but a direct answer. 'Well, I am scared at sharing it with you.'

Fynch nodded gravely. 'Tell me then.'

Elysius wasted no further time. 'I am dying. It will happen soon.'

The boy did not react other than to stare at the ground. Elysius saw him lace his fingers together as if to steady himself whilst Knave stopped his search and lay down silently next to Fynch.

'Have you read it in the Stones?'

'Yes,' he said. 'But they assure me in their strange

roundabout way that the magic need not die.' He leaned forward. 'Must not die, in fact,' he added emphatically.

Fynch sighed heavily and lifted his gaze to look directly into the milky eyes of his dying friend. 'And you can pass it on to me.'

Elysius felt an enormous outpouring of gratitude and pity for Fynch. The brave little boy had worked it out for himself. He could hear the regret in the child's voice and wished he could avoid placing this terrible burden on a youngster who had already given more than enough to Myrren's cause. But then this was not for Myrren – this was another sort of gift; a terrible and heavy responsibility to entrust to a child. But he was the right one. Elysius had known this from the moment Knave had encountered the tiny gong boy at his work in Stoneheart all that time ago.

'Fynch, will you accept it?'

'I fear it,' Fynch replied without committing himself.

Elysius was surprised that the boy had not baulked. 'You need not, if you wield it wisely.'

'I don't understand how I can use magic,' Fynch said, shifting to stroke Knave's large head and velvety ears.

'Yes you do, child. You have always known in your heart. You told me that your mother was fey. She passed her talents and her own sentient ability on to you. In truth, I do believe you chose me.'

Fynch took no notice of the gentle accusation. 'And I must use it to protect Wyl. See to it that he rules Morgravia. Is this right?'

Elysius hesitated and Fynch's gaze flicked up from Knave's head to stare at his freakish friend.

'You will help Wyl, of this I am sure, but Myrren's

gift has its own momentum. It will take him to his destiny come what may. You . . . well, you have a much more complex task, son, and I wish I could spare you it.'

'What is it that I must do?' Fynch asked, dread in his voice.

'You are soon to be custodian of the magic belonging to the Thicket,' Elysius explained.

It was not a time for further apology or placations. Elysius knew this weight of responsibility must fall on the narrow shoulders of this small child. 'When I first came to the Wild, guided by the birds and animals, they called me the Gate Wielder. It took me a long time to understand what they meant, and then I spent years trying to ignore it. The rest of my life I have devoted to avoiding it – I have never believed I am strong enough.'

'Gate Wielder,' Fynch said, testing the words on his tongue. 'And what does it mean?'

Elysius told Fynch about the Thicket acting as a gate, as he had detailed to Wyl earlier.

'Has there always been a Gate Wielder then?'

It was an astute question and Elysius acknowledged it with a smile. 'No. In past times there have been, I suspect. But I was the first in a very long time. The Thicket takes care of itself and ordinarily can keep people out via its own means. Those who may be allowed to pass through for whatever reason then have Samm to contend with.'

'Samm is persuasive,' Fynch agreed. 'So why change now? Why did the Thicket need you?'

'My guess is that until fairly recent times it hasn't needed someone with magic powers.'

Fynch looked at him, confused. 'Your guess?'

'Fynch, the Thicket has never spoken to me as I gather it speaks to you. My communication with it has been via the birds and animals. From the few things you've said, it sounds to me as though the Thicket itself talks to you. My feeling is that you are no ordinary Gate Wielder, if there is such a thing.' He laughed briefly, sadly. 'I believe that you are someone very special.'

'What do you mean?' Fynch asked, scared afresh.

'I don't know what I mean. I am speculating. Perhaps the Thicket needs you for more than simply watching over a gate that almost never gets used.'

That notion hung heavily between them for several long moments.

'If the Thicket has its own powers, why does it need you?' Fynch asked eventually.

'Well, again I can only surmise. My hunch is that it needs to channel its magic through someone to achieve change outside of itself.'

'You mean change in the world beyond its own borders?'

'Exactly.'

Elysius reached for a flask of juice he had squeezed that morning. He gestured to Fynch who nodded. As he poured them each a cup, he tried to make this difficult notion clearer for the child whose burden suddenly felt so much heavier than his own.

'I think it needs the wilder magic my mother spoke of, and that means someone whose talent revolves around nature. It found that in me and I presume any previous Gate Wielders offered similar qualities. I am passing my nature magic to you, so that would answer one part of this strange equation, but the other is how and why the

Thicket speaks to you. I can't imagine how it will use you.'

Fynch had never felt more frightened in his life. He took the cup from his friend and drained it. 'So Aremys went through this gate?'

Elysius nodded, surprised by the sudden switch in topic. 'I pushed him. It was the first time I have ever used that unknown magic.'

Fynch's eyes widened. 'Why did you push him?'

'He was a complication. You and Wyl were the only ones I wanted to come through and perhaps the Thicket sensed this. It has the ability to make up its own mind but it is linked to the Gate Wielder. Normally it can repel people with the greatest of ease but Aremys was strong – his friendship with Wyl very real – and I realise now that he was somehow protected by Wyl and the magic Wyl possesses within himself. The Thicket summoned me to open the Gate.'

'Where did you send him?'

'I was careful not to push too far. I hope he is in Briavel or Morgravia.'

Fynch switched his thoughts to another question niggling in his mind. 'So I must stay here after . . . after you leave?'

Elysius finished his drink and sighed. 'For a short while anyway. This is why I have asked you not to follow Wyl, although I am sure he told you to go to Werryl.' Fynch nodded. 'Stay here until you have learned more about the Thicket and its intentions.'

'How will I do that?'

The little man looked at Fynch sorrowfully. 'I am hoping it will tell you.'

Fynch bit his lip in thought.

Elysius sighed. 'There is more connected with the magic of nature. I could keep this from you and allow you to learn it slowly as I did, but that would be cruel. I am sorry, but each time you unleash your magic, for whatever reason, you will sicken.'

'Is that what has happened to you?' Fynch asked and once again Elysius was struck by the boy's ability to see straight to the core of a topic.

He nodded. 'It will take my life shortly. In fact, son, when I pass the burden to you, I suspect that will herald my end.' He saw the misty look in the child's eyes. 'No, do not be sad for me. I wish I could spare you the same burden.'

'Will I die too?'

'Perhaps,' Elysius answered honestly. 'This is why I must counsel you to use your magic sparingly and keep your life long,' he added, not quite so truthfully, as he could already imagine what lay ahead for courageous Fynch.

Fynch nodded, looking suddenly older for this terrifying knowledge. 'Is there anything else?'

Again Elysius resisted the urge to soften the blow; he would not offer empty words of comfort. He pressed on, finally vocalising his suspicions. 'I think the Thicket wants you to track down and destroy my brother, Rashlyn.'

The boy visibly shook. 'Elysius! I could never kill anyone.'

'I know what might be asked of you is difficult.'

Fynch shook his head rapidly as if trying to shut out the placating words. 'No. No!' he said, forcing Elysius into silence. 'I will not kill anyone, for your personal revenge or anyone else's.'

'Not even Celimus, after all that he's done?'

At this Fynch's mouth hung open. He wanted to respond but could not. Then he dropped his head in his hands. 'I don't believe I'm capable of it . . . not even Celimus.'

'Fynch,' the mellow voice said softly. 'I don't ask this of you. This is for the sake and safety of all that you love – Wyl, Valentyna, your family; Morgravia, Briavel. I dare to think that this is why the Thicket is becoming involved.'

'What do you mean?'

'Now that I have discovered where he is, I realise that Rashlyn has the ability to plunge all three realms into war. If, as Wyl says, Rashlyn can manipulate King Cailech, then there is only bloodshed ahead.'

'Why should the Thicket care if we all kill each other?'

'I do not know. You must seek those answers for yourself. I think it does care, though.'

'Why me? Why not Wyl, who is a soldier and knows how to wield a sword and kill a man?'

Elysius shook his head. 'Dear Fynch, I wish I could spare you this. Wyl is a wandering soul trapped in helpless flesh and bone.'

'You have never seen Wyl fight. He might walk as Ylena now but he is still Wyl Thirsk inside.'

'Child, you miss my point. Rashlyn is far superior to Wyl. He could snap a sword from fifty paces, deflect an arrow, smell the poison – he cannot be killed by conventional means. Wyl is no threat to him. No one is, in fact.'

'How can I do it then?'

'I am giving you the means, son. Shortly you will be a sorcerer, but far more fearsome is the fact that you also possess whatever power the Thicket deems to lend you. Find out what it can do. Use it.'

A dawning expression moved across the small boy's face. Elysius pressed further. 'Rashlyn is a madman. A destroyer. No one can stand up to the sort of power he wields, except you. You alone can stop him. You and Knave and the secret of the Thicket that calls to you.'

Whether Fynch was filled with uncertainty and misgivings, or whether he just felt frightened and alone in spite of Knave's heavy head resting on his legs and reminding him of friendship, Elysius did not know. A dread silence sat between them as the former gong boy considered all that he had just learned. Suddenly the memory of being a hardworking child and coming home to his parents' tiny cottage with their meagre belongings felt as though it had been the best time of his life.

But he could appreciate that there was nothing random about his relationship with Knave, which connected him to Myrren through Wyl and to Elysius and his mad brother. His part in saving Valentyna's life was not a coincidence. His own life was being shaped, orchestrated. He had been chosen. He looked at the strange dog who sat beside him and acknowledged the curious tingling sensation between them which had grown after they had passed through the Thicket.

He made his decision.

'I wish I could stay here in this serene place and not take on this terrifying role,' he said, 'but then I think about Wyl's suffering and how he too is on a strange path he didn't ask to journey upon. It seems we are both being asked to do things neither of us want to do and yet must to help others. I know I have to be brave and accept the burden of becoming a manwitch even if it does mean an early death. I'll help Wyl all that I can and I'll face Rashlyn for you. I can't promise I'll overcome him, Elysius, but I will die trying.'

The man felt ashamed of himself for asking so much of this brave child. He wished he could bite out his own tongue for what he knew he must still say.

'Fynch, one more thing.' Large, trusting eyes turned to look at him. 'You must not, under any circumstances, allow Rashlyn to seize your powers – and he will try, believe me. You must never lose sight of the fact that you will be weakened each time you wield magic and this is why I urge you to make for the Razors first. Don't follow Wyl. He must take his own path now . . . and you yours. You will need all of your strength to match Rashlyn; you cannot risk being compromised in any way. I beg you to heed this warning, for if he defeats you and takes your powers – as he can – then the world is doomed.'

Fynch hugged Knave close, who licked him as if to say he understood the import of what was being discussed.

'Wyl left very upset,' Fynch commented, wanting to leave behind the talk of death and destruction.

'I gave him no peace. He came seeking answers and I gave him the wrong ones,' Elysius said, filled with regret.

'It occurs to me that the Stones are open to interpretation – would that be fair?'

'Of course. They never provide a clear answer.'

'So perhaps Wyl's fear of becoming Celimus is also open to interpretation,' Fynch prompted.

Elysius did not answer immediately. He had learned in the short time he had spent with Fynch that the boy was a serious, deep-thinking person. He might be young but he was sharply intelligent and perceptive. 'How would you interpret the notion then?' he asked gently.

'I wouldn't. I don't trust the Stones or what they predict in their misted way. I trust only what I see or hear and what I feel in my heart.'

'Do you think they lie?'

'No, I'm not saying that. I'm simply saying that there are many scenarios we might not be considering. The Stones have put a notion into your mind and you are trusting it, but you yourself built into Myrren's gift the aspect of free will, didn't you?' Elysius nodded. 'We don't know what might happen or who might influence the future. Celimus could die tomorrow in a riding accident or from disease. That's the randomness of the world, isn't it? And then Wyl may not have to answer to Myrren's gift any longer.'

Elysius felt a rush of love and admiration for the bright, brave boy. He hardly trusted his voice to speak without trembling and he fought back the tears that sprang to his eyes. Reaching for Fynch he hugged him hard.

'You are the most extraordinary person I have met in my life, Fynch. You alone will give our world hope and I go to my death relieved that it is you who takes over this power from me. I am proud to know you. You are right: none of us knows anything for sure.'

It was Fynch's turn to feel choked. He did not feel brave and he did not want to be saviour of the world. He just wanted a quiet life. He hugged the little man back with affection and sorrow that both of them were suffering for his magic.

'How much time do we have?' he asked after a long silence.

Elysius already felt as if he had passed over his burden to the boy. He regretted it but knew he had no choice. 'Time is short. I must channel all of my magic into you.'

'And then you will die?'

'Yes.'

'When shall we begin?'

'Now, son,' Elysius replied softly.

EPILOGUE

THE CORPSE OF THE former Duchess of Felrawthy had been laid out in the small chapel at Werryl, where those who had known her — just four of them in Briavel — could pay their last respects. Father Paryn intoned a final gentle prayer to commit her body to a peaceful rest. He was aided by Pil who lit small candles at given moments during the prayer: one for her head, one for each limb, one for her soul. They would burn until they snuffed themselves out, by which time Shar's Gatherers would have collected her.

Physic Geryld, Commander Liryk and Chancellor Krell sat behind the Queen. At Valentyna's right was a composed Duke Crys of Felrawthy. On her left side was Elspyth, the only one weeping. Elspyth had liked Aleda immensely and could not contain the sorrow she felt at this fine woman's shocking end and her courageous, desperate bid to see her son alive.

Valentyna reached to put an arm around her petite companion. 'I gave Romen an identical kerchief,' she whispered, handing Elspyth a beautiful square of embroidered linen. 'You keep this. Now both my friends own one.'

Elspyth was touched by the sentiment but it made her lack of composure worse and she could only nod her thanks. Later, when the prayers were done and the candles glowed softly around Aleda's body, Elspyth was sufficiently calm to whisper back to the Queen, 'I shall stay on with Crys for a few moments.'

Valentyna smiled and nodded. 'Forgive me, I have business to attend to,' she whispered.

Everyone bowed for the Queen's departure. Once outside the chapel, her counsellors had to run slightly to catch up with their monarch's long stride.

'I don't need to remind any of you, I'm sure, that no one is to discuss these events outside those of us here who know. The death of Aleda Donal, plus the presence of the duke and Elspyth, are to remain a secret to the best of our ability.'

She saw Krell baulk and surmised what he was about to say. 'I understand that the folk of Brackstead are the weak link in this plan and that the nobility too have met Crys and Elspyth, but we can say they have departed Briavel. The gossip in Brackstead will die away soon enough.'

Krell had paled. She frowned at him but he said nothing and so she continued. 'The Morgravians will remain as our honoured guests for as long as they choose. No one is to discuss their presence outside of the palace. Is that clear?'

Everyone nodded except Krell.

'Thank you, gentlemen,' she said, effectively dismissing them. 'Chancellor Krell?'

'Your majesty?'

'A word, please, in my solar.'

With the agreement of both sovereigns, Jessom had
followed through on his idea to set up a system of couriers
to make the journey between Werryl and Pearlis much
faster. Special huts for overnighting had been established
in recent weeks, with supplies of dried food and watered
ale, which meant there was always a rested man and a
fresh mount ready to go. By handing over messages at
these courier points, the journeying time for written correspondence – and less sensitive verbal messages if need be
– was more than halved.

And so it was that Krell's communication to his counterpart in Morgravia was received quickly at Stoneheart,
and why now King and Chancellor were standing together
in Celimus's study, both seething.

'Read it again!' Celimus ordered.

If it were anyone else Jessom would have suggested
that reading it once more would not change the contents
but he sensibly bit back the acid-tongued comment and
did as his King demanded. 'He was right to tell us, my
lord King,' Jessom said after he had finished.

'Obviously Valentyna doesn't know he has. She
wouldn't have sanctioned him writing to you like this.
No, he's taken this entirely upon himself because he's
frightened.'

'Of the consequences, do you mean, sire?'

The King ran a hand through his dark, lustrous hair.
'I think it's more simple than that. Krell and that
Commander of theirs seemed determined to turn the
marriage into a reality. They said as much during our

visit. Their people want the peace as much as our own, but those two and Krell in particular understand that Briavel is in no position to fight a war with us. Diplomacy is their one weapon.'

'Yes, I understand,' Jessom said, even though he had grasped all that he needed to on the first reading. He knew he had to get the King to calm down because then his thoughts would flow smoothly and in a more cunning fashion. He had learned this the hard way. When the King was angry, people got hurt and this was not Jessom's style.

'And that snivelling bastard son who should have died,' Celimus spat, 'but somehow escaped our sword is now walking tall as the new Duke of Felrawthy. Not to mention some stupid woman from Morgravia poisoning the Queen's thoughts. They know everything.'

'Not everything, sire. They are piecing together various stories,' Jessom soothed, though he knew the King's words had a horrible ring of truth.

Valentyna might be young and inexperienced but she was the daughter of a canny sovereign and, if his own first impressions were right, she possessed an intelligent head on her shoulders. Which, no doubt, was why his counterpart in Briavel had reacted so swiftly and done what some might consider unthinkable, sending a private communication into Morgravia. It was obvious that the Queen would be appalled by what the Morgravians were telling her.

Jessom poured his King a goblet of wine. 'We do not know the full measure of the young duke yet, your highness. He might be useful to us in ways we cannot anticipate,' he said, thinking aloud.

'True,' Celimus replied, taking the proffered cup. 'But my inclination is to believe that at this point Valentyna must have no intention of marrying me. You agree?'

Jessom nodded gravely; the King was right. 'I do, your highness.'

'Then if she won't come willingly, we shall take Briavel the hard way.'

Chancellor Jessom was not ready for such a leap forward. 'War, sire?'

'Threat of it anyway, Jessom. She has understood all our couched words of intimidation – Valentyna is far from dull. She knows precisely what is at stake here. I freely admit that marriage would be easier and certainly a more economical means of bringing Briavel under our rule, but if she won't see the sense of this marriage then I shall teach her that she never was an equal – no matter what she has been raised to believe.'

Jessom, unhappily, had to agree with the King. 'Your orders, sire?'

'Summon my General and his captains. War with Briavel is now on the agenda,' Celimus said, before swallowing the contents of his wine cup and slamming it down on the table. 'And whilst we're at it, I might as well deal with the barbarian of the north,' he added, glee lacing his tone.

Valentyna's hand was at her throat, alarm spreading through her every fibre at hearing Krell's admission. 'You did what?' she said, her tone icy as she hoped somehow she had misunderstood her faithful advisor.

Krell had never before felt so unsure. 'Someone had to do it, your majesty,' he said, his voice small and filled with dismay. Suddenly the letter to Chancellor Jessom seemed like a rash move.

'Someone had to do what, Chancellor Krell? Betray me? Don't you think I'm coping with enough here without my own people working against me? Wouldn't it have been easier to take out a knife and just plunge it straight into my heart?'

'Your highness,' Krell beseeched. 'It was for the good of Briavel . . . for your reign. Your father—'

'Don't you dare, Krell!' she snapped. 'Don't you dare bring the name of my fine father into this. Yes, he craved peace, but for *me*, sir, for no other reason. He did not want his daughter fighting endless, pointless wars with Morgravia just to keep a tradition alive,' she said as sarcastically as she could.

Valentyna could see Krell moving to explain that there was more to the wars than that but she held her hand up. 'What possessed you, Chancellor? What was going through your mind when you sent that letter?'

He swallowed hard. He had never seen her like this before. Suddenly the young Queen was possessed by wrath; her dark blue eyes blazed bright with her anger and it was all directed at him. Surely he did not deserve this?

'I thought, your highness, that Chancellor Jessom might shed some light on the strange series of events. That he might explain whether there was some misunderstanding and prevent us leaping to wrong conclusions and making hasty decisions.'

'Chancellor Krell,' she snarled, 'the only person making hasty decisions is you, sir. You have presumed too much. Your office and your familiarity with this family, and especially with me, does not permit you to send secret missives to our enemy.'

'Enemy,' he echoed softly. He looked completely baffled. 'Me confer with an enemy?' The accusation was too much for him to bear.

Valentyna stepped forward. 'Yes, *enemy*, Krell. Celimus wants Briavel, not me and not peace, and not for the good of Briavellians or even Morgravians for that matter. He simply covets the realm. He is empire-building. He is also a madman but then I didn't think I would have to explain that to you. His latest actions speak a thousand words.'

Krell tried to resurrect some measure of his former composure. He forced himself to stand straighter, to stop cringing before the angry monarch who towered above him. 'My Queen, if you do not marry him, he will make war upon us.'

She closed her eyes momentarily, as if to gather her patience. 'And you don't think that is precisely what he will be ordering right now, as we speak?'

'But, your highness, what other option were you planning?'

'I was stalling, you reckless, interfering old man. I am trying to find a peaceful solution,' she said, tears welling. She fought them back. 'I wanted this whole business kept quiet so I could have time to think, to carry on diplomatic relations with Morgravia and keep the King at arm's length until I knew how to go forward. I still do not know what the answer is. If you had not interfered, Celimus would be none the wiser. He would still think I intended to marry him and I would have had time to plan. Perhaps I cannot escape being wedded to him, sir, but I would prefer to do so on my own terms. Not yours! You have now committed us to war. How does it feel to have so much blood on your hands?'

Krell began to weep.

Valentyna despised herself for reducing this good man to such a state but her anger was burning white hot now. 'Get out of my sight. Leave the palace.'

'Your highness, please, let me help.'

'Help?' She gave a bitter laugh. 'I don't need your sort of help, Krell,' she said cruelly. 'What I need are people who are faithful and true to Briavel and its ruler. You have betrayed us both and I will never forgive you. Now go.'

Valentyna waited until her heartbroken Chancellor had left before she buried her face in her hands and cried like a child. Through her tears all she could think of was her beloved Romen Koreldy and how badly she needed his arms and his strength around her now. He would know what to do. Romen would think of something to ease them out of this mess, but she had nobody. Not even her friend, Fynch, and his strange dog were here to offer their usual solace. And then her father's face swam before her and reminded her once again who she was and that she could never depend on anyone but herself.

The Queen of Briavel's resolve crystallised and by the time the startling news was delivered that Chancellor Krell had jumped to his death from the battlements, her heart was hardened. She shed no tear at the tragedy for it was because of him that Briavel would be going to war.